I0652322

Arcanium

SPIDER

AURELIA T. EVANS

Spider
ISBN # 978-1-78686-377-5
©Copyright Aurelia T. Evans
Cover Art by Erin Dameron-Hill ©Copyright November 2018
Interior text design by Claire Siemaszkiewicz
Totally Bound Publishing

This is a work of fiction. All characters, places and events are from the author's imagination and should not be confused with fact. Any resemblance to persons, living or dead, events or places is purely coincidental.

All rights reserved. No part of this publication may be reproduced in any material form, whether by printing, photocopying, scanning or otherwise without the written permission of the publisher, Totally Bound Publishing.

Applications should be addressed in the first instance, in writing, to Totally Bound Publishing. Unauthorised or restricted acts in relation to this publication may result in civil proceedings and/or criminal prosecution.

The author and illustrator have asserted their respective rights under the Copyright Designs and Patents Acts 1988 (as amended) to be identified as the author of this book and illustrator of the artwork.

Published in 2018 by Totally Bound Publishing, United Kingdom.

No part of this book may be reproduced, scanned, or distributed in any printed or electronic form without permission. Please do not participate in or encourage piracy of copyrighted materials in violation of the authors' rights. Purchase only authorised copies.

Totally Bound Publishing is an imprint of Totally Entwined Group Limited.

If you purchased this book without a cover you should be aware that this book is stolen property. It was reported as "unsold and destroyed" to the publisher and neither the author nor the publisher has received any payment for this "stripped book".

SPIDER

Chapter One

In retrospect, Elizabeth should have looked up what kind of circus Arcanium was before bringing the Bishop children.

It wasn't entirely her fault. Mrs. Bishop had recommended it based on a casual glance at the weekend events in the local paper. However, when she and Mr. Bishop went out of town for the weekend on business — which was almost every weekend — it was up to Elizabeth to entertain and care for the children, and she was responsible for the content of that entertainment and care, which meant she'd been responsible for investigating Arcanium's suitability for an infant, a three-year-old girl, a nine-year-old boy and a monster masquerading as a sixteen-year-old girl.

Standing in front of the half-naked sword swallower performing at the entrance of the circus, Elizabeth shared a look with said monster, who usually just went by Sharona.

"You're going to be in so much trouble." Sharona flipped her hair over her shoulder.

She was pretty, just like her mother. Though it was mid-January, the weather was unseasonably warm, and Sharona had taken the opportunity to ignore her mother's guidelines for shirt length and exposure, guidelines that Elizabeth couldn't really enforce without Mrs. Bishop's approval — and Sharona knew it. A teenage girl flaunting her already-beach-ready body next to a woman in orthodox dress turned a few heads from the initial impact of the sword swallower, as though Elizabeth was just another circus oddity.

If the Bishops thought hiring a Petrosian saint for a nanny would rub righteousness off on their children, they'd severely underestimated teenage determination — and chosen the wrong Wu daughter as a nanny, not that Elizabeth's mother had shared that little bit of information with them.

Thank God, Sharona's brother Todd was much more manageable. And the toddler and infant were at least predictable.

"Why's she going to be in trouble?" Todd asked, holding the toddler's hand tightly. "The guy's just swallowing swords. Man, three swords now? Wow, gross. Think he can do four?"

"I'll admit that if he were swallowing dildos, that would be more shocking." Sharona took her phone out of her purse and framed the sword swallower in the picture.

"What's a dildo?" Todd asked.

"I mean…this guy? Not hot. But imagine what Mom and Dad would say if they saw the snake lady in the background? Or maybe this nice couple walking by? How romantic." Sharona grinned at the shot of the woman in shiny purple latex leading a man in red leather around on a leash. The man carried a double-sided torch trident over his shoulder.

"Come on, Todd. We're leaving." Elizabeth didn't think the ticket master was going to give them their money back. The gigantic sign of rules and warnings that she'd apparently failed to read all the way through had been clear about one thing. *No refunds.*

"Why?" Sharona lowered her phone to follow the progress of the woman and collared man — most likely because, despite the scars on the upper half of the man's body, the leather cradling his buttocks left as little to the imagination as his mistress's outfit.

"I am not taking your nine-year-old brother and baby sisters into a place like this." Elizabeth hooked a hand around Sharona's elbow to lead her back to the elaborate Arcanium gates.

"It's not like they get it. He doesn't know what a dildo is. Do *you* even?"

"And when Todd tells his parents about circus acts gyrating in fetish gear, who do you think isn't going to get paid this week?"

Sharona giggled. "How do you know what fetish gear is?"

"How *you* know is the more important question. I'm thirty-five, and I'm religious, not ignorant."

"Same diff."

"It really isn't," Elizabeth said dryly.

Sharona grabbed one of the wrought-iron whorls on the gate before Elizabeth could lead her through. "I want to stay."

Trying to force a recalcitrant teenager to go somewhere she didn't want to go while maneuvering a dual baby-and-toddler stroller over grass proved too much for Elizabeth. "Over my dead body. Your mother wanted me to take you to a circus, which was supposed to mean clowns, trained animals, acrobats... There's nothing redeemable about a freak show pretending to be a floor show. I thought these places had all been wiped out."

"But I want to see the snake lady," Todd said. "I like snakes."

Elizabeth suppressed a shudder. "You know I don't. But if you want snakes, we can go to the zoo again. Would you like that?"

Sharona crossed her arms. "I want to stay."

"You just want to look at the boys," Elizabeth said. "There are boys wherever we go, Sharona. We don't have to stay here for you to let temptation get the better of you."

Sharona scoffed. "Look. This is the coolest place you've ever brought us to. Come on. This place has, like, three-headed dogs and games and a haunted house. I swear on a stack of Bibles" — she held up her phone as though it were the equivalent — "I won't tell Mom and Dad about this place if you let us stay. Besides, Todd knows how to keep secrets."

Elizabeth raised her eyebrow. "What kind of secrets?"

"Sharona sneaks out of the house by going out of her window and down the rose trellis," Todd said, whispering loudly. "She goes to meet a booooy."

Now Elizabeth directed her raised eyebrow toward Sharona.

"You little creep." Sharona shoved her brother. Elizabeth stepped in to keep Sharona from doing more than superficial damage and to snag Maggie before she decided to toddle off toward the shiny swords.

Todd scrambled behind Elizabeth. "You just told me I couldn't tell Mom and Dad."

"You're fucking dead."

"Language!" Elizabeth picked Maggie up and knelt next to the stroller, where Brianna had started fussing. "You can use those words with your friends all you want, but not around me and not around your brother and sisters." But now that Todd had revealed a tasty bit of ammunition, Elizabeth thought Sharona would be a little more amenable.

Sharona rolled her eyes. "Whatever. Can we stay? *Please*? Listen. There are elephants, right? Trained animals. I'm sure we'll find some clowns and acrobats somewhere. I mean, it's a freakin' circus. There's more skin at a public pool. It's not a big deal. Just because you've got a thing about covering yourself up doesn't mean the rest of the world cares."

"Believe it or not, I don't expect the rest of the world to adhere to my standard of modesty," Elizabeth said.

"Then what's the problem?"

"It's more what they're doing while they're half-naked that concerns me. Your brother isn't *that* young and neither are you," Elizabeth said. Thankfully, the baby had drifted back asleep rather than wake up screaming to join the rest of them.

"It's not even sex. It's just sexy."

"It's not appropriate." She straightened, hitching Maggie on her hip and grateful for the pins holding her head covering in place, because Maggie liked to tug on it as much as she liked tugging her sister's hair.

"Geez, no wonder no one ever married you. You have so many sticks up your butt. There isn't room for anything else."

Elizabeth pretended Sharona hadn't hit a nerve, but both of them knew otherwise. "You're not making your case, young lady."

"One hour. If we see something we wouldn't see at the beach or Cirque du Soleil, we can leave and Mom and Dad never have to see the pictures I took. Todd will just talk about the muscle man and snake lady and sword swallower, and Maggie'll just squeal about the clowns or something. Come on. You can flagellate when we get home, and it'll all be fine. I'll buy you all the mortification instruments you want."

Sixteen years old and somehow both a juvenile delinquent and a devout student. Sometimes Elizabeth thought she and Sharona clashed so much because they were too alike.

"We're already here. It'll take us another hour to get to the zoo then it'll be too sunny and hot for Maggie," Sharona continued. "I swear I won't tell Mom, and neither will Todd."

"Swear," Todd said. "What aren't we telling them?"

"You know how we didn't tell them about that movie with kissing and boobs in it?" Sharona said.

"I'm not hearing this." Elizabeth resisted the urge to cover the toddler's ears.

"I'll be good the rest of the afternoon. I'll take care of Todd and make sure Maggie doesn't run off and play with scissors. These photos stay on my phone, and we don't tell my parents you took us to a weird-ass den of iniquity. Deal?" Sharona held her phone-free hand out.

"You've been listening to your father talk business too much," Elizabeth said.

"I've never heard him use the phrase 'weird-ass den of iniquity.' When have you been listening to him?"

"That's enough of being a smart aleck, Sharona. If it's too hot for Maggie, it's too hot for me, too." She was getting a headache, both from imagining what the Bishops would do if she stayed and from how warm she was getting underneath her long-sleeved shirt, long skirt and head scarf.

"Hard to believe it's January, isn't it?" Doing an excellent impersonation of a caring human being, Sharona opened her arms to take Maggie. "Not my fault your beliefs tell you to swelter in the name of piety. You'd rather sweat like a pig than let someone see a scandalous ankle, as though it's the Victorian era all over again."

"It's not about scandal and it's not about sex. You know that perfectly well."

"Excuse me if I don't get why covering yourself almost head to toe shows respect to God. Didn't he make Adam and Eve naked?"

Elizabeth refused to let Sharona bait her into another 'my Christianity makes more sense than yours.' She remembered similar debates with girls Sharona's age back when she'd been that young, too, when she had still been in public school—so-called fellow saints pulling Elizabeth's head covering off or lifting her skirt, as though Elizabeth's representation of piety somehow insulted everyone else's. People got sensitive when their holiness was threatened. They'd never understood that when she was young, she hadn't had a choice, because her parents had bought all her clothes and controlled what she wore. And now that she was a full-grown woman, she still didn't, for reasons adjacent to parental control. After all, she was an unmarried woman, which technically still put her under the purview of her parents.

These days, modesty was the least of her concerns, but it was one of the few ways her family—along with the other dozens of families in their neighborhood who were part of the same church—could declare its beliefs, and one of the few ways an unmarried woman could defend herself.

"*Remove the temptation,*" Charity Wu always said. "*We expect our brothers to control themselves, but we remove temptation out of compassion. We cover our bodies as God concealed his in the temple. Moses was the only one permitted to see God the Father in the temple, and so we only allow our husbands to see our bodies."*

When Elizabeth had pointed out that Moses had only ever gotten an ass view of God on the Ark of the Covenant, she hadn't been able to sit comfortably for days—bruised in the only place Moses had ever seen God.

The Bishops didn't believe in the strap or the paddle, and Elizabeth preferred it that way. It just would have been nice if the Bishops had given her anything at all with which to convince Sharona to play nice. Instead, they'd given her a spoiled—and, more importantly, smart—brat to look after, who was too old for a nanny and too convinced of her own cleverness to talk sense into.

The sword swallower yanked four swords from his throat just as Elizabeth and the Bishop children came closer. A few of the bystanders tossed quarters or dollar bills into the basket at the edge of the platform on which he performed.

The sword swallower returned his swords to their place in the spinning holder and reached for a gleaming brass hook. "Excuse me. I couldn't help but overhear."

"What exactly did you overhear?" Elizabeth fought and lost against the flush on her cheeks. Sharona hadn't been tactful about the man's attractiveness.

He had nothing to hide, per se, but he was a touch thin, his complexion sickly, his hair shorn but stubble showing the dramatically receded hairline. He was hardly the masculine specimen that was luring Sharona into the circus, but a second glance had Elizabeth noticing muscle tone under his pasty skin. And he was fearless as he brought his head back and pushed the sharp end of the hook up his nose, then curved it down to emerge from his mouth.

She'd envy that fearlessness if he didn't look like he'd just caught himself on a fish hook.

The sword swallower gave a flourish, then picked up a handful of iron nails.

"Calling this a 'family circus' might be a bit of a stretch, but we stay pretty tame until after eight." The sword swallower carefully pushed one of the iron nails into his socket around the eyeball.

Elizabeth fought against the urge to retch, but she turned her face away. "Tame?"

"Relatively," he conceded. The wet sound that followed told her he'd slid the other one in.

"Don't you know you can lobotomize yourself like that?" Sharona said, fascinated in spite of herself.

"Gross! Cool!" Of course Todd would think this was the greatest thing since the spitball.

"I'm a professional," the sword swallower assured Sharona. "But don't try this at home, little man. Took magic and a bucket of luck for me to learn this without sending the tip into my gray matter, as the lady says, or piercing through the eye itself. Not a body horror fan, ma'am?"

"Not as a rule." Elizabeth still wasn't looking. She had no idea where he was putting the other four nails — and she didn't want to know.

"Nanny doesn't know how to have fun," Sharona replied. "Anything she's not afraid of, her religion forbids her from doing it."

"Well, we accept all ages in Arcanium until eight, as long as they're accompanied by an adult. Some of our oddities get a little frisky, so if I were you, I'd concentrate on the fringes rather than the juicy center of the circus. We have animal rides, performances, a carousel, food booths, midway games... Oops, looks like the little one likes shiny nails."

Elizabeth forced herself to look back at the sword swallower to make sure Maggie wasn't taking up swallowing sharp things herself. She couldn't resist a shudder as he unhooked himself.

"I told you I'd take care of her." Sharona shifted Maggie to her other shoulder, farther away from the nails in the sword swallower's hands.

"The haunted house might be a bit much for your youngers," the man continued. He bowed to the rest of the passing audience. "I'd recommend the midway. The prizes are eldritch, but nothing too questionable. Be sure to show them these." He put his hands behind his back, then whipped them back in front less than a second later. When he unclutched his fists, six gold dollar coins rested in his palms. Elizabeth hadn't even known they were still in circulation. "Well, would you look at that? You're quite the lucrative family. These ought to get you started."

With that, the sword swallower tipped the coins into Todd's eager hands then retrieved his nails again. One by one, he tossed them into his mouth and made a big show of swallowing them down.

Elizabeth turned away. This time she tasted bile at the back of her throat.

"Awesome!" Todd was at the age when everything was an exclamation. With her headache, Elizabeth was just glad they were outside so she didn't have to tell him to use his inside voice every five seconds. Sweet kid — needed work on his modulation.

"Hope I could settle your mind, if not your stomach, ma'am," the sword swallower said. "Welcome to Arcanium."

"Let's try that midway." Elizabeth didn't know whether she'd be able to handle the food court any time soon.

"Yay, scam artists and cheap toys," Sharona said in a cheery voice that had Maggie raising her arms in her own little cheer.

"I'm sorry. Who's the one who begged for us to stay?" Elizabeth maneuvered the stroller around to follow Todd as he sprang for the line of booths that seemed most promising as a midway.

They passed the woman in latex and the burned man in the collar on the way.

Maggie stretched out her little fingers for the leash. "I want doggie."

"You and me both, sister." Sharona spared another appreciative glance at the burned man's trousers.

They passed by the fortune teller's tent, which was verboten as far as Elizabeth was concerned. Jacob's son Joseph could divine all he wanted, but divination was still a form of witchcraft, and Elizabeth was no blessed son of Israel.

The midway was as the sword swallower had promised — with skulls, skeletons, tentacles and other such things as prizes instead of stuffed bears or cheap erasers, but no more extreme than one might see on a pirate ship. Despite the fact that the one-dollar coins were real currency, the attendants surprised Elizabeth by treating them as tokens instead — one coin per game, even though each game was three dollars a turn. Neither she nor Sharona nor Todd decided to look a gift horse in the mouth, and it saved some of the Bishops' money allotted for the trip.

The midway could only entertain them for so long, however, as expensive and difficult to master as the games were and with other things closer to the freak show to catch the kids' eyes.

Clowns, for instance. And not the clowns Elizabeth had been expecting.

Contrary to popular belief, Elizabeth liked clowns — friendly clowns with cute patched outfits, clowns who made balloon animals and emerged from tiny cars.

These were not those kinds of clowns.

At first glance from behind, they looked like some kind of punk rock fans lost from an outdoor concert. There wasn't anything intrinsically menacing about bustiers, hardcore leather boots and orange mohawks. But after a series of intricate tumbling moves in the miniature ring off the midway, they turned around and flourished for applause, and Elizabeth jerked the stroller to a stop.

"They could do Halloween makeup tutorials." Sharona looked back at where Elizabeth had frozen with the baby. "Oh, come on. Where are killer clowns on the list? Seven? Three? Do you know the odds any of them are serial killers?"

"The fear of killers is completely rational, no matter how statistically improbable." The cold sweat on Elizabeth's palms made her grip on the stroller handle too slippery to hold on to it with conviction. "And they've done studies. People are afraid of clowns because exaggerated, unnatural facial features unsettle the mind."

Sharona shrugged. "Not mine. I mostly just want the chick's outfit."

"You have your own phobias. It wouldn't be prudent to start on mine."

"Sure, I'm afraid of a massive storm destroying Metropolis, but I know mine is never going to happen. You, however, decided to fall into the arms of every clichéd phobia in the book. How do you even function?"

"Believe it or not, I'm unafraid of more things than I'm afraid of." Elizabeth managed to turn the stroller around. Unfortunately, that meant the creepy clowns with their creepy lantern eyes and creepy mouths painted to look creepily wide and — in the case of the older man with curly tufts of orange hair like a more classic clown — full of creepy teeth were now behind her where she couldn't see them.

"Name one," Sharona said.

"Schoolwork. I can look over that all day, while you sometimes seem to have a pathological fear of it."

That, at least, earned Elizabeth a genuine grin. "You want to move on?"

"Please."

"Great. The haunted house is next."

"You must be joking." Elizabeth closed her eyes and counted down from ten. It didn't help much, but it forced her to breathe with the count.

"Nope. Right there between us and the family-friendly carousel and circus animals." Sharona laughed with delight. "You want to go into the haunted house, don't you, Todd?"

"Yeah! I want to stick my hands in eyeballs and watch blood dripping out of someone's stomach," Todd said, as though describing a birthday party instead of carnage.

"Sounds like a blast." And by 'blast', Elizabeth meant 'nauseating image'. "I don't know about this place, kids. It looks like a strong breeze would blow it away."

"So do you," Sharona retorted. "But this place might actually have a spine."

The haunted house didn't look much sturdier than the midway booths, although it appeared more ambitious. It was composed of a collection of temporary structures — the sort that seemed to sprout up in construction sites or outside renovated buildings — clustered together to form a more substantial building. The vinyl siding had been covered with wood that wouldn't be fit for anything other than atmosphere. Any windows around the buildings had been painted over with ghoulish vignettes—a woman screaming, a bogeyman peering from behind curtains, a man attempting to run with partially amputated limbs, heads on pikes in the midst of hellish flames.

The style was sufficiently cartoonish to deemphasize the horror, but the bloodstain next to the stairway to the entrance seemed entirely too real, with a gleam that made it appear fresh. Real-looking cobwebs Elizabeth prayed were fake stretched across another length of wood. And a monster that looked like a cross between a Lon Chaney werewolf and a vampire bat loomed above the entrance. He rested on his stomach on the flat roof, clutching the wood on the side with his claws and staring unblinking at whoever dared ascend the stairs. Elizabeth could almost swear the monster breathed, that the pronounced muscles of his arms twitched. That it stared right at her.

She forced herself to tear her gaze away and apply her attention to the warning sign above the bloodstain. "Uh-oh, looks like there's an age advisory, Todd."

"'Some images and experiences within the haunted funhouse are too graphic or intense for children. No one under thirteen unless accompanied by a teenager or adult,'" Todd read. "And they use strobe lights. And it's our fault if we're traumatized. What is 'traumatized'?"

"Is that one of the things on your list, too? Terrifying flashing lights?" Sharona said.

"Still not funny. Even if I could get the stroller up those stairs, Todd, I don't want to go into a haunted house unless the name is preceded by Abbott and Costello."

"Who are they?" Todd asked.

"Oh, children of the cell phone generation, you have been grossly deprived. I'll have to rectify that. Shall we go home now so I can introduce you to comedy genius? Comedy, as in not terrifying." Elizabeth glanced up at the monster again. Had his claws been in that position before?

"But I want to go in," Todd said. "I don't mind blood and guts. I look at the roadkill on the side of the road. Dad lets me watch Bruce Willis with him."

"What a brave, cultured little gentleman," a man said from behind Elizabeth.

Sharona raised her eyebrows in appreciation, but she also thinned her lips to keep from smiling as Elizabeth looked over her shoulder.

Even though she anticipated something from her extensive list, nothing could have prepared her for a woman draped in a large albino boa constrictor, whose face was right in front of Elizabeth's.

She brought her hand to her mouth, bit down hard to keep unholy words from passing her lips, but that did nothing to muffle the undignified shriek. Only the sturdy stroller prevented Elizabeth from falling.

The man who had spoken rested his hand on her shoulder to steady her. Elizabeth automatically ducked from his touch.

He took her avoidance with alacrity. His calm, slightly amused expression didn't change. "I know it's sometimes pointless to say, but Raphael is quite harmless. He's accustomed to women handling him, which is why my snake charmer allows him out of her sight and why my assistant willingly wears him around the circus."

Only in a circus could an assistant's dress code include a red leather dress with corset laces up the sides, black bracelet cuffs that were made for chains and a literal boa as an accessory.

"Wow, his name is Raphael?" Todd exclaimed. "Like the Ninja Turtle?"

"I don't think the Ninja Turtle is who he was named after," the assistant replied. "Would you like to touch him? Really, he's as friendly as a cold-blooded creature can be."

"I'm sorry. I just can't," Elizabeth finally said. She forced the baby's stroller back with her, away from the man in the black leather pants and the girl with the serpent.

"Think he's the devil?" Sharona asked, joining Todd to marvel over the scales.

"I think he's a snake." Elizabeth rubbed at the gooseflesh that crawled all over her at the sight of the Bishop children touching the thing. "Look. I understand they're important, that they're fascinating and probably beautiful animals, but I can't—"

"There's no need to apologize," the man said. "Arcanium was made for shock and awe. I would be remiss to take offense when it is so successful.'

"You can hold him if you like," the assistant offered—to Todd and Sharona rather than Elizabeth. "I'm sure your sister can take the picture from a safe distance."

"Sister?" Sharona snorted. "I assume you're talking about the woman in black trying to blend into the wall. Do we look even slightly related? Here." Sharona hesitated before handing Elizabeth her phone. Kicking up a fuss if Elizabeth didn't give it back would be more embarrassing in front of circus folk. "Take a picture of us with the snake and the circus lady. Mom and Dad won't be upset by that, so we'll have something inoffensive to show them when they ask."

Elizabeth weighed her options—including tossing Sharona's phone to the monster on top of the haunted house and herding the children back to the car for their own protection, a survivalist combination of maternal and fight-or-flight instincts.

Sharona sighed. "It'll be more suspicious if we don't have any pictures at all. Come on. As funny as it is when your mother and my mother tag team for the scolding, I'd get grounded, too, you know."

"Sometimes, interacting with my client's teenager is like managing hostage negotiations," Elizabeth said by way of apology to the thoroughly amused, very bare-chested man. She carefully stretched her free hand out to take Sharona's phone without getting too close to the snake. She didn't like cell phones either, but any potential carcinogenic properties couldn't compare with an immediate reptilian threat.

"Managing a circus sometimes feels the same way," he replied. "I can hold the young one there if you want both hands."

Elizabeth's heightened awareness caught the way the man's assistant briefly tensed.

Elizabeth hitched Maggie up on her hip and offered the toddler the wooden cross pendant on her necklace to play with. "I can multitask. Thanks, though."

She found the camera on the phone and waited with minimal trembling for the assistant to drape the snake over Todd's and Sharona's necks then pose on the other side of Todd with a beautiful smile. There was only so much to be done about the prominent cleavage in the keyhole window of the dress, but a certain amount of sexiness was expected among circus women.

"You sure you don't want to try Raphael yourself?" the man asked Elizabeth. "I promise, no biting. If our snake charmer were here, you wouldn't even have to fear the dangerous ones."

"No," Elizabeth said quickly. Then she corrected herself. "No, thank you." She was familiar enough with the Bishop children to let some snark sneak into her interaction with them, but she'd been trained to be unfailingly polite with strangers.

"Thanks. That's so cool! I want to meet the snake lady now," Todd said as the assistant lifted Raphael back to her own shoulders.

Elizabeth and Sharona shared a glance as Elizabeth returned the phone.

"Hey, twerp, how about we go through the haunted house before Nanny Elizabeth decides to steal someone's Taser to rescue us from the circus in a blaze of electrified glory? Come on... Inside's the best escape."

"Inside is where we trap you for all eternity," the man said, still with that amused expression that crinkled the corners of his startlingly amber-hazel eyes. "But do go in and enjoy yourselves, if you dare."

Sharona appeared caught between the man's charm and the menace of his words, but she put an arm around her little brother's shoulder to lead him up the stairs to the entrance.

"See you on the other side," she said to Elizabeth.

"No photography, please," the man said before the kids entered. "I would hate to have to confiscate your phone."

"I wasn't going to take pictures," Sharona said.

"Yes, you were. Arcanium lets you take pictures of all our wonderfully weird displays outside of the haunted funhouse, but I would appreciate it if you would refrain from revealing all of a humble circus' secrets. The clowns won't eat you for disobeying, but you'd piss off the owner, and that's never a good idea, young lady."

"Do I need to take your phone again while you go through?" Elizabeth asked.

Sharona's competing feelings about the man seemed to deepen. After a moment to consider, she tossed her phone down to Elizabeth.

"Good girl," Elizabeth said quietly.

She couldn't help the twinge of disquiet when as the kids entered the screaming darkness, which cut off as soon as they closed the door behind them.

"What made you think she was going to take pictures?" Elizabeth asked.

"Teenagers are our biggest offenders," the man replied. "When I'm not here, there's not much to be done, but I'm here now. And I'm the circus' fortune teller. I'm exceptional at divining the future."

"Or at being observant, I suppose." Even knowing that most fortune tellers weren't actually psychic, Elizabeth edged away from him just in case.

"Oh, don't worry. I don't read people who haven't paid for the pleasure — unless they intend to break my rules. I take such trespass very seriously. Maya, love, I'll meet you in the tent."

Maya stroked the serpent's golden-white scales, visibly wary, but she allowed the man to lift her hand, with the snake's head resting upon it. He kissed the serpent's head. The snake accepted such unsnakely affection without resistance. Then the man wrapped his arm around Maya's waist, pulled her close with the snake still between them and kissed her.

Elizabeth recognized the intensity behind an otherwise chaste kiss. Yet, though all her upbringing told her to look away, she couldn't. Her pale cheeks were probably bright red.

At that moment, the toddler became entranced by the gold bracelet coiled around the man's upper arm, and the baby decided now was the time to get properly fussy.

"Be good," Maya whispered to the man. She stepped away from him and turned to Elizabeth. "If you pass by Oddity Row, our Bearded Lady, Kitty, does really well with kids. Have a good visit."

"Thank you." Elizabeth struggled to keep the squirming toddler from mauling the man in the pursuit of sparkly things — the very picture of human temptation, Maggie was. "I'm sorry. She has a thing for jewelry. We thought she'd grow out of it by the time she started talking."

"Want the pretty," Maggie said, making grabby hands.

"It's quite all right." The man slid the bracelet from his arm and handed it to Maggie. "This ought to distract her while you tend to the littlest one."

"I appreciate that, but it looks expensive…"

"Gold can be cleaned. She can't hurt it." The man hooked his thumbs in the pockets of his leather pants, though there wasn't much room for them.

Elizabeth had to work not to look where his fingers drew her gaze. She was only human herself. Instead, she busied herself with putting Maggie in the child's seat of the stroller — a godsend for just this kind of situation. While Maggie played with the bangle, crooning her favorite jewel song that she sang when she got to play with her mother's costume jewelry, Elizabeth lifted Brianna from her seat and started searching the diaper bag for the bottle.

"Managing so many eccentric personalities has its drawbacks," the man said. "It must be just as difficult to take care of so many children on your own, especially of such varying ages."

"Yes, well, the mother only has to take care of them one or two days a week, so she doesn't see any problem having more," Elizabeth muttered before she realized she'd said it aloud. She stiffened and straightened. "Oh, I'm sorry. It's been a long day, and Sharona's well beyond the point where she needs a nanny, but she still needs a firm hand, and I can only be so firm. It's like herding cats. Sometimes I wish I had a few extra limbs to go around. Between the four of them, I'd probably need to be an octopus to keep them all happy."

As attractive as the fortune teller was when playing mysterious, his intensity only increased when he smiled. Straight white teeth, the hint of dimples and the light in his eyes all showcased cheekbones that could cut glass. Elizabeth had suffered from a weakness for cheekbones before.

He's off-limits, Liz. On so many levels. An echoed memory of him kissing Maya played in her mind's eye. Guilt entwined with the unwelcome heat it inspired.

"Or a spider," he said.

That effectively killed the mood. Elizabeth shuddered. "Not a spider. I can't stand spiders. Their prickly little legs, multiple eyes, hairy little bodies, the way they move... I have to call in one of the groundskeepers if I see them in the house. I even asked Mr. Bishop to squish one before, and that's supposedly under the heading of my job. Good thing he was understanding."

"You might want to avoid a certain part of my carousel, then. We do have a squid, though. For someone afraid of snakes and spiders, it surprises me that you'd be fonder of cephalopods."

"Well, I'm fonder in comparison. I wouldn't want to be face-to-face with one," Elizabeth said. The baby finally decided she was as hungry as she sounded, and from the feel of the diaper, she needed changing, too. "Wicked creatures, too clever by half."

"There's nothing wrong with being wicked and clever."

Maggie stretched up her chubby arms to offer the fortune teller his bangle back. He accepted it as though receiving a gift from a queen. "I don't believe I've introduced myself. Bell Madoc, man of many talents here in the circus."

"Child charmer, fortune teller, circus folk wrangler. Did I miss any?" She draped the spit cloth over her shoulder to prepare for burping the baby. Black was uniquely unforgiving of spit-up, although the admonition against vanity should have forbidden her from caring.

"Magician, acrobat, fighter, lover, dreamer... I once played Ringmaster as well, before we found our current one. I much prefer a less domineering role. My obsessively controlling ways are best behind the scenes." The baby wrapped her grasping fist around Bell's finger, playing with the large red stone on his ring. Brianna was gearing up to be as shiny-fascinated as Maggie. "I've always enjoyed children. It is unfortunate my tastes are so esoteric as to limit their presence at my circus. Their desires are so simple."

"You've clearly never played Candyland with a toddler—or tried to explain to them why they can't have something. They're more complicated than they seem, and they only get more complicated as they grow. Babies, however, are simple. Messy, but simple." She burped Brianna and wiped her mouth. "You wouldn't happen to have a changing table in your bathrooms, would you?"

"Portable toilets, unfortunately. But if you have a changing pad, there's no reason the picnic tables shouldn't suffice."

"People get miffed if you change babies where they eat their food, even if it's on a pad, but it'll have to do." She was no stranger to accusatory looks, and a baby needed changing when she needed changing, not when it was convenient for everyone involved.

"I give you official authorization," Bell said. "None of mine will give you any trouble...about taking care of the baby, that is. I really must be going, but tell Sharona" — he opened his hand with a graceful fanning of his fingers, revealing Sharona's smartphone, which he must have taken from the pocket of Elizabeth's skirt without her knowing — "I appreciate how she and her brother enjoyed the haunted house. It's still a relatively new attraction, and I'm adding new things whenever I can. Do watch out for the things that creep and slither on the carousel."

Elizabeth took the phone, not knowing how to respond to him stealing from her then returning the stolen item. He bowed with the same uncommon grace and blew a kiss to the toddler, who waved happily, now distracted by fistfuls of Cheerios she'd found in the stroller basket underneath her.

Bell glanced above the haunted funhouse entrance. "Someone likes you."

He walked away as Elizabeth raised her head. She jumped, nearly dropping the baby in the process.

The monster grinned at her, baring sharp teeth like those of a python or a fruit bat — some kind of creature that gave her the heebie-jeebies either way. The wings folded over his back rustled half open, and he blinked.

Dear Lord, it's a person. Heavily made-up, with pneumatic or engineered wings, but an actual person who stared at her with those inscrutable red eyes — as though someone had spilled crimson ink in them.

Elizabeth slowly drew the stroller away from the side of the haunted funhouse, fingers going cold. The man didn't take his eyes off her, nor did he stop smiling his jagged smile.

Sharona and Todd came running around the haunted house, Sharona forgetting about being cool and disaffected in the wake of her brother's infectious enthusiasm.

"Oh my God, that was fucking awesome!" Sharona said. "There were these people, right? And they were all in a line while this guy legit *whipped* them. I swear you could see their skin splitting. It was so realistic."

"I saw a monster burst out of a man's chest," Todd said proudly.

"Don't use four-letter words in front of your brother and sisters, Sharona," Elizabeth said distractedly.

"We just went through the best gross-out haunted house I've ever been in, and you're worried about me saying 'fuck'?"

Elizabeth held up Sharona's phone.

"Oh, fine. I'm allowed to say 'fine,' aren't I? It's a four-letter f-word, after all."

"A little gore, and we're back to being a smart aleck." The teenager drew Elizabeth's attention away from the monster for a moment, but when she looked back, it had resumed its original position as though it had never moved, never blinked, never rustled its wings, never smiled at her.

"What do you know about gore? You barely let us see PG-13 movies, and you cover your eyes at the violent parts on TV."

"Believe it or not, Sharona, I wasn't always committed to the orthodox. I've seen adult movies. I've even had a beer. Disgusting, but I had it. Now, can you do me another favor?" Elizabeth glanced up at the monster again. It still wasn't looking at her anymore, but the hairs on the back of her neck under the head scarf stood on end anyway. "Can you take Todd and Maggie to the carousel? Brianna needs to be changed, and the picnic tables are my only option."

"Sure, why not?" Sharona waited for Elizabeth to give her the money for the three kids. If she'd overestimated the cost, Elizabeth probably wouldn't see the money again, but that was okay. It was Mrs. Bishop's anyway.

"Thank you." And Elizabeth meant it. "Meet me by the picnic tables when you're through. We'll eat before visiting the circus animals. And maybe—*maybe*—we'll visit the oddities. Take pictures on the carousel. Your mom would like that."

"Come on, Maggie Bear. We all know you don't like it when Miss Elizabeth does diaper duty. Todd, you hold on to Maggie." Sharona waved without looking back, trying to make it look like a dismissal, but adrenaline had apparently left her mellow, which made Elizabeth's job much easier. Having children under the age of ten compete for their much older sister's affection could lead to some serious friction, but it was a good thing Sharona secretly loved her younger siblings and sometimes even showed it if her friends weren't around.

She wasn't always such a monster.

Elizabeth rolled the empty stroller and continued to pat Brianna through her fussiness on the way to the picnic tables. The smell of the food booths was simultaneously enticing and worrying. She'd anticipated less-than-vegan fare to select from, so she had date bars in the diaper bag, but when she wanted something more substantial, date bars just didn't cut it. Looked like she'd probably have to wait until she returned to the Bishops' home, where their housekeeper fortunately kept plenty of vegan items for the Bishops' full-time, in-home nanny.

Elizabeth made a beeline for the one picnic table where no one was sitting. She plopped the diaper bag down on the seat then quickly spread the changing pad. A few patrons shot nasty looks her way, but she laid the baby down and did a swift diaper change.

She'd been the nanny for the Bishops ever since one of Elizabeth's younger sisters, Amy, had married off and left their family, which had been right after Todd had come along. Between the Bishops' three younger children and the six Wu children who had come after Elizabeth, she could probably change a baby with her eyes closed.

Petrosian saints, especially the women, were in short supply, but they were known locally to be good, honest workers willing to take a humbler paycheck in return for a generous donation now and then to the Petrosian Church. Hiring someone concerned with religious law had its perks, especially when a wealthy couple needed someone to look after their children. When a person wanted good furniture, they went to the Quakers. When they wanted good bread, they went to the Amish. When they wanted midwives, they went to Quiverfull women. When they wanted good childcare, they went to the Petrosians and asked for their unmarried daughters.

After the diaper change, Brianna was still fussy, so Elizabeth arranged a wrap to keep Brianna close to her. In the warmth of the day, having a wrap and a baby against her body made her feel like she was going to faint, but she drank from her water bottle and braced herself. Discipline in modest clothing was something every Petrosian saint learned early, especially in the dead of summer when everyone else walked around in shorts and swimwear.

A younger middle-aged woman holding a plastic stein of half-finished ale sauntered to the bench and looked up at Elizabeth as though she were looking down instead. "If you're not going to eat here, quit hogging the table."

"I'm almost finished then I'll be out of your way."

"You know, it's unsanitary to change a diaper where people eat, not to mention rude. If I see mess anywhere, I'm going to tell management."

"Management told me to use the table." Elizabeth gathered the dirty diaper and the changing pad off the wooden picnic table. "I apologize for being in your way."

"You people all think you can just do anything." The woman's fake nails clicked on the stein as she set it down. She pushed her sunglasses up her nose in a gesture that shouldn't have been as aggressive as it was. "Just walk around and get special treatment and protection on our tax dollars when you're all trying to spread sharia law to the rest of us."

"Ma'am, I'm not Muslim, and even if I were, religious liberty means religious liberty for religions you don't like, too," Elizabeth said.

Petrosian saints weren't supposed to wear jewelry to avoid the appearance of vanity or arrogance, but these days, many of the women wore simple wooden cross necklaces to avoid this very association. And while the Petrosian church had no love for Islam, Thomas Petros worked closely with some of the local Muslim, Hindu and Sikh leaders to promote religious acceptance.

"Don't 'ma'am' me. I'm not your mother, thank Jesus, or else I would have told you how far back you put the feminist movement by wearing that burqa, or whatever you call it."

"Muslims refer to head coverings as hijab, but, like I said, I'm not Muslim. I'm an orthodox Christian, and I just needed to change my employer's child. Please, let me pass."

"So now you're giving good Christians a bad name? God doesn't need you wearing that thing. Jesus freed us from the law, honey. It says so in the Bible."

"With all due respect, if you call me 'honey', I'm going to keep calling you 'ma'am.' Petrosian saints are aware of what the Bible says about the law, but my spiritual choices are really none of your business. Please, let me pass."

"You're making Christianity look just like Islam, as though it's up to women to protect men from themselves. Do you know how insulting that is? Come on, honey. You don't need that." The woman reached for Elizabeth's head covering.

Elizabeth ducked away, turning to put herself between the partially inebriated woman and the baby. "If you wouldn't pull down my skirt, ma'am, please don't pull off my head covering. Wearing it is a gesture of respect."

"You don't have to hide your head from Him."

Lord spare me from well-meaning saints who don't know the difference between adherence and oppression.

"Don't touch me!" All trace of politeness — a mixture of Southern charm and Petrosian respect — disappeared as the woman got her fingernails under the edge of the scarf and pulled it away. "For God's sake, I have a child with me."

"See? No thunder and lightning. You're no more disrespecting God than I am. God loves us. He doesn't want us in chains. We have to show the other side that we're free."

Elizabeth tried to retrieve the black square cloth without startling the baby, but the woman danced away to the cheers and laughter of the women and their teenage children who had accompanied them. Elizabeth frantically tried to keep her head and neck covered with her long hair, but her shirt didn't have a high collar, and she wasn't sure everything was concealed the way it was supposed to be.

"I'm not going around covering random women's heads in the name of God. It's common courtesy not to force me to follow your form of religion in the same name. Give me the head covering. Now!"

Brianna punched her little fists against Elizabeth's chest at the shout, opening her mouth and adding her shrieks to the rest.

"It's for your own good." The woman crumpled the scarf into a ball and tossed it to her friend. "God loves you enough to free you from the law."

"I never said I was imprisoned by it," Elizabeth said coldly, hindered by the baby. "But I'm pretty sure both of us are bound by man's law, and man's law says you just stole from me and assaulted me. Give it back to me! I need it!" Poisonous bile soured the back of her throat. Sickness born of fear moved through her belly like frigid barbed wire.

"You're what's wrong with America!" the woman shouted back as her friend tossed the scarf to her again. She dodged Elizabeth. "People like you are how the terrorists win."

The sickness was there, right on the tip of her tongue. "So help me, if you don't return that head covering, I'm—"

"What on Earth is going on here?"

The question itself might not have been enough to interrupt either the woman or Elizabeth from the childish war that had almost turned adult really fast. But the one who stepped into everyone's sight and posed the question was strange enough that they stopped what they were doing.

Elizabeth wrapped her arms around the baby as she swallowed back the bile again and tried to stop shaking. Embracing Brianna was as much protection for herself as for the little girl.

The unique personage that was the circus's Bearded Lady pushed through the circle of onlookers then stood between Elizabeth and the women playing keepaway, separating the two warring parties. She was covered head to toe in chestnut hair, the hair on her head and the moustache and beard thickest and longest, swaying side to side like her beribboned skirt as she walked. With a purple corset and the butterfly illusion combs arranged in her hair, she looked like nothing so much as a curvy pirate fairy queen covered in ginger cat fur. She stood almost as tall as Elizabeth and exuded presence.

Hands on her hips, she took in the sight of the head scarf, with the woman's fake nails bright against the black, and Elizabeth's hair loose and disheveled, flat where the scarf had covered it and freer where it had tucked into the fabric like in a snood.

The Bearded Lady held out her hand to the fake-nailed woman. "I don't believe that belongs to you."

"I just wanted to help her. Look at the poor girl, trembling as though God's going to strike her down just because people can see her hair." But the woman grudgingly handed the wrinkled scarf to the Bearded Lady.

"Of all the places to attack someone because of their differences, a freak show circus seems a strange place to do it." The Bearded Lady returned the scarf to Elizabeth, who went through the steps of putting it in place one-handed, tucking her hair underneath and wrapping it around her neck to conceal all but her face once again. Only when she was fully covered did she let out a shaky sigh of relief. She could make sure it was on straight later. All that mattered now was that it was on. Her relief translated to Brianna, who hiccupped pathetically but stopped crying.

"Thank you," Elizabeth said.

The fake-nailed woman retreated slightly to stand closer to her friends. "Read the Bible, honey. You don't have to submit to anyone but Him, and He doesn't have a dress code."

"I don't see you walking around without so much as a fig leaf," the Bearded Lady said, sparing Elizabeth from her own similar retort. "If I hear that anyone else is harassing this woman, you'll have to answer to the circus owner, and believe me, that will not end well. He doesn't like it when his customers are harassed by anyone other than the clowns."

Nervous laughter defused the situation. The spectators dispersed, and the woman and her friends turned back to the table, much more interested now in their fried food.

"Oh my, who is this with such a fussy face?" The Bearded Lady tickled the baby under her chin. "She is absolutely precious. Hi, sugarplum! Oh no, we don't want tears here, do we?"

Elizabeth was far more willing to pass the baby to her than the fortune teller. And while the Bearded Lady cooed at Brianna and helped transform her pathetic face into a delighted one, Elizabeth adjusted her head covering until it was more or less straight again.

"I'm so sorry for the inconvenience," Elizabeth said.

"There's no need to apologize for other people's rudeness. Believe me, Arcanium's no stranger to Neanderthals who can't distinguish their head from their...hindquarters."

People watching their language in the face of visible religiousness wasn't a new phenomenon, but while Elizabeth didn't require it of anyone but the Bishop children, she much preferred this reaction to the previous one by the fake-nailed woman. Not least because it reminded her to curb her own poisonous tongue.

"But we have more than a few men and women who can make someone's life a living hell if they do anything to threaten anyone in this circus. I was this close to whistling for our strongman." The Bearded Lady carried Brianna as Elizabeth rolled the stroller away from the picnic tables and the main thoroughfare. "Don't hesitate to do the same if any of these folks give you more grief. Would you like for me to arrange for your tickets to be refunded?"

"You're too kind, but that won't be necessary. Actually, could you stay with us a little longer? The other kids should be coming back soon, and they'd love to see you. The fortune teller's assistant—Maya, I think her name was—said you'd be appropriate for the younger ones. She wasn't wrong."

The Bearded Lady smiled, and for a moment, Elizabeth barely noticed the extra hair. Elizabeth supposed, though, that assuming her beauty was in spite of the hair or beyond the hair was just as uncharitable as the people who couldn't see beyond her head scarf.

"I'd love to," the woman replied, unfazed by the baby pulling at the beads braided into her beard. "I'm Kitty, by the way. The name wasn't even intended to be ironic when my parents gave it to me."

"Oh my God, you're the best," Sharona said, coming up from behind. "How much shampoo do you go through in a week?"

"You have a beard! I want a beard. Wow! How long is it?" Todd asked.

"Kitty!" Maggie shouted.

Chapter Two

For a trip that probably shouldn't have happened, they didn't get home until dinnertime.

After Elizabeth put the baby to bed in the nursery next to her own bedroom, she helped Maggie wash up and brush her teeth. They eventually wound up in Todd's room, where Maggie preferred to listen to the big kid books Todd had Elizabeth to read to him — books that nurtured his curiosity and kept his interest, so usually books about dinosaurs, bugs, boy detectives or adventures. Elizabeth much preferred the boy detectives or adventures, but after the circus, he had it in his mind to hear about bugs. Elizabeth muscled through the book while trying not to shudder at the pictures.

"Did you two have fun today?" Elizabeth asked, rocking Maggie in her lap.

"Yeah!" Todd was using his inside shouting voice this time. Hard to fault a boy for enthusiasm, as long as he wasn't enthusiastic right in her ear.

"Yeah? What was your favorite part?"

"The Rotting Man. Did you see his boils? They were seeping *puuuuus*." Todd made a delightfully grossed-out face. "The haunted funhouse, too. That was so cool. All the blood hit the walls like *blam*!"

"I'm beginning to sense a theme here," Elizabeth said, her gross-out less delightful.

"And I liked the snake lady and the lady who let us take a picture with the snake. That snake was bigger than me! And the bug tent, with the tarantulas and hissing cockroaches and ants and moths and butterflies."

"Ah yes," Elizabeth said. "All the things that stopped my heart were things you liked. You really want my youngest sister as your new nanny, don't you?" She tickled Todd until he squirmed in his usual 'no more' way. "What about you, Miss Mags? What did you like?"

"Elephant! Merry-go-round horsies was fun." Maggie was still working on her verb tenses, but she matched Todd's enthusiasm in an excellent bit of mimicry that showed her absolute love for her big brother.

"I'll bet they 'was'," Elizabeth said. "What about Kitty?"

"Kitty!" Maggie threw her hands into the air and grasped at Elizabeth's head scarf, but she'd already learned to only grasp, not pull. "Kitty twirls."

"Yes, Kitty twirled you around and twirled her skirt and her hair and gave you little braids." Elizabeth tugged where she'd removed the small braided pigtails Kitty had done for the little girl.

"I'm glad you let us walk Oddity Row," Sharona said in the doorway. She wore pajamas, even though it wasn't close to her bedtime. "I thought it was going to be just another freak show, and it kind of was, but they weren't just on display, where I'd wonder whether they were some kind of fake. They were walking around, interacting, doing little mini-performances. Wish we could have gone to the show, though, even under the threat of killer clownage."

Elizabeth beckoned Sharona into Todd's room. She came in and sat cross-legged at the foot of the bed, her phone in her hands.

"I'm sure your parents would prefer you in one piece. Did you go through your pictures?" Elizabeth asked.

"Yeah, although the half-nakedness doesn't seem so bad in context anymore," Sharona said. "I guess you wouldn't agree, but I barely noticed the woman's bikini with all those snakes around her."

"And I suppose you didn't notice the strongman's short leather pants showing off all the muscles... Oh wait," Elizabeth said with a grin. Sharona had nearly drooled at the sight of the oiled-up strongman. Elizabeth had been tempted, too, but she had much more practice than Sharona in the art of self-denial.

"Why was no one wearing much clothes anyway?" Todd asked.

"That's your cue, Mother Superior," Sharona said.

Elizabeth had no interest in giving the little monster the satisfaction of religious condemnation. "Circuses are kind of like gymnastics or ballet. It's easier to see the skill when there's less in the way to cover it. And some of the circus people there wouldn't be able to show off how they're different from us if they were covered up. For instance, you've never noticed my massive hunchback, have you?"

"You don't have a hunchback," Todd said, giggling.

"But you wouldn't know, because of all my clothes," Elizabeth said.

"Yeah, *anything* could be under there. How can we be sure she's even human?" Sharona tickled Todd's toes. "She could be a giant millipede."

"It's not true," Elizabeth assured Maggie, who had started poking Elizabeth through her clothing to make sure she didn't feel little legs under all the layers. "Probably. So today wasn't a total waste, Sharona?"

"Are you kidding? It was nice to go someplace that wasn't just little kid stuff. Even the actual little kid stuff was cool. Did you know you could ride wooden people on the carousel?"

"I rode the squid," Todd said, raising his hand.

"I approve," Elizabeth replied. "Well, all right, kiddos. With visions of boils, spiders and snakes dancing in your head, it's time to go to sleep. You got a bit of a sunburn today, didn't you, Miss Mags? Let's go put some aloe lotion on that."

Elizabeth tucked Todd in and kissed him on the forehead before leading Maggie back to the bathroom to find the soothing lotion. "See? I'll put some on with you. My cheeks feel flushed. Can you help me put some on?" She laughed as Maggie slathered it over her cheeks. Then she gathered Maggie in her arms and rocketed her to her room. Her chandelier had already been dampened into a nightlight. Just as Elizabeth turned on the princess lamp for an additional nightlight, thunder rumbled in the distance.

"Hey, kiddo, I'll be just across the hall in my room if the storm gets scary tonight, okay?"

But Maggie was a brave little princess. She'd stopped joining Elizabeth in bed during storms already, while Todd had taken a lot longer. Elizabeth was almost sad at Maggie's strength. It reminded her all the more of her own weakness. Her mother had never let her in bed during storms. She'd hidden under covers and nearly smothered herself with the corner of the quilt to keep her whimpers from waking anyone else in the household. She wished she had been more like Maggie. She couldn't help but imagine all the things that the tiny toddler was going to be able to do when she grew up.

"Love you, sweetie," she whispered against Maggie's forehead after her good night kiss.

Before she went down the hall to her bedroom, she ducked into Sharona's. Sharona had turned on her flat-screen, but her attention was fixed on her phone as she texted.

"Thanks for helping me with your brother and sisters today."

"No problem." Sharona didn't look up, but the fact that she hadn't said anything insulting or snarky was still an improvement on some nights.

"Waffles tomorrow morning? Or for lunch, depending on when you wake up?" Elizabeth asked.

This time Sharona glanced up with a grin. "Sure. Thanks."

Sometimes monsters were okay.

Elizabeth stopped by the baby's room again to check that she was well into sleep before slipping into her own room and locking the door behind her. A locked door wouldn't delay her more than a few seconds than an unlocked one in case of emergency, but it would more than delay anyone trying to get to her—long enough for her to hide what she needed to.

The first thing Elizabeth did was remove her head covering. The pores on her scalp opened to the air conditioning — in January! — like a parched tongue to water. She shook her head to loosen the clumps of her hair, then shimmied out of the black shirt and skirt, leaving them on the floor next to the hamper. She brought her flip phone and the baby monitor into the bathroom with her.

The bathroom accommodations were as luxurious as those in the rest of the house — marble countertops, custom vanity, porcelain soaking tub, shower the size of a New York apartment. The rooms had been planned as a mother-in-law suite until Mrs. Bishop had convinced the mister that a Petrosian nanny would be much better for the kids and her nerves.

Outside the shower, she removed her bra and underwear — plain, cotton, dark — and avoided the mirrors as she stepped across the stone barrier into the shower. She liked this better than the glass doors to the other showers in the house, because she didn't have to see herself in the bathroom mirrors. She could close her eyes and feel her way by touch while in the shower. Outside of it, a black robe waited for her.

Once wrapped in terrycloth, Elizabeth took a moment to check whether her hair still covered her head and neck. It would cover her better when it was dried.

Her mother called Elizabeth while she was in the middle of drying it.

How does she always seem to know? Elizabeth set down the hairdryer. She probably wasn't going to use it for the rest of the night, so she took the baby monitor and phone back to her room — bigger than Sharona's but smaller than the master, with ceilings and paneling that belonged in a centuries-old library, practically palatial for a humble Petrosian saint who lived in a nun-like cell when she was at home. Other than the laundry, the room barely appeared lived in. She was hardly one to collect possessions, and she was the third Wu daughter who had stayed in the suite. It was no more permanent than a hotel room, whether it took ten months or another ten years for the Bishops to request her to check out.

"Hello, Mother."

"I don't approve of your tone."

"Sorry, Mother. It's been a very long day."

"You always sound ironic. It's very disrespectful," Charity said.

"You know I don't mean it. How's everything at home?"

"Your sister Ruth is pregnant again."

"Baby number four?" Elizabeth asked.

"Don't you remember all your nieces and nephews?"

"At the end of a day like this, sometimes I forget I have parents."

"If you don't stop using that tone, I'm going to put your dad on," Charity said.

Elizabeth swallowed. Anything she could say would turn nasty, and none of the words would help the roiling in her stomach.

"Yes, Ruth's having her fourth baby, due in June."

"How's Amy?" She'd been the last Wu daughter to sleep on the very bed on which Elizabeth was sitting and, from Elizabeth's perspective, Charity's favorite daughter—the consummate woman from top to bottom, cheerful, submissive, passive, sweet and an excellent mother and wife. And all of it seemed so frustratingly effortless on Amy's part.

Five of the seven Wu daughters had married before age thirty. All the Wu daughters who'd married already had at least two children. Elizabeth would have been considered a complete failure if she weren't working for the Bishops, taking a single woman's position as a caretaker for parents who needed help. Her only other option had been playing Cinderella in either her mother's household or any of her sisters', and none of them had really wanted her underfoot, especially her sisters. They hadn't considered the presence of another sister conducive to forging familial bonds, and none of them trusted her to nanny for their children. Non-Petrosian children weren't at quite the same risk. Even a once-lapsed Petrosian was considered an excellent role model, as long as the lapse was never mentioned.

Charity waxed lyrical about Amy and mentioned a few more things about Ruth and Miriam before asking, "Are you behaving? Following your commandments?"

"Yes, Mother."

"It doesn't sound like you are."

"How can I sound more obedient?" She said that, yet she could hear Charity shaking her head.

"The laws are more than laws, Elizabeth. They are the way we respect God, making an effort toward purity we can never attain. It's a sacred calling. I thought you understood that."

"I do." Elizabeth rubbed her forehead, hunched over her knees. "Believe me, I do. I'm doing the best I can. If I hadn't been prepared to do that, I wouldn't have come back. I wouldn't have stayed with the Bishops for as long as I have. I would have stopped taking your calls."

"Obedience is a discipline, but it's meant to bring us closer to Him. That's all I want for you. That's all your father wants for you. He says he can start looking for a husband for you whenever you want to leave the Bishops. Your years are slipping by. Soon, marriage will no longer be available to you, with no possibility for children."

"I thought I'd made myself clear, Mother. I'm going to be taking care of the Bishops' children until they all grow up and move out. Then you can send me to another family. That's just how it has to be. As your least desirable daughter, I'm sure Father's wiping sweat off his holy brow."

"Elizabeth…"

"Forgive me."

"We always forgive you when you ask. Go to sleep now. It's late. And remember to say your prayers."

"Goodnight, Mother."

Elizabeth tossed her phone onto the nightstand and continued to massage her head, knowing full well that nothing she did would dull the knitting needle making its way from temple to temple. Part of it was from overheating most of the afternoon, part of it from handling four children and part of it from dealing with her mother, even for a few minutes. Forgiveness was divine, but Charity made no effort to hide how much Elizabeth was her disappointment. Being dutifully single was all well and good, but it would have represented her family better to be dutifully married. She'd thrown away that opportunity when she'd left the fold. Returning didn't give her that opportunity back, no matter what weight Father had within the community.

Elizabeth leaned over and pulled the chest out from under the bed. Her eyes barely open, she unlatched the chest to retrieve the bottle of whiskey she kept inside it. She took three deep swallows in succession straight from the bottle, screwing her face against the burn. She took two more swallows then put it back in the chest and kicked the chest under her bed.

Petrosians were teetotalers. Not even wine was permitted. There was plenty of biblical precedent for the drinking of wine, of course, but for all the damage alcohol could do to a family—Noah and his sons, Lot and his daughters—Petrosians believed there was no need to tempt those around them who might more easily stumble. Elizabeth would have stuck with a good high-content wine if she could, but she didn't like drinking a whole bottle, and she couldn't very well keep a partially used one in the Bishops' refrigerator without someone knowing she'd fallen pretty far off the church wagon.

She already had everything planned out for any emergency during the night, because once she'd had her whiskey, she certainly couldn't drive. If it was bad enough, she'd have Sharona take the wheel. If it was too bad for that, someone probably needed an ambulance. She didn't drink enough for a hangover or to get properly drunk—just enough to take the edge off.

While avoiding the full-length mirror by the window again and also avoiding looking down at herself, she pulled on a pair of black pajama pants and a long-sleeved turtleneck baggy enough on her slight frame to give her skin room to breathe while still keeping her covered. It wasn't the nightgown prescribed in the admonition that she dress like a woman, but this was one of the few areas in which her mother, her mother's husband and her father had agreed not to battle. The attire in which she slept away from the eyes of others was such a minor detail. They'd only fought back on long pants during the day, when she would be in the public eye. She'd acquiesced as a teenager but had thoroughly rebelled against the plethora of wardrobe strictures after leaving the Petrosian fold.

Yes, Elizabeth Wu was one of the movement's greatest embarrassments on many levels, her embarrassments well outweighing those of Father — which must have filled him with as much relief as righteousness.

Elizabeth had been given her mother's husband's surname. He'd agreed to marry Charity, despite her getting pregnant by another man. Oh, how they had labored over Mary analogies while Charity had grown larger and larger with Elizabeth inside her.

All of Thomas Petros' other children were given greater honor among the rest, sons and daughters of a reluctant prophet, although Thomas made no effort to ensure preferential treatment. His sons and daughters also withstood more scrutiny. Such scrutiny became more malicious upon the bastard daughter of an adulterous union.

"Even prophets sinned," Thomas said often to his congregation. *"There was only one who did not sin, and he spent all of his time among the worst of the worst."* The important thing was to never sin again, and he didn't. Not another bastard was born from him or from Charity.

But Elizabeth had still come forth in that magnified sin, a constant reminder through her more European features that she was not like her sisters, who all bore a purer Chinese heritage proudly upon their faces.

Much had been made of those years when she had cut ties from the Petrosian saints, with frequent comparisons to Jesus' parable of the shepherd and of the prodigal son. When she'd returned, Thomas had preached of Mary Magdalene — not the woman who would have been stoned for adultery, who had never been named in the Gospels, but the woman freed of demons and among Jesus' favored women. How Thomas and Charity and the rest of the community had celebrated her return—too loudly and not without a generous helping of virtuous forgiveness. Still, despite the warm welcome, the few proposals of marriage from before she'd left quickly dried up, and they'd had to wait for someone outside the fold to take her as a nanny.

And ever since she'd returned, it wasn't just the community's behavior that had changed. Elizabeth knelt before her bed and clasped her hands, but she still couldn't pray. Not honestly. She waited as long as she could stand, then wrapped her night scarf around her head and neck and crawled between her sheets to the sound of close thunder and rain pattering upon the giant windows across from her bed. The curtains covered them, but they didn't muffle enough the storm sounds from outside. That's how she liked it. Her headache subsided under the heat of the whiskey and the peaceful percussion of the rain.

* * * *

When she woke up, she wasn't sure what had done it. There was rain, yes, and thunder, but she'd slept through worse. No whine from the baby monitor or chirrup of a text message had startled her from sleep. Usually there was nothing unusual to waking up in the middle of the night to go to the bathroom or get a drink of water, but Elizabeth couldn't shake the feeling that something was wrong in her room.

Rain blew against her face as the curtains billowed inward.

Elizabeth jerked up. There was no way she had left the window open. There were multiple latches on each window, and they were difficult to push up. Besides, she would never have opened the windows during a storm, especially when that storm was bringing the cold back, tightening her skin until it was like stone, even under the blankets and all her clothes.

"Hello, Elizabeth."

The voice came out of the darkness between the flapping curtains. The storm illuminated him in strobe flashes, but she couldn't tell who he was, except that the relief of his silhouette seemed all the stranger cut against brief but stark lightning.

"Don't scream."

He must have known she would do just that, this mysterious figure made of weird angles and gentle, menacing, familiar voice, because she tried. She tried to scream loud enough to wake the baby, wake Sharona, wake the dead.

But nothing came out. Nothing but a thin hiss of air where a scream should have been.

"Once, I would have stolen you straight from your children at the moment of the wish, my dear. Without you, the children might have wandered the circus until afterhours when my clowns could have taken them. They are quite irritated that I denied them such a treat, especially since children are so hard for them to come by these days. You should thank me for waiting."

The man darted forward. Elizabeth tried to run, but her legs tangled in her blankets—or the blankets tangled around her legs. Part of her still believed she was dreaming, which would explain everything—the way nothing came out of her mouth when she screamed, the way her blankets seemed to pull her more deeply under her covers to bind her down, the way the man remained shrouded in darkness though her eyes had adjusted and fear had sharpened her sight. His feet made no sound as he approached her, but there were footsteps coming from the other side of the bed, another figure emerging from the corner of her room.

She twisted under the covers, rolling until she was wrapped into a cocoon. She wriggled and fought against the hands that grabbed her by the shoulders and pulled her out from under the coverlet, sheets and all. The new man's grip was firm as he lifted her over his shoulder. If her skin was like marble from the cold, this man's body was like a boulder.

"Is this really necessary? Can't you just—"

"I can, but I won't. Earn your favor, Victor, and follow. Bring her to me."

"Why didn't you just let the Creature do it for you?" the man carrying her asked.

"You know why." The strange man gave no further explanation, merely stepped back into the obscurity of the curtains. When their billowing subsided, he had disappeared, although Elizabeth's room was on the second story—not that logistics had prevented her abductors from coming into her room through locked windows.

"I'm sorry," the man carrying her said. "I know you're scared, but I don't have a choice."

With her bundled over his shoulder, the man vaulted through the window without effort. He ran down the slanted roof, then launched from the gutter to the lawn. When his feet struck the grass, he crouched to absorb the momentum, but he should have cried out in pain.

Some bone should have broken after jumping from such a height.

The man brought her to a worn blue truck that could generously be called vintage or quaint. He jumped with her into the bed, pulled the back shut and covered them both with tarpaulin against the rain. Two strikes against the back of the cab signaled the truck to pull away from the curb.

She cried silently into the metallic water that lined the truck bed, panic stealing her breath like the storm had stolen her screams. Gray mist clouded her vision. The man next to her rubbed her back, his empty apologies echoing in her ears.

* * * *

She woke up again, and this time it wasn't to her dark, cold room with rain on her face.

Elizabeth hadn't gone in because the kids were too young, but there was no mistaking that she was in a circus ring under the big top tent. The spotlight was fixed upon her, illuminating to the wooden dividers that marked the ring's edge. Someone had put a blanket on the sawdusty floor for her. She couldn't see much beyond the ring, but she sensed there were people in the darkness watching her—like some kind of black market auction or underground show, the kind of show that abducted people from their homes and stuck them in the middle of a circus ring. Not a single possibility rang hopeful in her head.

"Hello again."

Now that she was in the circus, Elizabeth placed the voice.

"You're the fortune teller... Bell." She lifted a hand to shield her eyes against the spotlight's glare.

"Amazing, isn't it, the clarity that follows when fear falls away?"

"The only thing that's clear to me is you're a fucking lunatic." Elizabeth struggled to her hands and knees. "I swear to God, if anyone comes near me, I'm going to fuck you up so badly, your grandchildren will still be wincing. No... You won't even be able to have grandchildren to wince."

"How lovely that I have the fortune of meeting the real Elizabeth. I was hoping to encounter her sooner rather than later."

Elizabeth squinted into the light, nonplussed, until she realized what she'd just said — more importantly, how she'd said it. "God will forgive me. I wasn't thinking."

She touched her fingers to her head. They struck fabric, and, despite the circumstances, Elizabeth could briefly breathe again. She was still covered. A sex trafficking auction wouldn't have let her keep on all her layers.

"Such a shame for this farce to continue." Bell stood from where he had been sitting on the edge of the ring. She could have sworn he hadn't been there when she'd scanned the darkness. "There's no need for it. I know your every thought. I know your future, your present, your past. I know why you maintain this charade that you're still devout, why you cling to your origins like an infant to her blanket."

"You know *nothing* about me, you sick —" Elizabeth literally bit her tongue to keep the filth from passing between the prison of her teeth.

He laughed quietly, remaining on the edge of the light without crossing into it as he circled her. "You still don't believe in me. For a woman who believes divination to be a sin worthy of fear, you seem reluctant enough to believe anyone has the power for it."

"I have faith, sir. I'm not weak-willed enough to pay to be conned."

"You let your children enjoy our midway readily enough," Bell said.

"You took someone with kids?" someone asked from the darkness, dismayed.

"Isn't that an invitation to greater scrutiny?" another woman asked, her voice tight with something that was either anger or frustration. "This isn't how you operate. You steal people without ties, remove them seamlessly from their lives. Dealing with loving families is a bit harder to manage, isn't it?"

"I've done it before." Bell shared a mutual understanding with Elizabeth before saying, "Besides, they're not her children. She's not the mother, only the nanny. She's never been a mother, never going to be a mother. She accepted the position of a glorified babysitter because it was the closest she was ever going to get to loving her own."

"What did you say?" Her knees protested as she stood, but she was used to that by now, and it barely slowed her down.

"I said many things, and I'll say more. Your mother truly believes you're contrite, but though you kneel beside your bed and clasp your hands where no one can see you, you don't pray. I know you haven't been able to pray since you left the community, that you can't even convince your lips to say the word 'amen', although you clearly can convince them to say all sorts of other things. I know the closest thing you have to devotion is the booze you keep under your bed."

The man stepped partially into the light, as fey and mysterious in the contrast between darkness and light as he had been under an afternoon sun. In nothing but leather trousers that showed no sign of damage from the storm raging beyond the tent canvas, his bare skin somehow made him appear more dangerous to her than if he had been as clothed as she was. "What do I have to say to convince you that you cannot hide what you are from me?"

"You're the psychic, right? You figure it out. You're certainly enjoying all this grandstanding, playing the enigma, when what it comes down to is that you're a sadistic, sick fu— man. I don't know what you intend to do to me, but I'm going to—"

Bell continued to smile his cat-like smile, knowing and amused because of it. "I'm an entertainer. I love to hear myself talk. And if there's one thing a carnie knows deep in his bones, it's to stretch out tension as long as he can before revealing the wonder. But let's dispense with pageantry, shall we? You seem to have lost patience for it."

"I lost patience when you had your man take me from my bedroom and bring me here for…for what? Why am I here?"

"Bell, stop savoring." Maya, sans serpent, stepped into the light, her dress more corseted and frilly than the one Elizabeth had seen her in before—all silk and lace and petticoats, which suggested she was more than a psychic's assistant. "I get that you like doing things your way, but this is cruel, even for you, teasing someone who just made a wish at the wrong time to the wrong person. You did the same thing to me, and I'd like to stay special, thank you."

"You'll always be special to me, love." Bell kissed her neck. Though Maya still showed obvious concern for Elizabeth, the woman couldn't suppress a shiver, closing her eyes and baring her neck for him.

Elizabeth swallowed against the spasm of nausea, forced herself to release the tightness in her shoulders and adopt a more submissive, apologetic posture — something to make a dangerous man feel powerful.

"Look, sir. I don't know what's going on, but I won't call the police or tell anyone. I'm not even a hundred percent sure this is happening. Just let me go. I just want to go home. Please."

The effort she made to appear unthreatening stopped being an act. She fell to her knees, and though pain shot up her legs, it was the least of her concerns. Even with a sex trafficking ring likely off the table, *something* was going on here, and it clearly wasn't something good. Whatever this Bell person was, the others had been cowed into acquiescence. They weren't going to interfere, or else they would have already.

"Please, I want to go home. Let me go home." The words sounded like they belonged to a little girl instead of a grown woman. As nauseated as she had been, groveling made it worse, but still she clasped her hands in supplication.

"That's not your home any more than those were your children," Bell murmured against Maya's skin before returning his attention to Elizabeth. "I was under the impression that home is the place you've been trying to run from since you were seventeen…unless you'd really like to return to Thomas Petros' weak effort at an urban commune, genuflecting under your mother's roof in constant apology for her mistake, patronized by Father and Daddy dearest alike. Is that where you'd have me return you?"

Blood drained from her face. "How do you—?"

"How long did you really think you could hide in the midst of saints, Lizzie? But you can't hide from me. I know all your dirty little secrets. Besides, my dear, I have no intention of letting you go, not when you've given me such a lovely wish to play with."

"What the hell are you talking about? Have you been stalking— Can someone please tell me what's going on? *Please.*"

Bell stroked Maya's corset with his knuckles, subtly urging her back into the darkness, and she allowed herself to be urged. Then it was just Elizabeth and Bell and the brief reflections in the darkness that meant other people were watching. He stepped fully into the light. When she focused her eyes upon him, she could no longer see anything in the shadows, not even a suggestion.

"You're not leaving this circus for a good long while. You're never going to see your family again. And you'll never see the children again."

"Tell me you didn't hurt the kids. They haven't done anything to you except be kids, and I swear, if you did anything to them…"

"They wished for not a thing in my presence. The children are safe from me and my circus. Forget them. Fade them from your mind, these half-pint surrogates that were nothing but fine sand in your desperate grip. They were never yours. None of it was ever yours."

He crouched down in front of her, heedless of any restriction that his trousers should have given him. The worst part was that his pale eyes showed tenderness, empathy, yet he didn't stop.

"All that is yours you hide beneath the rags you wear in the name of righteousness, but we both know piety merely masks fear—fear that has gnarled its festering roots through every part of you, every inch of your skin. It's no wonder I couldn't allow the Creature to take you from the house as he requested. I may never have gotten you back."

When he stretched his long fingers to her cheek, Elizabeth flinched. No one was supposed to touch her, not with the kind of intent a man like Bell would have.

"You can't fool me," he said, gazing at her with chilling intensity. "And it's time to stop fooling yourself. It's time to make you mine."

Elizabeth reeled away. She scrabbled at the blanket to scramble back.

"Oh, not that way. I'm quite content with Maya in my bed. But you've bound yourself to me—mine as the circus is mine, mine as its inhabitants are mine. Mine like everything you see before you. Now, take off your head covering."

"Stay away from me."

"I'm not going to harm you, Elizabeth. I'll do many things to you, but I won't harm you. And you'll remove that head covering on your own, because modesty has nothing to do with why you wear it. When I'm through with you, no one will recognize you enough to point and decry your blasphemy. Please..." Bell flexed his fingers in a way somehow graceful and threatening at the same time, as though his beauty itself was the trap. "Remove the scarf."

Elizabeth couldn't slow her breathing. Once she got started, she rarely could. Her head swam and her vision tilted, but she brought her hand to her scarf once more, this time to untuck it from around her neck. Still meeting Bell's eyes, as though to gauge whether or not he was really serious about his command, she slid the covering away from her hair. Her quickened breath trembled as she let it fall to the blanket.

"There. Was that so difficult?" Bell beckoned to the scarf. It lifted from the blanket like a rehearsed magic trick. As it slid across his palm, he closed his fist around it, nothing there when he flourished his hand open again. "Everyone here barely sees what you were trying to hide. Now, remove the rest."

"What?" Elizabeth clamored to her knees again. Waiting until she found an opening to escape was starting to feel like a luxury she couldn't afford. "I thought you said—"

"There are few people in this tent today who haven't been caught in various states of undress, sometimes even during the course of our performances. Either you remove your clothes or they'll end up removing themselves. I'd prefer it if you would bare yourself, my dear. Shedding your old skin will make what you will become so much easier."

"Why should I care what's easier for you, you bastard?"

He smiled. Beautiful though he was, why did he have to seem so *normal*? "Oh, it's not easier for *me*. But as a psychic, I'm not partial to people who lie, and those garments of your religion are lies. Show me the truth, Elizabeth. You have no need for your clothes. Remove them. Show me everywhere you let Dez ply his craft upon you. Every last inch."

"How do you know that?" Elizabeth clutched at the loose turtleneck, holding the large shirt against her chest as though it were a shield.

Bell must have thought her question didn't merit an answer. He simply stood above her with his legs parted and his hands by his thighs like a gunslinger, the light unflinching and honest over the planes of his lean strength.

Not one person—no man, woman, child, not even a doctor—had ever seen under her clothes since she'd returned to the Petrosian community. Religious exemption gave her all the excuse she needed. Petrosian Christianity wasn't exactly Christian Science, but the modesty rules, especially those for women, made doctor visits and other assorted inspections voluntary rather than mandatory, and as an unmarried woman, no one else ever had any reason to see what her clothes concealed.

Elizabeth traced the shape of the wooden cross she wore over her sleep shirt. Then she tucked it under the loose turtleneck and swallowed against the stone in her throat as she crossed her arms to take off her shirt. With her shirt over her face, she closed her eyes and kept them shut as she peeled sleeves down her arms and discarded it. Humiliation flushed her cheeks and boiled hot behind her eyes. Shame cut through her, tiny shards of glass flowing in her veins. Then she stood, the spotlight hot upon her bare skin, and pushed her pajama pants down to her ankles.

"All of it. Keep the jewelry, if you like."

No matter how tightly she clenched her eyes shut, she couldn't stop the tears from streaming down her cheeks.

"Bell..." Maya began.

He must have done something to quiet her, because she didn't protest again.

"Please," Elizabeth whispered.

"It'll make things easier for you. All of it."

Elizabeth pushed her underwear down to join her pants. Whether her clothes had been worn in righteousness or fear, she'd worn them almost constantly for over ten years. Revealing even the slightest bit of skin felt as naked to her as entering a church while wearing a bikini. In losing every last vestige of protection, she felt flayed — not just naked but stripped down to what was beneath her skin.

But it was her skin Bell had wanted to see. Every inch of her previously unexposed skin that she'd hidden from her mother, from both her fathers — from any man who had asked for her hand because he couldn't get anyone younger or prettier or with a purer history, and she'd been serviceable enough for the purpose of procreation and raising children.

A man had seen it before, though. In the seven years she'd spent running from the Petrosian community, many men had seen her bare, but only one man had seen all the ink that had been poured into her, because he'd been the one to put it there.

The only sounds in the tent were the whispers of Bell's bare feet on the sawdust as he resumed circling her and the choking gasps that escaped from her as she tried so hard to hold it in.

"Remarkable."

Elizabeth jumped at the brush of his fingertips over the blades of her shoulders.

"A nearly exhaustive catalogue of all the things you fear." He released her from the agony of his gentle touch. "Needles are apparently one of the few exceptions."

The tattoos covered all the skin that she normally concealed, from ankles to wrists, up her neck, under her hair, vining over her scalp under the long growth she'd cultivated over the years since her return.

"Bell, that is quite enough." The protest came from the Bearded Lady, Kitty, her warm voice unmistakable and jarring. It was hard to believe that such a sweet, kind woman could have anything to do with this, but she hadn't stepped in until now, which meant any number of disquieting things. "She wished herself in by accident. She's done nothing to offend you, nothing to hurt us. Can't you see what you're doing to her?"

"No one appreciates fine art anymore," Bell muttered near her ear, though she hadn't been warned of his proximity by heat, which made Elizabeth jump again. But his voice was farther from her once more when he continued. "The purpose of this exercise was purely practical. Birth is a painful process — rebirth, even more so. I needed to see my palette, and she would have ended up disrobed either way in the end."

"You didn't have to do this so publicly," Kitty replied.

"You didn't have to come. And humiliation wasn't my intent."

"No, but you're enjoying it anyway," Kitty said.

"An artist should enjoy his work, especially with a wish such as this. I have to tell you, Lizzie. I've been waiting for you for ages." This time his heat hit her like a furnace. Before she could flinch away again, he stroked through her tangled hair. "I want you to understand that what I told Kitty is true. Your humiliation, your shame, your pain... None of it is what I want from you. But you will have to suffer through them. Hold on to your fear, Lizzie. I'll give it something real to cling to."

With the next pass of his hand over her hair, the cool breeze through the ring struck bare skin, followed by the slither of her hair over her shoulders and back to strike the blanket in a hushed fall. Her hair fell out in clumps under the movement of his palm. The sensation of air on her scalp was like a ghost.

"I promised no one would recognize you," Bell said softly.

"I don't understand." Elizabeth shuddered and shivered—not cold, beyond fear, shrouded so completely in humiliation she didn't think she'd ever be cold again. "I don't know what you're doing. How you're doing it. Why you're doing it. Just stop. Please stop. *Please*. Someone stop him. I can't do this again. I can't—" The fast breathing shifted seamlessly into hyperventilation, mucus blocking her nose and thickening in her throat.

He brushed the last strands of hair from her head, leaving her bald, naked and trembling in the middle of the ring, as though he'd stripped years from her as well as clothes and hair. The only thing he'd let her keep was the wooden cross on its leather cord. It felt sacrilegious against her sternum. She covered her breasts with her arms and kept her legs tightly closed, but it wasn't enough to cover every story inked over the rest of her.

Seven years under Dez's needle. If the body was a temple, she'd spent seven years outside the Petrosian community defiling it, like spray-painting graffiti over the exterior of a Gothic cathedral. The snakebite, tongue piercing and the ear holes had filled in on their own, but there had been nothing to do about the tattoos except endure them and make sure that her mother and

Petros never saw them. Charity would have never let her out of the house if she'd known. Elizabeth would have become the secret once more, the spinster in the attic, with nothing but a Bible and the constant atonement for a sin she couldn't erase, a desecration she couldn't deny—and so many others that no one could see and that she'd never, ever share.

"I just want you to know, Elizabeth, nothing that's happened to you is your fault. And this won't hurt, but it will feel quite strange."

Chapter Three

He'd said it wouldn't hurt and it didn't. It felt strange enough, though, that it might as well have been pain.

Elizabeth doubled over, her legs weak for entirely different reasons than fear. But it wasn't just her who writhed. There were things moving *inside* her beneath her shoulder blades and on both sides of her hips, something trying to push its way out, stretching the skin like fingers against latex. She fell forward onto the blanket, which did nothing to cushion the hard ground.

The storm strengthened around the big top. Thunder roared in her ears.

Her whole back arched with a creak as the base of her spine snapped. Something emerged behind her legs like tentacles. Her screams were no longer confined to her head. She grabbed at the blanket as though it could ground her, but all she did was stir up the sawdust into something like mist in the spotlight. Tears streamed down her cheeks.

A bare foot pressed upon her mid-back to pin her down, limiting some of the movement, but leaving her arms and legs free. Despite her flailing limbs and bucking spine, Bell exerted little effort.

"Oh my God." It was a female voice she hadn't heard yet, but who it belonged to didn't matter.

The shifting protuberances under her shoulder blades pushed out on either side of Bell's foot. Elizabeth pitched against the feeling that they were tearing their way through skin and sinew.

Her heel connected with someone's leg, but she was the one who felt it. Her limbs tangled in the blanket as they'd tangled in her sheets. Her skin was covered with a layer of cold sweat mingled with dust, and she didn't know what part of her body was which.

I want to wake up now.

"I'm sorry, Lizzie, but you're quite awake."

Her eyes flew open at the clarity of the voice inside her head. Though confusion and panic remained, the pain—or what she'd interpreted as pain—subsided.

Bell slid his foot from her back. "Magnificent."

Elizabeth struggled to get air into her lungs. She pushed herself up from the ground for more room to breathe.

There were four hands on the blanket.

She yelped, whirling around to see who was over her. No one was there but Bell, and he stood well away, his thumbs tucked into his trousers, the feline quality to his pleasure all the more apparent.

And there were four legs in front of her, her tattooed legs in the center and the others bare, just like the arms she'd seen. It didn't feel like she was on top of anyone, but she whirled around again, struggling to her knees against unexpected weight on her slight frame.

The limbs tangled together this time when she tried to turn, legs and arms unsure what they knocked against because they'd never knocked against anything before. But when her tattooed legs struck the bare ones, she felt the blow on the bare legs, too. And when the bare arms brushed against her tattooed arms, she again experienced that doubled sensation of self-same skin on skin.

"No, no, no, no, no, no, no…" she muttered over and over again as she crawled off the blanket and into the ring, as though she expected the extra limbs to fall away. But they persisted, scrabbling at the ground like the rest of her. No matter what she did, they followed.

She tried to shake them off, but the more frantic she became, the less sure she was which limb was which as her brain struggled to send the appropriate messages. She clawed her way forward with four full sets of fingers when she couldn't determine which knees to bend.

Bell stepped in front of her, his feet on either side of Elizabeth's hands—the ones connected to tattooed wrists. The other set scratched instead upon the leather of his trousers in a silent plea. The sounds that came from her mouth were less than human, because her teeth suddenly ached as though she'd brushed them with a cheese grater. She sounded like a helpless, pathetic creature trapped in a cage too small.

He crouched down to lift her chin with gentle fingers. "There, now. No need to cry." He thumbed away the newest streaks of tears to blend with the old. "You're safe, Elizabeth. Simply altered. The worst of it has passed. I promise."

She could barely speak through the fullness and discomfort in her teeth, not to mention hyperventilation. "What...did...you...do...to me?"

"Calm down and I'll tell you. Better yet, I'll show you."

He took the hands she acknowledged as her own, ignoring the ones that clawed his leather or his forearms. It was more intimate contact than she'd had with a man in more than a decade, and in spite of everything, that's what her brain fixated on, because that was something it understood.

As she fought to stand on her own, she bit her lip so hard that the delicate skin tore, drawing blood. She tried to tell her legs to move, but the other, inkless legs would move as well, crisscrossing with hers like the limbs of a newborn foal—in no small part because she simply could not believe what she was seeing, feeling, hearing, none of it. There was no possible way those uninked legs were there.

She finally admitted to herself that, for whatever reason, she couldn't stand on her own. She allowed Bell closer so that she could climb up his arm to his shoulder until all of her was upright. Sadistic bastard and half-naked he might be, but he was solid and more real right now than she was.

Bell beckoned to something beyond the spotlight at the top of the tent. The subtle rumble of machinery blended with thunder to make the descent of a large antique mirror far more dramatic.

"Denial isn't going to serve you for very much longer," Bell said. "I assure you, this is an unadulterated mirror, not something out of my haunted funhouse. It shows you nothing more than the truth. Go on, child. See what I have made of you."

He shifted behind her, slipping his arm around her neck and pressing his chest familiarly against her back. He peered over her shoulder at his handiwork. When her legs tangled among each other, he held her more tightly, heedless of the extra elbows that threatened his ribs.

"Hello, beautiful." The purr of his voice did things to her she hadn't expected she could feel under the circumstances—but biology was biology, and she hadn't had the chance to put up any of her shields when Bell had done everything he could to strip them away. "You're one of the best I've ever created, even better than the twins. It wouldn't have worked with just anyone, but your frame suits the Spider."

The mirror left no room for confusion. When she stepped away from Bell, he relinquished her without protest.

She tripped and stumbled on the way, even though she took small steps. The second set of legs had been arranged higher than the originals and couldn't stand flat on the ground, but they still managed to get confused.

"What did you do to me?" she repeated, the question barely more than a breath that the thunder subsumed.

Her teeth looked different when she spoke, and every part of her mouth still ached. She brought her fingers to her lips, folded the bottom one down. In a matter of moments, her teeth had been filed to wicked, razor sharp, intersecting points. She jerked her fingertips away, the skin smeared with blood from her lip.

"What did you do?"

"Think back. What did you wish?"

"I didn't wish anything. What does wishing have to do with it?"

"Despite many of your life choices, you're an intelligent woman, Elizabeth. I'm sure you'll figure it out."

She couldn't deny that the thing in the mirror was her, but it looked nothing like her. It had been such a long time since she'd encountered her own reflection on purpose, even longer since she'd seen herself without clothing or without hair. A little lack of recognition was to be expected.

The parts of her that had always been hers were covered with Dez's art, monochromatic illustrations accented with small pops of color — the golden honey of the bees over her right upper arm, the turquoise of the scarab beetles on her hips, the red hints in the apple on her left calf. Dez had liked the black ink on her pale skin, liked her baring herself to the world with silver hardware and black lipstick and eyeliner to enhance the stark drama he had created, a body mural of all the things that scared her for anybody to use. She'd believed back in the heady, hedonistic days that she could steal their power if she held them in her skin. Dez had encouraged her experimentation, and he'd been a hell of an artist. Every piece he'd put on her had been ammunition.

Right down to the spiderweb and spider silhouette he'd needled onto her right thigh, overlapping and blending with the widow's lace that wound around her calf and over her hip.

The mourning corset tattoo, with the skeleton torso cameo over her abdomen, laced behind her back, and she worked her way into profile to follow it, her breath coming out shakily when she remembered to breathe.

She glimpsed the *anima sola* Dez had given her for her twenty-second birthday, the one he'd insisted she accept. It had once spanned side to side on her upper back, but now the sides blended partially into the second set of arms emerging from an extra plane on top of the scapula—another ball joint that moved with the same ease and flexibility as her primary set. Like her second set of legs, they were a little longer than her prime limbs, but the placement—even the blending of the tattoo into the uninked skin—appeared seamless. As best she could, she reached behind her to probe at the base, searching fruitlessly for some kind of mechanism or prosthetic.

Elizabeth briefly ran her hand over the smooth flesh of her head, not a trace of hair to be found, as though it had been newly shaved with a straight razor. Dez had always thought her uniquely exotic without hair. Sometimes she'd agreed, and sometimes she'd thought she looked like a hairless cat. Her fingers passed over the flight of bats rising from her neck and over her left ear, over the flurry of death's-head moths that emerged from trompe l'oeil cracks in her skull to the right. That was something Dez had excelled at depicting— movement that appeared natural to the contours of a woman's body.

Elizabeth slid her fingers down to her narrow hips. Right above the flare of her pelvis at the small of her back, the second set of legs had emerged, melding with the bottom edges of the mourning corset. They'd borrowed muscles from her flanks and created new ones, although not as prominent as buttocks. Like the new arms, ball-and-socket joints had been created from new protrusions to her pelvis. The legs' length and angle made them splay a little on their own, but she could bring them closer together if she concentrated.

When she loosened the muscles again, they spread, slightly obscene.

She'd never seen these legs, these arms, but though they were different from her prime set—different position, different length, different freckles, no tattoos—they looked like hers, somehow. If she'd been born this way, they would have looked like this.

She dug her nails in where seams should have been, where the art ended, but all she tore was skin and all she drew was blood.

Bell covered the offending hand, stilling it.

"I've been wanting a wish like yours for as long as I've had this circus." His lips brushed the shell of her ear. "I've been waiting for you, little Spider."

"What did you *do*?" Elizabeth asked again, as though this time he might make sense.

"I granted your wish."

"I didn't wish this. I would never wish this. I hate…" She struggled again to hold in the contents of her stomach as she finally realized what he'd made of her, and what he'd made her from.

"Sometimes I wish I had a few extra limbs to go around."

Hardly a wish at all so much as an expression of exasperation, but the son of a bitch had taken it and run with it like some kind of—

"The wish provides the framework." He seemed to know exactly what she was working through in her head, as though he were the one creaking the rusty cogs. "I can make of it what I desire."

Elizabeth sidled away, shoulder striking the mirror.

"Not like that, Lizzie, not for a long time yet."

"Stop calling me that." If he was as psychic as he claimed, he was a special kind of asshole to keep using that particular pet name. "Now, I don't know what's going on or what the fuck you're smoking and why you decided to share, but I need to get back. I can't have these. I can't be your goddamn spider. I can't *stand* spiders, and you *know* it."

"You're not leaving me. I just got you. You'll be a stunning addition to my Row and in my funhouse."

"No!" Elizabeth shoved the mirror away from her. It swung on the tether, then came back to her like a pendulum. She didn't care. She rocked back, slipping only a little, to deliver a solid kick of her heel directly in the middle of the mirror. Against her intent, her bare right leg twinned the prime leg as though her will had directed both. The double kick shattered the mirror in its frame. A few large pieces fell to the ground, but the rest splintered out in cracks that looked just like a spiderweb, as though mocking her.

Elizabeth tried to ignore the glint of bad luck scattered among the sawdust. "I'll fucking wish again. I'll wish something on you, if wishes are what trigger these things, as though you're some kind of…some kind of jinn."

"As a jinni, you'd be surprised how well I weasel out of such wishes." Everywhere Bell stepped conveniently happened to avoid glass—or else the glass avoided him. "Including ones where you ask to leave before I'm ready to let you go."

"This is ridiculous." When Elizabeth brought her hands to the side of her head, all four pressed against the eerily smooth baldness there, no scarf to obstruct them.

This was a dream. Wishes didn't come true. Arms and legs didn't spontaneously grow out of someone's body. Genies and monsters weren't real. People were bad enough without pretending demons were the ones behind it.

"I'm going to wake up. For God's sake, wake up!" She slapped at her cheek to try to jolt herself out. Her right hands overlapped. For a moment, her face contorted, on the brink of a meltdown, but she swallowed thickly, forcing it down her throat.

"I hate to disappoint you, but the trick to this circus is that there's no trick." Bell snapped his fingers. The spotlight dimmed and the lights in the bleachers rose, revealing the members of the circus who had chosen to be party to her humiliation. She recognized almost all of them—Kitty and Maya, of course, but also the burned fire-eater, the contortionist who had led him around, the snake lady, the strongman, the conjoined twins, the Human Torso missing his legs and the Human Torso missing all her limbs, the sword swallower who had greeted them.

Some of the people in the crowd stood—strange and normal-looking alike. Then they changed. For some of them, the change was as subtle as their eyes turning completely black. Others bared teeth that went from human to bestial in a matter of seconds, a transformation that wouldn't allow her to dismiss them as Halloween costume veneers.

"I'm the jinni that holds this world in my hands," Bell said. "And these are my jinn, most of them of more demonic persuasion than I, to varying degrees of resentment. As useless as it will be to tell you that you needn't fear them, it's important that I say it. They are as much mine as you are. You are safe here. Trapped, but safe."

She abruptly surged forward to strike at him, using her added weight for additional momentum. She'd intended to use only her prime hands, but the other set joined in, albeit more artlessly.

"You're batshit and a goddamn monster, but I don't care if you're a genie or a dead, pipe-fucked rat. Change me back. Wake me up. Just fucking do *something*…"

Poison poured from her mouth. It had been held back for so long, and she was so scared, stripped and changed, that she didn't try to stop it. Everyone could already see that the clothes, the head covering and the cross were lies, a holy insult, a hopeless ruse. What difference did it make for her to curb her tongue? Maybe if she spat enough of the acid out, it would hit the extra limbs and dissolve them away, dissolve this whole godforsaken circus in its wake.

She wished she could just wake up, wished she could move without tripping over her own legs, wished her mind would either make sense of everything or finally break so the world wouldn't have to keep shaking every time she saw her body—both the altered and unaltered parts.

He laughed, knocking her hands away, batting at each fist. He treated it like a game, as though she were just a fly he warded off. Finally, he somehow caught all her wrists in his two hands.

"Good to meet you again, Lizzie. I do hope we'll become better acquainted." He forced her wrists behind her back, which brought him obscenely close to her, and with the way he stared into her eyes, at her mouth, down at her body, she no longer believed his own words that he had no sexual stake in this game. He wasn't hard, but there was no mistaking his expression. And her body couldn't help how it responded.

"I hope you fuck yourself," she managed through the trembling that left her feeling unbearably weak—but then she'd always known she was. "You arrogant, flea-licking, syph-sucked son of a whore."

"A genuine delight. But there's no need to insult yourself while trying to insult me," Bell muttered so that only she could hear him.

Elizabeth lunged again, then pulled back when it brought her flush against him. Her conflicting impulses to throttle him and get as far away from him as possible broadened his grin.

She tried to knee him in the groin, but he pushed her hips too close against his for her to get her leg where it needed to be. He shook his head and clicked his tongue until she stopped struggling.

"This is usually the point in the orientation when Miss Kitty warns new recruits not to wish again for a while, because I have too much fun with them and it's a waste of a good wish. I won't lose you before I'm ready."

His voice vibrated over her skin and confused things all over again — which made her even more scared and angry, because she sensed the manipulation.

"Jesus H. Christ…" She tried to yank her wrists from his grip, but he still wouldn't let her go.

"Although you may not believe it of me now, no matter how many times I say it, I'm really not interested in harming you. You're not here for punishment, and you've done nothing to earn my hatred, so I might be more willing to grant a wish your way in time. But you still have to give me what I deem appropriate service before I consider loosening my hold."

"Bell, you're not making it better," Kitty said, exasperated. "Do we need to have a talk about personal boundaries and how people have different ones? Especially when the woman you're intimidating adhered to conservative modesty before you decided to make her your pet?"

"And here I thought I'd been as much like my kitty cat as I could." But he released Elizabeth's wrists and stepped back. "She was even thinking a wish, and I didn't let her say it. You know how hard that is for me."

"What do you want? A cookie?" Kitty asked. "You did it the way you wanted to. Don't try to dress it up as altruism when she's still in shock."

"Yes, and she's going to be for a while. You have a week, Elizabeth, to fruitlessly try to ignore what you've become. Then Arcanium *will* have its Spider, ready or not." He lifted her hand to his lips, meeting her eyes long enough to catch the moment horror set back in. Then he kissed her knuckles.

At the touch of his lips, she ran.

His laughter — so fucking achingly normal — followed her as she stumbled, fell, crawled, scrambled to her feet, only to stumble and fall again. But now she was outside the ring, right in the middle of the storm, and without a stitch of clothing on her altered body.

Even in the days she'd been barely as tall as her father's knee, Charity had been a religious mother, telling her first mistake of a daughter the more child-friendly stories from the Bible. But Charity's sister, Temperance, had never been as firm on the matter of edifying storytelling, and she'd been the more well-traveled of the two sisters.

Elizabeth had been Charity's lapse in faith — a young woman smitten with a preacher and the preacher smitten enough to be tossed from his more conventional Southern Baptist congregation. Temperance's lapse had taken her to Eastern Europe, through Turkey, then down into the Middle East, where she'd finally accepted dressing modestly again, although she'd never worn the head scarf like Charity and her daughters.

Thomas Petros spoke of demons like children spoke of monsters under their bed — in a way that suggested he believed in them but wasn't completely convinced of their physical reality. Most of the demons in the Bible seemed metaphorical, ancient explanations for physical and mental illness.

But on the evenings Elizabeth's aunt had tended her, Temperance told stories of jinn. Not the fun genies that the West had taken for their own, but jinn — forged from fire instead of formed from dust like humans or from light like angels. It was from the jinn that demons came, and whether jinn decided to do the work of evil or good or anything in between, they were nothing to be trifled with, as powerful as angels but with the free will of man.

Jinn were little more than entertaining wish-granters in countries where Christian theology had no room for them. In other lands, the jinn were spoken off in the same breath as technology, as alive and vibrant as they had been centuries before.

This wasn't belief, though. This wasn't a matter of faith. Bell was as real as she was, and he called himself jinn, called some of the people in the circus demons, claimed psychic powers without the slightest whiff of self-doubt.

And here in the storm, pelted every which way by rain and falling in the mud, lightning leaving strobed impressions in her eyes, she didn't think she could deny that she was awake any longer.

Which meant it could all be real — jinn, demons, spells, the arms and legs that had emerged from her like buds from the soil, the wish, the warning that she could never leave.

She faceplanted again, scraping her knees on pebbles and getting dirt only God knew where. Elizabeth preferred the cover of the mud, though, because it hid her tattoos, and the rain faded the limbs that came from behind into wraiths. But she still had to contend with them, because trying to run with her second set of legs was what made her keep falling, and if she didn't acknowledge them, she was never going to get out of the circus.

She forced herself back up, then bent down and grabbed her secondary legs by the knees, as though carrying herself piggyback. She'd deal with how everything had changed forever later — forever was plenty of time. Right now, she just needed to get out.

If she could find a way out, everything would be all right. She could run home. Run home and beg new forgiveness for old sins, make new amends and accept her place back in the attic like some kind of mad wife, praying every last hour of her life that this hell didn't follow her beyond the grave.

The intricate Arcanium gates were closed, chained and locked, obvious enough for her to see in the pouring rain. But as a nanny, Elizabeth was adept at jungle gyms and tree-climbing. She knew all the best ways to scale a scrolled gate rife with footholds. Twenty more paces, then a quick climb, and she'd run right out of this nightmare.

The monster landed in front of the gate before she could reach it, slamming into the ground in a swirl of rain and spreading his leathery wings to block her escape.

Elizabeth crashed into him with a scream. He barely stumbled, wrapped his arms around her like gray wolves closing in on prey.

"It's not safe for you to go, little Spider," the monster said, his voice startlingly deep, kind in spite of his appearance.

"No! No, no, no, not again. Fucking bastard..." She pounded on his chest, which resisted her like velvet-covered stone. Coarse gray fur covered his bare torso, as though he were a gargoyle come to life. The lightning showed her far more, more than she wanted to see.

He withstood her blows, his blood-red eyes nearly closed as he held her more tightly to give her less room to strike—yet another embrace she couldn't break. Beneath thin, parted lips, his wicked teeth gleamed with saliva, rain and electricity. His nostrils flared. He seemed heedless of her nakedness or his almost-nakedness. Little more than a loincloth wrapped around his waist, and that only the barest side of decent. She could tell where it stopped because her legs were pressed to his, her hips to his, and she was suddenly aware of the fact that the monster—whether demon or twisted human—was *very* unabashedly male.

And this very male monster leaned toward her, nudged the line of her cheekbone with his nose, breathed heat onto her skin as though he was going to kiss her. When she turned her head away, though, straining from him, he didn't try to follow her lips. He nuzzled her jaw, her neck, the place behind her ear, all of which had become so much more accessible without a head covering or hair in his way.

She had been so close to freedom. It was right there in front of her. But the monster slid his arms tighter around her, and he lowered his teeth—massive predator's teeth—less than an inch away from her jugular.

"I would tell you not to be afraid, but it is your fear that calls me to you," the monster murmured in her ear.

"Please, let me go." The rain took the tears from her eyes but none of the quaver from her voice. "I just need to get to the other side of the gate. Please. You don't have to tell anyone you helped me…"

"It's never a good idea to plot behind the back of a telepath." Bell inspected his nails as he leaned against the gates. "When I said you were trapped here, I meant that if you cross the boundaries of the circus or if you run from the caravan while we're traveling, you'll experience extreme discomfort—first from crossing the line, then from the lash of the whip when the Ringmaster gets his hands on you. You're not here for punishment, but I will punish you if you break one of my rules."

She fought harder against the monster's hold. "You're just trying to scare me. That's all this is. You're doing everything you can to scare me into doing whatever you want, and I don't know why."

"Is it working?" Bell arched an eyebrow as he brushed away something she couldn't see on his fingers.

"Exquisitely." The monster spoke into her skin, making her shiver for reasons that had nothing to do with cold rain or fear.

"Do I enjoy frightening you? Well, you scare so well, I'd be lying if I said no, and I don't lie to my people. So believe me completely when I tell you that you cannot leave. You're allowed to *try* to escape once." Bell glanced up only then, as though she were less interesting than the weather. "Once, without the Ringmaster having to whip you. Because sometimes my children need to experience what will happen to trust that it will."

"Just let me go," she begged. "I just want to go back. Make him let me go. Call off your fucking guard dog before he—"

"The Creature?" Bell uncrossed his legs and straightened. "He's harmless, neither demon nor jinn. He wouldn't hurt you even if he wanted to. Latched onto Arcanium when we set up the haunted funhouse and wouldn't let go, nor do I have any inclination to force him. Having him here confirms that Arcanium is what I want it to be. He feeds on fear, not flesh. But he can be a bit overenthusiastic with new cast members, and we haven't had anyone new in quite a while. I tried to spare you this particular welcome, but you scurried off into the storm. Please let the Spider breathe, Creature."

"You call him Creature?" Her body could only take so much adrenaline pumping into her system before she couldn't maintain that level of panicked excitement anymore—especially with the winter cold working through the rain that covered her, seeping to the bone. Now she shivered hard enough from both elements and emotion that she thought she'd shudder to pieces.

"Like the Ringmaster, the Creature doesn't have a name." Bell came closer to her, as though sensing the fatigue of her fight-or-flight response. She didn't flinch when he reached for the Creature's hand around her waist to ease it away. "He doesn't fit into my freak show because he's too inhuman. 'Monster' works as well as anything, and he doesn't seem to mind it."

The Creature also didn't seem to mind Bell removing him from her. He barely resisted, though he gave her one last nudge of his nose like a cat before stepping back. He spread his bat wings once more, then launched himself into the night clouds. The rain had thinned, the thunder softened and, though the lightning was as sharp as ever, the storm was clearly on its way past the circus. Without the Creature's heat, her shivering grew worse, so violent that her neck and back threatened to seize.

"In time, you'll understand this place is hardly the hell you fear it is. Why you religious sorts always think that baffles me. It's nowhere close to hell. Just ask the Ringmaster, if you dare."

He brushed the rain from her cheeks, away from her eyes. Without hair or head covering, nothing kept water from dripping down her forehead and the sides of her face.

"Even if you could leave, where would you go, the way you are now? Come on. We'll get you warm and dry in your own home. Forget what you left behind. The children will have a new nanny within days. Your family will only breathe a sigh of relief that their sin has finally disappeared into the darkness where sin belongs."

He kissed her forehead. She was too tired to resist him, too cold to speak.

"Welcome to Arcanium, little Spider. I think you'll like it here."

Chapter Four

The next day, Elizabeth stayed in her small RV. Bell didn't disturb her, but though she'd locked her door, Kitty somehow managed to open it to leave her food.

"You missed breakfast. I didn't know if you'd be hungry."

Elizabeth sat on the small couch in the living area, looking the other way, a new black robe wrapped around her. She had to hold it, because she'd tied the robe's belt around her waist to bind down her secondary arms. They tended to twitch and flail whenever she moved her prime arms. Her secondary legs had the same problem, but their weight kept them from getting in the way.

The robe had been the only piece of clothing in the entire RV, not so much as a pair of leggings or a T-shirt left over from a previous tenant. She supposed shopping for an eight-limbed person wasn't easy, but after ten years of completely covering herself, wearing a robe she couldn't even close still felt naked, and if Bell could make her a spider, she knew he could have made her some clothes to go with it.

"Do you want me to bring dinner?"

Elizabeth still didn't acknowledge her. Sitting on the small couch should have been a simple process, but her hips kept snapping forward. Not sliding off the cheap material while Kitty was in her vehicle took all of Elizabeth's concentration. Whatever Bell had done to her, something was wrong at the base of her spine, and she had to use more of her back and abdominal muscles to adjust for the change. She'd been avoiding a proper examination, because that would mean admitting to herself that Bell hadn't just attached limbs to her like some crazy science experiment. He might have changed the very foundation of her anatomy, and unlike spare limbs, that couldn't be fixed.

"Do you want to talk?"

"No." It was the only acknowledgment Elizabeth was prepared to offer.

"Okay. I'll be back with dinner. We're leaving tonight."

Elizabeth waited until Kitty was gone before taking the lunch she'd left behind. Her stomach was still queasy, but growing limbs was hungry work. Though Elizabeth ate everything on the plate, she saw none of it, tasted none of it, didn't care what it was or whether it would make her sick.

By now, the Bishops would have started worrying. The Wu daughters weren't a flaky breed. They might excuse one day of absence, one day where a phone call couldn't find her. But the fact was, she hadn't been there on Sunday morning to take care of the baby, take the children to church or arrange for their afternoon activities, and she hadn't been there when the Bishop parents had returned from their business trip, nor had she arranged for a temporary replacement. And that just wasn't like her.

They'd probably contacted Charity, who would have already written off her eldest. Failing to raise one out of seven daughters well was still a decent success rate, and bad blood could always be expected to go rotten in the end. Bell hadn't been wrong about that. Elizabeth doubted her family or community would look too hard for her.

Mr. and Mrs. Bishop would probably do most of the worrying, but once they opened Elizabeth's locked door and started searching for clues, they'd find the whiskey. She was never going to be accepted back as the Bishops' nanny. Even if Bell hadn't made her a freak, he could let her out today and have effectively ruined her life.

Elizabeth wrapped the robe more closely around her to avoid looking at the ink on her skin the way she had all these years. She didn't think she was going to be able to do that much longer.

* * * *

When they arrived at their new destination the next morning, Elizabeth didn't bother asking the random woman driving her RV where they were. It didn't matter. From what she could see through the blinds, the plot of land looked the same as the one they'd left. More trees on the edges but more or less the same.

She could tell by a glance out of the window who would be considered cast and who would be considered staff. The cast was far more colorful, in demeanor as well as clothing. The staff, on the other hand, were dressed in plain black like stage crew, and they didn't talk, not to cast or to each other. They didn't emote or listen to music or whistle while they worked. As it was, the circus was up and ready in less than three hours, big top to oddity tents. It was the height of efficiency and just a little too convenient. The staff looked the most human, but they acted more like robots or androids, though Elizabeth doubted Bell would mess with electronics when he could mess with human dolls instead.

It was starting to sink in. Strange, how easily she could start believing in the impossible, how possible it became when it was right in front of her, dusty and worn instead of too shiny to be true.

Accepting a magical explanation, though, didn't exactly settle her mind.

Someone knocked on her RV door then opened it. Kitty climbed the steps to the living area, carrying a black plastic garment bag over her shoulder.

"Hey, the perimeter's set up, so you're good to come out and look around, maybe grab a bite to eat from the big top. I'm not supposed to bring you any more food, but the golems are exceptionally good at breakfast burritos." Kitty peered down the narrow aisle to where Elizabeth sat on her bed to look out of her window. If she tucked her legs up at her sides, it was easier to sit on her bed than on the couch.

"This is a ridiculous question, I know, but all things considered, Elizabeth, are you okay?" Kitty took in the rumpled bed, the book by her pillow, the otherwise clean space. "It doesn't look like you've been crying."

"That doesn't mean I'm okay."

"I just didn't notice any tissues anywhere," Kitty said.

"Look…I'm here. I can't do anything about it. If I was going to have a breakdown, I would have had it already, but here I am, still frustratingly sane. You don't have to keep checking on me or pretending to care."

Kitty sat on the edge of the bed, draping the bag next to her. "I do care. This is what I do. I care for the people he brings into the circus. It's always hard at the beginning. When Joanne and Jane arrived, they didn't leave their RV or tent for six months. Christina barely spoke for a year."

"Then why did he only give me a week?" Elizabeth asked.

"He must think you only need a week."

"How long did it take you?"

"It's different for people like me."

"You mean demons?"

Kitty smiled. Elizabeth didn't smile back. "I'm not a demon. I'm as human as you are. I wished myself into Arcanium on purpose. Now, I've brought some of the costumes Bell wants you to wear. You can dress for the circus here or in the back of my oddity tent, where you'll usually find me. Obviously, I won't have to do anything with your hair, but I keep all the makeup in there, so if you want to meet with me this week to discuss how you want me to do your face—"

"I'll do it," Elizabeth said. "I know how the bastard wants me to look. Why would you do that?"

"Do what?

"Join Arcanium on purpose."

"It was the best freak show in a world where freak shows are dying—for some good reasons and some bad ones," Kitty said. "When you look like me, sweetie, there's not much else you can do. Sandra, our Skeleton, came in on her own, too. Caroline, the carousel engineer, joined us over a year ago. Victor, the man made of stone, joined a little after. Of course, none of us knew it's a demonic circus until we were already a part of it."

"But you stay a part of it even after you know. And you help him." Elizabeth turned away from her again. Kitty was as friendly now as when she'd just been another sideshow. But it didn't matter if the locals were demons, monsters or humans with an unhealthy attachment to a damned circus. As far as she was concerned, they were all complicit.

"I'm the human who's been here the longest, so I'm the one Bell usually has welcoming unwitting humans into the fold. Elizabeth, I've had my share of coldness and hatred directed at me. You don't have to like me or any of the others. All you have to know is that *none* of us will hurt you, and I do my best to be there for everyone when being a psychic still doesn't make Bell understand what it's like to be human."

Elizabeth gripped the blinds so tightly that they bent and snapped under her fist. "This isn't my first rodeo, all right? I know how this works. I'll come out if he insists. I'll look the way he wants me to look. I'll wear whatever sick joke you have in that bag. I'll go to the Tattooed Man to have these blank spaces filled in, just like he told me to do. But I don't want your help. I don't want anything to do with you."

"Okay," Kitty said softly, standing. She paused before leaving. "Troy will be available for you later today in his trailer. He said to look for the one with the tramp stamp."

Elizabeth could probably have hidden in the RV forever, but she didn't like it in there. The walls were too damn close. Everything was too brown and smelled faintly of wood polish, as though it was old and new at the same time.

As she stepped out of the vehicle, winter hit her like a wall, but her body didn't react to the chill the way she'd expected it to. She felt the cold, but it stayed on the surface rather than seeping into her like it had during the storm. If she had to walk around barefoot in a robe that no longer had its belt, with nothing to cover her bare head, she decided it was the least Bell could do for her—literally, the very least, but she'd take it.

On the way to the big top tent, the cast sent her a few curious glances, but when she avoided their gazes and made no move to join them, they maintained a respectful distance. Those who entered the big top before her walked through the ring to the red velvet curtain that led backstage. She followed.

Picnic tables lined the generous backstage area. The cast were all gathered, some together and some alone, on the benches. Staff served scrambled eggs and sausage in tortillas. Kitty had called them golems. That made more sense to Elizabeth than androids.

One of the conjoined twins beckoned to her as she left the food line. "Hey, new girl. The oddly limbed sit over here. And may I say, you learned how to walk with extra legs much faster than I did. I guess it's easier when there's only one mind telling them where to go."

Elizabeth turned away, but there weren't many other places to sit where she'd have enough room to qualify as 'eating alone'. The few people who *were* eating alone weren't the kind of people she wanted to sit with. Like the Rotting Man, who still seeped and who everyone else apparently avoided as well. Or the Cyclops, whose giant eye over his squashed nose was just a little too big, as though it would explode like one of the Rotting Man's boils at any moment.

Then there were the groups that were so clearly demonic that she wouldn't sit with them if they paid her.

She didn't want to go back to her RV, but she was still absolutely sure she didn't want anything to do with the humans of Arcanium either — these people who somehow found it in them to smile and laugh despite where they were.

Instead of sitting with anyone, she edged around the crowd and ate standing in the shadows next to a giant pile of crates.

"Hey, what are you doing all the way out here?" Maya wore a long peasant skirt and skin-tight shirt without a bra underneath, neither of which were appropriate for the weather. Making cast members impervious to winter cold as well as summer heat was probably useful for an all-weather circus. "Joanne, Jane and Christina said they were going to talk with you over brunch. I thought you'd want to hang out with people who had to go through similar adjustments. It's better to get through this with other people."

"You wouldn't know. He didn't do anything to you." Bad as the rest were, Elizabeth had even less interest in entertaining the lucky ones who Bell hadn't twisted like clay.

"Of course he did something to me. You think I was able to walk on a high-wire or tightrope before he got his hands on me?"

"How terrifying," Elizabeth replied dryly.

"It *was* terrifying. Not the high-wire part, but all the rest."

Still looking away from Maya, Elizabeth spoke without emotion. "Let me be perfectly clear. I'm not interested in making friends. I'm not interested in talking with other people Bell made like me. And I'm certainly not interested in a little girl telling me how awful it was to be stolen by the devil himself and treated like a princess in return for being his whore."

The strike against her ear rang through Elizabeth's skull. The girl was small, but there was darkness in her eyes that could have been demonic.

Elizabeth brought her hand to the side of her head against the unexpected pain. "I thought no one could hurt anyone else."

Maya laughed, a sound like throwing knives. "A slap, a scratch, a punch... That's nothing. In a claustrophobic place like this, Bell doesn't concern himself with those unless it's in view of guests or if it leaves marks. Now, if anyone tries to kill you and it looks like they really might succeed, he'll step in. Or he'll just watch and spontaneously give you tightrope-walking skills so you can escape the psycho with the knife. If you're *really* lucky, you might end up friends with said psycho after she gets better. The point being, 'harm' is a word open to interpretation. Sometimes Bell gets off on the conflict."

"What an angel," Elizabeth said, finally turning around to face her.

"No one ever said he's an angel, least of all him. But don't you *dare* think you know anything about me or any of the others. Don't you dare think I have it easy just because Bell decided to keep me out of the freak show. And don't you dare call me his whore, because I guaran-fucking-tee you, *you're* going to end up sleeping with someone you didn't expect, too, when the incubus and succubus really pour their magic out over the entire circus. What? You didn't think Arcanium got by on rustic charm alone, did you?"

Maya didn't seem to be the least intimidated by Elizabeth's strangeness, nor her height—not the way she'd sometimes used it against the Bishop kids. Maya was young but she wasn't a child, and Elizabeth was well aware from her own sisters that shorter girls sometimes compensated.

"He pulled me in, took me from my family, cut me off from my life, just like all the others. Then he pursued me. And when he sees something he wants… Believe me, loving him doesn't do me any favors, sweetheart."

Disgust curled Elizabeth's lip. "If you think that's love—"

"What would you know about it? Last I checked, you were covering yourself head to toe and getting your kicks from another person's family." Maya shoved her, advancing fast enough to surprise Elizabeth, who stumbled over her extra legs onto a picnic bench. Maya wasn't much taller that way either, but she had a way of gathering intensity. Perhaps she'd learned a thing or two from the jinni, like using truth as a weapon.

"But hey, Bell likes playing with broken toys, and you *are* new. Everyone has their own adjustment period. You can be scared, quiet, angry… Hell, you can be as mean as you want. But don't expect the rest of us to just take it. We've all paid our weight in flesh and blood. What you're going through isn't anything special. Usually there aren't enough fucks in the world for me to give when it comes to scared women tossing 'whore' at me because I'm convenient, but you're one of the ones who seems to mean it, and I don't fucking appreciate it."

Elizabeth pushed herself to her feet once more and braced herself against the table in case Maya decided to shove her down again. "I didn't call you that because I'm the shriveled-up, prudish, resentful spinster you think I am, who'll melt as soon as some big, strong man gets his hands on me. Been there, done that, not impressed anymore. All of you know what he is, but you're still with him, his lovely *assistant*. How many have walked through his circus, into his little fortune teller tent, and made wishes with you right there, helping them express their deepest, darkest desires, or perhaps just a weary dream? You were right there with my kids. What if they'd been the ones to wish? What if Todd had wished for a snake of his own? What if Sharona had wished her baby sister could just disappear? What would he have made of the wishes of innocent *children*? And what would you have done about it?"

Elizabeth took Maya's face in her hands with more scorn than compassion. Maya shook her off, but she didn't retaliate this time.

"That's right. You would have done nothing. You'll slip into his bed and play circus queen, but God forbid you use your position to stop him, even just a little."

"God doesn't live here." Tension vibrated under Maya's skin, clenched through her jaw, her fists. The darkness in her eyes remained, but the frustration she kept blinking back made her seem much more human. "And you try undermining a psychic. Just try. The truth is hardly as black and white as you make it. You'll taste the gray here eventually. We all do. He's more than the evil he does."

"No, he isn't. That's not the way evil works, sweetheart."

"Don't act so damn condescending. I do my acts of contrition daily. Good doesn't erase the evil, but evil doesn't erase the good either. I see more of both than most. You've barely had a glimpse, *Spider*."

Maya stepped closer to her again, her skirt brushing Elizabeth's legs. She glanced down over the glimpses of ink the robe didn't cover, gaze lighting briefly on Elizabeth's lips—long enough for her to question the breadth of Maya's tastes.

"Let me give you a few pieces of advice, one sinner to another. Don't judge till you've been here more than a few days, till the spells sink all the way in. Do right by Bell's circus, and he'll do right by you. Most of all, allies are what's going to get you by in here, because you might as well start thinking in terms of decades in service to him. So..." Maya traced the edge of Elizabeth's lower lip with her dark red painted nails, somehow finding the exact places where she'd once been pierced and pricking them. Elizabeth jerked away. "Keep your damn mouth shut. And Bell wants me to tell you Troy's ready to work on the new tattoos. He'll freshen up the rest in the meantime. You're fucking welcome."

Everyone was watching them by now. Elizabeth didn't care. She waited until Maya was walking away. "Doesn't matter what you do. You're still not forgiven."

The rigidity in Maya's spine told her she'd struck another nerve.

* * * *

The trailer with the tramp stamp. Elizabeth was still trying to figure out whether it was ironic or just trashy when Troy stepped out.

"Hey. We've been expecting you. Please, come on up."

If Elizabeth hadn't been familiar with the body modification scene, she might have been surprised that Troy was so soft-spoken. By this point, she was used to accepting that it took all sorts — from artsy types to accountants, all the way to bookish rebels trying to stick it to Leviticus.

Even so, climbing into his trailer felt a little more backroom-transaction than she was comfortable with. The blinds were closed, and Troy had covered them with felt to block out the rest of the light. The living space of the trailer had been reconfigured with a dentist's chair and a workstation instead of a kitchenette.

Troy switched on the surgical lights above the chair, making the situation seem even shadier. Framed pieces of flash art hung from the cabinets and small sections of the walls. The quality was exceptional, from street art to Japanese calligraphy to photo-realism to watercolor to traditional, even better than some of the artists Dez had employed at his shop. Backroom this might be, but it wouldn't be some shoddy prison tattoo. She found that oddly comforting.

"I hope you don't mind Christina being here." Troy nodded to the limbless Human Torso on his bed.

"After all, I worked so hard to get here." Christina wiggled the stumps of her thighs in her custom jumpsuit. She'd been a small woman before the loss of limbs. Without them, she was the size of a large teddy bear. Troy wasn't a big man himself, but when Christina indicated she wanted help sitting up, she wasn't any kind of burden to him.

"No. That's all right," Elizabeth said. "Sorry. I don't mean to stare."

"I was made for people to stare at. We all were. You're pretty stare-worthy yourself, even before you take off the robe."

Elizabeth ran her hand over her bare scalp. She was overdue for stubble. It wasn't coming back, nor was it just her head that had lost its hair. When she'd been able to stop and take stock of herself, she'd realized Bell had removed every last bit of hair on her body except eyebrows and eyelashes—the better to show off her tattoos. Dez had gone through his own depilatory lengths on her body as well, to ensure the perfect effect.

"You said…" Elizabeth hesitated now that she was in such privacy and proximity with not one but two members of Arcanium. "You said you were made."

"I made one of the wishes that tends to annoy wish-granting jinn, because they hear it a lot." Christina shrugged. "Looks like I lost the baby weight, huh?"

Elizabeth lowered herself onto the dentist chair. "You can't be serious."

"Oh, it's more complicated than that. It is for most of us. Seems he gave you what he took from me. All Asian women must look the same to him."

"Actually, I think these are mine. Or would have been mine if I had been born with them." Even the freckles seemed like hers, the tone and length of limb far more plausible than Christina's would have been.

Christina laughed. "I was just kidding. Bad joke. Mine wouldn't work on you at all. He always makes us look like we're born this way, but better."

"Convenient how he curates a freak show without being one himself," Elizabeth said.

"Oh, he does a little bit of this and that, depending on what the circus needs. But it rarely needs another freak when wishes provide him with such an endless supply."

This time, bitterness tainted the joke, and Christina's face—tanner than Elizabeth's, with watercolor lips and a less transparent complexion—hardened. She aged ten years in a minute, which made Elizabeth question her original assumption that Christina was young.

Kitty had said she'd been there the longest, but she looked younger than Elizabeth, too. Maya had told her to think in terms of decades. She wouldn't put it past Bell to interfere with aging just to create the desired effect—a circus of pretty, odd young things to intrigue and entice the perfect clientele. And they'd last as long as Bell wanted them to.

A ragged Siamese missing its back leg jumped onto the bed to curl up next to Christina as though she was its favorite pillow spot. It blinked indifferently at Elizabeth.

"Excuse Bella. She likes to watch, too." Troy dried his hands with the same thoroughness he'd washed them. "She doesn't like the sound of the tattoo gun, so she won't bother you. Are you allergic?"

Elizabeth shook her head.

"Where would you like to start?" He sat down on the stool next to her and clasped his hands like a church boy considering prayer.

"Where does he want me to start?" Elizabeth kept her eyes downcast to offset the clenching of her teeth.

"Well, by the time you're displayed, he wants at least your upper arms and thighs with some art so that it looks like you're completing yourself. I haven't seen what you have yet, so I wouldn't know what themes and styles to follow. If it doesn't matter, we can work piece by piece, but if you'd prefer something cohesive…"

Elizabeth considered the art on Troy's body, some of it his own work, by the style, and some of it impossible for him to reach or see for himself. Cohesion hadn't been a priority for him. He appeared to prefer creative chaos.

Almost everything that could be pierced or plugged had been — eyebrows, ears, nose, a heavy septum ring and a lip plug centering the piercings along his lips. She hadn't seen inside his mouth, but she'd bet her extra arms and legs that his tongue was split, pierced or both. Bars lined his sternum and the jut of his hips. Circular barbells adorned the skin between his thumbs and forefingers, as well as his nipples and his navel. Implants horned his forehead and ridged his shoulders and forearms.

His face and shaven head were a black-and-white lesson in facial anatomy — half skull, half musculature. The rest of him reminded her of *The Illustrated Man*, with realism melding with scrollwork, words weaving among images and almost everything from the neck down covered. After ten years without touchups, Elizabeth's had faded, some of the lines blurring, but his tattoos were too clear, too colorful, each one as sharp as new.

"I'm not wearing anything under this." It was a ridiculous thing for her to say. All she had to do was look at him to see he wasn't Dez. But she hadn't chosen Troy. She hadn't agreed to be vulnerable to him. Bell had forced this upon her.

Troy braced his elbows on his thighs and peered up at her. "Don't worry about what Bell wants from you.

If you don't want me to see you, I won't kick up a fuss. He can put the art he likes on the skin he created. But he sent you to me because I like the work, and he said you liked the needle."

Other than the vividness of the color and the unnatural clarity of the art, there was nothing supernatural about the man. Everything he'd done had emerged from natural means, from choices, from artistry — plain, common needle and ink from a man's hands. If Troy hadn't been proud of his work, he would never have displayed it on his walls.

"You wished yourself in here on purpose, too, didn't you? You wanted to be the Tattooed Man."

"I've never wanted to be anything else." He spread his hands to present himself, the surgical lights blinding on the titanium jewelry. "At a certain point, I couldn't be anything else anymore. Like Kitty and Sandra, I've been to a number of circuses. This one is by far the best. It's not afraid to get dirty."

"There's plenty of dirty here, my man. We never had a problem with that," Christina said. "You know, I think he's said more these last few minutes than in the last month."

Troy grinned, suddenly shy. "I don't mean sex-demon dirty. I mean Arcanium brings the freak show up close and personal. Shows off the oddities to remind people we exist, whether born this way or created. I like it better when we exist. On a screen, you wonder whether it's real or not."

"That's the second time I've heard about sex demons. That's not just an inside joke around here, is it?" Elizabeth said.

Christina shook her head. "Lady Sasha charms *all* kinds of snakes. Then there's Lord Mikhail, our strongman. Ever since *Magic Mike*, he's been even more dangerous than usual."

Troy turned around in a creak of black leather, a comically quizzical expression under all the piercings and ink. "When did you see *Magic Mike*?"

"Caroline streamed it. I was helpless to stop her. It's not like I can work the touchscreen. Okay, I didn't protest too much."

"She's going to ask me to dance for her one of these days, I just know it," Troy muttered to Elizabeth. "You won't make me dance for you, will you? Please?"

Christina giggled and squirmed with delight, losing all the years she'd gained in her dark moment.

Elizabeth saw beyond the tattoos and piercings with ease. She had so much practice seeing the Before even after the After was permanent. Troy was around her age, maybe a little older, but he took care of his skin the way an artist took care of his canvases. Like most artists, there was a childlike quality to him, but unlike the artists she was used to, he was exactly what he appeared to be in physical presentation and demeanor. Underneath the sharp points and wicked edges, guile didn't dare touch him. How someone like that could thrive in a circus run by demons, deceit and violence eluded her, but between him and Christina, Elizabeth couldn't convince herself of any threat from them—not like the razorblades in chocolate Elizabeth sensed from Kitty and Maya.

Christina had been in the big top for Elizabeth's rebirth, but Troy hadn't. When he told her she could leave without him seeing her, he really wouldn't have seen her yet, although she doubted he would remain innocent of her body for long.

Elizabeth glanced back down again, accustomed to defeat enough to recognize it even when the victor wasn't there. "Do you mind?" she asked Christina.

"We get used to it, seeing skin all the time. But I remember when it still mystified me, even horrified me. I can close my eyes if you want. I'm always good to sleep."

"You've already seen me. What's there to hide?" Elizabeth slowly drew the bathrobe over her shoulders. A stranger might assume the motion was intended as seductive, but she couldn't convince herself to expose herself with anything that seemed like eagerness.

She paused with her top half bare, her legs still covered, then lifted her inked prime arms into the light. The bee swarm and honeycomb along her right arm, tinged with honey, had been darkened, deepened and sharpened, as though inked with pen and brush rather than needle across her skin. The gaping hole illusion in the middle of her chest was as fresh as though someone had really cracked open her chest to expose her heart. The mourning corset and the partial mandala that marked her hairless mound were also achingly clear.

Looking at herself wasn't like peering into Bell's mirror. In the mirror, the horror had been the arms and legs he'd conjured from her—her ink had been her past. Now, the past she'd escaped had become present all over again.

"As long as you're in his circus, the art stays fresh, almost alive." Troy kept his hands away from her, but he lovingly gazed over what she'd shown so far. "This is good. I can mimic it."

"Don't. Do your own." She tightened the robe around her waist, then untied the belt to release her secondary arms. "They're still a bit wild. They might have to be strapped down, but please, not too tight."

She tried not to flinch as he took both left wrists to guide her back on the dentist's chair.

"Don't worry. I'm a professional. The only reason I'll touch you is to maneuver the arms. Okay? I won't do anything you don't want me to do, Elizabeth."

She settled back against the firm cushion, though her spine wouldn't quite uncoil. "Thank you."

"Now, what do you want me to do for you today?"

* * * *

Name a phobia and Elizabeth probably had some version of it, with varying degrees of severity. But she'd discovered as a child that a needle-prick was hardly worth the fuss, and she grew up to give at donation stations until she started getting tattoos, which prevented her from donating any more blood.

It wasn't that needles didn't hurt. It was that needles never hurt as badly as she feared. Getting a tattoo was facing her fears, and tattooing her fears had been intended as a reminder that she could conquer each one. It had turned out quite differently in the end, but she could still endure a tattoo with something approaching pleasure. Difficult to explain the appeal even to herself, but it had been too long since her last needle, and even though it pierced through skin where once there had been nothing but empty air, her reaction remained the same.

Once he'd cleaned off the blood and excess ink, Troy wiped his hands and helped her sit up. While she waited for the lightheadedness to clear, he gave her the rest of the screwdriver he'd made before they started —

something to keep her blood sugar level up. Plus, she needed to finish it before she would even consider looking at what Troy had done for her.

He'd worked on her left arm today, because that was the easiest for him to reach while she rested on her stomach, the robe like a blanket over her legs. Plenty of bare skin would provide additional canvas over time, but the point of this exercise had been to make her new limbs less bare, not completely covered.

A stylized and illustrated chain emerged from the fires of the anima sola, but it gradually became more realistic as it wound around her elbow and connected to the shackle that delicately circled her wrist, so lifelike that if someone didn't look closely, they might believe her truly bound. Which had been the point.

Warm laughter purred in her ear, though no one was there. Her point to Bell had been made, and it had pleased him — which hadn't been the point at all.

Soon the chain and shackle inked around her wrist would be joined with more fears, as though Bell had given her extra limbs because her body alone hadn't been adequate space.

"He'll want something more spidery on your other arm to balance the spider illustration on your left thigh, but we've made a good start." Troy retrieved a cobalt blue bottle from his cabinet. The handmade label read, *For cast only*. "This should heal the skin completely within fifteen minutes at most. Saves time for when we need to be performance-ready."

He wore a glove to smooth it over her arm. The liquid gel moved and absorbed like lotion. The pain she'd been counting on lasting a little longer faded away.

"Will I see you again tomorrow?" he asked.

Elizabeth pulled her robe on, eschewing the binding of her secondary arms and threading the belt through the loops instead. She didn't look up as she nodded.

"Do you need help home?"

Elizabeth struggled to stand, but she leaned away from Troy when he tried to help. "I'm fine."

"Troy…" Christina's caution convinced him to stay back while Elizabeth stumbled to the door.

Chapter Five

Bell sat on one of the outdoor picnic tables where Elizabeth had been eating her meals instead of backstage. He sat the way he moved, the way he considered, the way he touched — all casual grace and deceptive danger.

"It's time to show you where you'll spend your weekends — a little tour of the funhouse before you become a part of it."

"If you're planning to take me into that haunted house, you're going to have to drag me in by my cold, dead body." She discarded the rest of her breakfast — seeing Bell stole any trace of appetite.

He jumped down from the table to join her.

"It's always a pleasure to engage with the real you." He brushed his fingers under her chin and lifted it to force her to look at him. "But nothing gets in the way of my circus, not even a rebellious woman resentful of her own rebellion."

"The last time I got near that place, the outside was enough to make me shudder, and you fucking well know it."

"Why do you think I'm putting you inside?" Bell's crooked smile made her want to punch other parts of him crooked, too.

"Why not just put me on Oddity Row with the rest?" It wasn't where she wanted to be, but it was worlds better than a haunted house.

"Oh, you'll have your place there, in your own way." His scrutiny stole the robe from around her body. No matter how tightly she wrapped her prime arms around herself, she couldn't hide from the knowledge in those lantern eyes. She could have sworn they were a simpler hazel when she'd met him. "But not during the weekends. You'll serve the house better. It's where I want you when the circus opens today at two o'clock."

"That's in only three hours." Everything was happening too fast. There weren't enough years in the world for her to be ready.

"We have plenty of time for a tour. If I have to make you dance for me, I'll do it, but I'm not fond of puppeteering."

"Could have fooled me."

"Have it your way, Lizzie." He curled his fingers as though playing an instrument she couldn't see.

And she was the instrument. He jutted her hips forward, her spine moving on the hinge that hadn't been there when she'd been normal. It eased some of the weight off her lower back and placed it on the secondary legs. They could only stand on the balls of their feet, but they were no longer on tiptoe to brace themselves on the ground.

As he dragged her along to walk with him—and as she tried to resist, with no effect whatsoever—she made a mental note on how he made her move, the way he'd created her to move, for her own ease and to appear more spiderlike in her gait. Her hips weren't used to it yet, though, tired by the time they arrived at the haunted funhouse.

"Don't call me Lizzie." Elizabeth adjusted her robe, which had spread obscenely over her legs when Bell had taken the reins.

"Because that's what your ex called you? Or because that's what your father calls you?"

Elizabeth refused to dignify the question with a reply.

"I don't call you that just because it irritates you. Elizabeth is your mask, my dear. She always has been. Lizzie may have lived the worst of you, but she's truer than anything Elizabeth pretended to be."

"Don't you have a funhouse to show me?" Elizabeth crossed her prime arms. Her secondary set were still bound with a leather belt Troy had let her borrow so she could properly use the robe belt where it was supposed to be.

He swept his arm toward the entrance. "Absolutely. After you, milady. I'll be at the bottom of the stairs in case you fall."

What a goddamn gentleman.

After what she'd gone through over the last week, the haunted house seemed less imposing from the outside. If the Creature was there, he hadn't yet made himself known. But she still hesitated at the door handle, because however cheesy the funhouse looked on the outside, the inside would be quite different. Bell wouldn't accept anything less than terror in a haunted house of his own making. What would be the point of a demonic circus if the horrorful heart of its carnival side lacked bite?

And once she got in, any anger left for Bell would dissipate. Fear would return, as childlike and powerful as ever.

Elizabeth hadn't always been afraid. Oh, there had always been things she was afraid of. Spiders had scared her since she was three, and she'd had an ongoing night terror about a monster living under her bed for most of her prepubescent life. But afraid hadn't been her nature, not even after the stories Charity and Temperance had told her or the tales her father had spun at the pulpit in the name of love and truth.

Everything had changed once she'd changed — when she'd grown eight inches in a year, developed breasts, sprouted hair where it hadn't been before — when everything had become awkward and the world had expanded. When the colors of the world had started to fade and lose their luster. When she'd finally understood what her existence meant in the center of their strict religious community.

She couldn't blame it all on her biological father, her mother or her mother's husband, who'd been little more than a resentful authoritarian figure in her life in comparison to his real daughters. Something *inside* her had changed. She didn't know what it was, but it was as though her child's curiosity had wobbled then turned topsy-turvy. Anything unknown no longer filled her with wonder and questions but with creeping dread that had tightened the muscles in her back into tree branches, while the rest of the fear dug its roots in deeper every year.

She'd leveled out about the time she'd run away, when her fear seemed this close to being controlled.

Then she'd learned there was no controlling it. It just lay in wait before it attacked.

Seven years later, she'd begged to return to her parents' world. There was fear there, too, but the Petrosian world was smaller, and so her fears became smaller, too — as long as she didn't think too hard about what she was doing.

Nothing to do here in Arcanium but think, and what came after every thought was fear. Because Bell brought the wonder, the awe, the curiosity, the amazement that a cynical YouTube world couldn't always understand, with its virtual reality and CGI and video hacks. As a member of the cast now, Elizabeth saw the other side of the awe. For all the old-fashioned tricks and sleights of hand, Arcanium was real.

And when she walked into the haunted funhouse, that would be real, too.

She turned the handle and stepped in. Bell came in right behind her to close the morning light away. The darkness of the funhouse wasn't absolute — where would the fun be in *complete* darkness where you couldn't see what might kill you? — but it was close enough. Once her eyes had adjusted, she could discern the distinct, dark-colored lights illuminating the halls, beams of blue, green, red, purple, strobes to disorient.

"I turned off the sound system." He slipped past her into the narrow hall. "For you, I've no need to preserve the illusion that the screams aren't genuine. What I do need is for you to know what I didn't do to you. There might be a hell here, but while you'll be a part of it, it won't touch you. It matters to me that you understand this."

"Lots of pretty words, Bell. Not going to make me believe you." She darted her gaze from corner to corner, where the colored lights had been strategically focused to avoid, and where the strobe lights only illuminated in partial-second glimpses.

"I know. Follow me. Nothing would hurt you even if I wasn't here, but if it makes you feel safer if I stand between you and my haunts, I will walk before you."

He called them 'haunts', as though they were little more than ghosts in his crazy carnival ride. And he called them 'his'.

"Here we go," he murmured.

When they rounded the corner, her body threatened to freeze up. He took her hand to keep her moving forward. She stumbled through each plodding step as they approached a man in the shadows.

The man was tall, his bowler hat brushing the acoustic tiles on the ceiling, and his arms and fingers long, reaching to his knees. His frame was far too slender to be that of the Tall Man, who was only a little taller but more proportional. The man's funereal black suit had been tailored to his alien form, accentuating rather than normalizing his elongated limbs. Lack of limbs, extra limbs, long limbs, short limbs — the universal shorthand for weirdness seemed to be a funhouse mirror perspective mingled with mangled anatomy.

The tall gentleman leaned down from his great height, his pale face clarifying the closer he came, but no matter how clearly she could see him — down to fine hairs and pores and even a few freckles — a face never came into view. He had a brow ridge, cheekbones, chin, eye sockets… No face.

He made no sound, but his non-face came within inches of her own, and if Bell hadn't been jinn, she might have broken the fingers holding onto her hand.

She might have broken them on purpose if he'd tried to reassure her once more that there was nothing to be afraid of, which was probably why he didn't. He just moved her forward and around another bend.

They passed a few doors and interior windows that had been boarded up.

"I like to keep my options open for new inspiration to strike. We're always under construction here," he said. "I think it adds to the uncertain atmosphere."

"If I die of shock, I'm coming back and tormenting you for eternity."

"I welcome the company, my dear."

Cobwebs and thin fabric draped from the ceiling—no point messing with the classics, especially with the full-sized rope web that had been constructed to cover an entire wall where guests rounded a corner. Eerie black spider legs emerged from the shadows, but no spider emerged with it.

"We'll come back for this once you're all dressed. The web is for you, little Spider. The Gentleman unsettles them. The Spider gives them a good jump scare. And now things really get interesting." Bell led her beyond the spiderweb, dragging all four of her feet along the dark linoleum tiles.

"I don't want to see."

"I know." Compassion infused his voice, more insulting than if he'd been cold and unforgiving. "But you will."

When they didn't have boards to cover them, the windows weren't windows so much as walls that had been cut away and replaced with Plexiglas. As they crossed the threshold between wall and window, surgical lights switched on to show a body strapped to a metal table. The young man struggled helplessly against leather bound taut across him. He'd been stripped down to his boxers. Tears streamed down his temples.

"Please, please, I'm sorry. I'm sorry. Please let me out! Don't cut me! Don't cut me again!"

When the ambient soundtrack was on, the cries probably blended in with assorted screams, wails and cackles. But without any other sound to detract, anguish strained through the broken voice.

A figure stepped forward—a doctor wearing a mask that covered the lower half of his face and black-edged goggles over his eyes. His white scrubs and white latex gloves were sterile and blinding under the lights. He brought with him a gleaming surgical tray lined with scalpels.

"No. No, you can't do that," Elizabeth said. "You let children in here."

"You'd be amazed what you can get away with when people think it isn't real," Bell replied.

Eating breakfast seemed like a terrible idea now. She placed a hand on the wall behind her to brace herself against the creeping, quivering wave of nausea. Shivers ran up her spine and over her scalp. She managed to swallow back the urge to vomit, but she didn't know how long that would last. "I let Todd walk through here."

"He's a well-adjusted boy with a solid grasp of what's real and what isn't—or at least what shouldn't be. What he didn't know didn't hurt him."

"But it *is* real."

"He couldn't know that."

He pushed her free hand away from covering her eyes as the doctor lifted a scalpel from the surgical tray, brought the edge to the concavity beneath the ribs, then sliced down the middle of the guy's abdomen. The blood was too red, the line too perfect—too easy to dismiss what she saw as fake. But the boy's screams became less coherent. He sucked in his belly, as though that would help him escape from the blade.

Elizabeth turned away again, only to be confronted by a woman in a bloodstained old-fashioned nurse's uniform. Her mouth had been split open to her ears and forced into the semblance of a smile. There was pain in her eyes, which was the only way Elizabeth knew this was a real woman rather than a demon, but Elizabeth still screamed and scrambled around Bell, tripping over her own bare feet. The nurse stretched her dripping, bloody hands to both Bell and Elizabeth in imploration, but Bell cast her away, holding his palm up to her like a vampire hunter with a cross.

The nurse bowed back into the shadow, pleading silently with Elizabeth. But she lowered her eyes when she noticed the four legs beneath the hem of the robe. Help wouldn't come from another victim.

The light in the operating theater darkened on the doctor making a horizontal incision under the ribs, his goggles and mask splashed with a line of blood.

Bell led her onward. They passed a boarded door frame then stopped in front of the next illuminated window.

Another man had been bound, but this time shackled to the ceiling and floor, stretched taut as though prepared to be quartered. The roar of a chainsaw heralded the entrance of a large man in ripped clothing and a black butcher's apron.

The chained man was also gagged, but Elizabeth spoke for him. "No. No, please, no. Don't…"

The chainsaw split through the man's thighs, adding new stains to the already blood-soaked room. The light in this room wasn't nearly as clear and clean as in the operating theater. A dark, rich red glow camouflaged the full extent of the splatter from an unknowing gaze, and it made the exposed flesh and bone seem much more unreal. The way the legs jittered and kicked on the ground added to the unreality.

All eight of Elizabeth's limbs, not to mention her entire abdomen, seemed filled not with their own flesh and bone but cold jelly. If Bell hadn't urged her forward, she would have collapsed. Then she might never have been able to stop watching the man unable to scream as the triumphant butcher cut him down into parts.

"You sick motherfucker, let me out of here. I'll sit in a tent. You can even bring out the spider legs and the rope, but I can't be in here. I can't. I just can't." She scratched at her face, at his arm where he held her, at his hand, over her scalp. She didn't know why it all made her itch, but she paused when she realized she'd scratched through skin, collecting stained patches underneath her nails.

"They're trapped here for as long as I decide to have them." Tenderly taking the scratching hand in his own to keep her from doing any more damage, Bell moved them back into darkness that now seemed unbearably soothing — unbearable, because she knew what was on the other side of the darkness. Just because the rooms went dark didn't mean the violence ended. "They're here because they tried to hurt or kill the people of Arcanium, the ones I swore to protect. They would have disfigured, crippled, raped, slaughtered what belongs to me, for the sole reason that they dared to be different."

"So you punish them like this for doing exactly what you do?"

"You and I disagree on definitions. I *alter* those I bring into the circus by idle or deliberate wishes, but I only *disfigure* the punished ones. I will not rape, and although some trespassers become fodder for those who consume human meat, I do not slaughter. If you cannot yet see the difference between what I do to you and what happens to them, give me more time."

A little girl — or something that appeared like a little girl — ran down the hall, but when it looked up, its face was that of a bearded man with his mouth closed around a pink plastic pacifier.

"The foolish believe that because we wander, because we differ, we must be weak. I have lived many lives. My memory provides as clear a picture of the past as of the future. When I look at these...pigs, I see what they tried to do to my people. I see what would have happened if they had succeeded. The Ringmaster once accused me of not understanding the purpose of a dungeon. A dungeon was never something I wanted to make of Arcanium, but watching their suffering pleases me. It might also alleviate their debt more quickly than the others, although I doubt that reassures them."

He trailed his fingertips over the next window. Bodies had been strewn over each other in a dehumanizing tangle, their diseased skin disintegrated, twisted, fused with the others. They were naked, but the flesh fusion hid where nudity would have been prohibitive. Giant cockroaches crawled over and through them, inside them. Maggots squirmed in the open wounds, wriggling over the deadened flesh.

The chorus of their groans tortured Elizabeth's ears. Bell let her cover them, but only because it didn't shut the sounds out.

Puffs of air that mimicked tiny paws ran over her bare feet and legs to introduce the next room, where giant rats with glowing red eyes crawled on and nibbled at hooded men tied to chairs over a drain, a single pendant bulb swinging over them.

The halls continued with uneven, distorted perspective like German expressionist hallucinations, with sloped floors and ceilings and corner angles not quite at ninety degrees. It seemed impossible that all of this could exist within the size of the haunted funhouse, but Bell probably wouldn't confine himself to something as plebeian as square footage.

A man covered in thick, coarse fur lumbered through the hall like a werewolf.

A man—so many of them were men, and Elizabeth didn't think that was a coincidence—fought against the straitjacket that strapped him to a wall. He screamed and wrenched from things Elizabeth couldn't see.

A woman with a tentacle-like tree vine thrust down her throat hovered above the ground, kicking against the tendrils that tangled around her and emerged from her skin, from her nostrils, from her ears, from under her fingernails, as though it grew out of her. Her arms, legs and face had broken out in rashes wherever the oils of the vines touched her skin.

Three zombies shuffled past, snapping their teeth as though they could smell flesh but couldn't see where it came from.

After a while, each actor and tableau blended together like the pile of flesh-eaten bodies. There was always another corner, another window, another open door, another shadow. Elizabeth begged him to stop, stop hurting them, stop making her see it, nearly incoherent pleas spilling from her lips. But like those of the victims, they fell upon deaf ears.

"And here's the reason the Ringmaster quite happily remains at Arcanium now, in addition to the privileges afforded him with Kitty and Maya. It seems fitting that most of the men I collected for the funhouse come from the night their ringleader came for Kitty."

A darkly attractive man with tan skin and facial hair like the devil himself stood above five subjects, their shirts removed and trousers low on their hips to provide a broad expanse of flesh. The victims knelt with their hands bound close to a metal hitch made of plumbing pipe. One of the boys looked directly at her, sweat shining on his pallid face, his light brown curly hair matted and tangled, his fingernails dirty. Their mouths were all duct-taped.

The Ringmaster, resplendent in gilded red regalia, lifted the bullwhip clutched in his fist. He brought it down with practiced precision upon each boy's back, one after another. He grinned with wicked joy, black eyes an even greater contrast against perfect white teeth. His victims twisted, writhed, shouted as welts appeared on their previously unmarked skin. Blood seeped to the surface, smearing when the whip would strike them again.

"Most of my prisoners rotate among the funhouse horrors. I never let them become comfortable or accustomed to any one scenario. Of the many I punished before creating the funhouse, only the

Cyclops and the Rotting Man have failed to flourish. The human mind is capable of adjusting to almost anything."

Elizabeth staggered away, toward the bright red *Exit* sign. She climbed down the stairs leading out of the haunted funhouse, gasping as though all the air had been sucked from the building. She swiped at Bell for trying to help her down, then fell to her knees, retching. She didn't throw up. The heaves dissolved into coughs that wracked her like sobs.

At the leathery flutter of wings behind her, she grabbed a hard clump of dirt from the ground, twisted back toward the funhouse and threw it right at the Creature's forehead where he reposed over the exit. The dirt missed him, but he scurried back on the roof with speed that belied his size.

Bell jerked her back to her feet by an upper arm before she could find another projectile, holding her almost off the ground with one hand alone. "None of that. If you insist upon flinging your feelings at things, throw stones at me, not the Creature, who has done nothing but follow his nose."

"He reaps suffering. Something that does that can't be good, can't truly be harmless."

"Spoken as someone who shed their vegan principles as soon as I stripped away the guise of religion." He let her down but didn't let her go. "Does suffering taste better these days when seasoned with your own?"

"I'm not going back in there. I'm not going to be a part of this. You can't force me to do that to other—" She stopped herself.

"I'm glad you realized better on your own. I would have truly hated to demonstrate my mastery of your body once more." He pulled her back around the haunted funhouse and toward Oddity Row. "You have until opening to collect yourself. If I thought you'd get into your costume yourself, I'd let you go, but as it is, Kitty's ready to help you whether you like it or not. And if you resist or engage in the sort of childish nonsense you're entertaining, which I assure you Kitty would not appreciate, I'll put you back under my control until I've bound you to the spiderweb."

"I was right the first time." Elizabeth didn't actively pull back, but she also forced him to pull her forward. She'd show him childish. "You're a monster."

"I'm inhuman. There's a slight difference." He pushed her into the back of Kitty's tent, but the gesture seemed playful rather than impatient. "This one is not having a good day, Kitty. She needs a brisk pace and a gentle hand."

The whole back of the tent was like the funhouse, bigger on the inside than it seemed on the outside, and it was filled to the brim with costume racks, a mirrored Hollywood vanity and tubs and tubs of makeup and accessories. Behind the costume racks was a large cot that indicated Kitty also slept there.

Kitty glanced up from where she was putting the finishing touches on the conjoined twins' conjoined hair. "I've already talcumed the latex. I'll be right with you. If you want something approaching privacy, you can undress and start pulling on the suit behind the costume racks."

"I'll be waiting for her outside." Bell stepped back and lowered the tent flap.

Elizabeth considered it. She really considered shoving Kitty into the vanity, throwing her makeup all over the costumes and fleeing out of the front of the tent. She considered finding something sharp and mortally wounding anyone who got in her way. But Bell staying outside the tent quashed any thought of rebellion, because she knew he was as good as his word. She'd walked through an entire funhouse of torture chambers to that effect.

* * * *

She would have thought that a full latex bodysuit would be its own brand of hell, but as soon as the clearly custom black latex had been put in place over her four arms and four legs and the mask had been pulled over her bald head, the material melted against her skin like butter and moved easily with her. The material didn't breathe and it threatened to trigger her claustrophobia, but it wasn't quite as uncomfortable as she knew latex could be.

When Elizabeth had been encased in her bodysuit, Kitty stepped back, tilting her head. "You have a remarkable complexion. I'm only trying to figure out the best direction to go with your makeup."

Elizabeth brushed past her to the vanity and started searching through the giant makeup kits that some of the people in her other life might have envied. Normally, she wouldn't go through another woman's makeup, but as far as she'd been able to tell, disease wasn't something Bell would allow in his perfect machine of a circus unless he'd been the cause of it.

"If you told me what you were looking for…" Kitty began.

"I said I didn't want your help. I can do this myself."

After Elizabeth found everything, she got to work. The vanity lights were as good as the ones she'd used for Dez's photoshoots. Nothing but the best for a jinni's pet cat, apparently. The makeup was even better quality than she'd once used.

Once she'd finished, Elizabeth stared at her reflection. Her skin wasn't as smooth as it had once been, but avoiding sun and eating a cruelty-free diet had done her more than a few favors—in spite of her usual evening vice. With the help of makeup specially made for skin some liked to call porcelain, plus generous application of black liquid eyeliner and black lipstick, she almost couldn't tell the difference between what she'd looked like under Dez's lights and now in Bell's circus. Looking at herself in the mirror was like meeting a stranger for the second time.

"That's more dramatic than one might have expected from someone who clothed herself so modestly," Kitty said. "If I hadn't already suspected you had a more extreme background…"

Elizabeth resisted the urge to wipe the lipstick off with the back of her hand. "I told you, this isn't the first time I've done this." She tossed the lipstick onto the vanity with the liner, mascara and foundation. "I'll need these again."

"I'll put them in a case for you. The rest will be available if you want them. Elizabeth, are you going to be—?"

Elizabeth shoved herself away from the vanity and left the tent without another word. As she passed Bell, he fell into step behind her, all the way back to the funhouse.

She froze at the foot of the stairs leading to the entrance. She couldn't go back in. She just couldn't. Her legs wouldn't move.

Bell said nothing about it. Forcing her to adopt the easier but foreign spider walk up the stairs and into the

Spider

funhouse again seemed more an act of pity than
punishment.

At the spiderweb, the rope bindings unwound down
to take Elizabeth by all eight of her limbs, wrapping
around wrists, ankles, elbows and knees then drawing
her into the spiderweb like tentacles. She settled
perfectly into the slight concavity of the ropes, like
leaning into an upright hammock. The spider legs from
the darkness seemed to come from her, a too-many-
legged creature shrouded in shadow.

"You won't get away with this forever," she said.

"I've been traveling the world in my little circus for a
few centuries. Even before acquiring the circus, I was
always an entertainer, granting wishes for my own
amusement and the amusement of those around me. I
could quite literally get away with this forever." He
smoothed his hands down her prime legs, from thigh
to ankle. She twitched all the way down. "When a guest
comes down the hall, the spiderweb will automatically
tilt toward them. All you have to do, my dear, is
scream."

"Why did you want me to get my new arms and legs
tattooed if you were just going to put me in a latex
fetish suit that covered them?" Elizabeth asked.

Bell raised his eyebrow in a sardonic arch. "Would
you prefer to show them off in the slightest of your
wardrobe?"

She just glared.

"The time to expose your limbs will come soon. But
this is where you'll stay during the carnival's open
hours. At eight o'clock, when the circus performances
begin, your bindings will release you."

"Do I get a break? How am I supposed to use a bathroom in this web? Hell, how am I supposed to use a bathroom in this suit?"

"You won't need anything from the moment the web takes hold of you to the moment of your release. I'm not that sadistic, not even to my prisoners."

If he kept making her glare at him like this, her face was going to stick that way. It especially felt like that under the latex.

"Just like that, little Spider. Just like that." He stroked the boning in her latex corset. She jerked against her bindings, snapping her sharpened teeth. Bell didn't jump or indicate any kind of surprise. "Good girl. Scare my guests well."

She was going to kill him, even if she had to use a plastic fork in order to do it. God would forgive such a death.

"Remember. You're here to enjoy yourself."

* * * *

Elizabeth knew the second the gates opened, because that's when the screams stared. Not the real screams, the ones that had branded themselves forever in her mind, but the ones that came from the speakers — screams of the damned, moans of those driven hopelessly insane, wails of a million sorrows, enhanced by creepy music that shifted from music box to harpsichord to string quartet to theremin. It was the Halloween soundtrack of the century, and it added a patina of artifice to the house of horrors Bell had created.

Personally, Elizabeth didn't understand why he called it a funhouse. Who exactly was it fun for? Not the victims cursed to play out their mortal violence again and again, yet denied the mercy of death. Not the guests who went through to scare themselves silly — at least not a funhouse kind of fun. Only the Ringmaster could be said to have any sort of fun in a place like this. Maybe the Creature, who stayed outside the building but enjoyed the fruits of it nonetheless.

It took some time for the guests to show up after the soundtrack began. They had to pass Oddity Row, the midway, the fortune teller tent and the food booths before they could reach the funhouse.

Screams quite different from those coming from the tableaus or the sound system woke Elizabeth from her half-doze. She'd been hanging her head with her chin almost to her chest, but now she looked up. Anger was exhausting, and too many screams all bled together after a while. These differed because they were interspersed with nervous laughter and the sound of conversation — a few members of the group ribbing the ones the Gentleman had scared more.

Within her shadows, she saw them before they saw her.

Once they noticed *something* in the darkness and squinted to see it better, the strobe lights switched on and the spiderweb thrust forward. The spider legs clacked against the walls, her struggling, bound limbs meant to look more arachnid in the shiny black latex.

She tried to tell them, *"Get out! Everything is real! Get out and get help! Call the police!"*

But Bell had taken her words. All she could do was scream with all of her might, her voice among the real and false that permeated the funhouse. The group of young women stumbled back, shouting, clutching their chests. Then they laughed in relief and stared at her, taking in the sight of this banshee-like Arachne. They marveled at every last of Bell's details before moving on. She screamed after them, writhing against the rope binding her to the web, but they paid her no more mind, not when there were other haunts to see.

And so it went, from solo scares to couples clutching each other close to boys who really deserved to be poked by the business end of one of the spider legs when they tried to poke her. She actually had to nod at the Gentleman, unsure whether he could see or acknowledge her, for corralling the boys away. Oh, she'd scared them silly when the screams had ripped from her throat, but once they'd realized she was bound to the web, that had made her easy prey for revenge-bothering by boys posturing for their friends.

Bell was true to his word in all other ways. She never needed to pee. Her stomach never growled. No matter how still the bindings kept her, her muscles never ached or protested. And despite the violence of her screams, they did nothing to damage her throat.

It horrified her that she was part of a torture chamber. But when the lights dimmed further, the sound system turned off and the bindings released her to fall to the floor—somehow easier with more hands and feet to break the fall—what she hadn't expected was how cheap she felt.

She lowered herself into a sitting position, her four legs splayed out and her secondary arms limp at her side. The limitation upon her tongue had loosened along with her ropes, but she still couldn't speak. She just slumped there in the shadows and struggled to breathe as she cried. Muffled sobs from the other released victims in the funhouse rose and fell through the corridors like the moaning of ghosts.

Spider

As soon as there was nothing left to cry, she climbed shakily to her feet and stumbled back out of the entrance instead of going all the way through to the exit. The Gentleman had disappeared or already left, so she didn't have to endure anything or anyone as she escaped the funhouse and ran past the booths, tents and big top to the caravan. Christmas lights hung between posts around the RVs and trailers. It was all so cheery, false, brown, solitary. She slammed her hands against the side of her RV and threw up next to one of the tires.

When she climbed into the RV and turned on the light, there was a bottle of her whiskey on the kitchenette counter. The note beside it read, *No hangover.*

"You bet your ass there won't be a fucking hangover. You owe me that much," she muttered.

She peeled the latex from her body as though shedding skin. Any sliminess she felt came from emotions rather than sweat. Naked and unable to care, she took the bottle with her to bed and didn't bother to count the swallows.

Chapter Six

Bell deigned to use the bench opposite her this time instead of sitting on the table like a barbarian, which was usually his preference.

"It's a weekday. Aren't you supposed to leave me the fuck alone until the haunted funhouse opens again on Friday?" Elizabeth rejected all impulse to be polite to the man keeping her captive. The only drawback was that he seemed to like it.

"I've been thinking of ways to draw more guests to Arcanium, to bring the bizarre into more people's lives in places they don't expect to encounter it."

"Good for you. I'd like to finish my breakfast in peace. That would require my not seeing your face."

Bell clasped his hands as he leaned closer. "I noticed you're asking for bean and potato burritos these days."

"Yes, I'm back to being vegan and drunk, thanks to you. Go away."

"My truly arcane oddities don't have many opportunities to move among the rest of the population."

"Because you trap them here, and if they step outside the circus's borders, they experience a terrible, extremely painful punishment? Might be the reason? Maybe?"

"Precisely," he replied. "Kitty is my best advertisement, since she comes and goes as she pleases and makes no effort to conceal her oddity. Most of my demons don't play well with humans on their own, and they prefer to stay here. I want more of my oddities to reach beyond our borders, even if they are trapped here. You're perfect to show off Arcanium's strange beauty while also functioning within a larger curated display."

"No." She was going to get even thinner if Bell insisted on interrupting her breakfast-slash-lunch with another brilliantly awful idea.

"Come to the red tent between the fortune teller tent and Oddity Row. I want you in one of the leather pieces to show off the work of art you are. If you like, you can even pick from a selection of wigs, as long as you keep your back exposed."

"No."

"Did I give you any indication that these were requests?" He sighed. "If I have to force you to do everything, I will, but I imagine it'll grow tiresome for both of us."

"I'm fine with that."

"If you insist."

He sent her to Kitty's tent, where Kitty displayed a narrow selection of black leatherwear for her to choose from. Elizabeth still had the costume pieces Kitty had brought to her caravan, but Bell apparently lacked the patience to send her all the way back there every time he had to force her to do what he wanted.

When she refused to choose, Bell selected the most revealing bikini set and a long, black wig with electric blue tips that reminded Elizabeth of what she'd looked like before she'd shaved her head for Dez. It only made her hate him more.

He compelled her to do her usual makeup then drew her out into the Row. The way she moved when he forced her really was eerily like a spider, one foot at a time instead of mimicking the two-legged way of walking. If he could have, he probably would have dropped her torso onto an actual giant spider's abdomen and been done with it. But the hook of Arcanium was 'human oddities', and anyone who saw her looking too much like a spider would assume there was mechanical engineering involved. It was more Arcanium for her to appear completely human and completely weird rather than the product of robotic genius.

Walking outside Kitty's tent in a leather string bikini that didn't manage to cover the partial mandala that Dez had inked above her labia like a perverted Renaissance halo, she thought the absolutely worst thing about this would be for someone to recognize her, even one of the cast members. It was only a matter of time if Bell insisted on exposing her.

He led her like an unleashed pet to a red velvet tent, which was quite different from the rough, tan, all-weather canvas used through the rest of Arcanium. The Oddity Row tents all had red velvet curtains for the display, the same used to separate the ring from backstage, but it had never been used to form an entire tent. The red tent was about three times the size of those on Oddity Row. Four stakes around the tent helped provide a canvas canopy to protect it from the elements.

"*A curated display,*" he'd said. It belatedly occurred to her what a themed tent with her as the centerpiece would have to be, but before she could resist harder, Bell pulled her between the closed curtains and turned on the lamps.

When Elizabeth had taken the Bishop children by the creepy-crawly exhibit, she'd stayed outside the tent, but she'd glimpsed about two tables' worth of terrariums. Elizabeth hadn't gone in, and she'd kept her attention firmly upon Todd's back. It was bad enough that there were spiders and other crawly things in the wild.

Bell had collected many more crawlies since then and arranged far more professional displays for them — small terrariums for the creatures that preferred to be solitary, large terrariums for those that didn't mind sharing space, detailed and doubtlessly educational descriptions of each one attached to the corner. Shadowboxes of moths, butterflies and iridescent beetles, including a few that had been altered in Arcanium's steampunk style, lined the curtains behind the displays.

She made every effort to back herself out of the tent, but her strength had nothing on Bell's power. He kept her there with him, although he didn't force her closer to the spiders, scorpions, beetles, roaches and other vermin, some of which she wasn't sure were legally allowed in a small-time circus like Arcanium. Bell probably had his ways around that. He had ways around everything. Despite how ready he was to dispense consequences on everyone else, he didn't seem to know the meaning of the word as it pertained to him.

"I've collected the largest, prettiest, most dangerous of whatever you can think of that gives people gooseflesh," Bell said. "There's just one more piece I need for my collection, something no one else has."

Bell swept his hands in front of her. A Plexiglas box like a coffin appeared on a low platform where there had been nothing before. He slowly stepped around it. The metal latch flipped open, and the lid swung up.

"Be my Snow White, Spider, and climb in."

The glass had little holes in the sides and top, too small for most of the creatures in the tent to crawl through—including her. There was nothing there to hold her down, but she bet making the glass shatterproof had been the first thing he'd thought of when he'd created the coffin.

"Why do you even need people when you can just wave your hand and make whatever you want? You wouldn't have to hurt anyone. The whole thing could be a flea circus. No one would ever have to know."

"I'd know." He clicked his blunt nails against the edge of the open coffin. "You're a beautiful woman, as much a work of art as any of the wings on the walls. You're meant to be protected while shown off."

"I've had enough of being shown off. If I wanted to be shown off, do you think I would have covered myself from head to toe with clothes rather than reveal to everyone I'm covered head to toe in tattoos? You're just as bad as him. And don't you dare pretend you don't know who I'm talking about."

"Your artist made it clear what he wanted of you. You may think I want the same things, but I don't." He crooked his finger. She staggered another few steps closer to him and the coffin. "Don't compare me to that exploitative garden parasite. I'm my own despicable self, Lizzie."

"Aw, did I hurt the poor jinni's feelings?"

He stared into her eyes without blinking, tempering the intensity with a soft smile at whatever he found there. "You're going to think I'm punishing you for that, but I'm not. I'd already planned this. Into the box, Elizabeth. Eventually, the entire multi-legged empire will be yours, but for now, I'm still the director of this little exhibit."

"You can take every single one of these multi-legged monstrosities and shove them right up your —"

"Into the box."

She climbed in. Its dimensions weren't perfect for a coffin. He'd made sure to give her enough room for her extra limbs and for her to prop herself up on her many elbows without her head reaching where the lid would be.

"I realize you're mildly claustrophobic, which was why I provided such big windows on such a small RV and why I need you to see all the holes provided. You won't suffocate, and I would never bury you alive."

"Small consolations, Bell."

"Yes, quite small, considering what I'm about to do."

He subtly arranged her with his mind rather than his hands, posing her legs to add dimension, resting her prime arms over her belly while the secondary set helped cushion her head, her secondary fingers tangled through the hair that made up the wig.

There was a small black pillow built into the design of the coffin to keep her neck level, not for comfort. Nothing about the coffin was comfortable, but neither was it particularly uncomfortable—for which she wouldn't thank Bell, considering he was the one putting her in this thing.

He disappeared from her line of sight, and she couldn't move her head to follow where he went. "I want you to know I do this with the best of intentions to pave my way. You won't be able to scream, move without my permission or brush them off. You don't need to. They can't hurt you, Lizzie. You are completely safe from even the slightest danger, down to the most minor skin irritation."

"Whatever the fuck you're planning to do, don't you fucking dare…"

She knew what was coming before he came back into her line of sight with a large plastic tub in his hands. The plastic tub also had small holes in it, so that whatever lived on the inside could breathe much better than she could right now.

He brought the tub to her feet rather than her face, which was the only reason she didn't die on the spot, but once again, she couldn't show gratitude for that little mercy when he was about to *pour spiders on her*— definitely more than one, and large enough to make a dull thump when their abdomens hit the side of the tub as he tipped it over.

Sharona had liked to scare her with spider memes she'd picked up around social media. The part of Elizabeth's mind that was calmly in shock flipped through those images until she determined these particular spiders were probably of the Australian huntsman variety, scurrying up the sides of the coffin and along her legs with unnatural speed. No effort to flick them off or flail succeeded in making her move— not even a twitch.

The open lid above her eased down, and the latch flipped closed. Bell slid a fancy brass padlock through the latch, ensuring that she couldn't escape and that nothing from the outside could get in.

Then he knelt before the coffin, allowing her to turn her head as one of the spiders crawled up her stomach. Each prick of its feet was like the beeping of a bomb, because they told her how much closer to her face it was.

"Spiders usually have no allegiance, less inclined to bond than the snakes Lady Sasha keeps with her. But there isn't a spider in the world now who would betray itself to bite you. Calm your breathing. You're perfectly safe."

He kept using that word as though he had any earthly idea what it meant.

"You are the queen of everything in this tent—barring your humble regent, of course." He saluted her, then stood.

Two spider legs tapped her chin.

She couldn't understand why she hadn't gone insane yet. Bell had slowed her breathing, paralyzed her, but her mind still raced with every single alarm she had. Yet the tent was quiet, almost serene, with only the sound of little legs on glass, dirt and skin, unbearably loud to her hypersensitive ears.

"The sooner you realize your fear does you no favors, Lizzie, the sooner you can accept your place in Arcanium with the dignity everyone sees but you refuse to believe is there. You can hardly be blamed for not realizing what you are. Holding yourself back has always protected you in the past. But that was your artist's world. That was your father's world. This is mine, and it'll do so much more for you than theirs, if you'll let it."

He backed away from the coffin. "You'll be released at seven o'clock. Until then, my dear."

The bastard passed through the curtains just as the spider crawled onto her face. Her head hurt from the deafening screams she couldn't make.

No matter how their long legs made her want to twitch, wrench away, squish every single last one of their furry, alien bodies, she couldn't move. She remained an artfully arranged statue whose chest and stomach rose and fell like clockwork. She could close her eyes, but not knowing what was coming seemed worse.

Then the spider on her face moved over her eyes, and knowing what was coming seemed worse than not knowing, because now she could see the spider's ungodly long legs and its hairy body and patterned abdomen. Its leg span had to be at least eight inches. Bell wouldn't have put in anything but the biggest he could find. If he'd literally put in the biggest huntsman ever, there would be one with over a foot leg span in the coffin with her right now.

Without Bell, she would have lost complete control over her bodily functions and not even been ashamed at this point. But she stayed outwardly calm as the spider moved into her hair. Whenever her skin started to itch—whether from the spider legs moving over her or the spiders' hair or simply an anxiety response—it dissipated without a trace, not the slightest tickle.

Now that the chaos had settled, some huntsmen settled next to her while others explored their new home, probably looking for things to eat that weren't the size of an eight-limbed woman or for places to hide on said eight-limbed woman. Spiders usually wanted one or the other, like most animals walking on God's green earth.

Her rational mind sided with peaceful shock, an oasis in the chaotic whirlwind that was her shut-in panic attack.

The spiders weren't going to hurt her while she was so still, even if Bell hadn't made the spiders placid. Spiders in general were solitary creatures rarely dangerous to humans. Even the more venomous spiders sometimes had trouble breaking through the thick skin of human beings, and blisters and inflammation attributed to spider bites were often staph infections instead. Ecologically, they were one of the many predators of troublesome insects, and they themselves were prey to other creatures up the food chain. They were useful and necessary.

Elizabeth knew this.

None of her knowledge mattered.

Her vision blurred, narrowed, grayed as though clouded with cobwebs, but Bell wouldn't grant her unconsciousness.

The curtains opened. To her ever-increasing terror, she wasn't in Arcanium anymore. And all these people in the middle of a motherfucking shopping mall were looking right at her.

Little kids she would never have wanted to look at her body, although they saw women like her all the time on billboards and in television commercials and magazine advertisements.

Grown men whom she'd tirelessly concealed her body from all this time, by choice, for her own tenuous protection.

Women who looked down on her for selling herself out to the gazes of others, for allowing these tiny monsters to roam her body in the name of the almighty dollar. Whatever she was getting paid, it should never have been enough.

But despite any disgust, disregard or judgment, curiosity drove them all forward.

She couldn't cover herself. Couldn't hide. Couldn't escape.

Elizabeth closed her eyes. It didn't go away when she opened them. People peered into the coffin, spoke about her as though she couldn't hear them through the holes in the glass, stared right into her eyes. Yet they couldn't see the fear. They couldn't see her begging them to free her. All they could see were the spiders, the bikini, the tattoos—these terrible, amazing things meant to distract them.

"Do you see that honeycomb under the bees? Reminds me of those memes about holes in people's skin where bugs peek out. Gross."

"How long do you think it took her to get all those tattoos?"

"Are those arms and legs real? I can't tell. They look so real."

"I can't see where they've been attached. Shouldn't there be, like, a lump where the harness is? Holy Christ, they're moving! Is this real life?"

"So, do you think she was raised around spiders, or do you think she just gets a shit-ton of money to do this?"

"It's like *Fear Factor* or something. Would you do it?"

"No way. You couldn't pay me a million dollars to shut myself into a locked box with that many giant spiders crawling all over me. How many are there, anyway?"

"I think there's twelve. Even dozen. Yeesh. It feels like they're crawling on *me*."

"What kind are they? They don't look like tarantulas."

"No, those over there are tarantulas. Holy shit, that's one big-ass tarantula. There are babies smaller than this thing."

"These are those crazy big spiders they have in Australia or Iraq or something, right?"

"She looks so serene. Think she's drugged?"

"She's looking at us. Don't look drugged to me."

"But crazy."

"She's definitely that. But look at how tattooed she is. She was already crazy before she got in the box."

"You know what would be really weird? If she were drugged up with some kind of paralytic and locked in that box with a fuck-ton of spiders, and she's trying to tell us to help her right now, but it's not working. And we're talking about it and shit."

"A little too meta for right after lunch, Daniel."

"Come see the butterflies."

Bell had put his red tent right in the middle of people who were the ruler by which normal was measured, enticing them with the gross and arcane in one iridescent, freak-out gesture. They gazed upon her body, marveled at her uncommon courage and uncommon anatomy, speculated about her sexual experience, questioned her parentage, shuddered not in commiseration but disgust — the woman that she was secondary to the spectacle.

Bell was right. It was nothing like what Dez had done to her. It was worse, *more* dehumanizing and objectifying. Even the rational side of her brain was fading now, the cacophony of her panic shrinking it to Lilliputian proportions. She collapsed deeper and deeper into herself like a dying star, sweat trapped in her pores and tears trapped in their ducts. Eventually, her eyelids stopped wanting to blink—they moved by necessity only without the remotest consciousness or emotional state to move them. Her lungs were under Bell's control, but her heart thudded against her ribs as though to protest the speed of her breathing.

Just give out. She didn't need her lungs anymore. She didn't need her heart. She could die here and no one would know. Bell would keep her blinking until he brought her back to Arcanium. Then he could make her a permanent addition to the haunted funhouse, his lifelike puppet—not much different from what he was already doing, this mad taxidermist creating fantastic creations from the limbs of living. But living was a relative term. She'd be fine in a coma—or as an unthinking zombie. As long as her consciousness, her soul, no longer needed to be here. As long as the spiders couldn't creep over it and take a juicy bite every time she moved. As long as Bell didn't have to stick his tongue in and wriggle.

At one point, one of the spiders hid itself under her hair while two others settled on her face. The rest crawled around the playground of her arms and legs, preferring the shelter they created but stimulated enough to keep moving while being gawked at by all these people.

Maybe the spiders didn't have a choice in the matter either.

That little nugget of empathy did nothing to make up for their proximity. Nothing would be enough for that.

This was her punishment for everything—for being born, disrespecting her mother and fathers, running away from home, yielding herself to the control of an evil man, running back home under false pretenses, wearing the guise of piety to cover up her shame, lying by omission so often her soul was like Swiss cheese, bringing the kids to Arcanium, wishing for more in her life when she should have been content enough with its blessings, not stabbing Bell in the eye every time she got the chance, not fighting back now.

You're pathetic, Lizzie. Not pitiful. Pathetic.

Not until the mall's skylights had gone dark, when the employees in shops around her covered their carts or pulled down cage doors to lock up for the night, did the curtains close—no one looking at her, no one milling among the insect and arachnid collection Bell had set up, no one there to save her.

He was going to leave her in there. He was going to leave her in there until Friday, just to imprison her in her spiderweb once again. Bell had no intention of allowing her respite or relief. He'd wielded the worst of his weapons by telling her he would free her, by asking her to trust him. She should have known none of that was true, that he would pull it all out from under her when she was just starting to believe him—not believing that he had the best intentions, but that her phobias were entirely irrational, that she *was* safe, that she would be able to breathe on her own again without fearing a spider would crawl into her mouth and lay eggs in some ungodly place.

The padlock remained locked. The latch remained in place. And in the quiet darkness, the huntsmen were scurrying about again, their large bodies surprisingly agile.

But she could move. Slowly. As though Bell knew that if he let her have her full faculties, she would crush the spiders.

Her scream was nothing but a whimper as she struck at the glass lid. His Snow White indeed, choking on her own apple. Every time she hit the lid, it sent the spiders scurrying away from the lid — onto her.

Just like she wasn't sure whether eyes opened or closed was worse, she wasn't sure whether being paralyzed or able to move was worse. Because she still couldn't get out, but now the spiders responded to her movement.

The lights and the spiders' heat lamps dimmed by more than half. She shivered. The spiders scuttled along with the shivers as though riding a wave.

A shadow entered. He undid the lock to the latch, then lifted the lid.

"Slowly," he said. "You need to move slowly."

It didn't matter what he said. She wanted *out*, and if *out* meant stepping into a puddle of hot lava, she still would have done it as quickly as possible. But it also didn't matter what he said because Bell's magic on her kept her from exiting the coffin in any way that would hurt the spiders in her haste. She moved as though through molasses.

She clutched at his dark, furry forearms when he offered himself to help her from the coffin. He drew her out one leg at a time. The huntsmen scurried down her legs as though the coffin lid were still there, blocking them from leaving the coffin until they were alone along the sides of the glass, poking their little legs through the holes like prisoners begging her for their freedom as well. Then they faded away, appearing in an empty terrarium at the back of the tent where there'd been nothing before.

"You're all right. You're perfectly safe. No more spiders."

"Shut up. Just shut up!" She hit his chest without any strength. All the freaking out that had built up over the course of the afternoon and evening let out all at once, but each one of her eight limbs had been sapped of strength to fuel the fireworks erupting in her brain. She punched him in the chest, stomach, arms, the lift of his wings behind his shoulders, his face when she could stand to look up at it – his soft gargoyle's face.

"Why you? Why does it have to be you when he finishes with me?" Elizabeth shoved him back against one of the poles holding the tent up. "Why are you always here? Goddammit, why, you creepy fucker?"

The Creature grabbed her primary wrists like lined leather shackles – firm but without pain, despite her fighting against his hold. She could still hit him, but with her primary arms in the way, his face was safer, and she could look up into his red eyes, which seemed to reflect the velvet that surrounded her in this lush mausoleum.

"I volunteered."

"Why couldn't Bell come himself so I could claw his eyes out?" She leaned back onto her secondary legs the way Bell had shown her, hoping she could kick at the Creature like a kangaroo standing on its tail, but she didn't have the strength or the balance. The Creature crowded her back against the coffin, now free of spiders but still open and still dangerous in its own right.

"I imagine that is an excellent reason not to come himself." He closed his eyes to inhale, released her to touch her wig, heedless of the added fist for battering his ribs. Despite being a creature of flesh and blood, nothing fazed him as he brought his slightly flared nostrils to her neck, where he had smelled her before in the rain.

"Get off me. Get the hell off me!" Punching wasn't working. She tried scratching next, but his skin was tough, hide masquerading as human skin.

"I'm not going to hurt you. This will help." He slid his fingers under the edge of her wig to slide it along her bare scalp then discard it in the coffin. At her uncovering, he breathed in more deeply, pleased by the scent released. "Let me take it. Give me your fear, and I will take it from you."

"It doesn't go away. God, everyone's *so fucking helpful*. Everyone thinks it's simply hilarious when a grown woman becomes a little girl in front of everybody just because something scares her almost to death. They think the more they expose her, the fear will go away. Well, that's *not* how this *fucking works*! It *never* goes away. If it went away, I wouldn't keep coming right back to this hell, God punishing me over and over. I wouldn't be here."

Quality product or not, she was pretty sure her makeup was a mess, but the Creature didn't appear concerned about the ink her tears ferried down her cheeks and onto his fur.

His arms were immovable around her. Fur soft, muscles hard, skin yielding but tough, he was a beast rather than a man. He burned against her bare skin.

"*I* can take it away. Let me feed, Elizabeth. I'll feast upon your fear and leave the plate clean behind. I've done it before." He dragged his mouth over her neck, up the side of her head. "This is why I follow you. You have all this fear. To have you so close ... It's intoxicating. Let me taste it again."

She wailed into his shoulder, the curl of her fingers to scratch him seeking instead to dig into something, to find something to hold — his hips, his ribs, his back.

As she melted into his embrace, no strength to fight anymore, he parted his lips to inhale, his breath hot and the edges of his teeth sharp. But as before when he'd stopped her from escaping through the Arcanium gates, he didn't bite down, didn't even use those sharp teeth to threaten. All he did was move over her — like an open-mouthed kiss, but something more primal, something as simple as consumption.

His warmth seeped into her, heat against the winter that barely bit at her skin anymore. He smoothed his hands down her back, then up her neck to cradle her skull, breathing her in like a dying man gasping for breath. Fiber by fiber, her muscles relaxed.

"Do you even know?" he whispered against her neck. "Do you know how you call to me? You practically beg."

Elizabeth didn't know how a Creature fed just by breathing, or why a Creature like him needed teeth like that if he didn't use them. But the more he drank her in, the calmer she became. Her thoughts slowed, no longer racing in never-ending circles. She clung to them, because her thoughts were hers and he shouldn't be able to steal them, but they slipped through her fingers, losing their power without her death grip upon them.

Every time some other creature in the tent moved enough to make a sound, panic rushed back into the empty spaces, but not as violently as before. Her rational mind could take up more of the space that fear vacated.

The spiders were locked away, as were the centipedes, scorpions and hissing cockroaches. If Bell hadn't been done with her, he would have come to free her himself to get a front-row seat for her expression when he forced her to do something else for his entertainment.

Fear and recriminations had made her excruciatingly present in the coffin, second by second. With the Creature siphoning from her, she became present in another way, able to experience reality without her senses devolving into cacophony. Instead, they became oddly focused. The bugs in the tent distracted her, but not enough to detract from the much softer brush of his fur against her bare skin, the places where their legs interlocked and she could feel his skin and firm press of muscle. Despite extra limbs, she was still half his size. And he had his own extra limbs, didn't he? Those furled leathery wings draped down his back and legs to the ground, where the tips were flexible enough to bend — the train to his anatomical cloak.

His hands on her.

She'd had hands on her before. Bell was a handsy man. She wondered whether he even realized he did it, since he kept claiming he wouldn't touch her then followed it up with proprietary contact. Perhaps he meant he wouldn't touch her sexually, but his possessiveness carried an intimacy just as disquieting.

Before Bell, her congregation had laid hands on her to pray over the state of her soul when she'd returned and whenever someone in the community had wanted to pray for her during the Call to Prayer. Physical contact was common but controlled among Petrosian saints. They didn't touch anywhere that could be construed as sexual, which meant they pressed the tips of their fingers to arms, shoulders, upper back, hands, nothing more.

Her clothing discouraged contact. Lately, the only hands she'd had to contend with had been from the Bishop children. Tiny, grabby hands from the baby and toddler, pokes and pulling from Todd, withdrawal from Sharona.

It had been so long. So long since she had been seen, and being seen reminded her why she'd chosen to never be seen again. But it had also been so long since she'd really been touched. She'd thought Dez had poisoned that, too, that to have the Creature's hands on her would trigger memories of tenderness so twisted with manipulation that she still had trouble untangling them.

But the Creature's hands on her weren't like Dez's at all. They were larger, broader, hotter, somehow rested on her art differently. She drew her nails along his back, but not to tear. He was so close to her, almost kissing, almost embracing, his legs against hers but his hips away. He was doing everything he was supposed to, giving her what he promised but not taking anything he hadn't asked for.

As he breathed in whatever scent of fear fed him, the scent from his skin was that of smoke — not cigarette smoke or hickory smoke, but lightning smoke on the bark of scorched trees. Musk, the combination of fur over skin. And the scent of flesh that she'd forgotten. Not just skin, meat, but the scent of a man in the places where it was strongest, most undiluted and distinguishable — where sweat and dirt hadn't reached him, where he was clean and aroused. The scent not just of flesh, but of *the* flesh, the fruit that had been forbidden because it was exactly this tempting.

She didn't know why she did it. She couldn't use the Creature's excuse and claim that his scent drew her to him. It wasn't as simple as that. She was a woman accustomed to resisting temptation, to resisting almost everything. And for God's sake, she had just emerged from a day's worth of humiliation and panic attacks. She was still surrounded with the source of her deepest, most irrational fears, mere plates of glass and Bell's whim between her and them. It should have been the last thing on her mind.

Yet it buzzed under her skin, strongest where he touched her, where he moved those hands over her, and she brought her mouth to his neck where his scent burned strongest.

At the first touch of her tongue along the line of his throat, he stilled, his breathing gone silent, until all she could hear was the scraping and scurrying of insects and arachnids and the hiss of the Madagascar cockroaches in response to some unknown stimulus.

That cooled what madness had fallen upon her, or at least she thought it did. But the moment her hair stood on end in response to the images that the sounds conjured in her mind, he curled his fingers into muscle, releasing a breath only to drink it back in again with the resurrected fear, nuzzling closer once more.

"That... That isn't just fear I taste anymore, little Spider."

She wrenched her mouth away from his neck, turning her head away, but to one direction was the red curtain and to the other direction were the spiders, and his body stayed strong against her, moving with her when she shuffled around the coffin. However, he pulled away in apparent concern at her withdrawal.

"No." Elizabeth shook her head, braced herself on the edge of a table until the movement of the hissing cockroaches within caught her eye. She jerked her hand away as though they'd been crawling on her instead of their mossy terrain.

"Your fear rises again. What is it you fear from me? Even if I wanted to, I couldn't hurt you. And I don't want to hurt anyone."

"I don't believe you. I don't believe *any* of you."

When she tried to turn away from him, she got a face-full of pins through the bodies of butterflies in one of the shadowboxes. Her own reflection spooked her. For God's sake, where were the edges of the curtains? The whole tent seemed to be curtains with no end. The Creature had entered through them, but no matter how she pawed at the velvet, it wouldn't open for her. Maybe it wasn't meant to open for her. Maybe she *was* going to be trapped in here forever.

"You wouldn't look like that if you weren't made to hurt," she said as she searched. "You're a predator. You have the claws and teeth of a predator. You have the muscle mass of a predator. Even if you aren't a demon, what use are a predator's tools without predatory behavior? You're still a monster."

"I feed on fear, not on flesh or blood or bone. I don't know what I am or where I come from, but although I can eat if it appeals to me, my only nourishment is fear. The way I look inspires that which I consume. When people see me, they react out of instinct. They become prey. But that's for people who do not know I'm harmless. Why run from me when it is you who invited me, who invites me even now?"

"I'm not inviting you with my fear. The stench of fear should be telling you to stay the fuck away." After the cockroaches came the giant millipedes. The redheaded centipedes. A giant Goliath birdeater with a godforsaken leg span of a frying pan. A camel spider. A wolf spider carrying tiny nightmare babies on its back. A banana spider. The brown recluse. The black widow. She stubbed her toe on the platform that held the huntsman spiders she'd just escaped.

He slid his hand over her shoulder. He didn't grab her, but his touch electrified her skin into gooseflesh. "What did I do? What did I do that made what wasn't fear become fear once more?"

When she didn't pull away from him again, he slid his other hand over her other shoulder. Perhaps he believed that her shudder still came from fear. Her secondary arms flailed as both sets struggled to find an anchor in the platforms and tables around her without touching anything close to creepy. There was nothing that matched that criteria, and her handle on her secondary limbs still wasn't iron. Her secondary knuckles hit terrariums on either side of her, almost knocking the black widow's container off.

"If you let me calm you again, you won't terrify yourself so."

"I just want out. Please let me out."

"I am not holding you prisoner."

The Creature ran his thumbs up each side of her spine in a deep massage that had her raising her shoulders. Her sister Ruth had always said Elizabeth was one big knot no one could ever hope to untangle. Dez had said the same thing whenever he'd tried to work the kinks out of her back and shoulders.

"You're too afraid to see the way out. Please, Elizabeth, allow me to help you. I was helping before I scared you. What did I do?"

Elizabeth forced herself to stop moving, because if she flailed again, she might not be so lucky with the smaller recluse and widow containers, not to mention the harmless but revolting glass farm that contained nothing less than plain, old American cockroaches. She'd hate to knock that one over. Worse to her than the ant farm.

"Your hands," she said.

He removed his hands from her shoulders, holding them up as though to prove he no longer touched her in case she didn't realize it for herself.

She carefully turned around so that her secondary knees wouldn't knock the platform or table. "That's not what I meant. I…"

She felt like fear held every last one of her reins. But fear wouldn't draw her to the Creature, wouldn't slide her palms up his chest, his neck, to take his face between them.

"Don't," she whispered. Her fingers trembled against his cheeks even as she guided him down to bring his mouth near hers, as though inviting him to taste her fear elsewhere. "Don't," she said again, then kissed him.

It was as though someone else was in control of her body, in control of her body's reaction, although this was nothing like how she felt when Bell took over her will. A perfect stranger brought her body flush against his. A perfect stranger gasped from the flood of feelings she'd dammed up so many years ago, feelings she'd intended to relinquish for the rest of her life, that she'd thought were relegated only to the moments before she woke from dreams and couldn't be held accountable.

She didn't know whether this was even something that the Creature did — at least until he wrapped an arm around her waist and parted his lips to taste her in a far more substantial way.

He manipulated them around to grasp the edge of one of the tables, and he shoved her back against it as he urged her own lips to part.

Had she thought him more like a beast than a man, a mere imitation or sexless hybrid? All at once, he became a man against her hips, his erection lifting under the loincloth with unnatural swiftness in response to her tongue meeting his. He was no carving, no facsimile. He was more man than she'd had in a very long time—his cock against her hip, his mouth against hers to drink in her kiss, his hand branding a path up the length of her spine.

Her head fell back as he rolled his hips against hers, rubbing his erection along her skin with nothing but the loincloth in his way. He kissed down her neck, taking time to taste more than her fear all the way down to the hollow of her throat.

She brought her hands behind his head to guide him lower, but she shook her head. "Don't. God, don't."

The Creature raised himself up again, perplexed.

Elizabeth spun out of his arms, slamming her hands onto the table when she inevitably tangled her legs. She got an eyeful of the giant tarantula, the Goliath birdeater. Odds were, it was just bewildered by the giants rocking its world, but she couldn't shake the notion it watched them. It stared with oddly guileless eyes, showed no sign of aggression. Even so, she felt captivated by them, ice chasing the heat until she didn't know what she was feeling.

Only that her secondary arms reached for the Creature and pulled him close against her from behind. He hesitated, but encouraged by the insistence of her fingers digging under his ribs and the spreading of her secondary legs to accommodate him, he drank fear from her neck before taking the flesh between his teeth. With his hot tongue, he soothed the dents that the sharp tips had created. An undignified moan escaped her and she struck the table with a fist, but she moved back against him where his cock was trapped against her ass.

She brought one of those huge, hot hands to her breast, over the leather, then pushed it underneath.

Skin on skin on skin on skin… It was all too much after so long of nothing at all. She wanted him to touch her everywhere she'd covered, everywhere she'd protected herself, everywhere all those prickly spider legs had crawled over her. Elizabeth was neither innocent nor ignorant, yet the way the Creature touched her, it was as though she was experiencing it for the first time all over again – and her first times had been wonderful and frightening enough on their own.

They rocked against each other as though there was nothing between their hips. Elizabeth could practically feel his cock inside her. The memory of Dez taking her and her present, achingly intense desire to be taken combined in a volatile mixture that alone nearly made her come.

The redheaded centipede reared up, wriggling its little legs. Elizabeth nearly slipped off the table face-first into the Goliath birdeater's terrarium.

"No." It was little more than a murmur, but Elizabeth brought her primary hands to the sides of her head, shaking. One of her secondary legs curled around the Creature's, and her secondary hands kept hold of his waist at the same time Elizabeth tried to stumble back to the front of the red tent. The hissing of the

Madagascar cockroaches intensified the closer she came.

"Elizabeth!" This time the Creature wasn't tender. He grabbed her by the back of the neck then pushed her against the end of the table, irritating the cockroaches even more. He maneuvered out of the way of her secondary limbs, which had obviously mutinied from the rest of her — or else their priorities were clearer.

"Let me go," she whispered. Her bikini top was now askew, her right nipple exposed, flushed, tight. She couldn't stop looking beyond the monstrosity of his initial appearance — the breadth of his shoulders and chest, the demigod-like arms, the prominent tent under his loincloth. She didn't have to see his cock to discern what it would look like, so thin was the material of his covering and so intimidating his erection.

"I've tried to let you go when you tell me to, but you keep denying me." His frustration was plain, though his claws were gentle over her cheek. "I am not like the jinni. I don't keep prisoners. I am not human, but I am close enough that I believe I'm right in being confused. Your scent… You taste aroused…and afraid. Arousal almost tastes like fear, but I can tell the difference. Arousal and fear come off you in waves, one following the other. You won't let me take all the fear because you become aroused, but when you submit to arousal, the fear rises once more. I don't understand what you need from me. I don't understand what you *want*."

Elizabeth shook her head, leaning into his touch. "Don't. Please, don't touch me." Tears followed the previous paths carved down her face.

But when he stepped back — a perfect respect of her wishes, something utterly foreign to her — she snagged his loincloth to yank him back in.

Scratches and whispers and hisses filled the dim red tent.

In another life, her nightmares had also been filled with the click of a camera and the light of a video camera. He had turned what she'd thought was love into something artificial, commodified, something that could be bought and sold and that she could never escape without completely hiding herself.

Still he had called it love. Still her body had responded to him with the lust he had cultivated. She could have left at any time, bruises be damned, and eventually she had. Dez hadn't followed her. He'd pierced in his poison, woven the thread of himself into her until she could never truly leave, never forget how he had nurtured her fear and lust into the choking vines that the Creature tasted in her.

"Spider." His name for her was a groan, because she shifted her grip on his loincloth to take his erection in hand through the fabric. He was big, bigger than the ones Dez had convinced her to take, and the very idea of it inside her was terrifying. Yet she brought him to her thigh.

"Don't." She brought his hand back to her uncovered breast. She closed her eyes and forced herself to say what tasted so bitter to her tongue, tasted of submission – and with submission, humiliation that compounded upon all the humiliations that had come before. "Don't stop. Don't stop touching me. No matter what I do. Put your hands on me, all over me. Please."

Her plea devolved into a moan, because he made short work of the ties to the leather top. He dipped down to kiss the top of her breast where she'd been leading him, her nipple hard from proximity rather than ministration, but the Creature didn't leave her abandoned for long. His sharp teeth caught it, tortured it until she struggled just to breathe, her breast quivering from her gasps. Then he crowded her against the table again and surrounded her nipple with his excruciatingly hot mouth.

It had never been like this, not during the most adventurous and fearless of her experimentation with Dez in the early years, when she'd put his bed through the paces and could never seem to get enough. Her body had sung for him, but in Arcanium, it screamed.

He lifted his head, refusing to relinquish her nipple, but as soon as he had to, he yielded it in favor of her mouth, which he caught with the same voracious appetite he'd shown for her fear. For a creature who claimed to be unsure of what he was in relation to the world, he certainly seemed to know what he wanted from her. Then again, she'd been out of the game for over ten years, and here she was, lifting his loincloth and taking his cock in hand as though she was still the newly adult, sexually frustrated girl she'd been when Dez had found her.

She cried out when his teeth caught her lips. She could hardly throw stones when she met his tongue with her own sharp teeth — though he responded with a groan and a strong thrust into her hand.

Every time they rocked against the table, the metal joints squeaked, the terrariums thunked together and the cockroaches hissed. She spread her secondary legs to straddle the table. It didn't give her much leverage, but it anchored them a little. She wouldn't yield a single one of her hands from touching him with the same frantic need with which he touched her. Any time the sound of the crawlies in the room penetrated the lust haze in her brain, he drank it away with his kiss, somehow becoming hotter the more he took.

Surrounded by all the things that terrified her, fear etched into her skin, everything she was doing right now the result of still-undefined fear, she was a bottomless resource, a gourmand's dream.

"I will not stop," the Creature swore into her mouth.

He pushed her bikini bottoms down. She'd never had much in the way of hips, and once the leather passed the top part of her thighs, it slid down on their own. Then he twisted something at his own hip that left him without his loincloth.

He drank her, tasted her, kissed her, dragged his lips and teeth over her skin in a combination of fear-feeding and affection until it was indistinguishable. He moved down over the exposed heart, over the skeleton cameo on the mourning corset, over the mandala. He forced her thighs apart, nuzzling the spider and the teeth scars in turn before running his tongue from her slit up to her clit. Elizabeth shook her head, but she pushed down on his to keep him there, and she grasped at the arch of his opened wings with her secondary hands.

"I don't know what you're still afraid of, but keep giving it to me if you're willing, Spider." His mouth — pulling, sucking, licking, circling, teasing, torturing — became relentless. He caressed her thighs, mapped her musculature with his palms, then moved up to the secondary legs, where she discovered the inner thighs there were as sensitive as the prime set, despite the fact they led nowhere as interesting as where his mouth had her nearly melting down the side of the table.

Then he stopped. He'd promised not to stop. When he stopped, she stopped feeling and started thinking, and that was when the whole mess of her head returned, stronger than ever.

He raised his red eyes to hers. They were as inscrutable as they were opaque, which was perhaps why he exaggerated his expressions like the gargoyle he often seemed to be. But his expression now gave her nothing. For a moment, she was afraid he would stay that way, that he would stand and leave, or stand and simply fuck her before leaving, and she still wouldn't find a way out of this tent.

Then he slithered his tongue between her folds to dip into her cunt. He hummed in appreciation at what he sampled, which couldn't have been insignificant. As he stood, he unsettled her grip. Somehow, he seemed even taller after kneeling, and she felt even more vulnerable, especially with his cock thick and hard against her belly. She was almost positive it had grown since she'd stroked him.

"If you need further preparation, Spider, you'll have to stretch yourself. I can spare you most of the effects of size, but not like the demons, and I cannot prevent these from doing their damage." He raised his fingers, splaying them to display the claws—thick, sharp, unretractable and not something a woman wanted inside her.

"You mean...like this?" Elizabeth brought her prime hands between her legs. She caught her clit hard between the knuckles of her fingers, making herself whine. Then she slid her left hand back to sink two fingers into her cunt.

She didn't like him watching her rather than just doing it himself. Watching rubbed her all the wrong ways, like Bell displaying her in the coffin, like him having her strip in the ring. She'd been forced into mass exhibitionism under false pretenses before, poisoning what had been a pleasurable pastime until then. The old feelings hadn't gone away, despite years of protecting herself from the gaze of others.

The Creature's gaze was just as lascivious, just as intense and just as invasive, though she knew she shouldn't compare his intentions. Yet, as deeply as she despised a voyeur, his blood-red eyes upon her roused all the shivers of his touch, and as she tested the places inside her that hadn't been stretched by so much as a doctor all this time, she couldn't help but imagine that her fingers were his instead, and she added a third to approximate two of his. Lubrication wasn't a problem. She'd thought her long, self-imposed dry spell would have been more of an issue. Instead, her cunt seemed to clutch at her fingers, and the more intently the Creature watched her fuck herself, the more aroused she became and the more she wanted him inside her.

"I don't need this." Elizabeth withdrew from her cunt, though she continued to squeeze her clit and its hood, keeping the arousal there throbbing and keen.

The Creature took her shiny fingers between his teeth, sucked his way down to take what he hadn't been able to gather for himself. "No. From the way you taste, I don't think you need that at all."

He took both prime wrists and forced her hands onto the table. Once released, her clit pulsed with her racing heartbeat, and the change in angle made her hips snap forward on their new hinge. Elizabeth's secondary elbows struck the hissing cockroach terrarium. She reacted automatically with a sinking rush of fear that she'd toppled it over.

The Creature desperately grabbed her by the back of the neck and held the base of his cock to position himself. Once the head pressed against her cunt, he let himself go and grasped her thigh instead, keeping her steady as he entered her, hard and deep.

God, it should have hurt. She would have welcomed pain, because maybe it would have made her think clearly for once in this whole mixed-up encounter. But in the name of all that was unholy, it didn't. He filled her in ways she didn't know it was possible to be filled, stretched her beyond the limits of what she'd ever thought could be pleasurable, yet she hooked her legs around him, yielding him the last of her control and urging him for more.

She'd never been fond of the noises she made during sex, although everyone else had seemed to like them. But pleasure pummeled her from every side, a global series of sensations, battle upon battle that she'd never won once they'd started. Her cries and moans could have been ones of pleasure, but also of pain. She could no more stop them than she could prevent herself from reacting to intimate contact.

Those noises rather than the insectile now filled the small tent. But the Creature didn't let them dominate the room for long. He continued to make the table creak, to the point Elizabeth almost feared it would break. And he breathed in her cries with the urgent gasps of his feeding before smothering them with a kiss, combining his moans with hers so she wouldn't be undignified alone.

He fed like a beast and fucked like one, too. She'd had men lose control with her before, although Dez had never been one of them. But the Creature didn't lose control. He yielded to instinct, feasting on her and kissing her with a growl on the edge of his groans. His cock entered her with tireless rhythm. It could have been impersonal, cold. But with his body under the influence of instinct, he devoted every last bit of attention upon her. His kiss was terrible in its intention, as much a possession and invasion as his cock.

Elizabeth lost her breath again, but this time not from panic. The tent spun as though it was the carousel, and she was riding the gargoyle — or perhaps he was riding her. At this point, she wasn't sure who was taking whom.

She couldn't keep herself from touching him anymore — the monster of him, the man of him, in every inch. The thick muscles of his thighs and ass were powerful like the rest of him. She clutched at them, digging her fingers and fingernails in with the knowledge it couldn't hurt him, but that didn't stop her from trying, urging him faster, harder. Her prime thighs would bruise under the ink from the jut of his hipbones striking them, and her secondary thighs trembled trying to keep herself steady on the table. But God, she wished he'd never stop, that the pleasure could keep climbing like this, tightening in her abdomen, her cunt, in a spiral up her spine, and even into her mind, all her lusts conspiring together at the Creature's physical command.

The orgasm took what little breath she had left. An orgasm that hit this hard usually fell off quickly, but whatever allowed him to take her without pain also seemed to keep him rubbing the ridge of the head over her spot again and again, jolting pleasure through her until her moans grated with animalistic growls of her own. She jerked her hips to meet him, pushing herself with her secondary arms and pulling with the primes.

The Creature clutched the back of her neck as though she were a kitten, sheathed himself within her as deep as he could go. All of him stilled, except for his cock, which heated like iron and jerked with his own climax. Her cunt fluttered, clenched around him as her orgasm finally crested then calmed into aftershocks.

Their stillness more than him fucking her made her aware of just how big he was within her, how he stretched her entrance. In the aftermath, she was almost fascinated by the sensation, improbable and impossible as it was.

He lifted her from the table, keeping his cock inside her, and stepped backward until he reached the curtain. With his wing, he pulled it back from the center, where she'd struggled to find an edge and found nothing but more velvet.

The weight of the extra limbs made her heavier over his cock than she'd anticipated, straining her cunt even more around the base. And she looked down at him this way, still gasping for breath as she met his eyes too close. Then he lifted her from him, forcing her to release the hold of all eight of her limbs.

It seemed a corollary to how completely he filled her—without him, she felt emptier than she ever had after sex. The high was always so high, the low always so low. No one had ever been able to stop the crash that followed when they left her empty like this, vulnerable, utterly raw.

And without him feeding on her, distracting, the contents of the tent returned to her as soon as she turned around to pick up what passed for clothing in Arcanium. Turning around put her face-to-face with the fucking hissing cockroaches, who were still agitated at the earthquake the two giants had caused. Their hissing became deafening to her ears.

She couldn't convince herself to go closer to the dusty leather to bend over and pick it up, even though she knew that the top of the terrarium was still latched and they weren't going to escape and attack her for being a disturbance. On the contrary, they'd congregated on the other side of the terrarium to escape the source of the earthquake.

"There's never an end to it for you, is there? Already, new fear comes off you like mist." The Creature stroked along the moths emerging from her skull. "Does it not exhaust you?"

Elizabeth straightened. It took all her remaining, trembling energy to stand. The crash was like a weight, aided by her revulsion for the little monsters around her. Nothing was left from whatever respite the Creature had given, not even an echo of pleasure, not when he wasn't touching her.

"Little Spider, have you not yet learned that you don't have to run?"

He tried to come up behind her, but she jerked her shoulder away and edged around him, gaze fixed upon where the curtain had swung after he'd released it. The world of Arcanium showed between the edges.

Elizabeth darted between them and out into Oddity Row. She was naked again, but she wasn't going back for that leather as long as there were roaches anywhere close to it.

She didn't have to run? Where could she run to? She just had to get *away*.

Away from what, though? Her head was a mess, muddied, confused, jumpy and with a profound sense of déjà vu — except it wasn't from something in the past so much as a sense that this was her future. Everything was wrong. Everything that thrilled her, everything that frightened her, everything was wrong. She was hollow, not just empty, though her hands and feet were unbearably heavy.

"Elizabeth, wait…"

"Go to hell!" She didn't look back. She didn't think she could bear his confusion on top of her own, nor any hurt she might have caused more effectively with her words than her hands.

She didn't even know which direction she was going. Everything looked the same to her any direction she went. Oddity Row wasn't this big. She should have been able to keep going one direction and walk out of it, but she kept weaving in and out to avoid being seen and couldn't stop coming back to the red tent. The Creature had since disappeared. Perhaps he had taken her suggestion. In Arcanium, hell was never too far away.

But that particular hell she could navigate by. She started looking for the dark, looming figure of the haunted funhouse. This would be the only time she would approach it with relief, but she was too worn out to chide herself for that. All she needed was a north.

Once she'd made it to the stairway leading up to the funhouse entrance, Elizabeth collapsed on the steps. God knew how many shoes had turned the white-painted wood gray or what had been on those shoes, but she'd been crawled on by spiders all afternoon and evening, then fucked by a monster. If cleanliness was next to godliness, the devil could take her.

She could never do things by halves. There had never been a middle ground between piety and partying. She'd broken almost all the laws that Petrosians followed, as well as a few she'd given herself. She was lost, a haunted funhouse the closest she came to home.

She could go to her RV, take a shower, sleep in a bed, but she couldn't convince herself to leave, least of all make herself comfortable. As long as the spiders stayed away from her tonight, the steps would do, with splinters threatening her secondary flanks and step edges digging into her back. If Bell wanted her back in that tent, he could pry her frozen body from these damn stairs. He could and he might, but the important thing was that he'd have to.

Chapter Seven

Elizabeth woke up on the roof of the funhouse. The center of it was basically a nest, with a ragtag collection of pillows and blankets that looked like they'd been stolen from rest stops and people's porches. Everything around had been suffused with the Creature's scent, inoffensive but overwhelming. The rest of the roof showed other signs of being lived on — prints and scratch marks in the dust where the Creature preferred to crawl, a clear plastic tub of books that looked as piecemeal as his nest, a plastic drawer unit.

The Creature crouched on the edge of the roof. There wouldn't be any guests today, but he sniffed the air as though there were scents he could feed upon there. Elizabeth just smelled the traditional breakfast smells from the big top.

The early morning light had an unreal cast to it with the low cloud cover, but she could see the circus now, could orient herself against the big top and the animals' barn, the carousel, the canvas tents and wooden booths on the carnival side, and the caravan on the other side of the big top. She could see everything from here.

The Creature didn't turn to greet her as she approached the edge. "You would have been safer sleeping inside the funhouse than on the steps. But I have a place to sleep, and the clowns don't prowl up here."

"The clowns? The ones that are supposed to eat trespassers?"

"They prefer veal, but they'll eat tougher meat if it's all they can get, and they prefer fresh rather than the incubus' and succubus' castoffs. They might not have recognized you as one of ours. Do you want me to lower you to the ground now?"

"If you don't, Bell's going to make me crawl down, and I'm afraid of heights."

A curve softened the hard line of his lips as he continued to stare out over the tents. "Turn around and close your eyes."

"You going to do some kind of *Christmas Carol* spirit shit?"

"No — not looking helps with heights. As far as you're concerned now, you're on solid ground. The aim is to make the time between those two realities as short as possible." He took one prime hand and one secondary hand then lifted her from the roof. Cold wind from his wings buffeted her naked body as he quickly lowered her to the grass. Elizabeth opened her eyes. It had taken less than four seconds.

"But then what would you eat?" The question came out meaner than her curiosity intended.

"There's plenty to consume here," he replied quietly. "Without you, I still have the prison to feed upon. Unlike the clowns, I never go hungry."

"Prison?"

"The funhouse victims are not free, though they have cells where they recover, so to speak, in one of the semi-trailers. I'm the only one who visits them, but they don't know I do. They don't like Bell's pets. They're least fond of anything they believe to be a demon."

She closed her eyes again, rubbing her forehead. "Of course they are."

"I will not bother you again, Spider."

Elizabeth lifted her head at the billowing of wings, but he disappeared so efficiently, she suspected invisibility was another talent in his arsenal. After all, a creature like him flying around, looking for something to attach to... Someone would have noticed.

Her chest ached at the thought she might have hurt him, because he'd been nothing but kind to her — comforting, soothing, feasting on her fear, attempting to untangle her ambivalence through last night's mistake, though she could hardly claim it had been done against her will.

But she wasn't fond of Bell's pets either. The Creature was as complicit as the rest of them, gnawing at the scraps of Bell's sadism. All that mattered was that it wouldn't happen again.

* * * *

After slinking back to her RV for a shower to scrub spider legs and the Creature's touch from her skin, Elizabeth slipped into the big top for an early breakfast. At this time of morning, the only other people backstage aside from the golems were two naked people lounging in the big cat cages.

She ate as she walked past the caravan to the five semis parked neatly at the edge of the clearing. There were holes in the sides of all five, which meant they'd once been used for some kind of livestock, but other than that, there were no distinguishing qualities or marks, not even to advertise Arcanium along the highways. They were as nondescript as the caravan.

She went around behind them to investigate the doors into the trailers. Three of them were locked. The fourth wasn't locked, but it was empty. There were black clothes and shoes folded in tubs along the sides, as well as boxes labeled for different seasons and venues. There weren't any pallets or cots, not even sleeping bags, so Elizabeth still didn't know where the staff-bots slept, but she'd found where they dressed, at least.

She shut the fourth trailer and approached the fifth. The handle turned without resistance. Elizabeth yanked the door open and pulled herself up into the trailer. Whatever she'd been expecting, tiny pod apartments lining the walls wasn't it. They were like space station bunks or the micro-apartments she'd seen in pictures of Tokyo, where a person was confined to a pod about twice the size of a coffin to rest and sleep, with only a little shelf for belongings. Lights made some of the honeycomb pods glow, but most of the pods were unlit. Like the funhouse and Kitty's tent, Bell had been flexible with the physics of the place, the inside larger than the outside, but not by much.

In the darkness, the trailer sounded like hell. Not the wailing and gnashing of teeth of the haunted funhouse, but a steady ebb and flow of sobs and gasps of pain.

"Get out of here and shut the fucking door!"

Someone emerged from one of the dark pods and snarled at her, then pitched forward and threw up blood. It was too dark to be vomit. He clutched his abdomen, because his intestines threatened to fall out of him through the wide stitching keeping his belly mostly closed.

She shut the door, but she didn't leave.

"I said go away! Goddamn bitch."

She skittered around the blood pool and stared in horror as her eyes adjusted.

Alerted to an intruder, some of the prisoners crawled to the edge of their pods to peer out at her.

"You're not welcome."

"Get the fuck out!"

"None of Bell's bitches in here. You're trespassing, Spider."

"What part of 'get the fuck out' don't you understand, you stupid cunt?" The Man Doll, his little petticoated girl-doll body topped with a bearded man's head, jumped out of his second-level pod and ran at her like some kind of demented character from a video game. His pacifier hung on a chain around his neck. "We're not here for your entertainment. We get enough of that during the weekends when the funhouse is open, but we're entitled to some *fucking* peace from the rest of you *fucking* freaks."

Elizabeth fought off his little tantrum hands with bemusement, caught between wanting to scream and laugh—not because it was funny, but because it was just so *ridiculous* that she didn't know how to react.

"No, Hank, we're not." A young man with curly light brown hair and a back that had been rendered into raw meat dangled his legs over the side of his third-level

172

pod. He winced, groaned, as he climbed the ladder down to the floor.

"Speak for yourself, Kevin." The guy who spoke peeked out from the third level. He was still wearing bloody scrubs, which made him the doctor who'd cut open the guy's abdomen — the guy whose blood she was still trying not to step in with her bare toes.

"Yeah," Man Doll said, kicking Kevin's leg with his Mary Jane shoe. "Take your goddamn shitty guilt and shove it right up your cornhole, fucking choir boy."

"Ignore him. Hank's always a douche when he pulls the tea party princess straw," Kevin said. "You're the new girl in the funhouse, aren't you? The black widow in the rope web."

"She's Bell's new bitch. If she were one of us, she'd be sleeping in here, wouldn't she?" Falling Guts Boy said.

"No dogs allowed, you multi-legged freak." This time the Man Doll tried to kick her, but Kevin shoved him away.

Now that she'd recovered from the initial bemusement, she was starting to find the Man Doll annoying, like a Pomeranian. "Freak? You're one to talk."

"At least we're not bitches," Surgeon said.

"If by 'Bell's bitch,' you mean I do what Bell tells me, we all do that, don't we?" Elizabeth said. "But I make him force me to do it. And I came in here because everyone out there drank the Kool-Aid. I'm from a goddamn cult, but I can still smell Bell's bullshit. It's sickening."

She'd never called it a cult aloud before. Dez had called it that all the time, and she'd known before she ever left the community, but she'd never said it aloud.

"You wish yourself in, or did he give you the whole 'cake or death' speech, but with wishes instead of cake and clowns instead of death?" Kevin asked.

"I didn't wish in on purpose. He stole me from my family in the night. Fucking stripped me down in front of everyone and transformed me so the rest of his cast could gawk. I'm not on his side. It'd be nice to be with other people who aren't on his side either."

It would remind her that she had other options other than submission. These people weren't allowed to become complacent, weren't allowed to get comfortable. She could learn a thing or two from them. Complacency had left her shaking the tables in the red tent. Complacency had convinced the Creature she'd wanted those things, had convinced her that she needed them.

"I wouldn't call us good company," Kevin said.

"I'm not good company," Elizabeth said. "I'm not asking for good company."

"She's not one of us!" Man Doll crossed his arms over his pinafore.

"Jerk off, Hank. She's close enough."

"It's your fucking dick that got you into this mess," Chainsaw Guy said, sitting in the pod next to the Surgeon's. "You gonna let it get us into another one?"

"How was I supposed to know the circus had a succubus making everything hard? Not that Bell gives a shit either way," Kevin shot back bitterly. "But we trespassed and we hurt his people. What we were going to do to them, demon-influenced or not, is still shady as hell."

"Fuck that. We didn't deserve *this*," Hank said. "You want to talk justice? You could have been boohooing all the way to prison to be someone's bitch there, not in the goddamn demon version of Guantanamo Bay while people laugh at your torture like it's some kind of funny. You think you got it bad, Spider Lady? You think Big Bad Bell done you wrong because you have a few extra limbs and had to get naked, when you've clearly already done that to get tattooed? Your robe is fucking open all the way up to your shriveled cunt."

Elizabeth hit him, her knuckles striking above his beard with an audible thwap. The disproportionate weight of his head sent the Man Doll pinwheeling into one of the pods, falling onto a man whose limbs had been sewn together as shoddily as Falling Guts Boy. The victim's face was a mess of snot and tears, and he could barely move without whimpering, which was the only sound his sliced throat could make.

Elizabeth didn't give two shits about the Man Doll, but she hated to see the other man in more pain than he was already in.

So Bell repaired them just enough to survive. He didn't spare them the way he did her, with his promise that nothing would harm her, not a single bite or sting or irritating hair. He didn't even offer them a basic medicine cabinet, never mind prescription-grade opiates or even street drugs to let them escape from reality — nothing but bandages and sewing kits. For the ones who were the villains in the tableaus, that would be the closest they got to mercy — witnessing the pain of the person they'd maimed and tortured for the rest of the week instead of enduring it.

Elizabeth had to swallow against how the prisoners left her shaken. What happened to them seemed so much more real outside the funhouse.

"I didn't come here to have some little doll in a dress act like he's getting tortured worse than anybody else ever," she said. "Don't take your childhood trauma out on me. It may not sound too bad to you, but Bell knows I'm arachnophobic as hell. He still made me this. He still puts me in a tent that looks like the goddamn spider Taj Mahal and locks me in a glass coffin with the biggest fucking spiders he can find while the rest of you are licking your wounds. I'm not saying it's worse, but don't you fucking *dare* say I've got it chocolate and roses. Now, I don't have a lot of time before he makes me do it again. Do I need to put you in a timeout until then, Mr. Dolly?"

"You're such a fucking bitch," Hank spat, but his lower lip trembled like a child's, as though he had a little girl's sensitivity to go along with the dress.

"Yeah, I am. But I'm not Bell's bitch. Got it?"

"I like you." One of the other whipping boys crawled out of his pod. "You got rouse-a-crew-to-mutiny kind of spirit. We don't get a lot of girls, and Blondie doesn't talk much anymore. Being forced to blow poison ivy until the End of Days does that to people, I guess."

The vine-wrapped girl scooted to the edge of her lit pod. In better light, Elizabeth could see how her tongue had been forced out by the size of the vine emerging from her mouth. Blisters and sores lined the visible portions of her tongue and lips. They must have gone all the way into her mouth and down her throat.

Kevin stepped back to stand next to the other whipping boy. "She's not like the contortionist or the Torso Man playing scary in the funhouse whenever they feel like it. If Bell forces her in there, why shouldn't she be here? If one of his pets has actually taken the 'red pill', we shouldn't make her leave, right?"

"You're just saying that because you think you can screw this one." Hank pouted, crossing his chubby arms. "As if Bell would ever let us screw anyone but Blondie—if she didn't have a vine up there half the time, anyway."

"And you're only saying that because you know you can't, not the way you are. Keep your skirt on," the other whipping boy said.

"Next week, butch, you might be the one in the dress," Hank snapped back.

"Nah, she's not like us," a woman with short hair said from the second level. "She says it isn't roses and chocolate just because she's scared of itty bitty spiders, poor thing. But if Bell wanted her to be like us, he would have made her a nice little room in the funhouse, filled it to the brim with spiders and tied her in, like when we're with the rats or getting melted. You want some of this, girlie?" She thrust out her arms, which were necrotic and smelled of pus and rot.

"Believe me. I know it could be worse," Elizabeth said. "My rational mind knows that. Phobias don't give a damn. I'd lose my mind just as much if Bell put one little wolf spider in there with me, but he doesn't. He's got every spider you were ever afraid was hiding under your bed, and I'm pretty sure I'm going to spend time in the coffin with every one of them, and oh God…"

The way she couldn't get enough air when she gasped, no matter how much she inhaled, the narrowing and graying of her vision, the roaring in her ears… The stealth panic attack struck fast and hard. Elizabeth stumbled back against the side of the compartment, her robe parting over her legs and probably giving most of them an even better view than she'd given the Man Doll.

"Boo-fucking-hoo." The woman slid back into her pod and turned out the light.

But the two whipping boys flanked her, grabbed her hand when she reached for them, and some of the others emerged from their pods, if just to enjoy a break from their pain by watching someone else's.

"Not dying, not dying, not dying," Elizabeth murmured to herself.

Kevin scoffed. "Yeah, like Bell would let us die." But he awkwardly stroked her bare head and let her clench her clammy fist around his hand. The other whipping boy wiped away her hysterical tears while she destroyed his hand as well.

Time distorted during a panic attack like that. She didn't think it lasted long. She nearly fainted about three times, but the boys held her up, and she always seemed to get enough air when her body went limp and stopped struggling against itself.

"She's only been here a couple weeks," Chainsaw Guy said as she started to get more control over herself. He even looked like the kind of guy who would wield chainsaws and hack people to bits, with his flannel shirt, work jeans, sunspots on his pale skin and flyaway blond hair. "She's got no perspective. But her being here isn't her fault, and not having perspective isn't her fault. I'm okay with her hanging around as long as she doesn't come to stare or make our lives worse than they already are. Like that contortionist, making the fire-eater her puppy. Those lucky bastards — getting caught back before Bell decided to make the funhouse. Think they know how lucky they are?"

"Lucky?" Elizabeth lowered herself to the floor, adjusting her robe so she wouldn't flash anyone else — not that it made much of a difference now that they'd all seen her. And what the hell, she was at least ten years older than most of them, anyway, except for maybe Chainsaw Guy. They wouldn't think much of her either way, even if their bodies were in any shape to show interest.

Kevin slid down to sit next to her, while the other whipping boy went back to sit in his pod. "The funhouse has only been around, like, a year...or however long we've been here. Cheryl keeps track, but most of us stopped counting. It doesn't matter anyway. We don't age, and our situation doesn't get any better. But before he had the funhouse, the circus just had the freak show to torture trespassers with."

"And the carousel," the plague woman called out from inside her pod. Elizabeth assumed she was Cheryl.

"Yeah. The carousel's got a few living people working as wooden horsies," the other whipping boy said. "But the engineer's a peach."

Kevin looked down, picking at one of his fingernails. "I'm pretty sure some of the animals were human once, too. The way I hear it, though, he didn't used to like really torturing people, but some of the demons were making noises about leaving or taking over. Then we... We did our shit, and Bell suddenly had an influx of people he had to punish. Necessity, the bitch of invention, and all that."

Elizabeth leaned away from him. "What exactly did you do?"

Kevin stopped fidgeting. He didn't bother playing at offense. "It's in the past. And maybe we deserved the first month of torture, okay? I don't want to talk about it."

"Choir boy there thinks he's better than the rest of us because he'd beg for Bell's forgiveness if he thought it would make a difference," Hank said. "But even by his fucked-up standard, we've been punished way past what we 'deserve', which means Bell knows the rest of us would take it out on his pets if we got half a chance. That's why he doesn't give us half a chance. That's why he makes sure we're too weak to rise up. That's why we're out here."

"Have you already forgotten what it was like when he captured us? The choice he offered? What the clowns and the Ringmaster did?" Kevin asked. "You chose life, same as the rest of us."

"I didn't choose to get maimed, murdered, whipped, eaten, burned and turned into a freak for the rest of my natural life," Hank said. "You think when he lets us out, we'll even recognize the world? In fifty years? A hundred? You think you'll ever see your mother again? You think we'll have a red cent to our name? What use will your guilty conscience be then?"

"It can't possibly be that long," Kevin muttered. But his expression betrayed him.

"You really think he's going to keep us fifty or a hundred years?" Sweat coated Elizabeth's palm with another slippery layer, and her face flashed hot and cold in dizzying turns. "What's the longest someone's been in Arcanium, anyway?"

"If you're talking human, the Bearded Lady is the oldest, I think. Crazy, hairy whore," the other whipping boy said. "I heard she and the contortionist have been around for about twenty years. That demon Bell stripped powers from before he put him in the carousel, he's been here fifty-ish years, right?"

"Bell's immortal." Kevin shuffled his feet on the floor, grimaced when leaning against the wall tugged at his thinly healed whip welts. "He could keep us here for a thousand years, no trouble."

Everyone fell silent.

Elizabeth wrapped her robe more tightly around her. The gesture brought the neckline up to her collarbone, like she was wearing her old modesty garments. "Has anybody ever found a way out, a way out that doesn't hurt you when you step outside the borders? Or whatever happens to you when you do that."

"You haven't tried? Not even once?" one of the plague victims asked. "All of us tried."

"I've only been here a couple of weeks. Bell's kept me on a close leash, tying me down to wherever he wants me to be. I tried running right after he changed me, but I wasn't used to the extra legs. I didn't get to the gate in time," Elizabeth replied.

"Just another reason you're not like us, sweetheart," Hank said. "If you were like us, you would have tried harder to leave. You wouldn't have needed us to tell you. You're a precious little minx who thinks just because she's scared, she's in hell. But you're not. And no matter what you say or how you say it or how many tattoos you've got and where, you're not the badass you work so hard to pretend to be. At least I'm not so horny I'm willing to overlook that."

Kevin rolled his eyes. "It's not horniness to show a little sympathy, you know. There are other reasons to be nice."

"Not here," Hank said. "Not in Arcanium."

"It's cute you think all of this is me trying to be a badass," Elizabeth said. "It might have been about that when I was eighteen, but it stopped being about that pretty damn quickly. You don't know me. You have no idea why I've done the things I've done. And if you could not assume everyone's exactly like you, that'd be cool, too."

"Everyone *is* like me. They're just cowards who won't admit it." Hank stuck his lower lip out in another exaggerated pout.

"It's always the people at the bottom of the barrel who can't imagine anyone else being anything but trash," she said.

"And you want this woman to hang around here, knowing what she thinks of us?" A crocodile tear dripped into his beard.

Elizabeth tilted her head with a humorless smile. "Not them, doll. Just you."

"Fine." Hank pushed himself to his feet and flounced away, sniffing like his world had ended.

Kevin snorted from holding in laughter, then winced with a hissing intake of air.

"Troy, the Tattooed Man, used this potion from a blue bottle to make my new tattoos heal really fast," Elizabeth said. "Bell has plenty of that stuff. I'm sure I can get my hands on some."

"Appreciate it, but the only healing that works is whatever Bell allows us once the funhouse closes. Then we're left with whatever we can live with, although 'living' is a pretty loose term. We managed to snag a bottle once. It didn't do anything."

"There's really nothing we can do, is there?" she said.

He rested a hand on her shoulder. "Not yet. But the minute the opportunity presents itself—the fucking *second* Bell goes weak—you better believe we'll slip through the cracks."

"I don't think it's like Cinderella. We don't turn back into a pumpkin after midnight. Even if we manage to get out, we're still...this." Elizabeth kicked all four of her feet.

Kevin narrowed his eyes with grim determination. "Anything's got to be worth getting free."

Elizabeth ignored him. "Anything? Flesh-eating bacteria, vines, burns, amputation, disembowelment? Arcanium keeps you from dying. What would stop death out there?"

"I'd take my chances, Spider Woman," Kevin said. "*Anything*."

Elizabeth climbed to her feet. Kevin used the holes in the wall to help himself up as well.

Then she grabbed him by the throat. "That's good to know, pig scum. It keeps me vigilant, patching the cracks."

"Told you she wasn't one of us!" Cheryl shouted, but Kevin held up his hand to stop anyone from running at them. Elizabeth's hold gave him room to breathe—just enough. He coughed.

"I'm afraid I have to take my Spider back now. Always work to be done. If she still has the poor judgment to return to you afterward, that's her prerogative," Elizabeth continued. At least, her voice did. But she'd immediately recognized the telltale sensation of Bell pulling her strings, and it appeared Kevin had had the same thought.

She pulled him close, almost nose to nose. "You know she's far too good for you, don't you?" she said, too softly for anyone else in the compartment to hear.

He nodded, coughing again. "Yeah. I figured that when you gave her the tour."

"As long as we're clear." Bell released him.

Kevin backed out of her way like a chastised puppy, rubbing his throat. "Bell's taken her over. It's not her."

"Maybe that's just what she wants you to think," Falling Guts Guy said. He groaned, doubling over in his pod. "You're such a sap."

Elizabeth bent down to look him in the eye with a directness she never could have on her own. "In what world would any of mine voluntarily spend time with filthy vermin like you, Felix? I can't keep the Spider from fraternizing with belly-crawlers in her free time, but you're a fool if you think I put her here. I, of all people, don't need a spy."

Bell straightened then opened the door and jumped out. The door closed behind Elizabeth without her touching the handle again — just in case anyone inside the truck still believed she was playacting at being Bell.

He walked her body all the way to the big top, where he waited for her, carrying a bag with her costume and wig.

"Really, Lizzie?"

Elizabeth snatched the bag away. "I'd rather be with them than with the people who kiss your ass."

"You condemn me as though there's nothing in the world that could justify what they endure. But I assure you, justice as well as vengeance has been served, and they are much more fortunate than they believe themselves — ironic, given how they believe the same of you." He followed the path of the bats around the curve of her ear, but he didn't pursue her when she jerked away.

"I don't think 'it could be worse' is the most stirring of affirmations. And it's not close to lunch yet. You could have left me in there longer."

"I don't want you with them."

"You said you wouldn't control with whom I spend my time," Elizabeth said. "Are you going to start controlling me twenty-four-seven to make sure I surround myself only with all the monsters and slaves you prefer me to emulate?"

Bell took her by her secondary arm to stop her from stalking away. His expression seemed strange, as though he were both concerned and a little offended. "Those pigs fear the Ringmaster because they suffer his pleasure every time the circus opens. They only suffered my pleasure once, when they gave me their wish. They feared me for a time, but of late I've become only the devil of dreams, a devil they believe they can eventually defeat. So many people underestimate me because I rule from the wings, because I accept limitations. I don't want them to make you do the same, Lizzie. There's no future in which that ends well."

Elizabeth glared at him until he let her go. "Do you have a point somewhere in that sermon, Pastor?"

Bell stepped closer. It occurred to her that he was a little shorter than she was—for some reason, she'd always thought he was a little taller. Maybe it was because he was barefoot now instead of wearing boots. "What does it profit you to surround yourself with the same kind of people you surrounded yourself with after you left the Petrosian Church? You ran from your church, then ran from your artist and his people back to the Petrosians. Will you run right back to the sort of people who had you running back home?" He sighed, frustration plain in his expression. "Must you insist on always moving backward, Elizabeth? Don't you know I want so much better for you?"

"You sound like my father. But both of you are as far from qualified to decide what's better as people can get." She enunciated each quiet word, just in case he wasn't paying attention.

Bell didn't blink. "You don't have such an exemplary track record on the subject yourself."

Elizabeth made a fist and brought her knuckles to Bell's chest to push him back. She didn't even want to touch him with her fingertips. "You can make me do whatever you like — terrify innocent people, scare me to death forty times over, feed the Creature. I'm obviously here to entertain you, just another spider for your collection. But I don't want to be anywhere near you or the people happy to let you do all of this. If that means consorting with a criminal element… Well, like you said, it wouldn't be the first time. I can handle them, no problem. You, however, can go fuck yourself in your handbasket to hell. Now, you clearly want me to get ready, so excuse me. You'll have to force me to the tent and into the coffin, but I think I can dress myself. And don't think the Creature is the way you're going to get into my head. I'm not letting him do that to me again."

Bell cocked his head in curiosity at the mention of the Creature, but he raised his hands in surrender. "Wouldn't dream of it. I'll take you to the tent when it's time."

As she stalked off again without him, he called after her, "You know, what I do to you is nothing like what I do to them. Not even close. One day you'll see it."

"Just keep away from me, you and your people."

He smiled. "I don't control their wills either. But you may avoid them at your leisure, my dear. They cannot do anything to you without your consent."

Elizabeth had the distinct impression he was telling a joke only he understood, but he gave no clue as to what he found so amusing.

* * * *

Bell had her get into the coffin on her hands and knees.

"What can I do to make you understand that you're not here to be tortured, that I derive no joy from the fear you suffer?" He tucked a lock of hair from her wig behind her ear.

"You could fill the coffin with kittens instead," Elizabeth replied through the measured breaths he gave her.

"If we lived in a world where kittens were the terrifying beasts they believed themselves to be, I would gladly grant such a request." Bell lowered her into the coffin with a hand on her back, adjusting her spider legs to his liking. He arranged her head so that she would look out of the tent instead of toward the tables, so when he stepped away, she didn't know what he was retrieving.

"Just let me wish myself out," she said quietly. "Please. I'm no good for you. If you don't want me with the prisoners, then let me out."

She could almost convince herself that his tenderness was genuine as he replied, "There's nothing for you out there. Everything you need is here. Arcanium is your home. Now, this is a Goliath birdeater. Being the original circus we are, I call him Goliath. He's quite large, bigger than the huntsman but with a smaller leg span. As tarantulas go, he's unusually personable. And no, that doesn't mean he was once a person. He just grew accustomed to handling more quickly than most of our specimens, and he doesn't mind people. I'm quite fond of him. About as close to a kitten as I have for you, I'm afraid."

"If you weren't omnipotent…" Elizabeth twitched as he placed the spider in the valley of her spine.

"I know," he said gently. "You may hate me however you please."

"What if it pleases me to smash a hammer in your face?"

He laughed, then locked her into the coffin with Goliath.

* * * *

When the lock opened and the coffin lid lifted, she hadn't moved.

She'd felt everyone's gazes as prickly on her skin as the spider wandering over her, though eventually he'd returned to her back and crouched there. She could have sworn recognition had heated one man's gaze. No, she wasn't going to stay a secret much longer, and Elizabeth didn't know what she was going to do when the word got out about more than just the weird chick with extra limbs posing in a box full of spiders.

"Stay still. I'll take the spider away." The Creature tucked his hand underneath the crouched body of the tarantula.

Elizabeth twitched violently when the spider moved up her back instead of going into the Creature's hand. She turned her face into her arm and tried her hardest to control the trembling of her released body. The price of remaining still was that she couldn't hold back anymore. Gasps broke her wail, but it wouldn't stop, as though all the restrained trembling from the day made its way out through her vocal cords.

As soon as the spider no longer touched her body, she flailed, unable to keep her composure any longer. Her elbows and knees struck the Plexiglas with bruising force as she struggled to her hands and knees.

"You said you'd leave me be. Bell said he wouldn't push you on me again."

"I will not linger. I simply volunteered to continue releasing you, because I can continue to offer my services. If you want me to take your fear, I can take it from your wrists almost as well as I can from your neck. Or I can leave now."

Elizabeth finally managed to pull herself upright in the coffin, a shriek strangled in her choke-tight throat.

The Creature tilted his hand into an empty terrarium, patient as he waited for Goliath to climb off. He eyed her clenched fists warily, but he did not flee.

"Just your fear, Elizabeth. I never sought anything else."

Elizabeth pressed one of her fists to her mouth against a pathetic whimper. Then she bit the pad of her forefinger, digging her sharp teeth in. The pain grounded her in the moment—and at this moment, a giant spider no longer crawled all over her. All the little beasts were in their places, which wasn't on her. She shook her head, though the hand she bit rattled her head with its trembling.

"Very well. I'll leave you be."

Blood spread over her tongue. She was digging her teeth too deeply. If she kept going like this, she'd reach bone.

Elizabeth bent double and squeezed her eyes shut, as though closing her eyes would somehow stifle the cries that whined through her chest.

The train of his wings had almost crossed from the tent to the rest of Arcanium when she called, "Wait."

She clutched the sides of the coffin to turn around, her extra limbs ungainly and her fear removing anything left of grace. Instead, she moved like an invalid. Fear made some people angry, made them strong. Elizabeth wasn't fortunate enough to experience that side of fear. It burned out too quickly. She'd used every last bit of her energy just to endure Bell keeping her still all day.

God, is this going to be my life?

"Please." She slumped over the side of the coffin in defeat, stretching out her arms toward him as though she'd been wandering the desert and he was the woman at the well. "Please, take it from me."

The Creature ducked into the tent again, inscrutable as ever without expression. He took her primary hands, accepted her secondary hands when they also strained to grasp him. As he brought them to his mouth, he turned the delicate undersides of her wrists toward him.

She unclenched her hands, spread her fingers to touch his neck as he parted his lips over the edge of her sleeve tattoos. Cool air swirled over her skin whenever he exhaled. His eyes hooded in pleasure, and Elizabeth's breathing slowed and deepened.

She lowered her head, ashamed that she would beg, ashamed that she would offer herself to him when she'd sworn she wouldn't do this again. With every inch of relief he gave her, the faster and hotter the tears poured down her cheeks and stained the glass with diluted mascara. She couldn't even recover gracefully. She kept her face turned against her arm, her wig helping to conceal her.

The Creature lifted his mouth from her wrists. "I should stop now. It would not do for me to gorge when there is no end."

"Can you become full with fear?" She rubbed her face on her arm, which would do nothing to improve the mess.

He released her hands with clear reluctance. "*You* can. My body responds to it differently than yours."

"I remember," she whispered.

"That wasn't from your fear, little Spider. That was from you, from your touch…your insistence." It was more difficult for her to tell when he kept his head still, but she sensed the descent of his gaze over her body. "The passion in your fingers and in the taste of your kiss. I don't need fear as an aphrodisiac. What need has Arcanium for aphrodisiacs when it keeps an incubus and a succubus who feed upon trespassers and each other?"

Elizabeth lifted her head from her arm. "Everyone keeps mentioning… Are you saying that just having sex demons in the circus affects the rest of us?"

He blinked. "Has no one told you? Their magic strengthens when they hunger as well as when they feed. It spreads through the whole circus."

"And did they feed last night?"

"They did. Two trespassers who thought it would be romantic to sneak into a circus and make out in one of the oddity tents. Sasha and Mikhail feed, then leave the rest for the clowns. Their feed is far more fatal than mine."

Elizabeth grasped the edge of the coffin so hard her already pale skin went white above the knuckles. "So what happened last night, that was because the sex demons sent out magic to make us…"

"They didn't make us do anything. They didn't make you touch. They didn't make me assent. Incubi and succubi manipulate, of course, but the residue of their magic has no purpose, no aim. It's secondhand sexual desire at best. All it can do is magnify what already exists." He stepped back, wings spreading to open the curtain. "It was a pleasure, little Spider, but it was my pleasure and yours, not theirs. Theirs simply intensified what you started."

"What *I* started…" With the strength-sapping fear siphoned from her, Elizabeth vaulted over the side of the coffin. Indignant, she cleared the glass as though she'd lived with the extra weight and consideration of her limbs all her life.

"All I wanted from you was your fear until you touched me, kissed me, until the essence of your skin emanated a different kind of arousal than fear."

"You were practically making out with my neck. What was I supposed to do with that?"

"I do not shame you for your desire, Elizabeth. It is you who is ashamed, not I." He kept his distance from her, his wings tucked between the edges of the curtain, as though insulted by her shame. "Becoming aroused has always been a decision I must make, and in Arcanium, it tends to be an inconvenient one. If you had not shown an alternative interest, I never would have pressed upon you, never would have responded. But I see nothing wrong with what we did, nor in enjoying the effect of the sex demons' magic."

"Of course you don't see anything wrong."

He was a monster—not human, not demon, and without the accountability of either, no more than a beast of the field or bird of the air. He wouldn't understand what sex meant to a creature who suffered consequences, physical and emotional.

If it wasn't a need or even a biological imperative, how could a monster understand what he had done?

How could he understand how her mind and memory had been stirred in sticky tar, how the same destructive patterns always rose to the surface with all the subtlety of dinosaur bones? How a touch, a kiss, a man entering her, wasn't just a pleasure? How it wasn't—couldn't be—that simple for her? Or how letting demons drive her urges was little different than offering herself to them?

It wasn't his fault. It was foolish of her to try to absolve herself by blaming him. This was as much her responsibility as it had been when Dez had first revealed to her pleasures of the flesh. The fact that she still suffered the same weaknesses embarrassed her. After seventeen years, she hadn't grown at all.

"I've taken what fear I can, although you will continue to refill the well faster than I can drain it," the Creature said. "I will leave you."

Elizabeth wrapped her secondary arms around herself, held her head in her prime hands. "Are they feeding now? The demons?"

The Creature paused. "No. Their influence has dissipated."

She tucked her fingers under the edge of the wig, freeing her scalp from the helmet of heat that came from it. The wig didn't itch, but it was still constrictive and eventually became hot from the fever of her panic that had nowhere to vent.

With the wig a dark pile in the coffin, she stroked her palms over the skin. A bearded lady covered head to toe with fur, and a spider with only eyelashes and eyebrows to her name. A woman without limbs and a woman with extra. A spider and a flying monster. Bell liked balancing his weird.

The Creature still stood, watching as she soothed the skin over her head. She felt his regard as heat, less irritating than the kind contained under the wig.

"But they still have an effect?" Elizabeth said.

"Always. Even when Bell permits them to hunt beyond the borders of the circus. This is their home. The magic lingers."

"Is that all this is?"

The Creature pulled his wings in, and the curtains swung closed behind him. He tilted his head in consideration. "What is *this*, then?"

"I told you to leave. I told you to take only fear. But I..."

But I'm weak. I always have been — the sins of the father and mother, pouring over in the child of the same sin.

It was no excuse. This was her struggle, the one etched onto her bones, a curse from the beginning of time.

"I try to leave, Elizabeth, but you ask me to stay. Would you like me to leave now? I've taken what I need, at no shame to you. Don't make me your demon. I won't play Bell to your soul."

He came closer, furling his wings entirely, but still keeping a respectful distance. He made it clear time and again that he had no desire to pressure her — quite unlike when Dez's hands had slipped into every opportunity her confused, eager body had presented. The Creature gave her the space to deny him. She wouldn't have dreamed of denying Dez his bottomless hunger, especially once she'd realized her matchless own that sometimes had him struggling to keep up.

Lust and fear, two sides of arousal — perhaps it was no surprise that when one receded under a gentle hand, the other always rose to take its place, eventually entangling the two in an irreparable knot that had scarred over from her trying and failing to remove it.

Always failing, always running. Was there anything in the world she could be proud of?

She lowered her eyes like a penitent but reached up without looking to take his head between all four of her hands and bring him down to drink from his kiss.

"If only you'd fucking left," she muttered into his mouth, just before she parted her lips for the possession of his tongue.

God, it tasted so sweet, every inch of her skin and all the paths of her pleasure alighting without effort.

No, she couldn't blame the demons for the sweetness, for the betrayal. She knew she should resist the urges that had always destroyed her, but she didn't, because his body against hers was a comfort.

And he had no reason to resist.

Chapter Eight

It took many weeks alternating between the glass coffin on weekdays and the rope web on Fridays and weekends before she realized her muscles unknotted when she had to pull on the latex bodysuit.

Bell still had to puppeteer her into the funhouse, but the web was far more comfortable than the coffin. It was a chance to not suffer prickly legs on her skin, spiders hiding under her hair, paralysis and shut-in panic attacks, nor the weakness that followed her days in the red tent, when desire intensified into a whirlwind behind fear's wake — because the Creature was tender, because his feed kept her close, because his warmth called to her, because he was just as good without the sex demons' influence.

As soon as the funhouse closed for the evening performances, her bindings loosened and the funhouse prisoners were released from their torment. 'Release' was a relative term, of course. The victims capable of walking aided those who couldn't, carried them on stretchers back to the semi-trailer. Elizabeth helped. Even Hank wouldn't tell her to shove off when he was the one with extremities loosely sewn on where they'd once been firmly attached.

In the trailer, she endured their cries and screams as she wiped away blood and pus, wrapped burns and rotting flesh in bandages. Whenever she'd been sick or injured herself, Elizabeth had always felt better when clean and cared for. Despite mild mysophobia, she'd applied that principle to the Bishop children with success, and the prisoners were no exception.

Aside from two of the prisoners, most were in their late teens through mid-twenties. After the third weekend, the prisoners started coming to her as though she was some kind of Wendy figure and they were her Lost Boys—albeit with filthier vocabularies. It was a role she was much more comfortable in. They were adults, but they were still young. They missed their mothers.

Hell, Elizabeth was well into her thirties, but she missed her mother's daily phone check-in. Charity hadn't done that with her other daughters. As frustrating and deflating as it had been, it had meant that Charity had still cared enough to worry.

None of the prisoners found out what she did with the Creature. The Creature had no reason to share the information with Bell's allies, much less his enemies, and none of the prisoners ventured beyond the line between the funhouse and the semi-trailer. Elizabeth wasn't positive, but she didn't think the prisoners were allowed free movement through the circus, whether limited by Bell's magic or because of aggressive ostracism from the cast.

Between the prisoners, the funhouse, the red tent and her own tension with the Arcanium cast — plus her fears about what was happening among the people of her old life outside Arcanium — her small RV clinked like a distillery transport truck from leftover whiskey bottles whenever the circus picked up stakes and moved.

Bell stayed true to the word that accompanied his gifts. But the more she poured down her throat to calm down and knock herself out most nights, the more she wished he'd just let her have the hangovers, because that, at least, was suffering she'd earned.

* * * *

Her view in the funhouse never changed. Always the same kinds of people creeping down the hall worried about what was coming, what might emerge from the shadows or jump out next to them. They were indistinguishable in the dark, screaming the same, posturing the same, crying the same, whether young or old, male or female, in groups or alone.

But the man didn't hug the walls or dart his gaze from side to side to check baseboards and corners for hidden haunts. He didn't anticipate the boarded-up door next to him might conceal some shocking tableau. His gait was smooth, slow, casual. Leisurely.

He wore a trench coat that wouldn't be out of place in a noir detective movie. His leather shoes gave off a polished matte shine from half a corridor away, and a fedora perched at an angle on his head. A suit and tie beneath the coat completed the unlikely ensemble. In a world of leather and latex that often mingled with the medieval and bohemian, 'unlikely' was a difficult standard. He would have been more unlikely in tails and a top hat, but his sartorial choice and nonchalance still roused Elizabeth from the near-trance state she'd settled into.

He took his time approaching her, unfazed by the screams around him from the guests, the prisoners and the funhouse music. The dim light concealed most of his features, and the fedora obscured the top half of his face, but underneath, a slight grin curved his mouth.

She curled her fingers into fists around the closest part of the rope web she could reach. She wasn't even sure what disturbed her, but though her oversensitive instincts had been considerably dampened in Arcanium by an overabundance of *wrong*, ice slithered down her spine the closer he came.

The web rocked forward, bringing her with it, and Bell's magic pulled the scream from her.

Wailing, moaning, strobe lights, a woman with filed teeth and wearing S&M gear masquerading as a spider costume… Under such circumstances, the most unflappable of men were usually flapped. But the man stood there, staring and smiling at her with his hands in his coat pockets and face half hidden. All he needed was a toothpick to chew and a gold badge to flash to complete the image.

Eventually, she ran out of breath. She brought her teeth together in a sharp bite that clicked through her skull. Baring her teeth and hissing were the only other things she could do, but they didn't faze him any more than the scream.

His face wasn't two feet from hers. At this distance, she should have at least seen a glint in his eyes, but everything above the flare of his nostrils was black. He didn't resemble the Gentleman, who literally had no facial features. Of everyone in Arcanium, he reminded her most of Bell—appearance inescapably normal, but with some undefinable quality as far from normal as possible.

What the hell are you looking at?

"I'm looking at you, pretty Spider."

The man standing still and silent was bad enough. When he spoke, it was worse. And she still didn't know why, except he wasn't supposed to be here like this. And if he wasn't supposed to be here, Bell had to know.

"Don't bother screaming for him. He's not looking this way."

Five teenagers crashed into the corridor. From their haste, the Gentleman was probably chasing them. Elizabeth held on to that. The Gentleman was coming.

The teenagers stumbled down the corridor, laughing, catching their breath, pushing each other, one guy's arm around his girl to protect her.

Elizabeth wasn't in the shadows, not with the man still in front of her, which kept her web pitched forward. She'd lost the element of surprise, so the teenagers were more curious than anxious as they approached.

She thrashed against the ropes that bound her. One of her secondary arms actually managed to loosen its rope shackle enough for her to slip it out, and she reached out to scratch at the man with the acrylic claws that capped her latex gloves.

The man quickly stepped back, but if she'd caught him by surprise, he showed no sign.

As soon as she determined she couldn't reach him, she brought her freed hand back to pull on the ropes binding the others, but the only one she could loosen was her other secondary arm. Bell had anchored her primary limbs much better. Those ropes wouldn't budge.

She freed her other secondary arm just as the group of teenagers reached her. She was already in the strobe light, but their presence triggered her need to scream. She reached for them with her secondary arms, scratching and grabbing at their shoulders. The girl screamed higher and louder than Elizabeth, jumping back against her boyfriend. The other boys edged out of the way, laughing, though Elizabeth could tell she made them nervous. Perhaps because they'd seen her slip her bindings, and maybe she would come after them the way the Gentleman had.

Except the Gentleman didn't follow them around the corner. He didn't come after the man still standing there against the wall, the teenagers scattering and scurrying around him as though he were a rock in a river, as though they didn't see him but somehow knew to avoid him.

Even with her long arms and her claws, she couldn't snag anyone's shirt or jacket to use them as a shield or plead with them without words that she needed help. She gnashed her teeth, rabid froth building up over her lips.

It didn't convince the teenagers to stay. They ran, leaving her alone with the man, whose smile only widened. She screamed again, this time in frustration, but still the Gentleman didn't come.

The man slid his feet forward until he was *just* out of reach. She could brush the open sides of his trench, but she couldn't snag the fabric.

Then he raised his hand.

Her secondary arms flew back to the rope web. The bindings didn't close around her elbows again, but she still couldn't move them, nor could she reach for him with her prime arms, limited though that reach was. All eight of her limbs were pinned to the web, held there by nothing.

He came closer to her now.

And there was the hyperventilation, late but expected, wholly reasonable. She opened her mouth — whether to scream or bite was anyone's guess at that point, neither off the table — but at his leather-gloved touch on her chin, her jaw locked.

He cocked his head, eyes still obscured in darkness, as he ran the tip of a finger over the points of her teeth. "I thought he'd run out of worthy ideas after the carousel and the twins, that he'd lost his poetry. But this house, and now you..." He hooked his fingers under the edge of her latex mask, pulled it over her head, somehow as intimate as removing the top half of her suit.

He came so close that she thought he would kiss her, that he kept her mouth open like this to force himself as deep inside her as he wanted without having to fear her bite. But all he did was smooth his palm over the death's-head moths while she trembled so hard the ropes made a soft humming noise.

"You intrigue me, pretty Spider. He doesn't have much imagination, but he has excellent taste." He bent to whisper in her ear, as though telling her a secret. "We'll have such times, you and I."

The man withdrew, continuing into the rest of the haunted funhouse without a backward glance, not even when her locked jaw and her limbs were released from their invisible bindings. The web rocked back into the darkness, but that didn't stop her from thrashing against the rope like an animal caught in a trap. Too many minutes passed before she accepted either no one was coming or no one thought the man was worth the chase.

"What disturbs you, Spider?"

Elizabeth jumped, already on edge to scream. It was her constant soundtrack in this godforsaken funhouse. No shame adding hers to the chorus, even when it wasn't scripted.

The Creature clung to the acoustic tile of the ceiling. He should have weighed too much for the plaster and pulled the whole structure down with him, but something else kept him attached other than claws. She was in no state to ask what.

"When the quality of your fear changes, when it becomes unbearable, I sense it from all the way across the circus." He climbed onto the web headfirst from above, unsettling her. "It cannot be a small thing that frightened you if the fear still lingers like smoke."

The Creature touched her moving lips, her attempts to even just mouth words. Bell's magic thwarted every effort at coherence. In the funhouse, she was more beast than he was, and his fingers on her lips reminded her of the man. She turned her face away.

The gesture presented her neck, where he was more than happy to redirect his interest.

"Was it the Gentleman who stalks the previous hall? He sows fear and paranoia to heighten a visitor's funhouse experience, but he does not intend to trigger such sensations in you."

Elizabeth shook her head. The Gentleman's absence had concerned her more than his presence.

He brought his mouth to her neck, brushing his lips over her skin. "Shall I take the fear from you?"

An entire haunted funhouse to feed upon all day, and you want me now?

As though he'd heard her thoughts, he said, "On the roof, I take the scraps that seep through the ceiling, what escapes from the entrance and exit. The Gentleman feeds on all kinds of fear, but the rarest meat I crave is terror, not a mere adrenaline rush for a thrill. Bone-deep fear fades fast among the rest of the cast, and the crew is soulless, nothing of substance. You're the richest thing to walk through the circus since my arrival. I would stay in your web every time Arcanium opened its gates if Bell believed it would serve his circus. As it is, I cannot linger forever, but I can linger for a time. May I feed?"

He always asked. It seemed a strange thing to have to ask to take a person's fear away. It wasn't like the sex demons stealing life through seduction or the clowns eating whatever intestines they could get their hands on. It wasn't Bell granting wishes helter-skelter. The Creature was hardly as invasive as a vampire or an incubus. He didn't break the skin, didn't drain her energy, didn't muddle her mind. Yet he always asked.

And Elizabeth couldn't explain to him why she needed that so much.

But she shook her head. When he rescued her from the glass coffin, she yielded to his appetite because he took away fears she knew were completely irrational. She hadn't had so much as a rash from the tarantulas' hair, and no matter her position, the spiders exhibited no signs of agitation or aggression. Her phobia was the only thing to trigger such a continually violent reaction, and even that had begun to subside — probably because the fear of Bell's untrustworthiness had faded.

The strange man who had since disappeared... She didn't want to stop fearing him. Fear had a purpose. The only problem was when it went too far, and she had a sinking feeling this wasn't too far.

The Creature paused then lowered his head. "I thought... Never mind. I will return to the roof and leave you to the fear you choose."

She stopped him with a hand on his leg, another on his shoulder.

"You wish for me to stay?" He did not resist as she drew him closer to her, his leg overlapping with hers and his wings fluttering to adjust to the angle of the web. "I was allowed to enter to lighten the load of your fear. If I am not to feast, I serve no purpose and distract you from yours."

Her stomach twisted even as she curled her secondary arm around his waist to urge him against her hip.

She shouldn't be doing this. Sex in the red tent was morally ambiguous enough. There, it arose from the relief he offered, the closeness that relief required, the magic the sex demons sent out into the air. That was all it was, and that was why it stayed in the tent.

This wasn't the red tent. She shouldn't be doing this where this week's Man Doll or werewolf could run beyond his assigned corridor, catch her close to a cast member, and call her out on her hypocrisy.

Then there were the guests — guests who wouldn't know what to make of a winged gargoyle of a man with his lips to the throat of the Spider. Elizabeth recognized the irony, but in the urgency of the moment, she doubted those passing through the funhouse would. It certainly didn't follow the funhouse theme of torment and despair that was fun for the whole family.

Yet Elizabeth's eyelids fluttered as the Creature drank from her neck nothing that had to do with fear.

Shouts coming from the Gentleman's corridor warned her that guests would hear the Creature's low growl before they would ever hear her scream.

The Creature responded to her sudden tension with humming laughter. He nuzzled her neck, then ducked under her arms, climbing behind her. With her prime arms and both legs fixed to the web, he had to take care not to strain her limbs, but he manipulated the flexible web and slithered up to settle behind her, with his body cradling her rather than the rope.

The sensation of his hips flush against her ass and the slighter flanks of her secondary legs short-circuited her brain for a moment. But her slim build couldn't hope to adequately hide the Creature, not even with her extra limbs and the darkness working on his side.

Then his mouth was against her scalp. She had never adjusted to how sensitive it was. She could practically feel each crease of his lips at the base of her skull. He didn't feed, just breathed her in. He slid his hands up her abdomen to cup her breasts at the moment the funhouse visitors careened around the corner, with assorted shrieks and cries of frightened delight.

Elizabeth twisted her neck to try to warn him with sounds if not words, but he smiled, caressing her nipples through the latex until they were visible through the bodysuit.

She shifted, all too aware of his cock against her ass. He wasn't hard yet—he had a strange way of becoming aroused all at once instead of gradually—but the heat of his mouth along the back of her neck and the possessiveness of his hands sliding back down to her abdomen as the visitors came toward them suggested desire just as well.

Elizabeth closed her eyes at the gentle, wet pressure of his tongue over the contour of her ear.

The web rocked forward, the strobe lights intensifying, and she opened her eyes wide as the next scream was wrenched from her throat. She curled her secondary fingers, swiping at the guests to get them away from her as soon as possible.

However, though they shouted and raised their arms to protect themselves from her claws, their gazes remained on her. Nothing seemed to rest or fix itself to the Creature, who rested his head on her shoulder and laughed too low for her to hear. She only knew by the vibrations. He stroked her belly, then brought one large hand between her parted thighs, drawing her scream to a higher pitch than it had started. The visitors didn't seem to notice as they continued through the house.

The Creature used the momentum of the web rocking back to press the heel of his palm, broad and firm, against her clit.

"A creature like me knows how to hide. I can fly the skies in broad daylight over a crowd without anyone noticing."

But they can still see me. They could still see the way her nipples showed against the latex more obviously than before. The flush in her cheeks and the flutter of her eyelids. The parting of her lips in a way as far from frightening as even a fearful woman could imagine. The cant of her body into his touch. And if someone were there, they would hear her gasp, the creak of the latex, the groan of the rope.

With his free hand, the Creature followed the path of the zipper between her breasts up to her neck. He wrapped his long, massive fingers around her thin neck, squeezing just long enough to make her tense so he could sip her fear with his mouth against her cheek, curling his tongue to catch the gasp.

Then he slowly drew the zipper down.

No. I draw the line at being naked. She squirmed harder, shaking her head.

"They see more in the coffin." He nudged her cheek with his nose. "Trust me."

Elizabeth twisted to look at him, to search his face when his opaque eyes gave her nothing. She didn't know why she still expected the worst of him, because there wasn't a time in Arcanium when he had done anything unkind, wicked though he appeared. And in this place, she should have already figured out that nothing was the way it appeared.

He quickened his rhythm against her clit but relinquished the zipper to guide her mouth to his, the more pointed tip of his tongue deliberate and coaxing over hers. Screams of horror, pain and misery were the soundtrack for a sweet domination of a kiss. He wasn't always gentle, but even when he was, he commanded her as though he'd always been meant to. Asking for permission didn't diminish the way he kept an invisible collar around her throat that he could hook his finger through, and her entire body would relax and follow.

Kind though he was, she'd give a primary limb to deny him. God forbid she grow comfortable in Arcanium, heat and soften with lust in this torture chamber. But she did.

Still holding her mouth with his kiss, he brought his fingers back to the zipper. The click of its teeth seemed deafening despite the cacophony of the funhouse. It wasn't a sound one expected to hear in there, and the one time it had happened before, the Gentleman had come to scare the perv away. The Gentleman didn't come this time.

To her mortification, she found herself curious what would happen if he did, if the being that had acted as her informal bodyguard were to walk around the corner and witness the Creature pulling the zipper down between her breasts to her navel. The latex clung to her skin, but physics was physics and the material was skintight. Without the zipper holding the two sides together, the strain eventually parted the suit between her breasts, exposing the heart tattoo and a portion of the mourning corset.

The Creature pulled the zipper down farther, to the partial mandala then past the piece of fabric that was the only thing protecting her from zippering and unzippering over sensitive places. He insinuated the hand rubbing over her between the open latex and pushed the fabric away, leaving her completely bare in a thin triangle from neck to cunt, her breasts just holding the latex on and only his hand covering her folds.

If people couldn't see him, they'd be able to see her folds without his hand visibly in the way, which moved the two of them beyond sexy and into the realm of indecent.

"Trust me," he whispered.

More shrieks from the corridor, a warning. And he was still fingering her for the world to see. He had to remember how she was when he first encountered her. She didn't *want* to be seen like this, didn't want to be blamed for it. Yet her cunt grasped at nothing in a silent plea.

As the new mass of guests rounded the corner—a good dozen people crammed into the thin hallway—he grew hard between all four of her legs. Her secondary set had no shame, spreading higher and wider as the bindings allowed in reaction to the press of his thick cock against her. Their unique angle enabled her to clasp his waist with her knees. If they'd been free, she would have been able to wrap them around him, holding him flush against her while her prime set parted for him. But the bindings kept her anchored.

And God, the people were coming closer, laughing and pushing each other into the walls as the Creature brought his cock to her folds, still keeping her arousal urgent, his thumb massaging her clit under the hood and his mouth making love to her neck.

Her body didn't care at this point whether she was panicking or aroused or both. If anything, her brain seemed to be treating pleasure as a panic attack, ramping its intensity up with disquieting speed.

The visitors were coming, and she was this close to doing the same, with just the head of his cock slickening itself at her entrance and his tongue against her pulse.

As the web rocked forward, the motion pushed the Creature into her.

Elizabeth arched, her cry of pleasure roughening into a scream once she faced the visitors, local college boys from wherever the circus had put down roots. The Creature thrust into her, slow but powerful. She fought against her bonds to conceal the motion, even as she moved her body to take him in at the same rhythm, shook her head against the first signs of impending orgasm.

Most of the college boys had recoiled at her scream, surprised exactly like they should have been and moving on without interest.

But two of them didn't.

Through their pupil-dilating fear, something just as primal distracted them from her claws and teeth, from the spider legs and spiderweb. Their eyes glazed as her latex slipped just a little bit more, catching on her nipples, showing a considerable amount of cleavage and tattoo ink. The boy on the right's jaw seemed to unhinge, his mouth a dark hole, as he regressed back to the caveman that seemed to reside within every man — or else Elizabeth had always been good at bringing it out of them.

The Creature moved his lips to just below her ear, a place that, if properly stimulated, could render her a wordless puddle of melted lust — a place Dez had often wielded to quell any reservations. She didn't think she could clench more strongly around the Creature's cock, but his kiss and the boys' slack-jawed entrancement certainly challenged her to try.

At least the boys didn't try to touch her the way some of the others did, nor did they grab at their crotches as though the darkness would forgive them. They just stared, almost drooling, as she tried to play the part of the Spider Woman and hide the fact that a monster was inside her, stroking her into an orgasm that swelled and released like the flow and ebb of waves. Just when she thought it was over, he shoved into her again, stroking over the spot that sparked like licking a battery and which kept her coming, over and over and over again in an impossible loop.

She screamed with all the ugliness she had inside of her, shrieked so hard that the two boys had to cover their ears. She clawed at them with her free hands, kicked and struggled against the bindings with renewed fervor, anything to conceal what was happening to her, but also to try to outrun the pleasure, outrun the Creature, though they were both bound — her to Bell's web and him by her.

The latex couldn't hold. The sides of her bodysuit snapped past her breasts.

The boys lowered their hands from their ears, as though being able to hear would help them see her better. The ones who had started down the hall but had been waiting for their buddies now wandered back to her, hypnotized. The collection of them looked like nothing more than zombies, with her as the main course.

This time, one of them reached out to touch her.

"Yowch!" He jerked his arm against his T-shirt. Two sets of claw marks appeared, blood welling into the tracks. One of the tracks, the shallower set over his hand, came from her. The other set were deeper and across his forearm.

The Creature had stilled inside her, his growl low and steady against her shoulder. His claws held little shreds of skin underneath. But given the frantic direction of the boy's gaze, the Creature still hadn't made himself seen.

"How'd you...?" Confusion shifted into wariness. Eyes wide from desire narrowed in suspicion.

Well, it *was* a haunted funhouse.

Now the boys showed definite signs of being freaked out, though still enraptured by the sight of real breasts. In full latex, she could have been animatronic, but the very real way her breasts moved and the glimpse of her tattoos reminded them that there was a human being underneath the shine — or at least a body. Who knew how much 'human' made it through their brains?

She needed some serious bodily autonomy here if guests were going to start thinking they could touch her. She would bet none of them tried to touch the freaks in Oddity Row like this, but somehow she was open season because it was dark and secluded?

If Bell heard her thoughts, he still didn't release her from her spiderweb.

This time, however, the Gentleman came around the bend. With preternatural silence, he crept through the corridor, reached for the boys with his unnaturally long fingers.

Not a lot of things could convince boys their age away from free boobs, but a faceless monster grasping for their heads was one of them. The Gentleman chased them with his slow stride around the next corner.

The Creature kissed her in that place under her ear as the Gentleman made his way back.

She still wasn't able to speak, and it wouldn't have been kind if she had. *Trust me, my ass.*

Whether she melted under the Creature's kiss or not was irrelevant. Now the Gentleman could see what the boys had seen. No eyes or not, the Gentleman could clearly see, because he tilted his white, skeletal, alien, faceless head in a universal gesture of male appreciation. He didn't appear to show any other pointedly male signs of appreciation, but she tensed against and around the Creature as the Gentleman brought the sides of her bodysuit in to cover her breasts again.

He didn't linger, except in his natural slow-moving way, as though every part of him needed to catch up to his brain's commands.

The Creature licked her racing pulse. "I know what you must believe of me, my demonstrative woman. But they could not see where I touch you now, where I enter you. I promise you, little Spider."

Elizabeth shook her head.

"Do you want me to stop?" He ran his teeth over her scalp in a feral caress, used the base of her neck to find a grip as he thrust into her.

She shuddered, wrapping her fingers around the rope web again. One stroke after another, inside and out, made the rigid pole of her spine ease and her body welcoming to him again.

He drank from her as he came with his teeth in her skin like a vampire, though he didn't break through. In the warmth that followed and the sudden release of her fear, she couldn't help but writhe in the bindings, grinding back against his cock and into his palm. There was nowhere he wasn't, and he angled his cock to bring the sparks behind her eyelids again. She bore down as though to lock him inside her. Her orgasm made his fingers even slicker over her clit as he finished her off.

"I'm sorry," he gasped as soon as he parted his teeth from her neck. "I thought I could control it, but so close to you, it is so easy to just breathe in…"

Elizabeth reached behind her with her secondary hand and brushed her palm over his hip. She was more irritated by the boys seeing her when she didn't want to be seen than she was by an accidental reprieve in her anxiety. He didn't drink it all, not even close, and he'd stopped as soon as he realized he was doing it. Getting her gawked at was the betrayal, but she couldn't explain that while she was still a spider in Bell's web.

Her post-orgasm tension didn't go unnoticed. He withdrew his fingers from her clit and his cock from her cunt then replaced the flap of fabric, as though that would adequately absorb anything coming out of her. Walking in her latex was going to be a special kind of uncomfortable. Everything zipped up as though nothing had happened, but she knew it had. The Gentleman knew. The boys knew and would remember.

The Creature tasted his fingers over her shoulder but took no relish in the act. "I thought I could ease your fears without drinking them. But it seems I cannot ease them through the feed, nor by giving you the respite from it that you ask for. I don't understand, Spider. I don't understand what you want of me — why you call for me, burn for me, then turn cold as a north wind while still against my body. I am not ignorant of human ways, yet you are incomprehensible to me."

She closed her eyes and turned her face from his. He ran his thumb over her jaw.

"Do you call for me at all?" he asked, almost too quietly for her to hear.

When she didn't respond, he crawled back up to the ceiling. The warmth he'd left behind in her body cooled, though her face flushed in shame long after his wings had passed out of view.

Chapter Nine

As soon as the web released her, she went straight to her RV and cleaned herself of sweat, cum and the memory of gazes crawling over her. She hung the latex outside her door. Either Kitty or Lady Sasha would have it like new for her by the next morning. Elizabeth didn't know who did it, and she didn't care.

All that mattered was the bottle of whiskey left for her on the counter, like it always was.

She was a fifth of the way through before the thought hit her.

What the hell am I doing?

It was a question that encompassed a number of her problems and didn't even get into what other people were doing to her.

She'd *agreed*. She hadn't signed up for being ogled while doing it, but she'd agreed to web sex with her latex bodysuit half falling off. She'd agreed to let him touch her, kiss her, fuck her, without having adrenaline and desperation to blame for it. She'd felt *guilty* that her ambivalence in the aftermath wounded his feelings. And the truth was, he really did seem to have them.

Then there was the drinking itself. She usually didn't start before accompanying the prisoners to their semi-trailer to help them lick their wounds, figuratively speaking. She wouldn't be much use to them like this, but that didn't stop her from taking another two pulls from the bottle. She'd betrayed them anyway by accepting the Creature the way she had—in public, without fear to blame. She'd compromised for comfort, exactly what she'd said she wouldn't do.

No more hangovers, but she could still get plenty shitfaced. Ever since Bell had given her license to do so—no babies to wake her up in the middle of the night, no early mornings to get the children ready for homeschooling, in which she'd have to thoroughly participate without looking trashed—she'd been drunk most nights. Full-on sea-legs drunk, which she hadn't been since entering back into the Petrosian fold.

Only getting drunk wasn't helping anything. Add an unhealthy dose of conscience to the whiskey, and she had a perfect storm of dark thoughts floating around her head.

She groped around next to the couch for one of the empty bottles. Grasping it by its neck, she struck it against a handy corner. She didn't bother worrying about glass. There were so many bottles by now, she wasn't walking barefoot over that area any time soon anyway. Glass in her feet wouldn't matter anyway.

She brought the broken neck to her arm.

"Come on," she said into her quiet little home. "Are you telling me no one's ever tried this before? No one ever thought, 'Hey, I'd rather be dead than your psycho art project'?"

"Isn't suicide against your code?"

"So you do watch us. Nothing better to do than watch the dancing bears and laugh your fucking head off." The tip of the broken glass pressed against her wrist, just above where the ink began. She'd never done this before. Some vague memory told her that going across the wrist wasn't the most effective way, but it's not like she could look up YouTube videos on the subject.

"I have plenty better to do — namely, a circus performance. But I know when my people are planning a dramatic exit that I haven't approved. You don't think I'd leave such an escape hatch open, do you, my dear? Do you really think death gets in my way?"

"You telling me you can bring me back from the dead?" She dented her skin until the strange curved beauty of the glass pierced through.

"I'm telling you I can keep you from bleeding."

The single drop that had welled up, thick and dark, sank back into her body.

"And I can take away the weapon."

In the span of a blink, the broken neck had become a whole bottle once more, as though she hadn't broken it at all. She dropped it among the other bottles, but it didn't shatter again.

Elizabeth covered her face with her hands, tears seeping through the cracks between her fingers.

"If I need to take the drink away, I will. I only tolerate your desire for oblivion inasmuch as the oblivion is temporary. You're no use to me dead."

"Just go to hell, you son of a bitch."

"I never wished this for you, Lizzie."

"You know what you can do with your wishes," she muttered back thickly before downing another swallow from her mostly full bottle.

Somewhere between liquor and tears, she had the idea that she should probably take a shower. The bathroom accommodations were surprisingly spacious in an RV that barely had a kitchen sink. There was enough room for all of her limbs to turn around in the stall without catching and enough room for her secondary legs to hang over the sides of the toilet, though she was pretty sure most RVs this size were supposed to have airplane-type facilities.

She resented that she could find anything to like about her situation, but a good bathroom was something a woman appreciated. And hot water was a blessing, even if it came from the devil. She didn't come out more sober, but she came out more clean.

Once she'd pulled on her oversized robe, she felt a little better. Hungry, but being clean and letting her skin breathe did wonders.

The audience would still be in the big top tent. Not that they usually wandered in the direction of the caravan, but a girl couldn't be too careful about being mostly naked under something that could be undone with a simple sash. She staggered out of her RV. She considered bringing along her whiskey, but if she was going to work a needle and thread, the prisoners didn't need her tipsier than she already was. She could get drunk as piss when she returned.

Hank opened the trailer door when she knocked. He'd been given the crazed chainsaw role this weekend, which meant he was physically unharmed, and his psyche didn't appear to have scarred in response to lopping off limbs a few hundred times. It was probably easier for a person to accept doing that when they knew no one would die.

"Jesus, Spider Woman, you smell like a brewery."

"Suck it and gag, Hank. Let me in." Talking like an inebriated sailor seemed to be the password for the night, because he offered his hand to steady her against the pitching of the Earth's axis as she climbed up.

"Good thing you aren't sewing me up tonight," Hank said. "Don't walk into the cut-open person. They usually don't like that."

"The world's a little off, but if I had only two legs I'd be able to walk in a straight line. Shut the fuck up and stop helping."

Elizabeth used the air holes along the side of the compartment to work her way around the bloody vomit that tended to accompany prisoners with organ damage. Nothing else to be done for them, but the small triage center for the rest had already been set up at the far end of the trailer. They didn't need her sewing skills to be perfect, just a decent suture to get them through the night.

Bell provided them with the basics to bind and cover anything that seeped. No antibiotics or hydrogen peroxide, a corollary to Bell's no-disease promise — in the prisoners' case, no cross-contamination, no matter how many open wounds swapped fluids. The only disease the prisoners could suffer was the necrotizing fasciitis from the post-contagion tableau, but it wouldn't kill them. Like Bell had said, the prisoners weren't any use to him dead.

Kevin was one of the unfortunate souls from that particular tableau this time. One of the few female prisoners who wasn't Blondie — Elizabeth wasn't even sure if that was her real name or whether people just called her that because they didn't know her name either, and she couldn't exactly talk or even write — was blotting the suppurating flesh at his shoulder while he applied some cooling ointment on the back of one of the whipping boys.

Kevin's nostrils flared as she sat down next to him. "Don't suppose you have any of that to share."

"As a nanny, I encourage the practice of mindful sharing, but anyone who tries to share my liquor ends up losing a few fingers," Elizabeth said, pulling on a pair of white latex gloves.

Despite Hank's sour disposition, he still sat down next to one of the whipping boys and started tending to him — in the hopes they'd be more likely to do the same in the future, no doubt. "I thought you were in some kind of cult. Don't cults usually have rules about things like drinking?"

"Yeah, they do. They have rules about tattoos, too. And profanity. And excessive nakedness."

"You still don't belong here, but I'm starting to like you, Spider Lady," Hank replied.

"That gives me a special warmth in my chest that has nothing to do with heartburn, I'm sure."

"And fuck you, too."

"He doesn't let us have alcohol anyway," Kevin said wistfully. "Guess he figures it would take the edge off."

"Or make us more belligerent," Hank said. Elizabeth was just impressed he knew such a multisyllabic word. "Either way, we don't get to go by the booths for ale or beer or whatever they're offering for wine these days."

"I think, depending on the venue, they sometimes have cocktails, too," Elizabeth said.

"Fruity," Hank muttered.

Elizabeth rolled her eyes. "Yes, we all know you're an asshole. Do you have to try to convince us all the time?"

"Do you have to always convince us you're a cunt?"

"At least I'm helpful."

"I'm right here helping, too."

Elizabeth settled with two of the contagion victims, using the same cooling ointment as Kevin. It would ease the pain, at least for a little while. Then she dried the poor boys' backs and covered them with gauze.

Everyone worked quietly, sobered by the day, and every last one of them tired of screaming. It wasn't as though anyone had a radio or something they could listen to, nothing to distract or entertain but a few magazines and books. And God only knew if Bell rotated those things out or whether they had to suffer the same literature over and over during the full sentence.

Most everyone had their wounds tended to by the time three golems arrived with dinner. They were accustomed to bringing hers along as well with whatever the prisoners received — at least for those who could eat without food emptying into their abdominal cavity, and Blondie could only drink a chocolate protein shake with the aid of a straw. Bell granted the rest of the prisoners a good deal more than just bread and water, sometimes even pizza or sub sandwiches, but most of them only ate by force of habit. They didn't get fed all day and being tortured took a lot out of them, but also it didn't do much for their appetite.

Because of her specialized diet and because Bell cared to indulge it, the golems usually brought her a wrap or sandwich and a ginger ale. Hank gave his usual sour expression at the favor shown her, but hummus, avocado, spinach, beansprouts, tofu and vegan cheese weren't much more appetizing to him than what the golems offered. It tacked one more reason to hate her onto his shit list, but at this point, he seemed to enjoy

Spider

hating her. As long as he didn't get fresh with her again, Elizabeth was content to keep pissing him off.

Eating took away what tipsiness still lasted after tending to people's wounds. As soon as they finished with their respective dinners, the prisoners retired one by one to their pods. The general rule was top row for those who could climb, bottom row for those who couldn't, and middle row for those mobile but not hale and hearty enough for more than the shorter climb.

Kevin was one of the latter, but he crawled into an unused bottom pod. He winced as he tried to lie down.

"You okay?" Elizabeth asked as she packed up the leftover gauze, ointment and thread. She was used to organizational tasks like this — not much different than picking up toys at the end of the day. "Sorry, bad question. You just seem to be flinching more than usual."

"Disease kind of reached a sensitive area," Kevin said.

Due to the effect of the sex demons, the prisoners had a few of their own self-imposed rules. Elizabeth was sure the few girls got propositioned when she wasn't there, if the boys felt strong enough for sex. But the prisoners, like the rest of the circus, were held to the same standard that demanded absolute agreement from both parties. The matter was especially touchy among the prisoners, though, considering the reason most of them were in Arcanium was because they'd broken that rule.

Apparently, they'd spent the early months avoiding anyone else's touch and suffering too much alone, but for everyone's sake, they'd eventually agreed to conditional contact when it was in the realm of amateur nursing. And such tending sometimes required a certain amount of nakedness. Only the prisoners who had been the subject of multiple amputations and medical experimentation were allowed to be completely naked, since clothes could be painful and they weren't in any state to become aroused.

The pods didn't offer much in the way of privacy, and Bell didn't provide blankets, but when they were on their own, everyone was expected to keep their clothes on so no one would feel threatened or tempted, even in the dark. Stripping down to underwear was permitted. Beyond that, if no one else was willing to tend to certain areas and the person couldn't tend to it themselves, it was just another tough break from Bell's box o' torture.

Elizabeth slid over to the edge of his pod. "If it's nothing prurient, I can still take care of it, if you need."

"It hasn't reached *that* far. But it's close." He winced again with the certainty that it was just a matter of time. "If you have any more of that cooling ointment nearby, I wouldn't say no."

Elizabeth crawled back to the first-aid pile then brought a pot of ointment and a soft washcloth over to him. The line of his sight was pretty obvious to her, although he darted his gaze away as soon as he realized he was looking down her robe and that she could see him doing it.

She settled on the edge of his pod again, adjusting her robe. Her cheeks burned almost as much as his, and she didn't have a fever to blame. Bell still hadn't provided her with everyday clothes for her new body, and she wasn't going to wear leather or lace in the semi-trailer after spending the entire day in latex. It was bad enough everyone in the compartment knew she wasn't wearing anything underneath the robe.

Kevin couldn't quite meet her eyes. "Thanks."

There was something terribly innocent about him. Elizabeth understood how deceptive that was, because he was in Arcanium at all. But the way he avoided looking at her and the way he shifted reminded her of simpler times before she'd run away from the Petrosian Church, when 'courting' had actually been a thing that boys did, with the shy gallantry of someone who *really* wanted church-approved, post-marital sex with someone.

Oh, those boys had probably wanted more, but sex had featured either first or quite high on the list at that age. And although it hadn't been demure to admit as a woman of the church, it had been quite high on her list as well. Dez hadn't needed to work too hard to get her into bed. Once she'd made the conscious decision to discard sacred laws, there had been nothing to stop her from satisfying the urges that had dirtied her thoughts for so long.

Innocence, even the semblance of innocence, wasn't something she'd thought about in a long time. To have that sort of innocence — not necessarily lack of sin but a lack of experience or confidence in that experience — endeared him to her in spite of her wariness.

When her four legs shifted under the robe, parting it slightly, he glanced down to catch the sight before once again looking away.

Elizabeth fingered the edge of the thick terrycloth, then slid it back to expose two of her legs. The light from the pod hit the tattoos just right to bring out the vivid intensity with which Bell had imbued them.

Kevin swallowed thickly, but he still made every effort to avoid peering too closely. "You may want to turn around. I don't have to go full commando, but I'm going to have to push down the waistband."

Elizabeth ducked her head, smiling a little, but she turned around, wrapping her prime arms around her prime legs and letting the secondary legs splay in front of her. She had more grace these days, learning from Bell positioning and maneuvering, but there were still angles and positions where she had to relinquish elegance. Sitting on the ground or near the ground was one of them.

The sound of Kevin pushing his boxer shorts down seemed unnaturally loud in the close quarters of the pod. At his hiss, she reacted before she could stop herself — or maybe she just told herself that.

There was nothing to see, not really. Not directly. The deep patch of necrosis had dug into his hip right along the line between his abdomen and leg. But the angle of his thin shorts revealed a dusting of hair, and the outline of his cock was plain to see from the way the fabric bunched on either side.

She didn't know why she'd care about his cock when there was a patch of necrotic flesh right in front of her. On the same note, she didn't know why he'd be so self-conscious when there was a patch of necrotic flesh this close to eating his junk. Maybe both of them had become inured to the horror. After all, he was looking at her tangle of legs without being thrown by the fact there were four.

In such close quarters, the prisoners were accustomed to bare skin, disease and despair, sex arising from sheer desperation, but not with outsiders. And though they'd let her in, she was still one of those outsiders, if not necessarily one of Bell's people. Prisoners didn't ask non-prisoners to meet their desires when those desires had damned them in the first place.

For a while Kevin tried to keep his composure. He used the soft washcloth to dab ointment over the slowly disintegrating flesh, sighing as the coolness gave him temporary relief.

But she could tell he sensed her attention, because his movements slowed in distraction, and his cock steadily responded to her, to the rasp of her thighs moving over each other, the whisper of her robe on her skin. And when he glanced up, she could imagine what he saw. The parting top half of her robe would show almost as much as the open bodysuit, and though she kept her legs closed, she slid the bottom half of the robe back farther.

He opened his mouth to say something. He wanted to ask her. She recognized desperation as well as she recognized desire. How long had it been for him? Had any of the women in the compartment ever offered? She couldn't see why not, unless they knew something she didn't. He was sweet, slender but cute. *Cute*. That wasn't the adjective she'd use to describe the men who'd had her. Dez didn't do cute. The Creature didn't do cute. Bell certainly didn't do cute.

She wasn't the woman for this. She was older — not quite cougar territory, or at least she hoped not. But she didn't do cute either. Cute was what she could have had if she'd stayed in the Petrosian Church, if she hadn't practically tattooed a giant, scarlet 'A' over the anatomical heart on her chest. Sweet was what most of the boys in the youth group had been.

She was neither cute nor sweet nor young.

Her stomach churned as she rested her prime hand on his thigh near the edge of his shorts. She eased herself deeper into the pod. There was nowhere for Kevin to retreat, but he showed no sign of wanting to.

Now the more obvious indication of his interest caught her eye. There was no denying the bulge that twitched against the thin fabric every time she moved, when she delved her fingers just under the leg of his shorts. He didn't grow with the speed of the Creature, but he certainly grew quickly.

He swallowed, his Adam's apple bobbing.

She avoided the patch of disease on his hip and trailed her fingers along the fabric to where his erection curved upward along his uninfected hip.

"Oh God." His breath hitched at the sensation of her fingernails running along the length of the erection. His head fell back when she closed her hand around it through his shorts.

Her vision went cloudy before she realized that, while he was breathing hard and fast already, she wasn't breathing at all. She abruptly let go of him and brought her hand to her forehead, as though she could hold herself upright that way. Her skin was hot to the touch, her cheeks flaming.

It wasn't like this was her first time by any stretch of the imagination, but something was off about what she was doing, and she couldn't figure out why. It wasn't the lesions or the people milling about the pods around them, the light on that meant anyone passing by could see. For some reason, it wasn't that. Was it him? Was it her?

"Hey, hey, it's okay. It's okay." Kevin stroked her head as though she were a kitten. He'd probably never petted a bald woman before and didn't know how to touch it or react to what it felt like. She'd been there before. When she'd had hair, men had pulled it like reins. After she'd shaved the hair off, they'd touched her bare scalp like it was a Fabergé egg. "You don't have to… But…*please*, God, this place doesn't make it easy, and I… *Please.*"

He took her hand. He didn't grab or yank, just guided it slowly to his cock again, giving her time to withdraw if she chose. But she didn't.

"Whatever the spells are, they require contact with another person. You can rub yourself off all you want, but that doesn't make it any better. And it doesn't matter what Bell's done to us. When that damn succubus starts sending her magic out…with no relief in sight… Just another way to torture us."

She cupped him when he urged her. He fell quiet again, his hips twitching and chest heaving as he tried to control himself. But he covered her hand with his, tightened her grip.

"Is that what I am to you?" she asked. "Convenient?"

"You're a fucking hot woman is what you are, Elizabeth. And I like you."

He continued to harden in her palm. She started to pump him like that, with his shorts tightening and bunching against the head. His pre-cum dampened the fabric.

"Is that what I am?" She shrugged one side of her robe off her right shoulder, freeing her right secondary arm as well as exposing her breast to him. What the hell. She'd already done that to perfect strangers today.

"Oh God."

She pulled the waistband of his shorts down. Kevin braced himself on the pallet as she cupped his scrotum with her secondary hand while she spat and licked her prime palm. He looked chafed, but she could probably jerk him off with sandpaper and he'd still choke back a groan like he did when she took his cock in both right hands.

He groaned more loudly when she squeezed him harder while bringing herself even closer. Her extra legs didn't really fit in the pod, but he twisted his hips to give her more room. The next time he stroked her head, it wasn't as tentative, though he stayed delicate.

His sandy brown hair was tousled, his lips pale but wet from wanting her. She leaned in, not quite committing. He strained to kiss her, but she swallowed, her throat clicking with dryness, and turned her head at the last moment. His kiss was needy and left a smear on her cheek.

"Did I…" He bucked in her hand with a gasp. "Fuck, you're good at that. I didn't expect you to be this good."

"You were expecting something?" This time she didn't withdraw when he pressed his lips to the corner of her mouth, his breath like a burst of air from a furnace.

"What do *you* expect? I just told you you're really hot. And I think you know it. Damn, I want to come so bad, but I didn't want to come this quickly. It's been building—"

"How long?" She brushed her lips against his cheek, flicked her tongue against his ear. His cock jumped in her hand with every little thing she did.

"Haven't been tallying up the days or anything, but not since before you were here. *Fuck*." He found her anatomical heart, slid his hand down to her breast, squeezing hard. She'd never understood why men did that, squeeze rather than knead, but it didn't bother her. She wouldn't have exposed herself if she hadn't been willing to let him touch. Dizziness had her leaning her forehead against his. Her breathing was too shallow, but at least she *was* breathing.

Her stomach lurched. She coughed, ducking back and flushing, cold and hot behind her cheeks. Her strokes over him stilled.

This time he jerked her chin over to him and kissed her hard, less like a shy boy and more like a man. She opened for him immediately, his groans muffled inside her. He thrust into her firmer grip.

She spared him no mercy, her prime hand a relentless blur while her secondary hand held him steady, squeezing in little pulses at the base.

Cum struck his abdomen then ran in rivulets down her hands. He still kissed her, but more gently, easing back from the bruising crush of his eagerness. She slowed her strokes until he couldn't cum anymore.

She released him, hovered her filthy hands over him, uncertain.

"Sorry. Sorry, I was just..." Kevin shook his head, laughing a little. "I was just so close. I couldn't stop."

She didn't want to use her robe to wipe her hands. The only thing in the pod she could use was the cloth with which he'd soothed his lesion. Elizabeth shivered. It was one thing to play nurse with latex gloves, but it was another entirely to put her bare hand so near a gaping wound seething with bacterial infection. And it wasn't just his hip. His shoulder, parts of his arms, legs, neck, the early boils in the corner of his eye... In the contagion room of the funhouse, his skin peeled off and melted like wax to join with the skin of the other infected. All of that sloughed off when their evening was through, leaving the gaping wounds, but he'd *touched* the others. Their disease was all over him.

She knew the infection wasn't contagious. But now that the urge to let him take her had passed with his completion, her fears returned, just as they did when she was with the Creature. Except when the Creature was there with her, he made her feel safe in spite of her fear, whether the feeling was artificial or not.

Kevin wasn't the Creature. He wasn't even Bell. He was a twenty-something young man who was tortured, desperate, victimized and briefly in the grasp of rare satisfaction. Control wasn't always high on a young man's abilities, especially with the influence of sex magic and enforced celibacy. Her extreme ambivalence tested even the Creature's patience. She was the very definition of mixed signals, so she didn't blame Kevin for bringing her closer when she'd tried to retreat. But she suddenly didn't feel safe—not in that trailer, not with herself.

Elizabeth carefully folded the washcloth so the damp side was covered and used the dry side to wipe her hands. If she insulted Kevin by the thoroughness with which she scrubbed all traces of him off her fingers, he didn't show it. Instead, her tattoos appeared to fascinate him, distracting him from her nervousness. He stared over every detail of the bees and the honeycomb, Troy's intricate spider web lace over her secondary arm.

As she scooted back toward the opening of the pod, he curled his fingers in her robe. "Come on. You don't need to go yet. I know that was a little fast, but I promise I can make it up to you."

She eased her robe back over her shoulder, though the front gaped open enough to show most of her tits and the mourning corset. When his diseased arm brushed the terrycloth, she flinched, but he didn't push her robe open or grab at her breast again, just caressed her jaw with his thumb and kissed her chin, her lips.

There was the glimpse of the man he could be — more patient, more eager to please. She met his tongue with hers, angled her head and slipped into his mouth to make him shiver like her — although she doubted it was for the same reason. When she pulled back, sure enough, his softened cock was already stiffening again.

"Doesn't matter what the funhouse does to us. Unless we're the doll — and the less said about that, the better — it's easy to get hard when the temptation's right. Stay a little longer."

He didn't push the robe from her breasts, but he nudged it aside from her legs, fingering Dez's spiderweb along her right thigh before hooking his grip under her knee. "God, you're beautiful. Your robe hides most of the tattoos, but they're amazing. And you're amazing with them. Stay."

He kissed her again — or she kissed him again. She was too confused to tell which. Only that she guided him with her hand in his hair, the light stubble on his chin scratching her face, and she parted her two sets of legs over his thigh as she kissed him down onto the thin pallet. One of her knees pressed against his scrotum, and he canted his hips up toward her as she stretched her legs alongside his.

His hiss of pain jolted her from what she was doing. Her head was dizzy and light again, unpleasantly so, as though she were under the influence of something that compelled her do these things that made him feel good, made her feel good, made her feel sick.

It didn't matter that Bell made everything sterile. Somehow, she understood that even if that weren't the case, she'd still be all over Kevin, needing him more than she wanted him, and that terrified her as much as the bacteria festering in the wound just a few inches below her cunt.

The moment she lowered herself enough for her folds to brush against one of the deep lesions on his leg, fear finally overtook arousal.

She shuddered all over, shook her head violently as she crawled back. The sight of her must have been exceptionally ungraceful, but she couldn't breathe in that little pod. She gasped in the scent of ointment, talcumed gloves, cheap soap, the fresh cold air coming in through the air holes.

Kevin's forehead furrowed as he followed her out, his cock jutting out from the crinkle of hair at the base. "Wait. What's wrong?"

"I'm sorry. I shouldn't have done that. I should go." Her skin crawled as though Bell had put spiders underneath the robe, which now had to be washed or burned or something—which she should probably do to herself as well at this point. Maybe the fire-eater would be so kind…

He reached for her, rubbed her hips soothingly through the terrycloth. "Hey, it's okay. I don't know what spooked you, but it's okay. Is it the wounds? We kind of stop seeing them after a while, and they're not dangerous. You're safer here than anywhere else in the world."

Kevin drew her closer to the pod, lowered himself to the floor on his knees to gaze up at her. When she met his eyes, he leaned forward and kissed her thigh above the inked spider, then ran the tip of his tongue up the thread of silk toward the spiderweb. "Please, I can make it good for you, too. Please don't go."

"Keep it down out there," someone called from a dark pod.

Elizabeth used her secondary legs to brace herself as she crouched in front of him. "Why are you here?"

He blinked. Hesitated. "What?"

She brought herself close to him, her lips pulled just enough away from her teeth for him to be able to see the filed edges. Maybe that spooked him a little, too, because he leaned back, crawled back into the pod. She followed him in, pursuing him until his hand slipped on the dirty cloth, and he fell back on the mat. She held herself over him on her hands and knees, this time neither kissing nor caressing, although his cock still twitched with arousal. Seemed he liked his women both passive and aggressive.

"What I asked, soldier, is why are you here?"

He licked his lips at the husky sound of her voice, stretched up to meet her lips. For a moment, she let him have her then she shook her head again — more for herself than for him.

"I know why I'm here," she said. "I told you why. I have a general idea why the rest of you are here, but you were cagey when I asked last time. I trusted you had a good reason and didn't push, but now I need to know."

"You know why." Kevin couldn't meet her eyes again, and he couldn't quite hide how it wasn't just because he had better things to look at.

"I know you were naughty. I know you were young, foolish, caught up in the moment. Sounding familiar, Kevin?" She crawled her nails down his chest, visibly denting the skin on the way.

"If I tell you, you'll probably never come back."

She trilled a little purr as his abdominal muscles twitched away from her touch. "It's possible. I might not come back for a while, but if you tell me, there's a

235

much better chance I'll come back at all. But a woman wonders what a boy like you would really miss…good company or a pussy to sink into? Because if you've been playing me, Kevin…"

"No, no, no," he protested quickly. "I like you. I like *you*. Sure, that makes me want you more, but I haven't been playing you. I just… It sounds exactly as bad as it is when I say it out loud. That's why none of us talk about it."

She tapped her nails just above the line of his hip where the disease began. "Start talking."

He swallowed then fell back against the mat with a sigh. He rested his arm on his forehead, shielding his eyes from hers. "The Bearded Lady, Kitty, called one of my friends out for being a dick. So he decides we're all going to go in and fuck with the freaks, because what's the worst thing that could happen, right? Circus folk and gypsies… They're entertaining, but they're weird, and no one likes them enough to let them stay. I mean, Arcanium has fans, but people get a serious case of 'not in my backyard' when a circus like this sticks around, when the freaks mingle where they don't belong."

Kevin briefly raised his arm from his face to add, "I'm not saying that's what I think. Just saying that was my friend's thoughts, and enough of us agreed. Hell, I thought it would be fun, fucking shit up without anyone getting on our case about it. Much beer and coke was had, and we were loaded for bear to do whatever we wanted once we snuck in. Long story short, my friend is very dead, thanks to the Ringmaster, because he doesn't like it when people fuck with his girl, and some of my other friends were eaten by the clowns. The rest of us ended up in the funhouse."

Elizabeth lowered herself until she was kneeling, straddling his legs but not touching anything that might seep onto her. She curled her fingers into loose fists—not to threaten, but to counteract the tension calcifying her spine.

"Yeah, I got most of that from your last confession, Kevin. That's what your little group did. But that's not what I asked."

"We all did different things. Went after different people. My friend and his wingman went after Kitty, of course, but the rest of us weren't picky. Most of the circus people were in the caravan area, their guard down. None of us was boneheaded enough to go after Mikhail, but the rest of the circus was fair game. The fairies who do that aerial act, the chain-smoking tumbler, the conjoined twins, the fortune teller, the high-wire girl with the tits... They all seemed kind of fragile. Nimble, but small, you know? Hit 'em with a two-by-four and you can do whatever you like."

"Charming." If she'd been fighting between arousal and queasiness before, her stomach definitely leaned toward queasy now.

"I told you, that's not necessarily what I was thinking. Truth is, I wasn't thinking much at all. Coke, booze, mob mentality, pheromones... I was fucking high and feeling good. Chris and I went past the caravan toward the carousel, where the peacock girl lives. We thought she was such a cocktease—innocent face, guilty body, that kind of thing, working those levers of hers, corset and tight leather pants. We didn't know there were two guys on the carousel who came to life at night. Still, Chris had a hammer and I had a knife. Knocked the wiry one out cold, and the big one was surprisingly not much of a fighter, even for his girl."

He blew air out in a rush and slid his arm away from his eyes. "If it hadn't been for Bell, we would've lost it on the girl. Caroline. Her name is Caroline. After it was all over and we'd been here a few weeks, I went to her. Riley, the big one, gave me some good bruises for it, but I apologized. Sucky as it is to say, I apologized. I'm a prisoner to make up for things with Bell, but there's no way to make it up to her, and I know that. But I still had to apologize, even if it didn't balance any scales."

Kevin sat up, sliding his legs from under her. She lifted her hips to give him enough room. Somehow, in spite of his confession, he was completely hard again and showed no signs of waning.

"She forgave me," he said. "She told me she knows what it's like to take the whip all the time, because apparently she's this saint who tries to protect children from the clowns, which is weird, because the clowns kind of hang around her a lot... But it's easier to talk about her than about me. So now you know. In here, we get a little cabin-fevered, and the sex demons keep it tense, but we deserve it. I'm not sure if we deserve this much and for so long." He held up his arms, inspecting where the boils had burst around the gaping lesions. "But we deserved Bell."

Elizabeth lowered her head. "I think I need to go now."

Kevin followed her out of the pod, falling once again to his knees and hooking his hands around her primary thighs. "Please, don't. I can take care of you, I promise. It's been over a year since we wished in, which means it's been a lifetime. I'm not that guy anymore. Just please don't go."

Elizabeth laughed without humor. "Honestly, it's not even that. Believe it or not, you're not the worst kind of guy I've had sex with, not by a long shot. I shouldn't have touched you to begin with. Shouldn't have gotten you off."

It complicated everything. But even now, she had to convince herself not to push his face between the sides of her robe and let him eat her like the ex-would-be-rapist that he was. After having her share of men who went all the way, she'd really be moving up in the world.

"But you did. And you seemed to like it. Didn't you? I wasn't just making it up to feel better, right?" Kevin rubbed her flanks, digging his fingers in to massage the knotted muscles.

"Either talk louder and take off the robe or quiet down and go back into the pod," Hank called. "Some of us are trying to sleep, but I'll settle for jerking off."

Kevin's hands fell back to his sides, and he rolled his eyes. "Not the most romantic of venues, I'll give you that. It's okay if you think less of me for what I did. I do." His cock didn't, but he seemed to take his renewed erection as a matter of course.

"I already knew. Now I know better." Elizabeth touched his hair, but it was only comfort for him. She felt like she was stroking him with filth, even if it was filth he'd passed to her. "I really need to go."

She pulled away from him before he could reach for her or protest again, climbed down from the trailer into the night air and empty spaces where she could breathe properly, not that her lungs got the memo. She stumbled around the semi-trailer.

Elizabeth wrenched off the robe. If anyone in the compartment were to peek out through the air holes, they'd see her, but they didn't make a habit of looking out. She used the inside of the robe to wipe her hands, her legs, her head, everywhere she could before she'd used up all of the inside. Wheezing, vision blurry with panicked tears, she threw the robe over the iron fence into the trees on the other side.

Whoever found it would be at no more risk than she was, but she just couldn't stand the idea of what she'd done, what she'd touched, everything Kevin had told her running through her head. She couldn't tell what disgusted her more—what he'd almost done or all the things she had done. She scratched at her skin as though the wolf spider's babies had decided to use her as a playground. In some places, she scratched so hard it drew blood.

She didn't like grass, especially when she was naked, so she crouched against the fence, using her secondary legs to brace herself. Elizabeth rocked against the iron, still scratching at her arms and legs and waiting until the hysteria died down enough for her to walk, shaky-legged and weaving, back to the caravan. If she was going to be this zigzagged, she wanted to have a better reason.

Elizabeth staggered into her RV, vision nearly obscured from the mist of panic.

God, what she wouldn't give for the Creature right there with her now, taking her fear away, taking whatever was broken inside her and patching it with duct tape until the next shattering. She hated that she needed him, that she needed and wanted but shouldn't have done either.

But if the Creature felt her fear, he didn't come to relieve her, and she didn't blame him. Why should he waste his appetite on a woman who didn't want to want him?

She couldn't rest, couldn't linger, couldn't use anything around her to hold her up as her panic spiraled her down. She could *feel* the disease on her skin, felt it brush from her like ash to contaminate everything that was hers. As soon as she calmed down, she'd be taking antibacterial wipes to every accessible surface — and recycling those damn bottles. The part of her left arm with the illustration that looked like torn skin had, ironically, received a good deal of scratches. Her own blood smeared over her from her attempts to quell the phantom itch.

She'd never be clean. Sins unforgiven were like oil, leaving invisible, indelible marks on the body as well as the soul. Bell teased those deficiencies to the surface in Arcanium. They poisoned, sickened everything they touched. She was the spider, the vermin, the infestation — and always had been, with no hope of relief.

Elizabeth took the rest of the whiskey into the shower with her this time.

Chapter Ten

She lay with the huntsmen today—a dozen giant spiders who occasionally jumpstarted her heart whenever they'd move with startling speed over her—amid the handfuls of visitors in the arcane, tourist-trap red tent.

In spite of her continued fear of the mini monsters, she was getting used to it—or at least she wasn't having panic attacks every time after the ceremonial Dumping of Spiders on Elizabeth part of her morning. She guessed even a fear-soaked mind could get used to being confronted with its fears when forced to long enough.

Every day, she had to revisit her terror, and every day, Bell's promise stayed true. The spiders didn't bother her except by existing, and she didn't seem to bother them. They didn't bite. When she moved, they just got out of her way or settled on top of her legs or stomach to avoid being crushed. For mini monsters, they were surprisingly chill. Maybe she was losing her fucking mind, but Goliath even seemed to have something approaching a personality.

That didn't change her urgency to escape at the end of the day when the Creature came for her. He still had to feed upon her to calm her down. But when her hands started wandering over him for reasons other than an anchor, he would break away, the wrinkles in his face deepening, and leave her alone again—alone with the cockroaches, spiders and centipedes.

She began to understand what Kevin had described when he talked about how not having sex could ache. Without the Creature pursuing her, and without her pursuing anyone in return, her sex drive had nowhere to go. She thought she'd be fine. After all, she'd made it ten years without too much of a fuss. But the sex demons made it impossible to push away or deflect, and the boredom of the circus routine made it impossible to distract herself for long.

That didn't mean she let herself touch Kevin again. He kissed her, and sometimes she kissed him. It was all very awkward and frustrating, in more ways than one. But she couldn't convince herself to really touch him, and to his credit, though he tried to convince her, he didn't force the issue. She'd pride herself on her self-restraint, except it didn't take much restraint to retreat from something that made her feel that sick. Also, he'd moved on from the contagion tableau to the hellfire one, which basically had him running around on fire all day. The sheer level of partially healed burns killed the mood, even for him.

But damn it, she didn't know how she was going to handle it when he became the surgeon or the chainsaw serial killer and didn't have suppurating sores standing in his way.

With the sex demons affecting her in spite of herself, the gazes of the guests who passed through her tent made things a different kind of uncomfortable than the spiders.

She'd hated the exhibitionism of what Dez had made her do, and she hated the exhibitionism of what Bell made her do now. That didn't change how she sensed their appreciation of what they saw, their inspection like fingers upon every shadow, curve, concavity and crevice, upon the illustrations with which Dez had branded her. She sensed the moment each of them had with her.

They used her. Passively, yes, but Elizabeth didn't need to be psychic to know what they were thinking, what they conjured to mind in the privacy of their own homes. Most evenings, it was as though she could feel where they touched themselves and how they imagined touching her.

Whiskey helped, but she had to wait for nightfall before she could use it, and it didn't deaden the feelings. She was mindful of Kevin's warning about touching herself, which she'd never liked doing much—one of the few guilty avoidances from the Petrosian Church that had stuck.

She didn't smoke. She didn't masturbate. And she didn't eat anything with a face. As though any of those virtues made up for her vices.

Someone tapped the side of the glass coffin.

Behind closed lids, she rolled her eyes. God, people were all the same. Give them a clear glass box and an animal inside it, and they all had to tap the glass to try to get the animal to move. And did the animal ever move? No. Did that keep someone from trying it every fifteen minutes or so on her coffin or one of the terrariums? Also no.

The person tapped again.

"Unless you're her very convincing twin sister, Lizzie, I'm pretty sure that's you."

Her eyes flew open. She turned her head so fast, the huntsman nested in her hair scurried over her face. The man jumped back from where he'd been crouching close to the glass to speak through the air holes.

"Whoa!" He laughed the way people laugh after a genuine scare that they realize isn't actually dangerous to them. "Hardcore, babe. Never thought I'd see the day you'd put yourself in an enclosed space and cover yourself in spiders. Looks like you really did grow that spine after you left."

Please, Lord, let me be able to talk. I wouldn't ask this man for help if I was drowning and he was a lifeboat.

Even if God didn't hear her, Bell did, and he was the closest thing she had to an answered prayer, because her tongue loosened as soon as she asked. Which meant Bell was listening.

Somehow, that comforted her, but she also had to be careful.

"Hello, Dez."

"It's been a long time."

Ten years had brought her to thirty-four and brought him to forty-two. He still looked good. He was too narcissistic not to take care of himself, and he'd always had smooth skin for his age. But age *had* caught up with him, just as it had with her. The circles under his eyes were deeper than they used to be. There were spots on his shoulders, neck and nose where the sun's effects had surfaced decades after damage Elizabeth had known better than to give herself. Then again, she was pale as a ghost, and Dez's mother was African-American. He'd darkened under the sun. She only burned and had quickly learned to appreciate the shade.

Elizabeth had thought that if she ever saw him again, he'd be somehow diminished, the way she was to herself. He would seem like a little, little man with massive insecurities, and she would wonder why she'd ever fallen for him.

He hadn't diminished.

His tattooed, well-muscled arms meant that most people in the tent gave him a wide berth, side-eyeing the way he talked to the exhibit, but not questioning him. He wasn't like Troy. He'd never sought strange, but he cheerfully intimidated. He covered himself in his art and wore his piercings with the same pride that he wore the giant ugly rings that could rearrange someone's face. He'd once beaten a man who didn't pay him for her services. Blood had caught in phlegmy strings between the gold rings and the man's obliterated nose. No one touched his girl…not for free. He'd been an opportunistic pimp, but he was also an artist, and she and everything she'd done was his art. Clients hadn't come for cheap.

His very presence seemed to dim the entire tent. The places where his shadow touched her dropped ten degrees. The spiders shared her agitation, darting away from the large man on the other side of the glass, several of them hiding near the edge of the wig. She wasn't sure which was worse—her abusive ex or the three huntsman spiders on her neck.

"You been in here the whole time?" Intimidating though Dez was, his smile was a balm, smooth as dark hot chocolate. It changed his whole demeanor to something inviting, something a woman might dream about if she craved a bad boy. The beauty of him was what made him the worst kind of dangerous.

"Yes, Dez. I ran away from you and straight into a coffin of spiders."

"You look good, Lizzie. Really good." He bit his lip in appreciation as he studied her. "You got the work touched up. Was it the same artist who did the ink on those prosthetics, that faggot who posted the pictures of you on this weird circus' website?"

Elizabeth had agreed to Troy posting them on the condition that the rest of her not be visible. They'd been artistic, intentionally obscure and surprisingly good under the dramatic surgical lights. She'd hoped the style of the photos would conceal the extent of her other tattoos, but a few might have gotten through the filter. Dez wouldn't have had to see much. He'd immediately recognize his own style, and he'd remember every inch of her canvas.

"At least he didn't ruin them. Seen what he's done to himself?"

"Of course I've seen it," Elizabeth said.

"How much of it have you seen?" He still smiled, and for some people, that was all they'd see, but his blue eyes had gone cold as ice shards.

"As much as he shows everyone. I'm not yours anymore. I can see as much of other people's tattoos as I want." She carefully sat up, but she had to move her secondary arms and legs as though they were fake. No point in trying to explain to him how she'd grown extra limbs, because there *wasn't* a good explanation.

Dez grabbed the padlock and rattled it against the coffin. She jumped, just like he'd hoped she would.

Then, gripping the lock when it didn't yield to him, he knelt down in front of her platform so they were more level again and he could see her better. His voice came through the air holes as though he were right next to her ear. "Come on, Lizzie. You and I both know you ran back to Daddy, Father and God after you left. Unless your relationship with them was far kinkier than you made it out to be, I'm the only real man you've ever had in your life."

"Do I look like I'm still Petrosian?" she asked. "And you seem to be forgetting all those other men you brought into the bedroom."

"That was still me, Liz. When they had you, it was because of me. And when you came with their cocks in your ass, it was for me." Unlike her, he made no effort to speak quietly.

Most of the guests had already left when it became clear that the large, intimidating man and the Spider Woman were catching up on old times, but those who hadn't suddenly looked up, scandalized. Huffing about complaining to a manager, a woman herded out her three-year-old son, who fortunately wouldn't understand what he'd just heard.

"I guess that's why you got a hundred percent of the profits."

He laughed. "Never knew you wanted a cut, baby. You were too busy scratching my eyes out, then scratching your nails down my back in apology."

She'd hit the side of the coffin herself, but the spiders would freak if she moved that fast and jolted their temporary home like that. She settled for leaning in closer to the air holes. "Still not my only, Dez."

His smile fell away as though he'd taken off a mask. "Who else?"

"None of your business."

He struck the side of the coffin again. This time it wasn't a polite knock. The huntsmen lost their minds, scuttling like little racecars behind her or farther into her wig. She didn't just flinch from the sound of the blow. The coffin had rocked on its pedestal. If he really set his mind to it and pushed it off the pedestal, she wouldn't be able to physically stop herself from crushing spiders beneath her, nor would she be able to protect herself. The spiders hadn't asked for any of this. She was terrified of them, and if they'd invaded her RV, she would have taken a can of Raid and several thousand boots to them, but they'd been forced into the box against their will, too.

"I'm with you." The words were quiet, a thrown voice in a crowd and easy to ignore, but she grasped onto Bell's psychic presence like the edge of a cliff.

Dez's anger also caught the attention of the rest of the guests. In this smartphone age, anyone could take video or call the cops if he got too violent. He flipped them off, but he spoke more softly, stroked the glass instead of striking it.

"Ever since you ran into my arms, you've been mine. Ever since you confided in me, confessed to me, ever since I marked you, you've been mine. I made you. I showed you the world your family never let you see. I gave you the pleasure you craved, fed you until even I couldn't satisfy your appetite alone. I made you a work of art. And I'm the reason whoever's pulling your strings now has strings to pull."

Dez's fingertips left prints on the glass, but he touched it as though he were touching her. Her skin responded despite the memories. Oh, yes, she remembered him weaving his ownership through her, one needle at a time, teaching her body to want him, need him, love him, even as he stripped her mind from her, layer by layer.

"If you're out of that fundamentalist fuck-up your father calls a church, you didn't have to join a circus to get your fix. You know I can give you what you need…and more. People have already figured out you're here. How do you think I found you? I've got people sending me pics, asking whether you're Lucy Lewd, as though the tattoos aren't a dead giveaway. They're asking whether you're available."

"Lucy hasn't posed or performed since I left," Elizabeth said through clenched teeth, hoping no one had overheard her old name. She'd started her so-called career as an anonymous model, but someone had called her that in a forum once, and it had caught on until Dez had given it to her as an official stage name. Elizabeth had always hated it.

"The Internet is forever. We were ahead of our time back then. You're still my bestseller." Dez smiled again, the charmer once more. "None of the new girls hold a candle to you, Lizzie. I'd throw them out in a second if you came back. They don't have the fire. They don't have your innocence or your sincerity. You were always so pure when you got dirty, babe. That's why the camera loved you. Still does, even smartphone cameras at terrible angles and in terrible light. Whatever he's paying you to wear that contraption, ingenious though it is, I'll pay you more."

Elizabeth slid forward in the box. "Dez, baby, you couldn't afford me."

"Oh, you're a tough girl right now, covered in spiders. But I still see the girl you were underneath it. Ten years, and you haven't really changed. I was mad as hell you left me, but if you come back, I'll forgive you. No hard feelings. Well…some hard feelings, but the kind you like. It'd be so easy, picking up where we left off."

As though they weren't in the middle of somewhere vaguely family-friendly, he ran his tongue over the glass. She could practically feel it over her neck.

"I don't know how much clearer I can make this." She brought her mouth close to his, until she could feel his breath through the air holes. "You're *never* going to get your hands on me again."

But her conviction didn't come from genuine resistance. It was much easier to say she wouldn't go with him when she literally couldn't.

She cringed as he stood, suddenly looming, the impressive muscles of his arms bulging as he clenched his fists.

"He has no power here, Elizabeth. You're safe."

"You and I," he said, pointing between them, his gaze as though he could burn through the glass to get to her, "we're not finished yet. I'll buy you out if I have to. Money talks, sweetheart, and I've made enough of it to have a hell of a lot to say. The owner of the circus has got plenty of other beautiful women on his payroll, but he clearly doesn't have any idea what to do with you if this is his idea of drumming up business. Your father might not care what dirt I have on you, but we'll see whether your new boss does. Or maybe he'll want a piece of you—like they all do and always will. But maybe he won't know how to ask nicely, and you'll have no choice but to run again, right back into my arms. Either way, I'm the only one you got, baby. I'll make sure of it."

"Yeah, good luck with that." It was all she could do to sound flippant. Dez knew better. When they'd go out as a couple, she'd trade obscenities with his friends and take their dirty jokes and drink them under the table, but then he'd bring her home, and he'd find his way into the soft meat of her desperation. She was all talk in public. But if no one else were in the tent with them, if the curtains closed, if he had the key to the padlock, how sure was she that she wouldn't beg for him?

But she knew how he thought, too.

If she told him her boss was the devil incarnate, Dez would give the police an anonymous tip about the circus, and cops would be on Bell like white on rice. But Bell wouldn't let something like police officers get in his way, and Elizabeth didn't want any of them making a wish at the wrong time.

If she told him her boss was the one sleeping with her, Dez might try to beat Bell to a bloody pulp. Elizabeth wouldn't bet on Dez in that situation.

As it was, it sounded like he was going the blackmail route — or perhaps the direction of simple commerce.

Dez was a snake. If he could slither in to poach what he wanted, he'd do that before pumping his venom into whoever he saw as his enemy. He'd get her the hard way if he had to, but he'd try the easy ways first.

He came up close against the glass again, holding the front of his jeans for her to remember what was underneath. As though she'd ever forget. "We'll see who wins this battle. I always enjoyed our games, but I always won, Lizzie."

"Except once."

His smile crinkled the corners of his eyes. "Did you win, Liz? Did you really?"

* * * *

"Your fear tastes different tonight."

After his visit to her funhouse spiderweb, the Creature had been as professional as a monster drinking fear from a woman's bare skin could be. He had barely said two words to her since, despite feeding from her daily after the red tent closed. Even that had become just part of the routine, as inevitable and impersonal as the padlock on her glass coffin. She got more closeness from the spiders.

And he certainly hadn't visited her again in the funhouse.

Elizabeth stepped away to lean against the coffin pedestal, crossed both sets of her arms over her torso, holding her shoulders and her hips at the same time. "How does it taste?"

He took a matching step back. "More real. Like the day I visited you in the web."

"Sorry you have to feed on the fake stuff all the time. I'll try to do better, *really* get scared of these things on and around me."

The Creature shook his head. "I don't intend to diminish the fear the spiders give to you. But you're aware that these are not things to fear. Phobias taste quite different from genuine fear, as tears taste different depending on the reason to cry. Your fear tonight... What happened today?"

"It's nothing to worry about. Bell's already aware." She pushed out of the tent, breathing in the cold air laced with the smell of animals and fair food.

Usually, the Creature was the first out of the tent. He followed her now. "Of what is Bell aware?"

She spun around. A month ago, she wouldn't have been able to do that without tripping over at least one of her legs. "Why does it matter to you? It's not like there's a shortage of fear in this place. You could barnacle onto the prisoners' trailer and feed for days, and they probably wouldn't even know. Why do you keep coming to *me*, feeding from *me*?"

"Your fear is richer, purer, its source never-ending. As for the prisoners, I take their scraps, but Bell would rather I not relieve them the way I do with you." He caressed the length of her neck with his claw. "If I do not incite the fear I consume, I'm at best a mere scavenger. With the taste of a feast, how can I content myself again with more meager fare?"

"Then why don't you just incite away? You look that way for a reason." Elizabeth had never considered him unpleasant to look at, but he'd been built to reap his own harvest. If he put half as much effort into that as he put into feeding from her, he'd have as much as he wanted and more.

"The clowns enjoy the kill, but only the Ringmaster seems to take pleasure in pain. Not all evil deals in sadism, and it occurs here less often than you might believe. I don't *like* terrifying victims. I prefer to feed from terror I never caused."

"You got along just fine before Bell brought me here," Elizabeth said. "Why continue to chase me when you don't want anything to do with me?"

He spread his arms, the span as impressive as his wings. Built like an Olympic swimmer, he suddenly seemed so much bigger than her—or rather, she suddenly realized how much bigger than her he was, given intimidation was usually not his first impulse. However, when his face twisted in anger and the predator of him showed through, intimidating was all he could be.

"I want everything to do with you! Not just the fear, Elizabeth, but you. You're the one who wants nothing to do with me, only what I can do *for* you. I am content with the feast as long as you offer. I would be a fool to deny it. And I will not pursue your body again. But would you deny me your welfare as well? Do you want the only thing I know of you to be your fear?"

Elizabeth took another step back. "There's not much more of me than that. That's why you feast so well."

"You think Bell brought you in here because of that fear? I'm sure it amused him at the time, but it doesn't entertain him for long." The Creature lowered his arms and furled his wings back once he seemed to realize he'd been the cause of her retreat. "If he had wanted you frightened, there were far more ways to terrify you than promising your safety time and again. But despite that promise, something scared you in the coffin today, and it wasn't just the spiders you know you shouldn't fear."

There weren't many people in the circus she willingly interacted with. She had the prisoners, and she had the Creature. Bell was psychic and already knew, but she sure as hell wasn't going to talk with him about it. She felt deep down that she shouldn't tell the prisoners, given how they sometimes talked about her, how some of them looked at her.

Besides, who was the Creature going to tell?

"Oh, what the fuck. You already know how screwed up I am."

She kept her prime arms over her chest but let go of her waist. She continued walking away from the red tent but indicated that the Creature could follow. He crunched the brown grass under his feet more loudly than she as he joined her.

"It finally got around to my ex that I was working for Arcanium — or at least that I was a pop-up advertisement for it. If I didn't have any ink, I could just be an anonymous body, but the tattoos are something everyone can see and recognize." She rolled her shoulders, as though she could shrug off the *anima sola* with a little effort. "My ex is the reason people recognize me at all. He, um…"

She kept trying to figure out how to explain who Dez was, but there wasn't a good way to put it, and she didn't want her life before to start and end with Dez alone.

Finally, Elizabeth just started over from a different point in the story.

"I grew up in a cult. When I say 'cult', that doesn't mean it was a bad community to be a part of. It's a branch off Christianity built on the charisma of a self-described prophet, so it fits the definition. And the self-described prophet is my biological father. He's not my dad. My dad is the man who raised me, the man who married my mother. But Thomas raised me in his own way, too, participated in my life the way a person can in a small community. So we call him my father. And in a small, prophet-driven community, that had its own challenges."

"I can imagine."

She didn't know how a fear monster could imagine such a thing, but sometimes people needed to make her think they understood, even if they couldn't. It was a helpless sympathetic gesture. Elizabeth could let them do that much, in spite of her pride.

"I ran away at almost eighteen, as soon as I graduated from high school and they couldn't keep me there. There's only so much a woman can do as a Petrosian saint. You know what you're going to be from the moment you're born. While you wait for marriage and motherhood, you take care of your parents' home or you become a nanny, which is just a wife and mother surrogate. When you're conceived by the prophet's sin, you get even fewer options."

They were approaching the caravan too quickly, and she had no interest in sharing her story with any of the people hanging around there. She banked right to circle the big top, giving it a wide berth just in case anyone in there could hear really well. The Creature followed her lead.

"But the thing about cults... They don't want you to leave, and they make sure it's hell to do so, even if they don't mean to punish you for it. People who leave usually do one of two things. Some get paranoid—of God's wrath, of what they left behind following them— or they crumple under guilt. Others completely lose their minds, doing all the things they aren't allowed to do, things they haven't developed any shields against because the cult *was* the shield. A young girl done with piety is suddenly offered a world of temptations. I was lucky those first few months. I've pickled my liver as it is, but I probably would've overdosed if I'd ever tried certain drugs. Before I could, I stumbled across Dez in his tattoo parlor. Here was a man who could promise to make love to you all night then actually do it. He had stamina, knew how to figure out what made a woman melt then did it as often as possible."

At this point, her face and ears were burning the way only pale skin could. The fact that it was dark outside didn't alleviate any of her embarrassment at how embarrassed she was.

"He'd found himself a girl with no defenses, very little experience with human contact, love or lust, with essentially no friends or family and not much money. Oh, I was working at a restaurant, double-shifts when I could, and had enough to get by. Enough to buy a small tattoo, in fact, the most permanent way I could say 'fuck you' to the saints. I got drunk most nights on cheap shit, wore clothes that showed the most skin, embraced all the kinds of freedom I could afford—until Dez got his hold on me and swept me off my feet. He told me I didn't have to work, because he could take care of us. He bought me good clothes, bought me good booze. He promised he was saving up for the right ring. Sometimes, I didn't leave his bed except to visit the bathroom."

"He did his best to make you fall head over heels in love with him, all while he took away your independence," the Creature said.

"He saw in me a mostly empty vessel. He filled my head and he filled my body." Bile soured the back of her throat, but she'd already peeled off the bandage. No sense in stopping now. "He made it more than a craving. He gave me a goddamn addiction, and he did it on purpose. As soon as he knew he had me, he started to change. He pushed me past the basic vanilla stuff he'd introduced me to, convinced me to go more and more extreme in the name of experience, in the name of my love for him. He somehow convinced me that I couldn't say no, and at that point, I didn't want to. All this time, he was tattooing me, feeding on my discomfort at seeing my fears manifested on my skin.

I'd told him those fears in confidence, and he made them public, inescapable."

She shifted her prime hands over her shoulders, her palms over the straps of the leather bikini. It wasn't a coincidence, Bell doing this to her. He might not be as bad as Dez, but he wasn't much better and he fucking knew it.

"He told me how beautiful I was when I did what he wanted, fed my addiction to make me think I liked it. About that time, he asked me if he could take my picture. He showed me the photography room in the back of his parlor. He showed me where the cameras were in his bedroom, how he had these videos of us. Sometimes he had us masturbate to the videos—first to the sweeter sex, then to the extreme—the kind where he hit me and humiliated me and made me do…things in punishment. Then he started showing me other videos, stuff he and his friends shared with each other, the kind of videos that may or may not have been illegal. But by then, he didn't have to try anymore. Oh, he still told me I was beautiful and that he loved me, but if I did anything less than everything he told me to do, he punished me. And the punishments turned me on, just the way he'd made sure they would. Looking back, I can't believe how *patient* he was. He knew a good victim when he saw her. He wasn't going to threaten that until he knew nothing he did would drive me away."

The Creature's temples twitched from the clenching of his teeth, but the rest of his body telegraphed little of how he felt about her confession.

"He had me, body and soul, by the time I was twenty. The photos got more explicit, though he *was* an artist. He showed me his portfolio, and he had a gallery, did exhibitions. The pictures he took of his women were the fucking best. So he was, on the surface, legitimate. At first, the photographs he took of me were basically boudoir or nudes — artistic love of a woman's body. But he worked his way into posing me in more pornographic images. And in the bedroom, he started bringing in his friends."

She'd never told anyone about this — not her mother, her dad, her father, a therapist…no one. She was getting light-headed, but the Creature didn't interrupt to offer to take the edge off.

Elizabeth wished she had one of those bottles of whiskey right about now.

"Dez's friends were mine, so I knew most of them. They weren't as good in bed, but Dez made sure to keep me stimulated enough that a threesome or moresome didn't freak me out. Eventually, other people's touch was as though Dez was doing it. He'd molded me just right so that I was hooked on him, but the less pure stuff would do just as well in a pinch."

She stopped by the wooden fence that surrounded the elephant and camel enclosure. She didn't think she could walk anymore.

"Then, in addition to pimping me out to his friends, he started accepting money from strangers. He told me they were other models and actors. It took me forever to figure out that they weren't, that all the strangers thought I was this porn actress from the pictures and videos of me that Dez had posted online. They thought I was supplementing my income. And by the time I figured that out, I'd also figured out I couldn't say no to them any more than I could to Dez. As sweet as he could be when seducing me, *conditioning* me, he could do more damage than a volcano when he lost his temper."

The Creature lifted a hand to tuck her hair behind her ear but withdrew when he apparently thought better of the gesture. She didn't think she could stand a man's hand on her skin, which would spark and sing and beg for more. This was *not* the time for that to start.

"I was afraid of him, but still devastated by love for him — the love of someone who had never known good love and couldn't recognize that love shouldn't have felt so poisonous. It took longer than I'd like to admit for what he was doing to me to finally burn through that love. Four years into it, I still thought I was the luckiest woman in the world. But I started to feel suffocated in his small house, same as I'd felt in the church. I started seeking experiences beyond the realm of his influence, like college. I asked him for a more formal acknowledgment of our relationship, like that ring he'd promised me. He denied me. They say artists should never marry their muse. It would have been silly for him to marry his very own personal porn star."

The elephants shambled through the enclosure, eating hay and eyeing their visitors without much interest. The camels were more skittish with the Creature around, but he didn't make any sudden moves.

"I started to fight — not to get out of the life he'd given me, understand, but to just have a few things of my own *in addition* to the way he used me. When he wouldn't let me have that, in spite of everything I did for him, that's when the love started to die. But even when it was dead and buried and I finally understood that not all men made their wives do what he made me do, he still kept me on the hook with sex. I couldn't get enough of it, even though it didn't satisfy as it once did. That just made me need more and more, willing to do worse and worse things in order to get it. He saw me spiraling and took every advantage. I saw myself spiraling and finally realized I needed to get out."

"What did he do?" the Creature asked, with complete certainty that someone like Dez would have done something once his favorite toy started looking to escape the toy box.

"Threatened to send the photographs and videos to the Petrosian Church if I left. He knew I didn't want to crawl back to the church after leaving it in so much disgrace. He promised I'd return not just in disgrace, but I'd probably be outright shunned. It's bad enough being the prophet's love child without also being a whore. I couldn't do that. I couldn't admit to them how badly I'd failed, how low I'd fallen.

"Dez kept me with him with blackmail, hospital visits and sex for another few years before being with him was worse than the idea of going back. I was in the hospital because of things he'd shoved inside my ass and cunt that wouldn't come out, and I was bleeding and screaming in pain every time he'd try. It was already established at the hospital that I was in the extreme porn industry, so to most doctors who didn't look too closely at my charts, it probably looked like a sex experiment gone horribly wrong. And most doctors didn't look too closely back then. To them, I was doing it to myself. But that time, someone came in after the surgery and asked whether there was a problem and whether I needed a way out."

Elizabeth couldn't look at the Creature anymore, couldn't stand to see the reflection of herself in his opaque eyes.

"I was lucky as hell Dez had no interest in binding me to him with a child. He'd had a vasectomy, and I was on birth control for the others. If I'd ever gotten pregnant, I don't know what I would have done. But I'd started over on my own before. I took the chance on an impulse. Ran back to the Petrosian Church. All I know is that Dez didn't follow me or follow through on his threat, because the church took me back and never asked too many questions about the life I'd led outside of the community. All that mattered was that I'd repented. Big prodigal daughter party — as big a party as an ascetic church can throw, anyway. Big potluck, good brownies."

She laughed, surprised by the genuine affection within it.

"No one ever looked at me like a former porn-star-slash-prostitute. I would have known. There's a way people look at you when they know you do sex work. It's not a good look. Men look at you like they can ride that ride whenever they want. Women look at you like a threat. Some of them see 'victim', but God forbid any of those 'victims' try to find more legitimate employment."

Elizabeth shook her head. "I got that from people when I went out with Dez as his hardcore arm candy. But I never got that from the saints. They just thought I was a wild child, back from her unofficial *rumspringa* to embrace virtue after overdosing on vice. They could handle that."

"And you never saw him again?" the Creature asked.

"Maybe he thought I'd come running back to him again when the saints couldn't satisfy my cravings. It was surprisingly easy to kick the sex addiction, though. As long as I did it completely cold turkey, barely even touching myself, I didn't awaken anything. The booze addiction… Well, I got good at hiding that one, because I was still unhappy in the life available to Petrosian women. But being a nanny is better than being a wife, and I loved the kids. I really did. Even Sharona at her bitchiest, I loved her."

Of everything she'd said so far, that was the thing that made her tear up. She was tired of cleaning kohl off her cheeks.

"I thought I was done with him, except for the disease he'd left inside me, mind, body and soul. Then he shows up in the red tent and tells me it isn't over."

Elizabeth squeezed the wooden barrier so hard, it was a wonder she didn't get splinters.

"But Bell knows?" the Creature asked.

"He knows. He says I'm safe." Elizabeth scoffed. "There's a lot of things Dez can do while I'm still 'safe' with Bell. And since Bell's done this to me" —she gestured at her mostly naked body — "using what Dez did to me, how much can I trust him not to use the rest? It's only a matter of time, really, before he puts that tent somewhere he can get away with spiders crawling on my entirely naked body. Where he starts making me stick things up my cunt. Where he does what you did to me in the funhouse, but on a regular basis. He's working up to it, like Dez. He made himself a black widow spider out of a sex addict who's been in this position before. It's just a fucking matter of time."

The Creature's eyes widened when she referenced the funhouse web. "If I had known…"

"Well, you didn't. And I asked for it, didn't I? I wanted it. I still want it. And I don't know how much of that is me or what Dez did to me or what the sex demons are doing, so that just makes everything more confusing. I'd been doing so well. I thought I'd kicked it for good. But Arcanium isn't the best environment for dealing with that kind of craving, is it?"

He shook his head. "I am unique, in that being a part of Arcanium has allowed me to shed rather than contend with the parts of my existence that I don't care for. Before Arcanium, I often had to hunt. I'd leech upon high-crime neighborhoods at night, the closest I could come to the fear of war-torn countries. I didn't want to venture too far from home back then, even for better food."

"Fear, fear, everything is fear with you." she said. "Would you even be here with me if I wasn't the messed-up phobic I am?"

He lowered his eyes, looking away. "It's not all you are, but you wouldn't be who are you if it weren't for your fears, little Spider. Without them, you likely would never have interested Bell enough for him to draw you into his circus, much less caught my attention."

"Dez and I might have visited a place like Arcanium together on a date. Seems like the kind of place he'd take me."

"From what you've told me, he probably would have found a way to bring you to one of the Funhouse events," he mused. "Seems like something he'd have heard about and wanted for you."

"The whats?"

"Arcanium is occasionally invited to private events or conventions. A Funhouse event brings the spirit of the haunted funhouse but the eroticism of the big top and Oddity Row performances. Sasha and Mikhail turn their influence up as high as they can, and our oddities and performers offer more sexual fare, mixed with the usual darkness of Arcanium. We've had only one since you arrived, but demand should pick up soon."

Elizabeth struck the barrier, startling one of the elephants. "Damn it. I knew it. He doesn't want the model. He wants the goddamn porn star. I *knew* he was going to do this. Hell, Dez knew he was going to do it, too. If he's going to play the blackmail card, maybe Bell does owe him for the rights to his whore."

The Creature rested a warm, heavy hand over the one that smarted from hitting the wooden beam. "The Funhouse performances are not compulsory. Some of the oddities do not participate, even ones forced into Arcanium against their will. I certainly don't. That sort of funhouse, horror elements aside, offers me very little."

She swallowed back frustration. "I don't care. The fact he wants me to play that part again, that he chose me because of what Dez did to me…"

"You would be quite a different woman, Elizabeth, if you hadn't suffered. It is as much a part of you as your fear."

"That doesn't mean I have to like it or what it's done to me." She crossed her arms again, but this time in a less defensive way. "If I could amputate what saints and sinners have done to me, I'd be the first to find a knife, even if it made me more unpalatable to you. I'd like to stop feeling like I've taken a bath in a septic tank."

"Is it so distasteful?" The Creature shook his wings out, retreating from the animal enclosure. "As you believe I want one thing from you, does the Spider seek the fly for one purpose alone?"

Elizabeth blinked. She hadn't been thinking of him at all when describing the spiritual scum that had coated her skin ever since she'd run away from home. Of all her mistakes, he was probably the most innocent.

"Wait." She pushed herself away from the fence and shook her head, taking his forearms in her hands. "That's not what I meant. I've sometimes felt that way when you were with me, but it wasn't you making me feel it. You didn't hurt me, okay? You followed Bell's rules to the letter." Elizabeth paused. "But what if Bell didn't have those rules?"

"Do you wonder if I would have crushed you beneath me and incited the fear to feed upon while I took all of you?" The Creature kept his tone even, but tension made his words shudder like a cello string. "Do you think that's the kind of monster I am, the kind of man?"

"That's not what I meant either." She sighed. "I don't assume you'd force me out of malice, but you might have been…driven by an urge you weren't accustomed to controlling. Maybe you would have noticed how I responded, whether or not I was on board, and you'd push, telling yourself 'she'll enjoy herself anyway' —"

"No." He sliced through her rambling with a decisive blow. "I've said before that I don't have a sex drive like most human men. There is no proliferation of my species, no reason for the male to whip himself into a frenzy, no reason to subjugate our women. And given how well the men of this circus restrain themselves under Bell's laws, given the right incentive and despite the effects of the sex demons, I suspect the argument for biological helplessness is more contrived than many people would admit."

"Speak for yourself."

This time the Creature was the one to keep her from backing away, taking her hands before she could.

"You're not helpless, nor are you a slave to your cravings. I've yet to feel threatened by your appetite. Even under the influence of a traumatic addiction, little Spider, you've never forced yourself upon me." He offered her a hint of a smile. "You might attempt to persuade, but when I refuse, you don't pursue me with a nail-studded baseball bat or slice the leather of my wings and bind me to a pole to force me to submit to your whim."

"You're bigger than me."

"Do you *want* to bind me down and torment me despite my reluctance? Are my greater size and strength your only deterrent?"

There was warmth in his voice now. It only deepened when she shook her head.

"And Bell's law isn't mine." He stroked his thumbs over her eyebrows with affection, then slipped his claws under the edge of the wig to relieve her of it. Her scalp breathed a silent sigh of relief as he handed the wig back to her. "It's not easy to deny you, but you allow me to, and I allow you to as well. It's not easy, but it's not so hard, is it?"

She lay the wig over the railing. "Would you say the incubus and succubus are active tonight?"

The Creature tilted his head in curiosity. "What do you think?"

"Doesn't feel like it, but sometimes it's sneaky."

He laughed. "Yes. However, if I had to guess, the sex demons are either sleeping or on one of their hunts outside the borders of Arcanium. There is residual influence, nothing more."

She folded both sets of arms behind her. The gesture felt girlish, strangely elegant when doubled, but it meant she no longer tried to conceal or protect her torso. It felt almost like removing her robe. Really, the leather bikini was mere suggestion at clothing—strange how such a minor distinction determined whether she was viewed as a model or an obscenity. Stranger still how people had once thought she was a saint just because she covered all her tattoos.

"What if I asked you?" she said.

"Asked me what?"

"For more than just a feast tonight." She swallowed.

"After revealing certain uncomfortable aspects of your past, I understand if you're feeling vulnerable...stimulated...hungry." He seemed to caress another part of her with his gaze after every descriptor. "But you confuse sex with comfort."

"As long as I'm having sex, there's no reason it can't also be comfort."

"You don't want that. You don't want to give yourself to me only to regret it later, as you have time and time again." The Creature covered her shoulders with his strong hands. If he'd intended to push her away, he failed. But he also didn't yank her against her body, though the flex of his forearms suggested it had crossed his mind.

"Your regret tastes bitter to me, Elizabeth. You will accuse me of taking advantage of you." He lowered his head until his brow almost touched hers. When he licked his lips, he lingered a little too long over the prick of bared teeth. "And you'd be right."

"So you're saying I'd hate myself in the morning."

"And me. You'd hate *me*. You've been so candid tonight. I would not want the silent treatment to resume in the morning because of a moment's passing desire, not when I believe you need not a lover but an ally in this circus, one who is neither prisoner nor performer—not quite impartial, but not an inside man either." He smiled when she raised an eyebrow. "You're one of the few of Bell's people to avoid the rest of his troupe, and you're the only one to mingle with the most despised. Your judgment of Bell and those he calls his own isn't much of a secret."

"Guilty by association, as far as I'm concerned."

Elizabeth's hips canted forward of their own accord. She bit her lip when she brushed against his cock. The Creature closed his eyes then gently pushed her away from him again. At parties in the Petrosian community, the elders had called it 'making room for the Holy Spirit'. Elizabeth was struck with a strong urge to laugh, but she feared it might sound hysterical.

"I understand why you find refuge with them, although I don't like it. I don't like *them*. I would rather you occupy your time with the Tattooed Man, the Torsos, the conjoined twins, the aerialists. They are quite human, some of them as tragic in their wishing as you. I think you will come to appreciate the oddities more when the prisoners prove an insufficient representation of humanity."

Elizabeth rested her prime hands on her hips, though she kept the secondary set clasped behind her back. "You don't even know them."

The Creature's lips thinned. "I know their fears."

"Well, I know what it's like to make a terrible decision and hit rock bottom then keep hitting a lower rock bottom every time."

"Your ex wasn't punishment for your sins, Elizabeth," he said quietly. "Systematic torture and brainwashing could hardly be considered a fitting sentence for such a human transgression as being a rebellious teenager."

"My sisters managed to avoid such human transgression. They stayed with the church. They never imagined leaving it. They're happy."

"You see them as happy." He touched the claws of one hand to the tip of his tongue as though to savor. "If I were to taste them, I imagine I would find strife you haven't begun to imagine. It wouldn't mean that they aren't happy, but perhaps they have their own suffering."

"Or perhaps their older sister scared them straight."

"The world is not divided between the safe church community and the darkest dungeons of hell, little Spider. Simply because you've been trapped in one or the other does not mean there are not places in between, and those are the places where I've fed the most."

He relinquished the taste of his claws to run all of them over her scalp, making her shiver. He seemed to become distracted by her lips as his hands closed behind her neck. They were close again, gravitational pull inexorable. She brought her palms to his abdomen, smoothing up to his chest and trembling. She lifted her eyes as his forehead found hers again.

They angled to kiss, but she hesitated.

And he hesitated as well, slight grin widening with a touch of bitterness. "With both far sides of the divide pulling you on the rack between them, it is no wonder ambivalence frustrates you so."

She raised her mouth to his again. "We've kissed before without me breaking. I'm vulnerable, not fragile."

"I know." He pressed a kiss to the corner of her mouth, expertly avoiding her attempt to capture him. Then he kissed her forehead, reluctance like pain in his expression. "I want you, Elizabeth. And I would have you, wherever you wanted me to take you. But you're afraid you don't want me. *He* insinuated himself through your desire until you are unable to tell where you begin and he ends. His hold is not inextricable, but I won't confuse the issue. I will continue to feed from you to ease your fears, but do not ask me to kiss you, touch you, love you, until you are sure it is you — and you alone — who wants it."

Elizabeth sighed, but she couldn't force him back against her when he was determined to widen the space between them. "I had no idea Bell's rule extended that far."

"It doesn't. I'm imposing this condition."

She picked up her wig and cradled it in her arms like a kitten. "Figures I'd attach myself to the only monster in this circus with scruples."

He laughed. "You'd be surprised."

"By your lack of scruples or other monsters' scrupulousness?"

"Both." He gave her a farewell that looked like both a bow and a curtsy yet was somehow appropriate. "I hope one day you will find out just how unscrupulous I can be."

"The incident in the web is just the beginning, is it?"

The snap of his wings opening was his only answer before he launched himself into the sky.

One thing she'd say for Arcanium… It never lacked dramatic flourish.

On the way back to the caravan, she stopped by Troy's trailer and knocked on the door, hoping she'd caught him before dinner. He was voluntary, so he really could have been anywhere, even outside the fences, but it didn't hurt to check.

The trailer creaked a little as Troy came down the stairs to open the door. "Hey. Haven't seen you in a while. What can I do you for?"

"Are you busy?" Elizabeth fussed with the wig in her hands. "I can come back later or another day. I wouldn't want to interrupt."

He smiled. "Nah, Christina isn't here, if that's what you're wondering. I'm just finishing up a sketch, that's all. Want to join me? I'll bring the whiskey."

With a folding tabletop resting on top of it, his dentist chair doubled as a desk. He propped the tabletop against a cabinet, then took his place on the stool.

"What can I do for you?" he asked.

"When I was more involved in altering my body, I had some lip piercings—"

"The snakebites, yes. They healed over well. I wouldn't have even guessed you had them." Troy lifted her chin to peer at the skin under her lower lip, but Elizabeth stiffened.

"How did you know what they were?"

"They're in the photographs." He glanced up, troubled. "Are you all right?"

"What photographs?"

Troy spun the stool around to reach for his laptop and set it where they both could see. He pulled up the Arcanium website, then clicked onto his subpage, where he advertised his services in tattooing and piercing. He clicked into his gallery. The album of the Spider Woman of Arcanium headed the site as one of his most recent works.

"When I posted my pictures of your new ink, a few of my artist friends linked me to the Dez Arnette photography you posed for." He looked back up at her.

"The pictures were over ten years old, but he's always been timeless."

"You know him?" Dez had enjoyed fame in certain local circles, but she'd had no idea it had extended beyond. Elizabeth supposed she'd been naïve to believe he wouldn't seek to spread his reputation over the Internet.

"Not personally, but I've followed his work. He's a triple-threat — tattoo artist, photographer, videographer. His stuff appears in magazines and online for goth, extreme, erotica, porn sites, all kinds of places. He has a reputation as a genuine auteur, so people gravitate toward him."

Elizabeth tried to swallow, but jagged gravel obstructed her throat.

"I thought I recognized you, but I almost couldn't believe it, because you didn't...you didn't seem like the kind of woman who would model or perform for him," he said sheepishly. "Then again, in full religious costume, you didn't seem like the kind of woman who'd have a full body of tattoos. After you came to me the first time and I got a look at the art up close, I had to check."

"Perform for him?" She was parroting, but, in her defense, it had been a really bad day.

Troy considered her with a combination of concern and wariness. Between the anatomical lesson, the glinting silver and the subdermals, his face was a series of distractions, but underneath it all, he was a surprisingly gentle-looking soul. She suspected that in another life, he'd been bookish, hair weeding over his glasses to conceal his eyes, his face like a model posing as an academic. She also suspected his delicate, awkward prettiness had been the butt of a great deal of taunts.

"Did you...not...know?" he asked.

"I knew about the photographs. I thought those particular videos were more...exclusive." Had he really put *everything* they'd done where *anyone* could find it? Where *everyone* could find it? "Show me."

"Are you sure?" Troy asked.

"The pictures first." She kept herself stiff in an effort to appear composed, but she didn't think she succeeded.

Troy continued to glance up at her in wary concern, but he typed Dez's name into the search bar and found the site. The picture on the homepage was of Dez holding a camera while surrounded by the tattooed, pierced and mostly naked bodies of his models posed around him like a throne of flesh. They were all about as young as she'd been, legal teens through mid-twenties.

Under his portfolio, much like Troy's, he'd arranged the pictures by model shoot, most recent to oldest. Except her. She topped the page, set off by a darker band, labeled with her porn name and the years he'd shot her, like a gravestone.

"You don't get the buzz you used to, but images are still shared now and then. Tattoo artist and pin-up circles, mostly. But your, um...videos keep you relevant. They're not kept with his portfolio."

She didn't think it was good for her to flush so violently multiple times in one day. "Have you seen them?"

"Watched them, you mean? Well, when they were new, I did."

"Oh, fuck." Elizabeth covered her face with her prime hands and her head with her secondary hands, as though that was adequate concealment from the entire Internet.

Troy put his hand on her shoulder, hesitating at first before deciding to rest it there. "I haven't revisited them since you came here or anything. You were in a different place in your life. I respect that."

"But you've seen... Fucking hell, you *saw*."

He patted her shoulder in an attempt at consolation. "I'm a tattoo artist and an Arcanium freak. I see a lot, and I don't clutch pearls. I thought it was legit, consensual. Was it not?"

She skirted the question, whose answer was far too complicated for her to address. "Does anyone else know?"

"Know what?"

"That there are pictures and videos of me, Troy," she snapped. "The thing we're talking about right now. Does anyone else know? Did you show it to anyone?"

"Bell knows, but only because he *knows*," Troy said. "And no, I didn't show it to anyone. Like I said, you were in a different place, and a woman should be able to walk away from the life if she wants to. I can't guarantee no one else in the circus knows, but I guarantee I didn't show them."

"Not even Christina?" She softened her tone, though not by much.

"She likes me, but she's not a part of the culture. I didn't show her. Had no reason to." He sat forward on his stool, tilting his head to try to meet her eyes. "Did Dez do something wrong? Or are you just trying to escape a past you're not proud of?"

Spider

Elizabeth rubbed the tension in her neck at the same time she rubbed her forehead, where a headache had definitely decided to settle in. "You said you'd bring the whiskey."

He twisted around on his stool to pick up two tumblers and the whiskey bottle. "Ice?"

She nodded. He grabbed some ice from the freezer, poured her a few fingers. She indicated that he should keep going. He filled it to the brim.

She gulped all of it down at once. "Please don't tell anyone," she said as soon as she caught her breath.

"Okay," he replied gently. "They may find out, because news travels, but I won't tell them. However, if Dez did something wrong, the community needs to know. His models need to know — and women wanting to become his models."

She slammed the glass on the top of the cabinet. "There was nothing anyone could ever prove, and I'm guessing that hasn't changed. Now, can I get those piercings or not?"

"You'll be more recognizable." He followed her more slowly to the bottom of his tumbler, even though he'd poured less of it for himself.

"I don't care. They were one of the few things I asked for, and I miss them. People are starting to recognize me anyway. No point trying to hide now."

Troy considered her, clearly dwelling on questions she hadn't answered, the important ones. Finally, he said, "Surgical steel or titanium?"

Chapter Eleven

Most people weren't coming to the red tent for the bugs anymore. They weren't even coming for the Spider.

If women were fascinated by an extra-limbed porn star in a spider coffin, they were more circumspect about it. The ones who ogled, leered, undressed her the rest of the way with their eyes, took pictures and short videos of her... They were all men. Younger men. Older men still took pictures of her, but they didn't linger. Mama bears and young women rolled their eyes at younger bucks. They let boys be boys. But there was apparently an age limit when men couldn't be 'boys' without officially creeping.

Elizabeth didn't see the distinction, but then again, she was the one being creeped on.

No one did much more than memorializing the event for stroke material, though. A few of them tried the pocket trick, but it was a difficult art to master at the best of times, and in the middle of people crowding around to look was rarely the best of times.

It was a marked changed from before, when people were unsure whether she was who they thought she was. Now they clearly knew.

My, my... Wonder who could have possibly tipped them off.

But as long as they stayed legal and didn't try to undo the padlock or expose themselves, there wasn't anything Elizabeth could do but look away and hope they were more arachnophobic than they were horny.

When she put on the latex suit for the funhouse, she prayed no one would recognize her that way despite the multiple limbs — maybe she'd just be another haunt in the funhouse.

She should have known she didn't have that much luck. The Gentleman had to work overtime to convince the groups of men to keep moving, and more than one tried to touch her through her shiny bodysuit. Between being bound to a web and locked in a box, the box was safer, but at least in the funhouse, she got to scream her frustration all she wanted.

* * * *

As she climbed into the trailer, Kevin blinked at her piercings. "Those are new."

Though he was thin, the blood-spattered butcher's apron made him appear more imposing than usual. His arms had become vascular from wielding the chainsaw all day, and he hadn't cleaned himself up yet, so he was still covered head to toe with blood, except where he'd removed his black rubber gloves.

His victim writhed, leaking out onto the compartment floor. Kevin had managed to get his torso sewn up, but his limbs were still in the sack next to him. They didn't bother with delicate work when it came to the chainsaw massacre victim. Everything always regenerated, but it quickened the process when the parts of the victim were reunited. And the one who did the dismembering was responsible for re-membering. It was one of the unspoken rules.

"They're old, actually." Elizabeth touched the titanium rings over her lip. The healing unguent had done its work, but the area had been sore for a day — if Elizabeth had to guess, probably from the unguent not being able to completely close the holes with the rings in the way. "But you had to know the scars were there to see them."

"You're an endless surprise," Kevin said. "I'll be finished here soon, but I'm pretty sure you want me to shower."

"I prefer to bathe in the blood of my enemies, so it's really about what's comfortable for you. Pizza's by the bandages when you get your appetite back."

Elizabeth settled in at the triage center in the back of the trailer.

At first, she attributed the odd looks some of the boys gave her as a reaction to the piercings. They'd adjusted to her bald head, her lack of clothing and her tattoos, but the rings were new. A little curiosity could be expected.

But only a little. They were just two thin rings over her bottom lip, hardly scandalous in Arcanium. Yet the boys kept staring.

Elizabeth pressed the taped gauze onto the boy's shoulder in front of her, then looked around at everyone looking back at her. "What?"

Hank jumped out of his third-level pod, landing without a groan of effort. He'd been assigned the werewolf that weekend. His already bearded face had been supplemented with thicker, darker red hair. His teeth were as sharp as hers, but differently shaped, curved and interlocked, less human. His arms were simian and corded with muscle, his nose small, dark and wet. Extra hair aside, it was one of the less painful, more powerful things Bell turned them into.

"Did you know we can hear through the glass in the funhouse? Even when he steals our voices, we can hear what's going on outside. It's mostly just more screams from the guests. Laughing. Talking. Bell wants us to know that our suffering is trivial."

Elizabeth stood up before Hank could loom over her. She glanced back at the bathrooms. The shower was off, but Kevin hadn't emerged yet. "I don't see what that has to do with me."

"You think I can't tell the difference between a woman screaming because she's scared and a woman screaming because she's coming?" Hank asked.

For a moment, Elizabeth couldn't breathe, much less speak. "Most men can't."

"Ha ha. Well, you were moaning, too. A woman doesn't moan like that when she's scared. What happened, Elizabeth? The Gentleman get less gentlemanly with you? I heard he's got a sweet spot for a damsel in distress."

He stepped closer to her, close enough to kiss, but she couldn't back up. She had maybe a foot behind her before she'd hit the wall.

"No, you know what I think it was?"

"I'm on tenterhooks." She didn't like the beady way he looked her over. A man only got that confident when he thought there was nothing in his way.

"I think you let a guest have you. Several, in fact. I also recognize the look on a man's face when he's gotten a face-full of a sexy woman. And what do you know? Not too soon after your screams stopped, here come the gobsmacked guys."

"What a lurid theory. I can't imagine what would be more likely." But it was so uncomfortably close to the truth that her gut clenched.

What was worse, the way he looked at her was turning her on. She wanted to kiss him to shut him up, bite him and ride him because the twisted places in her brain somehow thought that would teach him a lesson about assuming what kind of woman she was.

"It's not like you haven't done it before," he said.

"What are you talking about?" She wasn't going to be coherent much longer, not if the litany in her mind of *oh shit oh shit oh shit* got any louder.

"A few of us prisoners compared notes. And guess what? So have people who come through the funhouse. Just today, in fact. They knew who you were, came to Arcanium just to see the Spider Woman and figure out if she was really Lucy Lewd."

There was no way to not cringe at that name.

Hank grinned. "Then it clicked. Kevin's the one who figured it out. He's the only one who's had a look at those tattoos up close and personal. He says you have magical hands. Based on what little I remember, I can believe it."

"You're a pig," Elizabeth said.

"You know what I'm noticing?" Hank picked an invisible piece of lint from the shoulder of her robe. "You haven't denied it."

"Because it's ridiculous." She laughed, but it was nervous, mirthless. The men who had been staring earlier were much closer now.

"Oh yeah. It's crazy." He whistled like a cuckoo clock and wound his finger next to his ear in the classic gesture. "But it's true, isn't it? You really did fuck those guys in the funhouse. Or maybe you just put on a show. But I'll bet that's not the first time guests got a good look at you — the one fun part of the haunted funhouse. Am I right?"

"Not at all."

"Did you really fuck a vacuum cleaner? Put one of those extensions inside you and turn it on while you sucked a guy off, like it made you the vacuum?" Hank didn't give her a chance to back away. He pushed her against the wall while holding the tie to her robe, trying to pull it open. She grasped at the sides of the robe with her secondary hands inside.

She leaned in until her nose nearly brushed his. "Don't you know you can't always believe everything you watch in porn?"

His smile was more a grimace now, but not because he was any less amused. "I knew it."

"What's going on?" Kevin ran a cheap towel through his hair. He was shirtless but wearing boxer shorts again. He was downright normal by funhouse standards, indistinguishable from a guest.

"Your girlfriend really is Lucy Lewd. That's what's happening. If I remember things correctly, Lucy was ready for anything — and I mean *anything*. Goddamn, she was wet as the Pacific every time they checked."

Hank pulled on the robe tie again, but Elizabeth wasn't letting it budge. "What was that you said about how she wanted it, how she smelled when she did, even when she was acting coy?"

It was Kevin's turn to blush. Elizabeth barely got a chance to glare at him before Hank leaned close to breathe her in at her neck, at the opening of her robe.

Tears sprang to her eyes, not from fear but from the betrayal of her own body. She'd never liked him, never liked the way he talked to her or looked at her or just the way he was. But his beard prickled against her chest, and his hands were large and strong, his breath hot, and she knew exactly what scent he was talking about. The low rumble of a growl rippled through his partially transformed throat.

"God, if I could bottle that…" he murmured. Then he opened his mouth and ran his tongue along the hollow above her collarbone.

Elizabeth grabbed his hair to yank him back. Instead, she threaded her fingers through the coarseness and pressed his mouth to her skin, her head falling back against the side of the compartment.

"I *knew* it," he repeated, his voice an octave lower. He jerked the sides of her robe down over her shoulders. "Now that's what I'm talking about. You've got a hell of a girl, Kev."

Hank whipped them both around, which put Elizabeth back in the center of the trailer, suddenly topless — and nearly more, as the robe slipped down to her hips. The men who'd been watching came closer. It was like one of those nightmares where the monsters were still as statues when she was looking, then hurried toward her while she looked the other way. Every single one of them had the same flat light in their eyes, as though they were dead. But not where it counted. Some of them had even taken their cocks out, pulled on them to get them harder.

Elizabeth tried to find one of the few women, but none of them were anywhere to be seen, which meant they'd probably known what Hank was going to do. And instead of warning her, they'd made themselves scarce.

"You really do like that, don't you?" Kevin said. "It's not just an act." He helped pull the rest of her robe off until she stood naked, surrounded by shark-eyed men. This had only happened a few times in her career. And it didn't matter how many orgasms they'd given her, she'd hated every one.

"Of course it's an act. Even porn stars who like sex have to fake about ninety percent of the moaning and groaning and coming every two minutes most of the time." Elizabeth sidled away from him, but he came at her from behind, and Hank blocked the way in front of her. Kevin rubbed her back, her shoulders, digging his thumbs into the stress knots. He was his own knot at the small of her back, though, as considerably hard as a deprived young man could be.

"Most of the time?" Hank said with a laugh. "You just can't help yourself, little Christian cult girl, can't help but not lie. You smell like *three* girls after the wettest goddamn orgasms they've ever had. You're leaning into your boyfriend's hands, and you're looking at me like you want to eat me up, even though you're scared. You *are* scared, aren't you?"

"Life isn't a porno, Hank, and I wasn't doing it by choice. Everything you ever saw of me was because I was coerced."

Aurelia T. Evans

Kevin's touch hesitated on her back, but he let out a breath as she grabbed his hip to grind back against his erection.

"Not very much. I mean, come on. You'd hit me with a shovel as soon as look at me—right back at you, by the way—but if I took out my cock and told you to blow, I bet you would. Look at you."

"You're not telling him to fuck off." Kevin sounded confused, but he was hard as hot stone against her ass. There wasn't much blood going to his brain. "Does that mean yes?"

He palmed her breasts, and she arched to fill his hands, shaking her head but going dizzy. Her cunt ached, the hollowness as sharp as hunger pangs.

Pre-cum smeared over her skin. She had four hands, and each one had somehow found itself with a cock in it.

If she couldn't stop, why should she try? She clearly wanted it. She couldn't ask for it with her mouth, but her body asked for it, begged for it, and she couldn't deny that. She couldn't pretend she didn't crave the men's bodies presented to her, no matter what they looked like, no matter that they were seeping pus, lymph and blood. She got hot from their moans, from the way they couldn't hold back the bucking of their hips as she wrung their cocks. And there Hank was with his shit-eating grin, his shirt off and his jeans unbuttoned, cock dark red and curving out from a bed of dense ginger hair and werewolf fur.

Elizabeth closed her eyes. She should have lost this need a long time ago. It should have shriveled and died from starvation. Maybe it had. Maybe Dez had taken the shameless joy and unbridled pleasure from the early years and replaced it with something that made a mere mockery of what pleasure should be. He'd made her body explosive and spread the ashes all through her.

He'd created the fantasy, but at its core, that fantasy was necrophilia, nothing but dead inside. She'd vacated the home of flesh. Someone else occupied the shell left behind. Someone else moved her, made her grab at random men's cocks, made her grind back against Kevin, who breathed harsh and hot down her neck as he met her thrusts — first through his shorts then he pushed them down. Flesh rubbed against flesh — not inside, not yet. Someone else made her salivate as Hank came closer, stroking himself in broad, firm motions, as though examining how she reacted to the sight of it.

Elizabeth shook her head when she realized the reason she wanted so much to submit to every dirty thing he'd likely imagined her doing was because Dez would look at her just like that — with cold calculation, wondering just how much he could get away with. No, *knowing* just how much he could get away with. Because she was aroused as hell, and even if she wanted to push him out, her body would accept him one way or another.

"This is what you did to Kevin, isn't it? Said one thing while your body said something else? How typical. Why women can't just sit back and enjoy sex without agonizing over it, I'll never understand. You clearly like it. And if what my boys say is true, you enjoyed it quite a bit for *years*. Everything's immortal on the Internet. You'll be getting every hole filled, getting slapped, spit on, facialed, cream-pied, tied up and gangbanged long after you die."

Hank got up in her face, his brushfire beard crinkling against her chin. She turned away at first, but when he tilted his head as though to kiss her, she couldn't help but do the same. He chuckled. "See? Despite all the protests, this is what you want, isn't it? No wonder you went into the business. Never have to work a day in your life, as they say."

Kissing him was like kissing a demon — though, ironically, that was one of the few things she hadn't kissed yet.

His mouth was too wet, feverish, and it felt like his beard was smothering her. He bit her lip too hard, caught her tongue between his teeth as though to show that she'd put her tongue in his mouth first.

Hank covered the top of her head with one heavy hand, sliding it possessively over the smooth skin. The other he shoved between her legs to stroke through her folds. Her stomach sank, because when he dragged his fingers forward, they brought evidence of her arousal with them.

His lupine smile was triumphant when he he lifted his probing hand between them and spread his fingers to show how her wetness clung between them, an undeniable gleam in the low light.

"Holy fuck," one of the men she was masturbating groaned. He jerked in her hand. Cum struck her forearm and her hip.

Kevin kissed her shoulder, squeezed her breasts, made the hard nipples bend in his palm. "God, that's the hottest thing I've ever seen."

Elizabeth looked over her shoulder at him, searching his face as though he was a stranger. "What, your kind-of girlfriend jerking off four men and getting kissed by a jerk-off? That's what you want? That's your idea of girlfriend material?"

"Girlfriends are overrated," Hank said. "Seems like an awful lot of maintenance just to sink into something soft. And let's face it, Spider Woman. How much time do you want to waste talking about your feelings when all you really want is something hard inside you?"

He brought the juices on his fingers to her mouth, pushed them rudely past her lips to rub her taste over her tongue. "Can't deny it anymore, can you? That's right, suck it, suck it like you're going to suck my cock as soon as Kevin gets what he's been spilling himself for. God, you wouldn't believe how annoying it is to hear him do that over and over and over, groaning your name, while you always stand just out of reach in that fucking robe. I think you like it. I think you've been coming to us hoping we'd just yank it away so you can finally scratch that goddamn itch."

She made a noise of protest, but it lost its bite when the next sound was a groan as he pushed his fingers down all the way to the knuckle, trying to get her to gag. She'd thrown up countless times deep-throating in the early days, but she could gag now without retching.

Someone new filled her abandoned hand. Kevin curled his fingers around her secondary thighs and hitched them up, bringing himself flush against her from behind.

Hank pulled his fingers from her mouth and plunged them between her prime legs once again. Kevin turned her head toward him, swooping down to kiss her with sloppy desperation.

Another man came. He grunted in satisfaction as his semen splattered over her in thick jets.

The next erection that found her hand had been partially dissolved by necrosis, but that hadn't waned the man's desire. He shouted and thrust his cock through the cum-slick circle of her palm.

Hank's teeth pressed too hard against her ear. He panted like a dog, stroking himself as he sank his fingers into her. The leaking head of his cock smeared against her stomach.

Her own moans joined with those of the men surrounding her, with the meaty sound of flogging flesh, the wet sounds of Hank and Kevin kissing her, of Hank's fingers entering her.

This was what she'd been made for. This is what every man wanted — a girl who couldn't say no, a girl who had been hacked and hardwired into sexual insatiability, a girl they could take any way they wanted, because anything would keep her high. This is what men wanted, and what the women in the compartment preferred, because it meant they didn't have to do it.

Kevin broke from their kiss, gasping, spilling over her back. She doubted that would be enough for him to quit for the night, for any of them.

Hank laughed as she turned back to him, opening her mouth to let him in as far as he could take her. She canted her hips to the rhythm of his fingers inside her.

But all the things these men were doing to her, none of it was for her.

Kevin wiped her off, kissed her, nuzzled her, rubbed at her thighs and muttered things she didn't understand into her skin, yet as gentle as he was, he was still sharing her. He didn't mind how many men came on her as long as he could have his hands on her breasts, on her thighs, their tongues together. As long as he could eventually sink in where Hank had his fingers, where Kevin now brought his own to fill her even more.

They knew she'd melt to anything they did to her, but was a single touch, a single kiss, a cock in her hand, for her benefit alone? Or did they think any pleasure at all was payment enough?

It didn't matter. Her pleasure didn't matter to them. They wanted her because she reached out and took them in hand, because her cunt was wet and welcoming, because her tongue stroked them, because her body moved the way they wanted it to. They wanted her because she was a living sex doll, and she was cheap.

She could hate herself all she liked, but her body didn't care. Tears streamed down her face as she undulated between Kevin and Hank and coaxed cum from the cocks she held.

Her body wanted them. Her body wanted anything. It was a series of conditioned lusts set at hair triggers.

But *she* didn't want them. She *didn't* want them. She didn't want *this*. Any of this. Any of them.

For God's sake, Lizzie, for once in your life, make a fucking decision!

The words—her own voice, her own mind—resonated within her skull, bolder than anything Dez had ever whispered into her ear to echo in the same chamber.

She broke away from Hank's domineering kiss, gasping through her quickening arousal. "No."

"I've heard that song, Spider Woman. Your cunt's singing a different tune, isn't it? I can feel you clenching."

"It doesn't matter what my cunt's saying, Balls for Brains. *I'm* saying something different."

She forced herself to open her hands, all four of them. The guys protested, grunting and groaning from the unexpected lack of stimulation. Between the cum and the bloody pus she realized was on her, her mysophobia reared its ugly head, but she welcomed the mounting disgust, because it made her thoughts so much clearer.

"For God's sake, Kevin, stop. You're not doing anything that could possibly be considered mindless at this point. Fuck, *stop*." She couldn't help the way she pushed back against the boys' combined fingers inside her, but she could try to twist away when they went shallow.

Kevin slipped his wet fingers from her. "But you're still—"

Hank knocked her arms away, his wolf man muscles more than a match for four sets of hers. He shoved all three of them toward the pods, bringing his body up against hers with his fingers in her all the way to the knuckles. She collided with Kevin against the wall, smashed against him with his fully hard erection sliding through the cum he'd already released. Her head fell back against his shoulder. His moan was near deafening in her ear.

"But I haven't even been inside you yet," Hank whispered in her other ear. "Enough pretending."

She shoved at the forearm pressed to her abdomen, yanked at his hair, struggled not to come, but he bent down to put his cock in position to replace his fingers. Kevin let out his breath in harsh pants, bucking against her ass.

"Let go of me." Elizabeth shook her head, even though she salivated at the sound and scent of male desire, ached everywhere she'd ever been filled. "Don't—"

Hank laughed, his smile furious and predatory, his eyes a brilliant bright blue that couldn't be confused for dead-glazed in lust.

"Enough pretending," he'd said. He wasn't pretending he couldn't help himself or that he was a slave to his dick, wasn't pretending to her or to himself. He just wanted to fuck her. That was it.

Between Kevin deciding to wrap his arms around her, pinning all her arms at her sides, and Hank lifting her up so that all her feet were on tiptoe, her cunt angled for his cock, she couldn't hit either of them where it counted.

Something filled her, but it wasn't from the men who pressed against her. It imbued her like seven hundred shots of espresso, or the all-encompassing sense of terror she might feel if confronted with all of her phobias at once—like something she'd experienced before, magnified multitudes over, yet somehow contained within her slight frame.

She snapped her hips forward on its hinge, forcing her weight back onto her secondary legs, which gave her leverage to raise her prime legs with her knees against her chest. With her feet, she shoved Hank away by his shoulders.

He flew backward and struck the side of the trailer. The great metal siding resounded like a gong as he fell to his hands and knees. Elizabeth landed back on her primary legs with a thud.

"What—?" Kevin began.

Nothing could get in her way anymore. If she chose to walk through the trailer walls, she'd leave a body-shaped hole in her wake. Kevin's hold was no match for her. She broke his embrace then landed her elbow just under his right eye. Stunned, he collapsed into an ungainly heap.

Elizabeth didn't check whether he was still conscious. She strode to where Hank had almost climbed to his feet. She grabbed him by his throat and raised him from the ground without the slightest effort, despite the fact that he outweighed her twice over.

She slammed him once again into the side of the trailer, gazing up at him with her head cocked in disdain, nothing sensual or suggestive about her body against his now. He gasped for breath. She wasn't choking him, but fear required so much more air than her grip allowed. He scrabbled at her hands, but just as nothing could stop her, neither could anything move her if she didn't want it to.

When Bell's voice joined hers, she wasn't surprised. For once, they were in perfect accord.

"Have you learned nothing?" In the close metal compartment, their combined voices made everyone in her periphery clap their hands to their ears. "Must I make every one of you melt like the Rotting Man? Must I have you whipped every hour of every day without relief? Or should I simply give my demons a feast and resume populating my circus with freaks rather than entrails such as yourselves?"

Despite Hank's longer arms, he couldn't seem to reach her. He struck at her shoulders, but his hairy paws didn't get close to hitting her face.

She gouged lines into his cheek with one of her secondary hands, then flung him into a group of prisoners. They fell together, partially naked or all naked. They scrambled away from each other as soon as they could, as though the exposed flesh of other men contaminated them.

There wasn't nearly enough fear in their eyes — both Bell and Elizabeth agreed on that. But Elizabeth had to work with what she had, and what she had was a freakish, enticing body covered in their fluids, so she could understand why they hadn't yet reached a full appreciation for who had taken a place among them.

She turned back to Kevin, lifted him up by his throat as well. His feet dangled near her shins, but his eyes were unfocused — not yet enough presence of mind to kick her.

"You," she murmured, narrowing her eyes.

"I'm sorry, Elizabeth. I'm sorry. I thought… I didn't know what I was thinking. You were just so…"

She bared her filed teeth. "You don't even know what you're apologizing for. You're apologizing to placate me, but you understand no more than the rest. You showed promise, Kevin. You showed contrition. You asked for forgiveness. That makes this all the worse of a betrayal."

"She wanted it, you sick bastard." Hank rose up from the fray, wiping the back of his hand across his face to gather the blood from her scratches. "Moaning, groaning, bucking like a fucking whore. She's had so many dicks in her, it's a wonder her pussy's still tight. And speaking of pussy, she was a goddamn waterfall in there. She had four cocks in her hand at a time, quadruple-fisting us like she couldn't get enough. She was freaking out, but that doesn't mean she didn't want it."

Elizabeth and Bell slowly turned around to face him, still holding Kevin by his throat. "I gave you every chance. Both of you." She shook Kevin like a puppy. "I should have sent you to the Ringmaster when first she touched you. But as long as she agreed to go along with what she didn't want, as long as she didn't make her thoughts known, I allowed her to suffer your self-absorption and excuses. She'd found reasons to need the most pitiful of my possessions, so I let her stay to struggle with her impulses, with your fumbling control, if she was willing to accept it. Then you have the *gall* to apologize to her now in the same way. 'I'm so *sorry*,'" she mocked. "'I'm so sorry you're too tempting for me to resist.' You're worse than that hairy foreskin of a dog, because you still think you're nice, that everything you've done is okay, that you didn't have a choice."

"Please." Kevin's throat narrowed until his voice was a death rattle. "Please."

She threw Kevin into Hank. Both of them tumbled back down onto the pile of men.

"I have the right to present everyone who touched her to the clowns. You're young enough that they might still appreciate your flesh." She cocked her head, drawing her gaze down Kevin's thin, lanky body. "You wished yourself into the circus to save your skins, but in the wish, you promised to serve Arcanium. Your suffering was the one thing I required of you, but barely a year passes, and you've already failed. Your lives are forfeit."

Some of the boys under Kevin and Hank protested, color draining from their faces.

She stretched out her prime hands. Kevin and Hank were lifted to their feet in mid-air, their toes dragging on the floor. Whites surrounded Kevin's irises. His lips were the color of gravestones. Hank, in contrast, flushed under his dark fur, bared his teeth, and fought against whatever magic held him like a hanging puppet. Bell peeled Hank's mind open for her to read his intentions, his schemes and desires, each more maggot-ridden and plague-black than the last. His erection hadn't flagged. Fury kept him hard, kept him feeling powerful, even with Bell inside her.

But she beckoned to Kevin first. He floated forward, trying to twist away from the nothing carrying him. "No. No, please."

"Suffering was your mercy. There's none left to beg for."

Bell hadn't taken her will, which was why when she hesitated, he didn't proceed. Instead, he dipped her into the pool of Kevin's mind, the way he had with Hank.

Kevin was a boy in a young man's body, a slave to instant self-gratification. Despite the long year of austerity, he still believed comforts should come to him whenever he wanted them, that Bell's denial was a temporary setback to the norm. He meant well, which was worse than Hank's malice, because he would never believe himself capable of exactly what he'd done.

He'd just lost control. He just found her so mind-blowingly sexy. He'd just been teased and strung along by an indecisive woman who couldn't comprehend what she did to a man. Everything happened *to* him. Although he'd proven himself capable of self-reflection, Kevin was still active in his own passivity, a series of excuses absolving him and leaving him confused as hell every time he was punished.

He whimpered. "I thought she wanted it."

Elizabeth struck his cheekbone, not with her elbow this time but with a clenched fist. It hurt like hell, and she wouldn't be surprised if she'd cracked something in her hand.

"You really didn't learn anything." Just her voice this time, just her grabbing him by the shoulders and hair and flinging him into the side of the trailer. She was so angry she couldn't see clearly. "It's the same reason you're in this fucking mess, asshole! I understand you being confused. I really do. *Until* I said out loud, in clear English, that I needed you to stop and that I didn't want it. What about *that* was unclear?"

"You were still grinding and moaning and pussy-clenching," Hank snarled, crawling and trying to stand at the same time. "And that goddamn demon wants to punish *us* because *you* don't even know what you want?"

Elizabeth grabbed his hair and shoved her knee into his mouth. Again, it hurt a lot more than expected, because his teeth sank into her skin and left a partial bite mark. But she broke a few teeth, too. Phlegmy blood dripped from his mouth in bubbles and strings. He shouted, covered his mouth with his hands, calling her all sorts of things in his mushed-up mouth.

Elizabeth yanked him to his knees. "It's called biology. I can't help that. If a person tickles me, I laugh, but just because I laugh doesn't mean I like it. I told you to stop, multiple times, and you chose to ignore me. But that doesn't matter, because he reads your mind, dickcheese. If I'd said stop from the very beginning, you wouldn't have listened, because you already figured out it's pure biology with me. Add in a pornographic past, and you thought I didn't have a choice. You could enjoy a willing body, and who cared if the woman wasn't? You're *sick*."

He lunged at her, jagged teeth bared and muscular arms flailing. He bowled her over, buckling all four of her legs. His dense body slammed on top of her, stealing her breath, but she jerked up—either by instinct or with a nudge from Bell—and closed her teeth around Hank's nose. Her filed teeth were perfectly angled to minimize skin resistance. When he yanked back in pain, he inadvertently contributed to the rending of flesh that left her with a nose in her mouth and a font of blood spilling from his face.

"You fucking bitch!"

She sat up with the help of her extra arms and spat the rest of his nose to the side. Now she was covered in sweat, cum, mucus, pus and blood. Her hands were starting to shake.

Bell swiftly tightened his control. The knowledge that bodily fluids were no danger to her sank bone-deep with certainty she couldn't give herself alone. In the absence of the Creature's feed, she appreciated having a calmer head. It left so much more room for the anger. The fact that the anger had built up over the course of seventeen years didn't mean that Hank didn't righteously deserve the bulk of it, and Bell seemed to agree, with a dulcet hint of amusement in her mind like a wind chime.

"Come on, Hank. Keep trying. I could bite you for days. Just be glad Bell didn't make me venomous."

"I knew you were one of his." Hysteria and tears edged his accusation. Elizabeth could get used to that sound. "I said it from the beginning."

Elizabeth managed to get to her knees, panting. She'd wipe her mouth, but she knew where her hands had been, and her forearms weren't much better. She spat out more of Hank's blood. "Joke's on you. I wasn't. But you know something? I've been afraid of the demons and monsters this whole time, and *they're* the ones who listen when I tell them to stop. They're the ones who protect me — even Bell, even though he stuck me in this dung heap. You guys are reminded every day of your mistakes. They slice through your skin, tear off your limbs, eat at your flesh. But you made the *same* mistakes *again*. On purpose. Deliberately. You're sick. You're *disgusting*."

She slammed her heel into the mess of Hank's face when he tried to attack her again.

"Come on!" she screamed at him, but also to the rest of the men around her, daring them to try to fight back.

With what looked like his last strength, Hank howled and raised his arms to smash her with his fists. Bell stretched out her hand and *pulled* at the air. The 'wolf man' ripped from Hank's body like cellophane, leaving him without any of the advantages the transformation had given him. As he fell, he still had what Elizabeth had given him, though, thick threads of blood caught in his beard.

She reached for the first thing she could find, which was a thick piece of vine trimmed from Blondie that evening, still oozing sap. It would do.

Bell withdrew, giving her the floor.

Elizabeth had little awareness of what she was doing and little memory of what had just happened once she'd finished. She dropped the vine, most of which had been stained red and dotted with bits of flesh, then fell to her knees in abrupt exhaustion.

"The Ringmaster would be so proud," Bell said in their double-voice, pleased.

Hank's face was nearly unrecognizable, and his arms and chest weren't much better—swollen, red and purple, bloody, rubbery. He was doubled over in fetal position, clutching his cock and balls, his genitals taking precedence over the rest of him, so she could only imagine what she'd done to him there.

Some of the other boys had welts on them as well, either because they'd been too close to Hank or they'd tried to stop her. The rest had rushed to the trailer door, but it wouldn't open, no matter how they pounded upon the metal.

Elizabeth nudged Hank's hands away with her foot. He coughed and tried to protest, but Bell forced them to his sides. Men seemed so deflated when flaccid, and Hank proved no exception. They were even more diminished when flayed.

"Killing you would be too easy an escape from Arcanium," Bell mused, their voice a purr. "And the haunted funhouse clearly isn't enough for you. I kept the lot of you separate from my people because *they* didn't want you mingling with them, not the other way around. But such separation has made you believe you're beyond my reach, and I can't let that stand."

Kevin cowered against the side of the compartment where she'd left him, staring up at her the way she assumed people looked at gods—with terror and awe. "What are you going to do?"

Briefly ignoring Kevin, Elizabeth ran her tongue along her sharp teeth. The taste of blood there didn't offend her, and Bell had taken any fear of it she might have had. "How often have you used that prick of yours as a weapon, Hank? No need to respond. I already know the answer. I think it's time we take that weapon away."

"No. No, no. *No*."

Gross though blubbering was on a grown man, she wouldn't have had him any other way. "I think it's time for the Man Doll to join Oddity Row."

"No, no, please, no!"

Elizabeth would have preferred it if his dick and balls had dropped off like ripe peaches, but it was still satisfying to watch them sink into his torso, development in reverse. Then everything smoothed over — hairless, holeless, sexless. The same phenomenon spread to the rest of his body as well as he shrank down to nearly a third of his size, too small for his torn jeans. Only his head stayed the same, wailing in agony, although she didn't think any of the changes hurt. The teeth Elizabeth had knocked out and the nose she'd bitten off regrew, but Bell left the bruises, welts and blood otherwise untouched.

"You'll find your pretty wardrobe in your oddity tent," she said. "You'll travel with the Rotting Man or the Cyclops, whichever you prefer. As soon as you emerge from this trailer tomorrow, you'll no longer be allowed back in. And you're to report to the Ringmaster after every evening performance for punishment, since you'll no longer have the funhouse to give you the pain you owe."

"*Chemical castration is supposed to be more effective at rehabilitating sex predators. Physical castration just makes them angrier, more violent when they do get a chance to attack.*" Elizabeth couldn't help admiring Bell's handiwork, though.

"*He hasn't yet earned rehabilitation. Mental castration would spare him the effects of the sex demons, and I wouldn't give him an advantage that even I cannot have. He'll learn, Lizzie. They all do, eventually.*"

She couldn't find it in herself to protest too much. Her own sense of revenge had no trouble at all with physical castration. If Bell had asked, she would have helped.

Elizabeth slowly raised her gaze to where Kevin gaped, plastered against the wall. "The others didn't press themselves upon her after she told everyone to stop. Their punishments will continue as before, with Hank's example before them, although they now have freedom to wander through the rest of the circus. But you, dear boy, crossed the line well beyond the realm of excuse."

"I'm sorry." Fear rendered Kevin's plea into a whisper. "I'm sorry."

Elizabeth crouched before him. "Do you even know what you're sorry for?"

"I'm sorry you... I'm sorry I..." A childish expression of petulance crossed his face before bewilderment replaced it, as though his own reaction surprised him. "I'm..."

She stroked through his messy hair. "At least you know you're supposed to be sorry for something. It's a shame you're still not sure for what, despite the fact that I've said it plainly. If you're so set on your belief that you're a slave to animal urges, then an animal you'll become. Not like the elephants or the lion and tiger...although I do like cats."

"What are you—?" He stopped, shuddered, eyes widening as though he'd been goosed, then twitched sharply once, twice.

Then the shudder wasn't from him, but over his skin in a wave, shifting the pale skin to something thicker with a texture Elizabeth couldn't immediately place— crepe-y, wrinkly soft, gathered at the joints and crevices of his body. His fingers shortened, tightened together, though they still had mobility and dexterity. The nails thinned, lengthened into something approaching claws, which Bell quickly clipped.

The transformation dipped under the waistband of his shorts, shrinking the bulge until it was impossible to see the shape of it through the fabric. His athletic leanness thinned even more, the pockets of softness more pronounced. The shape of his face changed as well, cheekbones defined and the chin more pointed. Eyes grew wider above a flattened, darkened nose. His hair fell out onto his shoulders and the ground around him, and his upper lip split into a cleft. The last alterations were whiskers, which pierced through his skin. He winced as though they were needles.

Elizabeth turned his head back and forth, inspecting him while he trembled. He tried to rise and run from the transformation, but weakness in his limbs trapped him where he sat.

His ears were pointed, his scalp gathered in wrinkles at the base of his skull. Gray discolorations covered portions of his body like birthmarks. But as much of a Sphynx cat as he appeared, he remained unmistakably human in the underlying architecture.

"I would have given you a tail, but I thought that would be a bit much. If you'd like one, however, I'd be more than willing to oblige. If you're lucky, pussy cat, one of mine will take you for a pet. Of course, you can't quite be like John is to Valorie." Elizabeth nodded in the direction of his boxers. "I left you unfixed, and human, more or less. But you won't manage much penetration with what I've left you. It'll take more than helpless rutting to get what you want. You'll need to make sure the woman wants what you have to offer, and you'll have to offer so much more than just *this*."

She covered his split lip with a finger before he could yowl whatever ill-advised, indignant, impulsive protest threatened to spill from him. "Remember the example of your friend over there. You're fortunate I left you with anything at all."

Kevin recoiled, shock dissolving into horror as the changes to his body finally registered. Elizabeth patted his cheek, crinkling the whiskers, then stood.

"You'll also have a tent on Oddity Row. I'll expect you there by tomorrow's opening, and in the ring with Hank after the performance for the Ringmaster to deal with. Does anyone else here have an opinion about how to use this body, or must she retrieve the vine?"

There were new glints in the shadows from people who hadn't tried to save her. They'd stayed in the darkness, where they'd been told to stay ever since Bell brought them into Arcanium. Perhaps he was right, that keeping them separate had done neither Bell nor his prisoners any favors.

"Time to leave, my lovely Spider. There's no place for you here anymore."

She didn't want to be here anymore anyway.

The men scattered from the compartment door as she approached it. When she grabbed the handle, it opened easily. Elizabeth jumped onto the ground, shoved the door closed again to lock the prisoners in for the night.

The ensuing quiet and dead crackle of grass beneath her bare feet jolted her back into her mind, where the last thirty minutes had been branded in her memory, except for that fuzzy stretch with the vine. The strange euphoria that had imbued her along with Bell's presence left as he did.

"It was a pleasure."

Chapter Twelve

In Bell's absence, horror returned to fill the vacuum.

The world spun around her, pulling her to her knees. She yelped when the one Hank had bit struck the ground. Dirt and dead grass clung to the drying liquids on her skin, making even more of a mess. One part of her suffered the irrepressible urge to flee to her RV to wash the remnants of the night away — as though that would make the memory fade. Another part of her wanted to go back into the trailer with a motherfucking knife to stab everyone in their pods. Instead, she stumbled back to her feet, dazed, disconnected, and headed away from the prisoners' trailer and toward the caravan.

"You need so much more than a shower, love." The accent was undeniably British — rough, but one that her American ear appreciated nonetheless.

Elizabeth jerked her head toward the darkness between vehicles. One of Bell's people stepped out of the shadows and tapped ash from his hand-rolled cigarette. He was in the same place he'd been the last time she'd seen him, and under disturbingly similar circumstances.

He held up his hands as though to show he was unarmed.

"Not getting close to you, darling. Just pointing out that Melanie has a self-cleaning aquarium with plenty of room if you need a proper dunk. She won't mind, and she's no demon. I hear that's an issue with you."

He was as pale as she was, with black hair almost as dark as hers had been, tousled past his shoulders. Coloring was about all they had in common. He was shorter, with defined, dense muscles roped tightly around his bones. His eyes were black to the edges, marking him a demon, but in all other ways, he seemed normal. That meant goose egg in Arcanium, but hell, after fighting her way out of a mass of humans, she could almost take a demon. With demons, she knew where she stood.

But she didn't bother replying. For all she knew, the demon was stalling her for Bell.

"Nice talk," the dark-haired demon called after her. "We should do it again sometime. I like a woman of few words."

She darted around the closest cluster of trailers, away from the demon's line of sight.

Elizabeth wouldn't find what she was looking for with someone who had wished in involuntarily or for punishment, but if she came across a trailer that belonged to a voluntary, she might have more luck. She didn't want to use Troy that way, because he'd always been kind and nonjudgmental. Maya or Valorie—those were the trailers she was looking for. Kitty's would be even better, since Kitty didn't sleep in her RV and they probably wouldn't cross paths.

She started with the nicer vehicles, because Elizabeth doubted Bell would give his favorite people some of the pieces of junk that helped comprise the caravan. Two of them were either locked or had a secret to opening the door that she couldn't figure out in the two seconds it took to check their handles.

The nicest trailer's door opened for her. She snuck up into something that looked like the wagon of a traveling king and quickly realized why he felt no need to lock his door.

The Ringmaster knelt on a sumptuous bed that appeared much bigger than the outside of the trailer suggested. He held Kitty by reins of her own hair, which also acted as bit and gag as he entered her.

As a male specimen, he was beautifully powerful like the circus strongman but with thunderstorms under his brow, menace in the shadow of his beard, evil strapped to him in muscle and sinew, practically emanating with the sweat of his effort. But Kitty was Kitty, and though her cries were like those of a woman in distress, she simply couldn't and wouldn't have been in actual distress with anyone from Arcanium, which made entering the Ringmaster's trailer even worse.

Elizabeth thought she could creep out without either of them noticing, given how distracted they were in each other, but as she backed down the stairs, the Ringmaster turned his head to stare death and destruction directly at her. At the Ringmaster's pause within and against her, Kitty also looked over.

Kitty couldn't say anything, but at the sight of Elizabeth's state, she reached behind her to close her fingers around the Ringmaster's arm. There was no urgency or tension to the gesture, although the Ringmaster was a copper coil burning hotter the longer Elizabeth remained. He didn't become less intense, but he didn't come after her when she did a hard reverse out of the trailer.

Shit, shit, shit.

There was no Voice of Bell in her head, so she hadn't broken a cardinal rule or anything, but she was pretty sure she'd broken one of Arcanium's unwritten laws — *Thou shalt not invade the Ringmaster's privacy.*

Losing control of her excess limbs in mounting panic that she'd be caught now that the Ringmaster had seen her, knowing that Bell could hear her thoughts at any time, she ran to Troy's trailer. Subtle rocking indicated Troy was in there with Christina.

Fuck.

Caroline had a tablet and a phone, but she lived at the carousel, and Elizabeth didn't know quite what that meant. However, with Kitty in the Ringmaster's trailer, she wouldn't be in her oddity tent.

Elizabeth hitched her secondary legs up with her secondary arms, both sets otherwise useless to her at the moment, though holding them messed with her center of gravity and she had to lean forward to make up for the change in balance. She likely looked ridiculous on so many levels, but there was no one to see her, or if there was, no one made themselves known. Except for the pale demon, no one was anywhere to be seen, which seemed odd — even with everyone's usual urge to fornicate after performances.

Caroline sat with her two men at one of the picnic tables in the food court. She was holding her phone, which eliminated that possibility.

Elizabeth ducked into Oddity Row. Darkness shrouded most of it, with the occasional beam of light from the food court pushing between the tents, but not enough to see well. She knew where Kitty's tent was in relation to the others, though, and a lamp inside limned the doorway.

Voices inside warned her before she opened the tent flap. She peeked through the edge of the doorway. One of the conjoined twins was removing her makeup while the other drank a tall glass of beer. Male voices came from the side of the room Elizabeth couldn't see.

Elizabeth fought the urge to hit the canvas.

Her skin prickled under the dried fluids and pieces of dead grass that clung to it, as though from millions of spider legs. In the wake of fear would come futility. The siren call of the whiskey back in her RV was almost too strong to resist.

On her way back around the big top to try for the carousel engineer's tablet, Elizabeth pulled up short.

Maya was as naked as Elizabeth, with red cloth to binding her wrists to a pole in the middle of the makeshift ring some performers used during the day. The same kind of cloth formed a blindfold and a gag. Her clothes had been left in a pile outside the wooden partition.

She looked like a witch waiting for fire, a sacrifice before a demon's altar, too lush for innocence and deceptively helpless — because, like Kitty, no one would dare harm Maya. Which meant her binding was as accepted as Kitty's, and the man fucking her who wasn't Bell was there with her permission.

The sword swallower cupped her breasts in his inadequate hands. They plumped between his thin fingers as he thrust into her. He didn't look like he had it in him to take her as thoroughly as he did, but he grunted with need as he brought himself to orgasm, and Maya arched as he ground into her. The gag muffled any sound she made, but the legs wrapped tightly around the sword swallower's skinny waist spoke loudly enough, along with her hips. Maya was so much freer in her desire than Elizabeth could ever be anymore.

Elizabeth lowered her gaze, grinding her teeth that she envied Maya for even a moment.

The sword swallower eased Maya's legs from around him until her feet touched the ground again. He whispered in her ear, stroking her hair. Sickly or not, even in the dark, Elizabeth could sense his post-coital glow. And though Maya's eyes were covered and her mouth was stuffed, the lift of her cheekbones could only mean a smile.

The sword swallower kissed her over the gag and tucked himself back into his loose cotton trousers. Then he just walked away — left Maya naked and vulnerable and sacrificial in the center of the ring, in the middle of winter.

Elizabeth assumed the same magic that allowed her to wear skimpy outfits in winter without freezing a tit off also applied to Maya, but the woman's nipples were still tight and hard, her body quivering without the warmth of another body on hers. There were bruises, marks, cuts, unmistakable gleams on her skin. She'd been designed to appear as debauched from up close as she'd appear innocent from a distance. There was no way the sword swallower had left all those marks, those smears over her thighs. He hadn't been the first. And with her still tied to the pole, Elizabeth guessed he wasn't supposed to be her last.

She fought the urge to vomit, because the display was too familiar by half, almost as though it had been intended for her to witness. She also fought the impulse to undo the knots. Maya had chosen her own vice. Elizabeth had no stone to throw.

And she didn't want to alert Maya that she was there.

Elizabeth ran as quietly as she could for the pile of clothes. She wasn't convinced Maya would have her phone with her, but it was worth a shot, since there was also a small purse amid the small heap of sequins, silk, leather and lace.

Maya angled her body toward the crunch of grass, the rustle of her clothes. "Who's there?"

Elizabeth didn't answer. The phone wasn't among the clothes. She unzipped the bag. Dark red lipstick and mascara. Cash. Driver's license. She must have been intending to leave the circus tonight before she'd been otherwise detained.

The search hit pay-dirt under the cash.

Maya's phone was password-protected, but the swipe patterns on the screen protector showed that Maya had gone for that ever-secure 'numbers in sequence' solution to memorization. A simple swipe of 1234 got Elizabeth in.

When she reached the dial pad, she put in the only number she could think of that wasn't the police.

A man answered. "Hello?"

It didn't matter that Maya's number wouldn't be familiar. A good preacher and good prophet would never deny a soul.

"Father." Just saying it made her throat threaten to close completely, but she swallowed past her pride. "It's me. I'm in trouble. Please…"

Maya made an alarmed sound against the gag, struggled against the bindings on her wrist.

Elizabeth spoke faster. "Be careful. Arcanium's —"

She was going to say 'evil,' but the phone was plucked from her hand.

Bell's chilling warmth replaced her biological father's voice in her ear. "I told you I'd give you one chance to fail to escape without punishment. That was your chance, my dear. It's quite all right, Maya. I've taken care of it."

"You can't ride in like a white knight then turn around and expect me to play geisha like you do your own women," Elizabeth said without facing him.

"You quite misunderstand the purpose of this exercise if you think it in any way resembles what your ex required of you," Bell said. "Just because Maya takes many lovers in Arcanium doesn't mean she does so solely under my influence or under duress, as you were tonight."

Elizabeth spun around and grabbed for the phone.

Bell clicked his tongue, keeping it out of her reach. "You only had the one chance. If you try to call your good father again, I'll have to punish you, and I wouldn't want to do that tonight of all nights. Besides, you already denied the Ringmaster the pleasure of whipping a man. He'd be even more upset if you interrupted his evening with Kitty for a second time, don't you think?"

She gritted her teeth, but she stopped snatching at the phone. Bell tossed it onto Maya's pile of clothing then took Elizabeth by the elbow to lead her away from the ring.

Elizabeth glanced back at Maya. She'd stilled against the pole once more, although the knitting of her brow over the blindfold showed she was still troubled.

"She'll be fine. This is not the first time we've played this game," Bell said.

"You think it's a game?"

"Of a kind. Maya has many things she believes she must be punished for."

"And you punish her with anonymous sex?"

"She is never in danger, never taken advantage of. She suffers no pain other than at my hands or under the Ringmaster's whip, of her own volition. It is a game of punishment, but the atonement is real."

"Only a demon would convince a woman that she can atone for her sins like that," Elizabeth said.

Bell laughed quietly as he pushed open the flap to the fortune teller's tent and guided her in. Elizabeth resisted, stopping one set of feet outside the opening and the other inside.

All the candles in the tent lit up as his magic swept across the room, illuminating everything at once — lanterns, icons, votives, scarves, beads and bells, crystals and skulls, the table in the center with the tarot cards. Add in the dry winter grass, it was a five-alarm fire waiting to happen.

"There are many ways to atone, and I convinced her of nothing. She delivered herself into my hands. I simply give her what she needs, in my own way." He sat at the delicate round table, setting his tarot cards aside to leave nothing at the table that she might object to, other than himself. "Come in, Elizabeth. It's time for us to have a talk."

She was as conditioned in her religious responses as she was in the sexual, and her stomach clenched coldly as she stepped into a fortune teller's tent. But God didn't smite her with a bolt of lightning here any more than he smote her for any other trespass.

Bell didn't mock her for her thoughts. He waited patiently for her to reach the chair opposite his. All the fluids covering her smeared onto the metal, but Bell didn't blink. She settled back in the chair, uncomfortable but without much other choice.

"You've put me and yourself in an awkward position," he said.

Elizabeth crossed her arms. "You didn't have a problem with what I did while you were possessing my body."

"Not my prisoners. Your father."

"Oh, you didn't see that coming?"

"When I realized your intent, I could have sent someone to stop you, or I could have entered you then as I did in the prisoners' trailer. I chose not to, because now you cannot story to escape again without consequence. However, any outside scrutiny upon Arcanium makes protecting its secret more complicated. You put my people at risk, and that endangers your father."

Elizabeth's arms across her chest tightened so hard she almost kept herself from breathing. She unwound them to clutch instead at the sides of her chair. "What are you going to do?"

"If he leaves Arcanium unchallenged, nothing," Bell replied. "But in my experience, when daughters are in harm's way, fathers trespass. They threaten my people. And they risk exposing Arcanium to those who would try to destroy it or take it for themselves."

"Please don't hurt him."

She hadn't known who else to call. There'd been no one else who might believe her, who might still seek her while she was lost. She'd hoped for a way out of this hell, not to drag someone down into it with her.

Bell clasped his hands on the table. "That, my dear, is up to you. We've had parents burst their way into the circus before without bloodshed. If he does not trespass, his fate is in your hands. To protect him, you must protect Arcanium. Do you understand?"

She didn't acknowledge the command, too stiff to nod or shake her head against his warning. Her reaction was acknowledgment enough.

Bell suddenly pushed the table aside and moved his chair closer to hers, his knee between hers and no illusion of protection between them. When she flinched, closing her body from him, the hardness to his strange eyes softened. "Don't fear *me*, Lizzie."

"Easy for you to say."

He caressed the sides of her face, framing her. "You are fully capable of protecting your father, as you are of protecting yourself. My power was not the only thing that held those men at bay."

After what had happened, she shouldn't have wanted another man to touch her, especially a man who thought he owned her and could show her like a prized pony. She hated Bell as much as ever.

The problem was that she had a number of points of comparison, even with his fingers on her skin. She hated him, but not as much as she hated *them*. She hated that she let him touch her, but not as much as she'd hated herself for letting *them* do it. And of all the things Bell had done, of all the things she feared he would do to her, there were things she *knew* he wouldn't.

At the stroke of his thumb along her cheekbone, a cold, tingling breeze swept over her body. The jelly coating of dried fluids that itched and streaked over her disappeared. She felt fresher, if not quite clean.

"I'm sorry," he said quietly. "I'm sorry your introduction to the circus was one that led you to believe my prisoners would be better company."

She found the strength to jerk her face away, just enough. "Don't patronize me. You're glad this happened. You were just waiting for your people to look good in comparison."

"If I had told you what they planned before it happened, would you have trusted my warning? Your boy crossed *my* line the first time he urged you to touch him, but you would never have trusted me if I hadn't waited until they crossed *yours*. Do you think I *liked* waiting for them to do so before I could interfere?"

Elizabeth narrowed her eyes and leaned in until their faces were less than a hand's breadth apart. "I think you live for it."

"No. Almost everyone who comes into Arcanium struggles in their beginning, but nothing pleases me more than when they find their footing. Some of them know exactly what they want. Some need guidance. And others need to walk over broken glass before they find any rest."

"And some have to drain their burn blisters and have their limbs sewn back on," Elizabeth shot back.

"The day they can say what they've done out loud without choking on justifications, I might consider loosening their chains. It'll take more than just a year before I can finally use them the way I want to."

"The way you'll use Kevin and Hank? The way you use me?"

He smiled, his skin golden as a lion's in the candlelight. "There's no shame in being a freak."

"What do you know about it? You chose to be a fortune teller. You didn't deform yourself."

"You have no idea what I've done."

His response sent a chill down her spine.

"I've been in this game much longer than you think, and this is hardly my only form. If you want to decry the horror of deformation, I suggest you speak to Kitty or Sandra before you dare preach to me about the tragedy I've cast you in. You weren't born with your extra limbs, and you won't leave Arcanium with them. The initial reaction from those who see you isn't repulsion, as it is for many of those whom I value most here, those who have to fight past first impressions when they never earned such a fight. Your tribulation was never in your oddity, so let's move past the way I've changed you, because that torment has since faded in your mind to mere inconvenience. It's the woman you were who haunts you still."

She clenched her teeth. Because God help her, he wasn't wrong.

Bell reached under his chair and pulled out a bottle of her whiskey and two tumblers that hadn't been there before. He poured several fingers into both, then handed one to her.

She brought it to her mouth and downed it. Bell matched her without a blink. When she put the glass on her thigh, he poured them both another.

"Sasha, Kitty and Maya provide the bulk of sexual tension in this circus. Believe it or not, I didn't bring you into the circus because of what your ex-lover made you do for him. I didn't want Lucy, Elizabeth. I wanted you. I wanted the woman who hid her tattoos and the sins against you in layers of shame. I wanted to tear down the curtain you thought you needed to hide them."

"If you didn't want Lucy, you shouldn't have made me look just like her then put me in a box or tied me up for men to visit their fantasy in person," she said. "They don't even try to pretend they're not taking pictures of my tits and ass. When they think they can get away with it, they jerk themselves off with their hand in their pants. They're practically moaning in public. It's only going to get worse, because the word's getting out. Someone's going to complain to the management."

Bell poured her one more. After she gulped that one down, her movements slower than before, he gently took the tumbler away and set it down with the bottle.

He took her secondary hands in his, raised them up to meet her prime hands so that he could clasp all four. "The spiders are as much your protection as the glass. You cling to your fear of them because you believe that if you stay afraid, you won't grow accustomed to the circus and you can still resist me. But I'm not asking you to be anything more than what you are."

"Your pin-up Spider." She didn't slur, but her speech had slowed.

"Exhibitionism comes with the territory—always has. But sexiness isn't sex. I won't require that of you. All I require is that you serve Arcanium, and you've done that. Your fear was never part of the deal. I don't want you to be afraid—not of Arcanium, not of Dez, not of the Creature or the bastard pigs you surrounded yourself with. Not of spiders, of whiskey, or yourself. You've developed a taste for fear, but it's not what you're meant for."

He spread her hands to open her body to him, and for some reason, she swayed forward, her blinks long and something humming inside her lips. She wasn't turned on, but she was…something. Something familiar, better now than it had once been.

"You are a beautiful, strange, dark, intimidating woman." His words brushed her skin, hot against her mouth. She could almost taste them over her tongue. "You were that woman before Dez thought he created you. I gave you the form you needed to match. I didn't bring you here to be afraid. I brought you here for them to fear you."

He released her hands. They drifted down to the edge of the chair. She didn't stop him as he caressed the corners of her mouth with his knuckles, brushed his fingertips over the terrain of her lips and beyond. She parted her lips for him. He was so gentle, almost too gentle to feel as he traced over the sharp edges of her filed teeth.

"You're not anyone's plaything, Lizzie. These are weapons. And so are these." Bell pressed against her upper canines. He grunted, the sound almost sexual, as her canines extended out of her gums with a soft click through her head. The slight salt of his blood spread over her tongue.

His unnatural pupils had expanded almost to the edge of the irises. He eased his dripping fingers from her mouth. A clear fluid, tinged yellow like lymph, watered down the red. Bell sucked them into his mouth. When he drew them out again, they were clean, the places she'd broken through emerged smooth and undamaged. Her teeth retracted with the same soft click.

"Venom tastes sweet to me, my dear, but it won't sweeten the ones whom you kiss. You wondered what your bite could do with a little poison at your disposal. I like the way you think."

Her venom joined the salty blood down her throat with the same bitter, dark sweetness that she suspected he tasted as well. Antifreeze was supposed to taste sweet, too.

"So anything I bite—"

He shook his head. "Injection must be deliberate. A single bite won't kill unless you linger, pumping the poison into them. It will cause great pain, though, so use it wisely. I know how little you enjoy unnecessary cruelty."

The worst part was that he wasn't being sarcastic at all.

He cradled her head and kissed her cheek as though he wanted something more. But then he stood, offering his hand.

"Do you need help returning home?"

"I've walked through this circus drunk before. I doubt it'll be the last time." She eschewed his hand, but she didn't jerk away when he helped steady her as she stood.

Elizabeth paused before leaving the tent. "You created the storm, Bell. To pretend you're not responsible for floods and fire is the worst kind of denial, because I know you're not that naïve. You protected me, but don't think you're my savior in this story. If you want to punish everyone responsible for what happened tonight, you might try looking in a mirror."

* * * *

Instead of stumbling back to the caravan, she skirted around the food court lights to approach the baleful shadow of the haunted funhouse.

Nothing on the inside had anything to offer her. That was her job, nothing more. No, if she wanted to reach what she'd come for, she'd have to climb.

Oh, she could call him. And if she called and he could hear her, he would come. But she didn't want to call him.

She went up the stairs to the entrance then ducked under the railing. Would the slats lining the outside even hold her? Did they protrude enough for her to get a finger- and foothold? Her heart lurched against her chest as she stretched out half of her body to feel along the walls like an insect with antennae, finding the seams and testing them.

At least it was too dark to see the ground.

As soon as she determined she could hold onto the sides of the building, she slowly eased onto the slats, ready to jump if she heard anything cracking. The nailed-in wood held.

She felt her way up—slow, steady, swaying, strong despite the heaviness in her limbs from the whiskey. She could hold the side of the building with her secondary hands, but her legs were more difficult to maneuver, and they threw off her sense of balance as they dangled behind her. But they didn't become a problem until she reached the edge of the roof and tried to pull herself up.

She could have been running a marathon for how she breathed and how blood raced through her veins. Elizabeth clung to the roof edge, her eyes squeezed shut—as though she could see any better with them open. Fighting against ever-familiar panic, she drew her secondary legs in, curling them around her prime legs to adjust the center of her balance closer to what she'd once had. Her prime legs needed to work harder when she raised them up the side, but she didn't fall.

As soon as she could, she launched herself onto the roof, rolling before settling into a heap. A little dust and dirt was nothing in comparison to what had covered her before.

She pushed herself upright and climbed back to her feet, slipping only once. Then she made her deliberate way to the nest in the center of the roof.

The Creature looked up at her with mild bemusement. His eyes reflected like garnet in moonlight, though the moon was only a crescent and not enough for her to see much more of him.

"I would have helped you if you'd asked," he said.

She fell to her knees. Both sets protested such abuse, especially the one Hank had bitten.

"Are you drunk?"

She nodded, trusting his sight was better in the darkness than hers.

He sat up. "I felt your terror tonight."

"Why didn't you come, then?"

"I did. Bell told me I wouldn't be necessary, that protecting you was his responsibility this time." The blood light of his eyes shifted as he took in the sight of her. "I didn't expect you. I didn't expect…this. I could have helped you. All you had to do was call."

"But if I'd called for you, what would I have had to offer you when I came?" she asked.

"Offer?"

She crawled into his nest. When she jostled his legs, he held her shoulders to direct her to less bony places. She stopped when his breath ghosted cold over her face. His eyes were hooded, and though he steadied her, his hands weren't steady.

She swayed again, toward him, almost kissing him. God, she wanted nothing more than his lips on hers, but she shouldn't.

The Creature didn't know why she shouldn't. Despite his refusal before, he tilted his head to meet her.

One kiss. She allowed herself one kiss, leaning against him, into him, staying soft, barely parting her lips. One kiss.

Then she shook her head against the urge, against the need that pounded on the inside of her skull. She almost wrapped her arms, all four, around his shoulders and begged, but she bit her tongue and forced herself back.

"What happened?" His husky voice nearly undid her again, but she kept her sharp teeth on her tongue. "What terrified you tonight so much that Bell had to save you? Why did you come to me drunk and climb the side of a building just to offer me a token of atavistic fear?"

"Can I sleep here tonight?" She couldn't meet his eyes. If she did, maybe he'd see inside them. Maybe he'd see the shame there. And if she kissed him again, maybe he would taste blood and venom in her mouth. "I don't want to sleep alone."

"Of course," he said quietly.

He guided her into the center of the nest, reclined back down again. There was enough room for her to put space between them, but though she wouldn't freeze, she still preferred his heat.

The Creature covered her with one of his blankets, and she tucked herself against his side, resting her head on his shoulder. He brushed his lips against her scalp.

"Would you like for me to feed?"

She nodded.

They weren't quite kisses anymore. His lips shifted lower, behind her ear, under her jaw, against her pulse. He held her close with the blanket between them and fed deeply—from the climb, from the tent, from the trailer, from the tangled web. He fed on whatever he could find.

* * * *

When she woke up, he was stroking her head as though he'd been awake the whole time, yet he appeared far fresher than her.

"The Ringmaster hasn't needed to use his whip outside of the funhouse or a performance for a long time. This morning, the cracks of his pleasure echoed through the circus like a massacre. Might that have had anything to do with why you came to me?" He brought his clawed fingers to her eyes and somehow rubbed the sleep from the corners without pricking her in the process.

"It might have." She groaned as she sat up. She ached all over—from fighting, from climbing, from sheer tension. She thought her muscles would be used to the latter by now.

"Who must I kill?"

She stared down at him thoughtfully. "You've never been violent."

"I can start."

"Bell's plans will do for now." Saying the words nearly caused physical pain, but she'd always valued the truth, even when she despised speaking it out loud.

The smells of circus day breakfast wafted to the funhouse. She twisted around to better gauge the time of day based on where the sun was in relation to the big top.

The Creature grasped her arm before she could look behind her. "Do not be alarmed."

"Why?" she said carefully.

"The Gentleman stands right behind you. He shows his teeth."

"And that would alarm me?" She'd lowered her voice. It seemed rude to speak at normal volume about the Gentleman with him right there, even though he could still hear them.

"It might."

She brought her thighs together and covered her breasts with her secondary arms, but she wasn't as afraid of another monster's eyes on her as she thought she would be. She braced herself and turned around.

The Gentleman's face wasn't blank anymore. His mouth had appeared from nowhere, spreading far wider than a man's and lifting his cheeks. Lips pulled away from too-large teeth, a caricature of human, magnified to monstrous proportions. He stood before her with a breakfast burrito wrapped in butcher paper held in his white hands. He smiled at her as though features on his face were the most natural thing in the world and not at all like he wanted to swallow her head whole.

The Gentleman leaned down—and he had to lean down quite far from his height—to present the burrito to her with all the courtliness that had given him his name. His massive teeth were less than a foot away from her when she took the food from him.

"Thank you." She wasn't sure if that was what he wanted, but her upbringing had taught her to always be polite when uncertain.

His teeth clicked with menace as his smile shifted. He straightened, turned on his heel like a soldier, walked to the edge of the roof. Then he stepped off, though it was a good fifteen or twenty feet to the ground. Only a muffled thump followed the descent — no human or bestial cry of pain.

Her hands shook just a little as she twisted back around toward the Creature.

"What exactly is he, the Gentleman? I thought he was one of the demons, but their teeth have all been sharp. It's even creepier his way, so I don't know why he doesn't use that in the funhouse."

"The Gentleman is as unknown as I am, though his designs are more malicious, to be sure. He craves fear from a far deeper place than simple sustenance. It's why you attract him the way you attract me, though he prefers children and teenagers." The Creature traced the edge of her face. "Your fears are like those of a child — pure. With age, they've woven and spread through your mind, layer upon layer of psychological tangles, but you give in to them completely. Or you used to." His nostrils flared. "There is still a shroud of fear wrapped around you, but it's not what it once was, is it, little Spider?"

"I don't know what you're talking about." As far as she was concerned, that tangle was a permanent knot woven around her intestines, and it hadn't moved an inch.

"The quality of your fear is changing. I wonder, which would you rather be locked in a glass room with now? I recognized some of the prisoners' screams as the

Ringmaster flayed their hides. I know they are responsible for whatever happened to you. Would you choose them? Or would you choose your spiders?"

"They're not mine."

"They know every inch of your skin, as I do, and they'd protect it as though it were their own. Bell favored you with them, and they are yours, as I am."

He withdrew his hand from her, resting back against his pillows, his abrupt silence as unreadable as his expression in the early morning light.

Elizabeth slowly lowered her hands. As he had already pointed out, he was more than familiar with everything exposed. "Bell told me they were my protection. If he gave them to me, did he give you to me, too? Were you always Bell's plan for me?"

"If I am part of Bell's machinations, he has not informed me. I have no doubt that he encouraged my pursuit on your first evening in the glass coffin, but I assure you, I'm not his agent, Elizabeth. Nor am I your temptation, as you fear."

There was no point asking how he knew she feared a master darker than Bell behind the Creature's motivations. But if he were half the demon he appeared to be, he wouldn't have denied her when she'd been uncertain. He would have plied her uncertainty, threaded it through her desire as Dez had done.

"Bell wouldn't protect his humans as he does if the demons were the ones he sought to appease. Fear Bell's power and the Ringmaster's punishment, but there's nothing else in this circus to be afraid of." His wings rustled as he gathered himself to his feet. "You are quite safe, and where you are not, we shall willingly draw blood for you."

"He did draw blood...with my hands." Elizabeth held up her nails. She expected to see reddish-brown stains under the white parts of the nail, but Bell's magic had cleansed even within the crevices. "He was inside me, puppeteered me the same way he forces me into his glass coffin, into his spiderweb. But sometimes he didn't. Sometimes I drew blood on my own." She looked up at the Creature, a looming shadow but without the Gentleman's menace. "What does he want from me? What is he trying to create?"

The Creature tilted his head in thought. "He's already created what he wanted to create. What do you want to become?"

Fearless.

She didn't speak the thought out loud, as dark and wild in her head as Bell at his most furious, but far from the sound of his voice. Then on its heels came something darker and wilder, the other side of the same coin.

Feared.

She ran her tongue over the seam between tooth and gum where her upper canines would extend, where venom lay waiting.

In the light, it was more difficult for her to believe that the woman in the semi-trailer had been her. It was hard to believe that she wouldn't see Kevin again as he had been — a mild-mannered man too young for his age, too clueless for his urges. Hard to believe that she'd been surrounded, touched all over, touching back, and that none of them would come near her again because of the man who had imbued her with more than flesh or semen. He had violated her to the edges of her will, yet she'd accepted him inside her far more readily than Hank's fingers or Kevin's cock.

She couldn't have resisted him, but she hadn't even tried. Perhaps in accepting his help, she'd already sealed her fate as one of his. Somehow, that didn't seem as dire as it would have just a day ago.

Elizabeth stood up, parted her legs a bit to feel the cold breeze against places warmed under blankets. She welcomed winter's icy fingers between her thighs. She remembered Bell's fingers in her mouth with her assent, Hank's fingers in her cunt without it. It was all the same to her well-used desire. She couldn't control what Dez had done to her lust, but she could control with whom she exorcised it. She could control who to accept and who to deny. She could choose a worthier partner, someone who would say no to her, someone who would only say yes if her yes was sure.

She'd contorted the Creature's desire for her, sucked him into the same plague of uncertainty that tormented her. But he'd had a chance to manipulate her in kind, take what he wanted with her tentative consent, and he hadn't.

"I don't want to be afraid anymore," she said.

Elizabeth wanted to kiss him now, fast, hard, wrap herself around him and arch him in. But she moved slowly, all four of her hands reaching for him, stroking down his ribs and up to his shoulders. Deliberate. Slowly, yes, but without hesitation.

She'd had enough of hands where she didn't want them, gazes touching her in places she hadn't unveiled, that cold knot in her belly that seemed to force her actions against her will. For once in such a long time, could she just choose the vice, without the shame and guilt that accompanied it?

At the brush of her thumbs against his jaw, he closed his hands around her wrists. He didn't squeeze, but his strength pressed against her bones nonetheless. "We agreed we would not do this until you could say yes without saying no — not until you were certain."

He could hold only two wrists. She trailed her secondary fingertips down his abdomen, smiling inside at the twitching of the muscles under her touch. It was an oddly human reaction.

Elizabeth took a trembling breath to ease herself closer to him. The last time she'd made the deliberate decision to slip between the sheets of a man's bed, he'd taken that choice and made it his. She'd been a sex slave kneeling in the palm of any man's hand since, even when she wore modesty and convinced them not to try.

"After Dez, after Kevin, after Hank, after... Do you need me to say it? Do you need me to say I want you? Because I've had more men looking at me like something to eat in the last twenty-four hours than I'd like. A few of them even got a taste. But if they got a taste, I want you to have more. You deserve —"

When she lowered herself to her knees again in his nest, the Creature joined her. Elizabeth laughed in spite of herself. He couldn't even let her suck him off without trying to put them on an even footing.

"It is not about what I deserve," he protested, though he had shifted attention down to her lips. Hard as it was to tell exactly where he looked, her body knew what her eyes couldn't see. She licked her lower lip and imagined him sliding over her tongue.

"You don't deserve my body," she said. "You've earned my respect. And because of that respect, I want you to have it."

"You."

Elizabeth paused in her effort to find a tie or catch to his loincloth—he'd always been the one to loosen whenever they'd bothered removing it. "What?"

"You want me to have *you*. If I have your body, I want more than just the sum of your parts, however many parts you have."

He used his grip on her wrists to part her arms and pushed her slowly but inexorably down, back into the soft, uneven pile of cushions, pillows and blankets, undirtied by the elements—only by the cold slide of sweat down her back as he adjusted his position above her. He wasn't quite the shadow anymore. The sun haloed his edges with the kind of clarity that only came in the morning.

"If you let me take your body, I want the rest of you, Elizabeth. Everything. Your taste, your softness, your hardness, your fear, your stubbornness, your passion." He shuffled his wings, sliding his knee up to spread both sets of her legs. He dipped down, poised above her nipple, which had tightened in the cold and tightened more with the heat and moisture of his breath. But though he was less than an inch from her, and though he pressed the tip of his tongue between his teeth, he lavished nothing but consideration. He squeezed her wrists in unthreatening warning when she tried to raise herself up to him. "Your enthusiasm. It pains me when I believe I might be taking you against your wish, if not your will. So I ask this of you again, Spider... What do you want?"

The nervousness in her belly had a different quality when she dispensed with the efforts to remove his loincloth and instead reached under to stroke along his cock, to take his scrotum and the base of his cock in her palm with her own slight power. Men had once sworn oaths like this, and even with his cock only just beginning to swell under the permission of her touch, she could understand why — vulnerability and virility, both a hot weight in her hand.

It took her a moment to realize her nervousness felt different because excitement accompanied it.

"I want you to fuck me." She hadn't spoken plainly like that since she'd done so for a camera, for the pleasure of others. Doing it for herself felt unfamiliar in her mouth, but she kept going. "I want you to kiss me until I can't breathe. I want your hands on me, all over me. I want you to take it all. Jesus fucking Christ, just fuck me. *Now*."

Blasphemy tasted better than anything the prisoners had ever offered her.

She stroked up to the head of his cock, which was suddenly hard as a rock under the soft skin of his body. Yet still he hesitated.

Elizabeth stopped trying to make him take her, stopped trying to touch everything at once, although her skin screamed at her for withdrawing from contact. She slowly sat up despite his hold on her wrists, forcing him to adjust back, curious and slightly wary.

She crawled her gaze over his body, peering beyond the oddity and following instead the lines of his muscle, the contours, the density she knew she'd encounter if she touched him again to convince herself that he was there, that she was there with him and she wanted this. She wasn't tumbling into a fuck, stumbling accidentally against his lips and over his cock, manipulated, played, bribed or blackmailed.

His erection tented the cloth she'd left draped over him. He'd chosen not just to be aroused but to show her how much.

As she considered the reality of the Creature, she felt him staring at her, following his own heated paths, somehow more intimate than any macro lens with which Dez had caressed her. She had never seen the Creature close up in bright enough light before to notice the shimmer, like red mercury, shifting whenever he moved his eyes to search her face.

"What do you see, little Spider?"

"Not enough."

He licked the tips of his teeth with almost a purr as he settled back on his heels and slipped his fingers into the complicated knot at his hip, effortlessly releasing it.

There was nothing unfamiliar about what was underneath. She knew every inch of his cock from when it had slid through her hand, her folds, inside her. She knew his sac would be heavy in her palm, how it would swing forward and strike her as he thrust. She'd seen the creases where his legs met his torso, the flex of his thighs. She'd seen it all before. But now he presented himself to her as unobstructed as she.

Their bodies were no mystery to perfect strangers, much less to each other, yet all four of Elizabeth's hands shook as she reached to stroke the V of his hips above the crease that led her to the heated, flushed erection. It twitched with his quickened heartbeat, quickened breath, as he leaned in again, not to kiss her but to urge her onto her back once more.

"What do you see now?" His voice had dropped low enough to shiver inside her. Weight brought his cock against her abdomen. She trapped it there with a firm grip, still not breaking the intense eye contact he maintained.

"The one I want to touch me. Kiss me. Fuck me. I want it. I want *you*. Now." She pressed down on his erection until he winced. "Don't be slow or gentle. I can't take any more of this waiting." She arched against his cock, smearing his pre-cum over her skin. "Please. I'm asking. I'm begging. Just take it. Take *me* — "

He swatted her hand away and took hold of himself instead. He stroked the head through her folds to her entrance, gauging how receptive she was to what her words demanded, to determine the truth of what she might say solely to please him. Finding her wet and more than welcoming, he jerked forward. They groaned together as he pushed into her, able to slide in completely.

"Has there been anyone else since…" Elizabeth couldn't finish the thought, because the Creature pulled back just to fill her again, shoving her thighs farther apart with the press of his hips.

She dug her fingernails into his back, his buttocks, catching skin and fur underneath. He had his own trouble completing his sentence.

"No one before you. No one since. I don't need… Don't need release, but I still…still lose my mind once you enter it. I think of other men touching you, making you shiver, when I can do that for you. And you don't have to force yourself with me, don't have to swallow back shame. You can have so much more…" He lowered his forehead to hers, their heavy breathing mingling between them, but he still didn't kiss her, even when she parted her lips for him, bared her teeth in kind to his own. "You have no idea how much more you deserve. How much better your sensitivity can be in the right hands. How delicious the fear is when you allow yourself to feel it without fearing more in its wake."

His words stopped making sense to her, strings of moans that eventually devolved as he quickened his pace and force. He spoke instead through actions, claimed her as though it had been years, staring into her eyes, though she couldn't help hers rolling back, her eyelashes fluttering.

She didn't even want to let him go long enough to bring one of her hands between them to stroke her clit. She was already so turned on, though—from the unwanted events of last night, from him, from whatever magic always lingered in the air, just from the way she was—that she didn't need the extra bursts of pleasure. She was actually afraid she might come before him.

She wanted to wrap herself all the way around him, crawl into him. In spite of all her limbs, she couldn't get close enough. Fresh sweat smoothed some of the way, but friction heated their skin even more. He stroked her, not just inside, but everywhere he moved. Every thrust stimulated her whole body at once. Even the flesh above his cock rubbed against her clit—not as directly as she needed, not as firmly as she wanted, but in a constant tease that maddened her more.

Without a kiss to muffle her, she released all her pleasure and frustration, as though cries and moans could bring her higher. And in some ways, they did, when they joined in discordant harmony with the Creature's groans—softer than hers but unmistakable, because he couldn't muffle himself against her either.

Elizabeth had the vague sense that other people were near the haunted funhouse, but that wasn't part of her world right now. There was only the rooftop, the nest, the Creature himself and the fierce cocoon of lust and pleasure that wrapped around her at his urging.

"Feed on me." She fought to bring his head down to her neck. "Please."

"But you aren't afraid," he said with a smile. He nipped her neck then withdrew, spreading his wings for balance. The cords of his neck tensed and released, his smile shifting to grimace, but not from anger or annoyance. He was hotter inside her, thicker, his moans edged with a growl that told her he was close. Never had he seemed more the monster than he did in the light, but she'd be far more suspicious of a normal human face.

She trailed her fingertips over his strangeness. "Scare me."

"What?"

"Make me afraid. Then feed from me."

He surged inside her with a shiver, but he managed not to come. "Are you sure?"

"I trust you."

She trusted him implicitly, knew he wouldn't do anything to truly hurt her. But her fears didn't care what she knew, no matter how much she'd tried to arm herself with facts, truth and logic. There was no reason for the Creature to ever go without.

He jerked her upright and against him with a firm grip at the back of her neck, then curled his arm around her waist to anchor her there, all four of her legs wrapped in some way around him already.

"As you wish."

That was the only warning before he slammed his foot onto the roof and launched them into the air. The sudden force of his body pushing upward shoved him with almost unbearable pressure into her cunt, but with the roof receding and the ground even farther away, her fear of heights gripped her even more tightly than the Creature. He wouldn't fall, wouldn't let her go, but her mind's eye saw herself plummeting, all eight of her limbs in broken angles on the roof, blood bubbling from her mouth.

Every time he flapped his massive, powerful wings, it was like a thrust into her — up, down, in, out — and he was still hard as iron. Her helpless reaction to sex intertwined with her irresistible response to fear in an all-too-familiar combination that brought him to her neck with his own fundamental craving.

He pulled back his wings to dive toward the roof as he buried his mouth against her neck, his tongue hot and his teeth just barely restrained against the flesh. He almost pricked her when he spread his wings again to parachute them back into his nest, but she drew blood from him with her nails, orgasm crashing through her, the flush of his feed siphoning fear away and leaving behind only pleasure. His body was artless against her now, that of an animal as much as a man as he took from her, consumed and claimed all he could.

He came, gasping for breath into her shoulder, jerking so furiously that the jut of his hips would leave bruises against her thighs.

She twitched with aftershock as he bent to claim other parts of her. They weren't kisses, though he used his mouth. He left marks on her pale skin that darkened through the black ink, all the way down to her folds. She cried out all over again as he tugged at the flesh there between a monster's teeth, lapped at the cum he'd left behind in her as well as her own arousal, then brought himself up to her clit. She clutched at the sides of his head, canted roughly into his curling tongue, but nothing stopped him from his relentless feast.

If she didn't know any better, she'd say he'd found fear there as well.

He didn't stop until she'd come again, a savage quaking of her body, her throat raw from a different kind of screaming than the funhouse wrested from her, and without the protections it afforded her. She twisted, writhed, tears streaming down her temples and along her smooth head. She tangled the blankets and pummeled the Creature's back with her heels. He softened his sucking, then fed instead upon the fresher draught of wetness that he'd coaxed from her, only stopping when there was nothing left to take and he'd licked her through an aftershock almost as strong as a climax.

The Creature folded his wings and raised himself onto his hands and knees. They both panted, and though her nerve endings still sang with sexual need that she wasn't entirely sure could ever be sated, she forced herself not to ask for *more, more, more*, to let the winter cool the moisture on their skin and the flush on their bodies.

"Still alive, little Spider?" He licked her tight nipple, bending it with his tongue.

"I could do it again." Elizabeth traced his sharp cheekbone with her thumb, her own brand of reassurance—that he hadn't gone too far, that she still trusted him.

"Could you do more?" The Creature crawled up her body then settled on top of her, his weight just to the right of her so she wasn't crushed.

"I think I could do it all morning."

He laughed against her collarbone. "That's not what I meant."

"It's what *I* meant." She stroked over the ridges on his back that led to his wings. "I don't know. I think I'd be willing to try more. With you."

"I shall consider it." He brought his hand between them to firmly cup her folds. "All morning?"

"As touching as this is — and as thrilling as what preceded it was for everyone down below — it's time to open the gates," Bell called from the ground. "Elizabeth needs to put on her costume and get in place. I can prevent your caterwauling from crossing the barrier of the circus, but once the gates open, anyone would be able to hear you, and I'm not interested in another indecency citation."

Her cheeks and ears flushed hot for whole new reasons as she took in the sounds of the stirring circus. There were voices, mutters, near the back exit of the funhouse, which meant that the prisoners had heard…

But why should she give a flying fuck what they'd heard? They already knew what she looked like, what she sounded like. As long as they knew they couldn't have it anymore, what difference did it make that they knew she'd just had much better sex with the Creature than anything they'd attempted to offer?

"Tonight, perhaps," the Creature said, nudging her clit with his palm before pulling away and rolling onto his back.

"We'll see. That's not a brush-off. We'll just see."

"You're not ashamed?" He watched her as she stood, watched how she didn't cross her arms over her breasts or hunch out of sight from any of the prisoners who might have been able to see her from the ground.

"Not right now."

There were worse things than fucking someone she wanted to fuck. Much worse. And if God didn't understand that, if He didn't understand there were many kinds of broken and many kinds of repairs, perhaps she shouldn't truck with that kind of deity. She felt better after a morning with a monster than ten years of celibacy under her family name.

Her latex bodysuit, powder and a towel were waiting for her at the edge of the roof near the entrance. She wiped herself down and dry, then worked the latex over her skin.

The Creature reached around from behind and zipped the front up to her neck. He'd tied his loincloth back around his waist, his anatomy composed and calm, but he kissed her jaw as she pulled the hooded mask over her head.

"The Gentleman will keep an eye on you when I cannot, as he always does, should any of the prisoners wish to retaliate."

Elizabeth clenched her teeth. The mechanism that extended her canines and released her venom clicked, but she didn't make them grow. It was enough to know how easily she could.

"Let them try."

Chapter Thirteen

The prisoners didn't do anything to try to bother her, which was probably helped by the fact that Hank no longer haunted the funhouse. Now that he and Kevin graced Oddity Row, Elizabeth wouldn't have to see them most circus days.

But the number of men who came through looking for her had increased, and she didn't like it. She didn't like that the Gentleman had to work so hard to keep them moving through the halls, didn't like their phones pointing at her, didn't like the way they clutched at the front of their pants or slipped their hands underneath. Unlike the red tent, the funhouse was dark, and there were far fewer disapproving glances in their direction.

It was worse, though, when the strobe lights and the soundtrack of spooky music and screams turned off, when the ropes released her so that she could lower herself to the floor. After leaving from the entrance now rather than the exit, she didn't have anywhere to go.

She couldn't go to the prisoners' trailer, which was what she'd always done after the funhouse closed. And she hated her RV, hated the clink and fumes of whiskey bottles, hated that she still took what Bell offered.

She had the Creature, but did she have anything else? Did she have anything human?

The Creature waited for her above the funhouse entrance when she came to him after picking up her dinner. This time she didn't have to climb. He reached down to take her hand, lifted her as though she weighed nothing.

When he stroked the moths on the side of her head, she tucked herself against him but turned away. "Do you mind if we don't..."

"Of course. Whatever you need."

"You can feed, but I don't think—"

He pressed a chaste kiss to her neck. "Elizabeth, you don't have to justify your reluctance to me."

He wrapped his wing around her like a blanket, sometimes feeding from her, sometimes just sitting back against the cushions as she ate. Then she settled back to sleep against him—her giant, terrifying guardian angel to keep her safe in the night.

* * * *

She lay in the glass coffin, Goliath climbing happily over her abdomen. His prickly paws tapped her breasts as he considered approaching her face.

A boy and girl, both roughly between ten and twelve years old, were transfixed with wonder. Kids' fascination was contagious, and she wasn't nearly as distressed by having Goliath there as she once had been. Fear was still present, no doubt, but she'd much rather have the arachnophobia and the kids staring at her than one of the anonymous guys who didn't know how to treat a lady in a box when he saw one.

As though on cue, a pair of larger men came in behind the kids' mother. They weren't muscle, per se, but they had plenty of it — muscle that men like them built to feel powerful. The way her body immediately distracted their attention, she knew that power wasn't meant for other men, no matter how tight their T-shirts were.

There was something sensitive, though, in their eyes.

She used to be surrounded with men like that.

Which meant she wasn't entirely surprised when Dez sauntered in. He pulled the curtain closed behind him, shutting away the bright outdoor shopping mall on the other side.

"Hello again, love." He made no effort to conceal the unmistakable sexual warmth that colored his greeting, even with the children and their mother there.

Elizabeth swallowed. The restraint that usually kept her from talking had been lifted, although she wasn't quite sure when. Even so, she knew she shouldn't call for help. She'd already used up her free chance.

Dez nodded at the other two men. Perhaps they all worked out together, because they had the same build, the same walk, the same sweetness to their eyes, as though they'd built their muscles to form the right breadth of shoulders for a woman to cry on.

Elizabeth fought to stay calm — no need to alarm the children or their mother unduly. But the boy seemed to notice her tension. The line of his eyebrows drew in, and he looked back at the three men looming behind him.

They weren't menacing or intimidating the guests, but their very presence so close and fixed upon

Elizabeth apparently made the mother nervous. "Come on, Collin, Darya. We still have some stuff to get. Do you want a pretzel?"

"I don't want to go shopping for Darya's clothes. I want to check out the bugs," Collin said.

"No, we've been here for twenty minutes already. We should give some other people a turn to look through."

So small, and the boy already had a little bit of the hero inside him... But he was young, and his mother was still in charge. He was apologetic as he left, which nearly broke Elizabeth's heart. He didn't even know why, but somehow he *knew* and wanted to help, but he *couldn't*. Looking at Collin, she could almost imagine what Todd would grow into.

Thinking about the Bishop children hadn't become any less painful over time, even thinking about the monster—who was, after all, just a teenager. And while still ambivalent about demons, Elizabeth had grown rather fond of a monster or two while in Arcanium.

She waved at the boy as he left. Then she slowly sat up, adjusting her right arms for Goliath to tuck into the crook of her elbow. "Hello, Dez. I was hoping I'd never see you again."

"Could have fooled me. I'm surprised that woman let her children in here with you looking that delicious. Are you cold, or are you just really happy to see me?" He smiled as one of the other men eased his hand out of his leather duster, pulling out a bolt cutter.

"Are you fucking serious?"

"Oh, we're not going to do a foursome here in the middle of a public tent, if that's what you're worried about. I'm more than willing for us to go back to being just us for a little while."

"You mean me being yours. Exclusively yours. Purely yours."

"You haven't been pure since I found you, Lizzie. Don't make my friends laugh."

Elizabeth wasn't positive his friends knew how to smile. "But keeping me was a kind of purity, wasn't it? It meant you could make me think *anything* was normal, right, nice, pleasurable, exhilarating, just by being my first and keeping me from anyone else. I was untouched, uncharted. If you think we can go back to being that again…"

"There's more than one way to chart new waters."

He nodded again at the man with the bolt cutters. The man handed them to Dez. Then, as though given a signal, the two muscled men left the tent, leaving her alone with Dez. There were the insects and spiders, of course, but they were a relatively passive audience — although they seemed to be getting restless, their little feet whispering over the ground in their terrariums, tapping against the glass, the Madagascar hissing cockroaches growing louder in agitation.

"This is quite a place." Dez flexed his fists around the rubber handles of the bolt cutters as he approached her. "You used to lose your mind every time a tiny spider with the tiniest hairy legs showed up in the bathroom. You'd consider burning down the house just to kill one if you couldn't get me on the phone. And now look at you. Cockroaches, spiders, ants… What on Earth still keeps you here, trapped in a glass box with this kind of company?"

"Between the cockroaches and you, Dez, I'll take the motherfucking cockroaches every time," Elizabeth said.

He smiled, a dazzling, brilliant smile that should have belonged to a Prince Charming. How cruel God could be, to create such a man. But tradition said that the devil had been the most beautiful angel. And here he was before her now — or at least devil's spawn several times removed.

"I like it when you have a tongue on you, and not just when you talk dirty to me. When did that start?"

"About the time I started mentoring teenagers. When did you start being a grade-A douchenozzle? Or has that always been a side hustle?"

"If you keep doing that, Liz, we might just have a go of it in the tent before we leave." He tapped the end of the bolt cutters against the padlock.

"What exactly are you planning to do?" She couldn't hold Goliath much tighter. Oddly sweet though he was, he wasn't a kitten or a teddy bear. He was a spider and thus easily crushed. He required gentle handling, especially since he couldn't harm her in retaliation. Elizabeth pressed herself to the farthest side of the glass from Dez, but that still wasn't a lot of space between them, and the giant tarantula also wasn't too keen on the man tapping the padlock. He climbed up Elizabeth's arm and shoulder to the wig, where he settled like a Halloween fascinator, legs tucked close to his fat body.

"The Arcanium gates and fences are surprisingly hard to get through. And the other times my people came through to figure out how we could take you, you're either bound in a funhouse with layer after layer of security, or you're here all alone, but locked in the box."

"You've had people *scouting* Arcanium?" He was a fastidious planner, a psychological genius in his own way, but she hadn't quite thought him capable of being a criminal mastermind, much less with minions.

"Brace yourself. This is going to be loud."

She cried out when the bolt cutter snapped through the padlock hook. The padlock fell to the grass with an impotent thud.

"What are you *doing*?" she repeated. Goliath was scurrying now, and that had her phobia rearing its head on top of her incredulity. She cowered against the glass, eyes closed as she waited for Goliath to stop prickling her, afraid he was going to crawl across her face, poke his feet into her mouth, climb into her…

"You're a freak in bed, Lizzie, but you're not a freak. You aren't meant to be here. You're wasted on this place. You were meant to be displayed, of course, but you're a work of art. That's how you need to be displayed — as art. As *my* art. Skin deep, soul deep, you're mine, and I'm not going to let some two-bit carnie turn you into a Spider Woman when you were always enough woman for me." His sunny smile darkened. "And I'm not going to have that two-bit carnie getting you dirty with sawdust and greasepaint. You need silk sheets. You need city lights, babe, and that diamond collar I had you wear… Nothing but the diamond collar."

Dez slid what was left of the hook out of the latch, then slowly opened the lid.

Goliath was no fool. He recognized an out when he felt the breeze of it. He bolted for the side of the coffin, picking his way over the air holes to gain some traction that the glass otherwise wouldn't provide him. He launched himself over the edge, then quickly crawled toward the back of the tent.

"Do you know what you just did? Do you think Goliath birdeaters grow on trees?" Elizabeth was actually worried. He was her responsibility. If he got out of the tent and someone hit him with a broom because all they saw was a spider, Bell would be furious.

"Well, I'm stealing *you* right now. A spider's not going to rate in comparison. You're the goldmine he doesn't know how to use. I always thought I'd find you in some strip joint or on a cam site once your religious rebound lost its grip again. But running off to join a circus? Why the dramatics, love?"

"It wasn't my choice, and you're not stealing me."

"This isn't your choice either. Give me your hand now, or I'll make sure your carnie loses more than a spider."

"He's not *my* carnie." Believing Bell was her lover was the last thing she wanted Dez to think, lest Bell find it amusing — after he was through torturing her for losing his birdeater. "He's my boss."

"I'm your boss."

He used that voice. *That* voice. The one that made her spine straighten and her body want to cringe away from whatever implement he might bring out to strike her with. The voice of a master prepared to punish a wayward, submissive servant. He'd had her switch for some of his clients, but she could only ever play that part well because she was his submissive in the end.

She'd always been a puppet, one way or another, and always to powerful, charismatic men who knew exactly how to control women like her.

"I'm your man, Liz. I'm the one who makes you feel like no one else, and if anyone else gets close, it's only because of what I did to you. You belong with me. You belong *to* me. Every inch of you is mine. You gave it to me to mark, to brand, and no one else is going to use what's rightfully mine. Now, come with me." He held out his hand to her.

"I… Dez, I can't." The sight of his hand made her remember his touch as though she'd never left him, as though ten years hadn't passed and he was the only man to damn her. She would go with him if she could — despite self-loathing and lessons learned with the prisoners, she would still go with him. He would take her away, steal her back to his home and keep her like a princess in his tower, and eventually, he would hold sway over her once more, have her craving him as much as she craved sex.

"If you're worried what your 'boss' will do if he finds out, LaVon and Brady are guarding the outside. If he tries to stop us, I'll let him know how little I like people touching my things." He brought his hand close to her, running his fingertips over her cheek with gentleness as painful as his violence. She leaned into him, her mouth parting when he nudged her lower lip, smearing the black lipstick. "There's my girl. Come here, Lizzie. That's right, on your knees."

She raised herself up on her prime legs, following his touch to just short of his mouth. He breathed her in, angled his head, parted his lips as though prepared to enter her, slow and inexorably sexual, as much a penetration as his cock between her legs. But he didn't. He smiled, arrogance like cologne emanating from his pores.

"Do you think I could get half this kind of response from the usual girls I use in my shoots? They play at innocence, sweetheart, but they can't fake what the camera captured in you. After all these years, you still have it. You're irreplaceable. How many girls escape from repressive cults every year for me to sweep up?"

"I'm not nearly as special as you say I am. The only thing that made me special was that I stayed…until I didn't. And I can't go back with you."

"Can't or won't?" He slid his hand down to her neck, brought it around her throat just under her chin, but he didn't squeeze, though he had before.

But she was still breathless, panting shallowly. "Can't."

"Of course you can. Just take off those prosthetics and come with me." He parted his lips again, and this time, when she responded as he'd trained her to, he met the tip of her tongue then slid into her, possessing her mouth. He tightened his grip around her throat enough to scare her. Light-headedness swayed her forward to clutch at his arms.

Once she got her hands on him, she couldn't stop. His shirt was soft, thin, his jacket leather, and underneath, he was more human to the touch than the Creature. She tucked her arms under his jacket, bringing herself against his chest.

The glass blocked their hips from meeting, but that didn't stop his free hand from roaming familiarly over her back, down to her ass. Its path took him over the places where her secondary thighs emerged near her hips, with their own musculature integrated into her lower back and her buttocks.

He curled his hand around the secondary thigh, no doubt thinking it was some kind of silicone fake, bound to her with latex and glue or something else explainable. But as he searched for a seam and couldn't find it, she twitched from the probing of his fingers. One particularly forceful scratch made her whimper.

He pushed her away from him with the hand around her throat, squeezing reflexively. She choked, bringing one of her secondary hands up to claw at his fingers. He let go, confusion a surprising expression on his beautiful face. He looked young like that, as though he hadn't experienced the emotion enough times in his life for it to grow with him.

"What are you looking for, Dez?" Elizabeth lowered herself to her heels, holding her neck. "The catch? The edge of the latex? Does it look like there's anywhere for me to hide a zipper?"

"How do you take that thing off?"

Elizabeth laughed, flashing her filed teeth. Dez must have felt them when he kissed her, but he still stepped back at the sight.

She didn't care if she sounded hysterical. Her mind and body were a series of maelstroms coming together. She was afraid of what would happen when they did, but there was no stopping it now. "That's the secret. I can't."

"I don't get it, but it's time to go before someone starts sticking their nose where it doesn't belong. Take it off." He'd said that to her so many times, but never with this kind of impatience, this kind of frustration — frustration that wasn't entirely aimed at her.

Dez was used to understanding how things worked. He was an artist, a photographer, an autodidact. He'd studied anatomy while teaching himself how to draw so that he could better understand line, light, shadow, the composition of a body underneath what the camera could see. She'd been lying down the last time he'd been in here, and when she sat up, it was easy to dismiss the movement of her secondary limbs as perhaps connected to fishing wire or something similar. But now that she was moving more freely, he had to notice that the extra arms and legs weren't acting like those of a marionette, and in her string halter and low-cut bikini bottoms, Dez's art flawless across her bare skin, there wasn't the slightest harness for even the most observant eyes to discern.

"Lizzie, what did you—"

"Said a few things I shouldn't. Trusted someone I shouldn't. Story of my life, isn't it? And it's why I can't leave him like I left you, babe, even if you thought a Human Spider could be even more special than a girl who climaxes on cue."

"You can't be serious." With confusion so unfamiliar to him, he defaulted to what he knew, and that was his hands on her. He grabbed her shoulders, forced her onto her hands and knees. He pushed, pulled, prodded at the scant secondary arms his needle had never touched until he couldn't deny that each secondary finger, each secondary wrist, each secondary elbow functioned as an individual, independent unit from her prime limbs. He snatched at her secondary thighs, parting them with an insistence that would have been lewd if it hadn't hurt so damn much.

She struck him away with her secondary arms. He recoiled.

"What's the matter? Never seen an eight-limbed woman before?" There was that hysteria again. Tears threatened to fall, even though she wasn't sad, wasn't angry, wasn't sure what was building in there behind her eyes, pressing against its thin layer and ready to burst.

"At no point during our well-documented seven years did you have more than two arms and two legs. I know your body better than anyone else. You're *not* an eight-limbed woman."

"Are you sure?" She raised herself up again, using the side of the coffin to help her climb out.

"What did you—"

"You keep thinking I did this to myself. I've heard of people getting tummy tucks and boob jobs over a bad break-up, even shaving their heads." She carefully removed the wig, tossed it into the coffin. Her scalp was smoother than freshly shaved, no grain to cling to her palm. It had never been this smooth with Dez. "But, darling, I don't think there's added appendages in any plastic surgeon's revenge repertoire."

Dez shook his head, took a step back when she advanced. "I don't get it."

"There's nothing to get." She closed all twenty fingers over the sides of his jacket, then pulled him closer. "Don't be afraid, Dez. It's just real."

"No, I..." He trailed off as he curled his hands over the smaller wings of the added shoulder blades. She rested her cheek against his chest while he probed with much gentler fingers over the seamless transitions.

"This isn't even surgical work, Liz. This is... People don't just sprout arms the way trees sprout branches. There's no stitches, no scars."

"This is why I can't go with you," she murmured into his shirt. He was warm, and, though instinctive fear had soured his scent slightly, underneath it was the Dez she remembered. And he was distracted by her body in a whole new way that she preferred. How much better it was to be a freak to him, a science project, a Frankenstein's monster, instead of a woman whose will he had to crush under his thumb.

Aurelia T. Evans

But Elizabeth could almost hear the gears in his head turning, the way she could hear his heart beating beneath her ear.

"We can get them removed. Or —"

He was already starting to think like Bell, think how he could use it. From the cock stirring against her, she thought he still wouldn't mind her in his bed — freak and all. He slid one palm up between both sets of shoulder blades to the tie of her leather halter. With one pull, it loosened, folded away from her breasts. With one more pull to the string underneath her secondary arms, it fell to their feet. Dez leaned back to peer down at her with calculation, the heated glimmer of lust in his eyes.

"This really isn't possible, Elizabeth," he muttered. He brought his fingers to her mouth again to lower her snake-pierced lip and inspect her teeth. Those, at least, could be explained — a valid mod, although not a part of his preferred culture. "Use them, your hands — the other ones. On your breasts. Show me they're yours."

She tucked her primary hands behind her neck, stroking the bats and moths and tingling under his intense, darkening gaze as she brought her secondary hands to her breasts. They weren't as gravity-defying as they used to be, but her nipples tightened the way they always had, the same surprisingly dusky brown against her pale skin, a flush making them almost purple as she caught them between her thumbs and forefingers.

"Fine." He was too proud to adjust himself, but he rolled his shoulders. "We'll take you as you are. My fans already know this is where you've been. I can still give them the circus girl. I'll rig up a special harness for you." He replaced her secondary fingers with his, rougher, pulling her forward by her nipples until her hips were against his again.

"You can do whatever you want to me in this tent, right now," Elizabeth said. "God knows I can't stop you. I'm not capable of not wanting you. But I can't leave Arcanium, and you can't steal me from it. Believe me... I'd go with you if I could, if just to run away from you again."

"Yes, love, you certainly look like a girl who wants to run away from me." He twisted her nipples, and her hips jerked forward to meet his erection.

"I told you. Anything you want to do with me, Dez. But I'm not yours anymore. Someone worse than you has his invisible chains on me. I couldn't run away from him if I tried." She shoved his jacket down his shoulders. He had to let her go to shrug it off. "So if you want me, this is it."

"All this talk about how much you hate me... You're sure insistent on getting me out of my clothes." His belt clinked like the padlock opening as he removed it.

She backed up to the coffin. As he came after her, Elizabeth saw instead the strange, beautiful form of the Creature as he'd been so many nights when he'd released her from this godforsaken coffin. A place near the realm of her heart panged so hard, she thought something was physically wrong.

"I hate what you did to me, the original freak you created. I hate that you're here and that I'm salivating. I hate you, Dez, but I can still have sex with you if it'll get you out of my life, if it'll get me out of your system. Then you need to leave Arcanium and never come back, and you and your goons have to stop stalking me like some little bitch—"

He struck her across the face with the smooth end of the belt. She shouted in surprise, whipping to the side while holding her cheek. The skin seemed to split right under her palm from the swelling. The welt wasn't an inch from her eye. He could have done serious damage without a thought.

"I don't like it when you lie, Lizzie. And I don't like it when you cheapen what you and I had. What we still clearly have." With expert precision, he looped the belt over her head and tightened it around her neck like a noose. "I don't need chains, sweetheart. I don't need our special collar or an engagement ring. You belong to me. Now, I'm going to take you home and fuck you every way I can think of until you're on all your hands and knees, begging me to let you come one more time. What's our record? Fifteen in one night? So many times that it hurt, but you still begged. You're going to come with me because you don't have a choice. You'll come when I fucking say so. You always have."

He jerked her away from the coffin, flinging her to the ground.

"What? Are you going to drag me out there, a shopping mall filled with families and me with barely anything on, a swollen eye and a fucking belt around my neck? Are you skull-fucked?" She cringed when he lifted his hand.

But this time, he just wanted the cringe. He smiled again, gathered himself to appear composed. Normal. Charming. "I'd call it performance art. And people would believe me."

He wasn't exaggerating. He'd talked his way out of every shady situation he'd put them in, even with people who would usually be suspicious of someone like him. He could convince butter into an oven.

Dez inclined her face up to him with the buckle under her chin. The angle alone partially closed off her throat. He brought his hips close to her mouth, the denim over his erection brushing her lips.

"Is your mouth watering yet? If I sank into you, could you take me all the way in on your first try? Would you drip down your chin in your eagerness?"

She remembered kneeling in front of the Creature much like this then the Creature kneeling in return before he could take her mouth. It seemed more of a betrayal to him to perform fellatio for an old lover than it was to just let that lover fuck her. She closed her lips and turned her head, but Dez tightened the belt and jerked her back with a click of his tongue.

"If you can't be nice, I'm not going to make this easy for you," she rasped, lightheaded. The red tent seemed to spin, the fury of the hissing cockroaches rattling in her ears.

"You'll ride my cock like it's the first and last cock you've ever had, no matter if I have to tie your legs apart to do it. There's no reason to fight, Lizzie. It hurts you more than it hurts me."

"Oh, I don't know about that."

Dez whirled around, making her gag as he dragged her with him.

Bell had entered the tent, accompanied by the last person Elizabeth expected to see at that moment — and a sight that immediately filled her with so much shame she nearly threw up right then. If Dez hadn't been throttling her, she might have. Her cheeks flamed, and Elizabeth brought all four of her hands to herself to hide what she could, crossing her secondary arms over her breasts and her prime arms over her bowed face.

"I know you." The man's voice had the same warmth and charm as Dez, but none of the guile — deeper, the kind of voice made to cut through silence and noise with equal ease. He'd been the whisper in her head all her life.

Elizabeth dared to peek through her fingers at her biological father, afraid that the anger that tarnished his words was directed at her.

But Thomas Petros — wearing the plain, sober attire common to Petrosian men and sporting a modest but cared-for beard streaked with white — wasn't looking at Elizabeth. She didn't think she'd ever seen his face contorted like that. His congregation had witnessed righteous anger, devastated grief, concern, but nothing as ugly as the hatred that charged his rigid, knotted expression when he stared at Dez.

"Walk away," Dez said, as though he was doing Bell and Petros the favor. "You don't understand." *Trust me*, his tone hissed underneath. *This isn't anything close to what it looks like, although I understand how you might assume something terrible. Trust me.*

"I'd love to, but that's my employee you have in your...belt," Bell said mildly. "And you see, I'm not fond of outsiders hurting my people."

"So you're the one who put her in the glass box." Dez stroked her head as though she were a frightened dog, holding her closer to his leg. "I'm afraid there's been a mistake. This one belongs to me. I signed my name all over her skin. I don't care how much of a freak you made her, or what you had to sacrifice to whom. She's *mine*."

There was a vicious, hollow snap as Thomas Petros slammed his fist into Dez's face. Dez let go of the belt, teetered like a cartoon villain then fell back. He wasn't unconscious, but he gazed around, eyes out of focus.

"Beautiful right hook, Father," Bell said, just as mildly.

"I know you." Petros stood over Dez with both fists clenched. "You're the defiler, the corrupter, the filthy snake who first got his hands on her. You're the one she escaped."

Dez slowly regained his bearings, covering his swelling, bleeding nose with his hand, although that did little to stop the flow. "Who the hell are you?"

"I'm her father."

"Which one? The accountant or the fanatic who screwed her mother?" He laughed, sending a thick spray of blood between his fingers.

Petros raised his fist again and started for Dez. Bell stopped him with a hand on his arm just as the Creature burst through the curtain. The tent wasn't really made for five people, especially when one of them was an eight-legged woman and three of the men were quite large.

Dez staggered to his feet, rounded the coffin and grabbed the first terrarium he could reach — the hissing cockroaches. He threw the terrarium at Bell. The glass shattered at Bell's and Petros' feet, sending the hissing roaches scurrying. Elizabeth screamed, jerking back into the Creature's waiting arms. Though Petros reversed as fast as he could in an automatic response to giant cockroaches roaming freely in a small space, Bell barely blinked, not even when Dez grabbed the common American cockroach farm and flung that one at them, too.

The resultant cockroach explosion nearly made Elizabeth's mind shut down, but the Creature wrapped his arms around her, enveloping her as though to remind her that she was safe, even when the smaller roaches scurried over her feet. But she wrenched against his hold, shaking her head, too panicked to even scream.

"Come on, Elizabeth. We're going," Dez snapped. "I can get you out of here. I can get you away."

"I, like you, don't appreciate it when people take what's mine," Bell said. "At least I don't destroy other people's property in the process. Do you think my own cockroaches scare me, Desmond? Do you think *you* scare me?"

Bell beckoned to the horde of small brown roaches as well as the massive hissing cockroaches at his feet. They stopped running every which way and instead climbed up his body until they covered him like a suit. The hissing cockroaches floated from his hands into the reconstituted terrarium that Bell then lowered into the glass coffin. Before their eyes, the thousands of pieces of glass that had made up the more intricate cockroach farm came together as well. Bell funneled the many insects through the air back into their home.

Dez stared with wide eyes but thinning lips, no doubt making those same calculating connections that had led to him accepting Elizabeth's transformation. Her father avoided looking at Bell, but he appeared utterly unsurprised by the swarm of obedient insects and the recreated tanks.

Elizabeth stopped struggling in the Creature's hold. He wasn't embracing her, just bracing. He let her go as she found her footing again. She yanked Dez's belt off her neck, but she covered herself again as soon as she could. Petros quickly shed his jacket and held it out to her.

"Thank you," she muttered. She took the jacket with one hand and covered her front with it before turning her back to Petros to pull it on.

She couldn't fit both pairs of arms into the sleeves, but her secondary arms were used to being on the inside of her robe. She buttoned the jacket over them and tucked the collar closer together before daring to turn back. Just the fact that her father could see her at all made her hunch over, clutching the jacket, ashamed to even raise her eyes.

Petros didn't let that keep him away. He gave her a chance to refuse, but when he guided her away from the Creature and into his arms, his beard bristly against her scalp, Elizabeth allowed it. Neither of her fathers had been particularly affectionate, nor had her mother been, but she found herself needing what his embrace meant. More than any other man in her life, an embrace from him would go nowhere else, an end in itself.

Something that had been clenched tight in her for so long that she couldn't remember when it started suddenly released. She wrapped her arms around his waist, still hunched over as she closed her eyes against the hot, stinging tears. She couldn't cry like she had when she had been a child. But tears managed to find their way out, as they always did, soaking through his humble shirt.

"Let's go," Petros said softly.

She didn't resist when he led her back to the curtains.

"Don't you walk away from me, Lizzie!" Dez started after her. "Running to the circus, hiding behind the baby daddy... I'm the fucking only one who makes you feel alive. You never have to hide from me. If you just —
"

The curtain fell closed behind her, cutting off his words as though by magic. She'd stepped out into Arcanium. Maya was there with Kitty, standing a few tents away with her fingers laced through the other woman's. The smoking man was also there, sitting on the top of a tent with yet another cigarette.

Elizabeth closed her fingers over the fabric of Petros' shirt.

"Tell me you didn't break in," she whispered.

"Of course not. I came in at the gate. The redhead with a beard invited me in. I apparently had only one crime in me to commit today. God forgive me, I think I would have killed him with my bare hands if you hadn't been there, if you hadn't needed me."

Her throat was thickening from Dez's abuse and obstructed by the rush of emotion. She let out a choked, coughing sob that was supposed to be a sigh of relief.

"There now. You're out here, and he's in there. You never have to see him again." Petros stroked her head as though he didn't notice there wasn't any hair, as though he hadn't realized she had extra appendages, as though nothing had changed since last he saw her in clothes as sober as his, silent next to her family in the pews of the Petrosian sanctuary.

"You knew him." Elizabeth raised herself up, wiping under her eyes. Her makeup was probably already scary enough to belong in the haunted funhouse. Nothing smeared onto her fingers, but she tried to stay careful. "That's what you said. I never told Mom or Dad where I'd gone. I never confessed to you. How did you know him?"

"God never saw fit to tell me where you'd gone after you ran away, and I trusted his judgment, though I prayed for you without ceasing." He gently nudged her hands away from her face to use his own sleeve, dabbing her cheeks and around her eyes, careful where Dez had left his mark. "It wasn't until after you'd returned that a member of our congregation came to me with his computer to show me what he'd found."

"What was he doing that he found me?" Elizabeth asked, more than a little annoyed.

Petros gave a wry smile. "He showed it to me to admit to his sin."

"And to bring you down to his level."

Petros shrugged to concede the point. "I'm only human. God's most favored people riddle the Bible with their sins. Anyone who tries to use you to control me will fail. I've repented and been forgiven for my sins, but you are not one of them, child. You never were, no matter how much some tried to make it so. And I hope they never tried to make me yours." He kissed her forehead like a baptism. "When I saw what the saint wanted me to see, I was mortified, of course. But you came back to us with the same shame I see painted across your face now. I finally understood why you were so afraid that you would return so much later than our other prodigal sons and daughters, that you would drape yourself in our attire and hide as though in a convent."

"You give me too much credit." More composed, Elizabeth withdrew from her father, crossing her arms over her chest where the lapels opened too far. "I went willingly with him for years, and I never said no until the day I left. If ever there was a cautionary tale…"

"There are many ways to a yes, Lizzie — some of them good, some of them evil. There's evil in that man. I've watched it haunt you all these years. He tried to contact me soon after the saint confessed. He sent pictures and links to attempt to discredit you in the eyes of the church, including one in the body of the email that showed him with you. But I deleted them, the rest sight unseen. He tried calling me, but I deleted his messages and blocked his number. I'm sorry that you thought I would see the ink on your skin and condemn you, that you never felt you could confess to me. I'm sorry you had to suffer like this. But you don't have to suffer alone."

"Do Mom and Dad know?"

Petros had responded with pity and compassion, but Elizabeth was pretty sure her mother wouldn't be able to look at her, and her dad would probably never speak to her again. He had six other daughters he could praise, six other daughters he could call his own. What was the loss of one that wasn't even his?

"I wouldn't divulge something that wasn't mine to share, any more than I sought your confession before you were ready to provide it," Petros said gently. "It's up to you whether you want them to know. Either way, you have a home with us."

"I'm pretty sure the Bishops don't want me back." She laughed—no trace of hysteria now, nothing but bitterness. "Without their reference, no one else will ever hire me again. Even if I wasn't a freak. Even if I could go back."

"You're a child of God. It doesn't matter what happened to you or why. You called me for help, and I wouldn't deny you that. What kind of saint would I be to deny you sanctuary?"

Elizabeth glanced up at him warily. "It's not just the tattoos, Father. It's not just what Dez did. Do you know where you are? Do you know what I've become?"

"God doesn't show me everything, but he shows me some." Petros looked over his shoulder at the tumbler sitting on the tent. The pale man appeared thoroughly entertained, nursing his cigarette like a bowl of popcorn. "Whatever controls this place does well containing it, but as soon as I came in, I sensed demonic influence through everything, like cobwebs in an attic."

"Is it evil?" Elizabeth asked slowly, just above a whisper. "Is it all evil?"

Petros returned his attention to Elizabeth. He placed his hands on her shoulders. "No. Evil is here, but it isn't in everything. Your soul is still yours and God's. It always has been. You're not lost."

"I wouldn't bet on it." She stepped back with a deep breath. "Bell keeps me lost, and I don't know how long he'll keep me. I can't just leave him like I did Dez."

"Bell... The man with magic in his hands who led me to the tent?" Petros asked.

Elizabeth tilted her head. "You said you saw evil, that you could see the demonic. Could you not see him?"

"There are as many kinds of demons as there are humans, Liz. There's a pronounced mark of evil upon the magician, but his power dwells in chaos. Long before God made light from the chaos, he resided in its darkness. These things are not evil in and of themselves."

"You've got to be fucking kidding me," she muttered. "Forgive me. I just... This circus... He was the one who..." Elizabeth rubbed her temples. "He's not like the Ringmaster. He's not a demon. But he's jinn, and he's *not* good. He never touched me like Dez, never forced me to fuck him—not asking forgiveness for that one—but he did *this*." She gestured to her transformed body. "He forced me into *this*."

"He's why the phone cut off when you called me, isn't he?" Petros lowered his eyes, but he didn't let go. He'd seen the mark of evil upon her, yet he didn't recoil from touching it. "He's the reason you called. Not the man I struck, but the one with whom I walked in."

"This place is woven through with evil. It's sewn into the very fabric of it." Elizabeth breathed in, breathed out, found speaking her fears aloud easier to do than she would have thought. "It's sewn through me. I don't know whether I'm evil because of this place or whether I was just...*born* to kneel at the feet of the devil. But if I have to be trapped here, maybe evil is what I need to be."

Petros stopped her before she could turn back toward the tent. "You're not evil, Lizzie, no matter what you do. No one with the pain you carry can be as evil as the darkest shadows of this place."

"I won't let him sin against me again, so I'm going to have to go sin some more, Father. I hope you can forgive me."

Elizabeth bowed her head as Petros kissed her forehead again, the brush of his beard achingly familiar.

"It's not for me to forgive," he whispered against her brow. "That was never for me, nor is it for me to judge my saints. Perhaps you weren't meant for us, but that doesn't mean you have to be lost."

But as long as I am, I think it's time to embrace this darkness. Perhaps it's the part God called good. Her spine was a vibrating coil, and her fingertips were cold with fear, but she forced herself out of her father's embrace again.

"Don't leave Arcanium yet." Elizabeth backed toward the tent, already loosening her hold on the coat. "I don't think this will take long."

"I love you. I've always loved you," Petros said. "No matter what has been done to you, no matter what you do, I always will."

Elizabeth wanted to say that she loved him, too, that he'd been more a father to her than her own, regardless of the labels that her family had created. But if she tried to speak, she was afraid she'd scream and the monstrosity of her would become all too apparent. She couldn't go into the tent like that. She needed her heart cold.

When she pulled the curtain back to duck through, the sound of another person screaming hit her ears so hard they ached, and she had to rush in to contain the sound.

But Bell wasn't the one torturing Dez.

The Creature held Dez off the ground by his neck, his mouth open and teeth bared, the red liquid in his eyes swirling like whirlpools. Dez squirmed, kicked, wrenched against the Creature's hold, but he couldn't shake him, nor did any blow faze the Creature. And no matter what he did, Dez couldn't tear his gaze away.

Elizabeth hadn't known that a man could look so terrified.

Bell was off to the side, idly offering his arms for Goliath to climb on as he watched the Creature and Dez with voyeuristic fascination. He smiled when she joined him.

"Your father isn't what I expected."

"You can read my mind. How could you not expect him?" Elizabeth asked.

"There's a vast canyon between the way a person is perceived and the way he is. I had your perception of him—a pious pulpit pounder, a holy man prone to indiscretion in his youth, the false prophet of your cult."

"I never said he was a false prophet." It wasn't easy talking over a man screaming bloody murder, but she and Bell were close enough to each other, and Bell pitched his voice lower to counteract Dez's piercing cries.

"I've lived many lifetimes, Elizabeth, and psychotics and confidence men pretending to be prophets are an all-too-common phenomenon. Then your father crosses the threshold of Arcanium. I'm so partial to creating the illusion of hoaxes, it's a rare treat to encounter something real in a rawer form."

The ground seemed to drop away, and her stomach followed. "I thought he was just sensitive, that he attributed acute intuition to divine intervention."

"Oh, there's a touch of that, too. All the real prophets suffer delusions of grandeur to accompany the actual grandeur with which they've been gifted. It's the curse of the blessing."

He relinquished Goliath to her when she held out her hand for him. She gently placed him back in his quiet terrarium. He hadn't deserved any of the commotion from the day.

"Petros is undeniably real. I like him. It would be a shame to have to kill or imprison him," Bell said.

"You had no trouble imprisoning me."

No smirk should appear so attractive on an arrogant man's face, but Bell defied all shoulds. "Arcanium would drive a man like him mad. But a little darkness, a little chaos, does wonders for a woman like you. Wouldn't you agree?"

Elizabeth latched the top of the terrarium harder than she would have otherwise. "You're not cute when you listen in on conversations. I hope you know that."

"You and Maya would get along so well if you opened yourself up to my side of the circus." Bell held his hand out to her on the other side of the table and brought her around back to him, like a gentleman leading his lady to a dance. "Have I mentioned how magnificent your Creature is? I'm glad I was patient and kept him long enough to see what he was capable of."

"What is he doing?" She spoke so softly she almost couldn't hear herself.

"After feeding on so much of your fear, he's releasing it all into your ex. Every bit of it. Like that scene in *The Exorcist*, but unfiltered horror instead of pea soup. Perhaps, as its ultimate origin, the Creature thought it belonged with him."

"I didn't know he did that."

"Neither did he. How does it feel to see your fear on his face?"

Elizabeth undid the buttons on the jacket, emerging from its cocoon with only the slightest quiver of trepidation. Watching Dez cower strengthened her resolve. Bell's appreciative gaze lingered on her when she handed the jacket to him.

"I thought so," he murmured.

Elizabeth came up behind the Creature, curled her fingers over his shoulder. His wings didn't allow her to press against him the way she could an ordinary man, but she stood on her tiptoes to rest her cheek on the back of his neck. "You can let him go."

The Creature dropped Dez to the floor without ceremony.

Dez dug grooves into the ground trying to crawl away, but he shook too hard, his limbs twitching too violently for him to get very far before he crumpled in a heap.

When the Creature faced her, his eyes still swirled furiously. Elizabeth sank into the red hole down which the Creature had led her ex-lover. It didn't affect her quite the same. After all, she was used to the dark places her brain took her.

The Creature caught her face in his hands, blinking to break the spell. "I'm sorry. I did not intend to share that with you."

Elizabeth covered his hands with hers. "You shouldn't apologize. I can't tell you what this means to me. But I should have taken care of this myself over ten years ago. Can you go back into the circus and watch over my father, make sure nothing hurts him?"

The Creature peered down at the fetal man partially hidden under the insect and arachnid tables. "If that worm so much as thinks—"

"Bell will make sure he doesn't do any more damage. Or he'd better, since he promised no one could hurt me, and I have significant evidence to the contrary."

"Have I mentioned that your line is much more generous to those who hurt you than mine?" Bell said, inspecting his nails.

"Will you make him bleed?" the Creature asked, his growl harsh, metallic.

Elizabeth raised herself on her toes again, this time to take his lower lip between her teeth as she kissed him. The hard set of his jaw slowly eased.

"We'll see," she whispered into him.

"I would stay to see that."

"I can't do this with you here," she said, "just like I couldn't do it with my father here. You don't need to see what I am with him."

His wings spread slightly, granting them the briefest privacy. "And Bell?"

"He already knows."

The Creature caressed the hollow under her cheekbones with the claws on his thumbs. "*I* know. I've tasted it, little Spider."

"I need you to protect Father. I trust you to do that more than Bell."

He folded his wings in again. "To that I will concede." He kissed her one more time, as lingering and intense as Bell's attention upon them. Then he swept around the glass coffin and out into the circus.

Dez was starting to come around, the whimpers under the table more infrequent and his movements more coherent. He struggled to his hands and knees, bumping the table and threatening the ant farm.

Bell took her right prime hand in his. "Are you ready for your armor, Lizzie?"

She didn't know what he meant by that, but she nodded, tightening her other hands into fists as she watched Dez squirm — this big, strong, handsome, hardcore sociopath, squirming like a kicked toddler.

"Oh, it's nothing much, really. You're still difficult to dress," Bell said. "Just something to make you feel a little more...powerful."

Leather and metal emerged from her like scales. It wasn't a second skin, not part of her like her extra arms and legs — more like something that surfaced on the still lake of her skin.

Gloves covered all four arms from knuckles to elbows, leaving her fingers free—and on the tips of those fingers, her nails thickened and sharpened into something like claws. The metallic blades that lined the gloves provided additional weaponry.

A specialized harness, no doubt similar to the one Dez had envisioned, wrapped around her waist and around her chest and arms. The thick, strapped corset granted slightly more modesty over her breasts than nothing at all. Reaching to just above her knees, her boots matched the gloves, with arachnoid spikes and blades down the front. The boots on her secondary limbs had an additional heel so she could stand steadily on all four feet at once with her weight focused on her prime legs.

He was right. As armor went, it wasn't much—more like the armor she might see in some of Todd's friends' video games—but Elizabeth understood it wasn't armor to protect her. Arcanium was her protection, and where Arcanium needed help, bit by bit Bell had transformed her to protect herself. The armor was just another part of the Spider that Bell had made her, the Spider he wanted her to be.

Only when she was sure the armor wasn't fused to her skin did Elizabeth let go of Bell's hand. Balancing herself with her back legs, she crouched down where Dez had finally managed to recover from the worst of the Creature's force-feeding.

"What the fuck, Lizzie?" he gasped. "What the actual *fuck*?"

Elizabeth straightened his shirt. "I'm awfully sorry you had to meet my new lover that way."

He jerked away from her at first then settled, staring at her as though she was a lifeline. She watched the sanity return to him, and with it, his anger. In this case, she didn't blame him, but she couldn't allow sympathy to sway her. She already had her own warped responses to contend with without adding pity into the mix.

"He's usually a perfect gentleman," she said. "I'm afraid you touched a nerve by touching me the way you did. He thought he'd give you a dose of your own medicine. You showed me a side to him I've never seen, and you'll always have my gratitude for that."

"That? You fuck *that*? That monster? That…god-fucking demon thing that looks like a cross between a gargoyle and a rat? Are you telling me I broke you so much you'd spread your legs for that thing?"

"Yes. All four of them. Or do I have to remind you that I'm kind of a hybrid monster these days, too?" Elizabeth tapped her fingers on her knees, unconcerned with how unladylike her present stance was. Dez had seen her in much less, and he'd brought her much lower. There were no depths to which she hadn't sunk for him. Hard to feel ashamed of something as innocuous as crouching with her legs open.

"You're different," Dez said.

"So people keep telling me. What's different about me? The fact I have tits and a cunt?"

"That'll do for a start." Dez got to his knees, used the table to pull himself to his feet. Elizabeth raised herself up with him.

"No matter my anatomy, Dez, facts are still facts. I can't go with you. You physically *cannot* take me from Arcanium. If you actually managed it, I'd be tortured by some kind of spell until you brought me back. But since the world outside that curtain is different now than when you first came in, you wouldn't actually be taking me out of Arcanium. You'd be bringing yourself right into it. And the people here aren't keen on men like you. So my original offer stands."

She slowly unbuckled the straps that held her corset on. In spite of everything that had happened to him, Dez fixed his attention not on the insects next to him or Bell in the wings, but upon the skin she bared, as though he'd never seen it before. Her eyelashes fluttered as she discarded the stiff leather on the table. Then she stepped toward him, against him. She slid her primary hands up his shirt while working her secondary fingers over the front of his jeans.

"You can have me here, one more time. Then you can go out there and tell all your friends and fans and followers that I'm not who they thought I was, that I'm someone else—a devotee of your art, perhaps, sickening as that is. But I'm not Lucy Lewd, because I can't be. Not even the best surgeon could have done this to her."

He grew in her hand, his erection swelling from the stimulation, but he also seemed newly enchanted by her words, by the lips shaping them.

It occurred to her for the first time that in conditioning her to respond to him, to need him, he might have accidentally done the same thing to himself. The sex demons weren't giving out enough magic to make him respond like this after what the Creature had done to him, after everything he knew. But though his face still showed the haggardness of fear—a drawn quality Elizabeth had seen all too often in the mirror—he stared at her like a starving man offered a feast.

"Go on. Touch me. I'm giving you permission this time. Or does that turn you off?" She nipped his jaw, ran her tongue over his meticulously shaped beard. "What's the matter, Dez? Isn't this what you wanted?"

Her sudden change of heart must have made him suspicious, because he was more tentative to kiss her back, to press his mouth to her neck where his belt had left her tender. Hesitant to bring his palms up to her breasts, to test their weight and movement in his hands.

"Not quite how I remember them, babe," he said with the early stirrings of a grin.

"You want me to list all the ways you got older, too?" She bit the firm curve of his ear harder than she might have otherwise.

"Ow." He batted at her face, but she just smiled. She tasted blood and wondered whether it had stained her teeth.

"Let's face it. Neither of us is the same as we were ten years ago. But at least we're still pretty, right?"

She undid his jeans, licked her secondary palm, took his cock in a firm fist, twisting him as sharply as he'd twisted her nipples. He grunted from discomfort, but she ran her tongue over his Adam's apple, catching it with those same teeth that had drawn blood. She hummed with pleasure at his sharp intake of breath, a moment of fear that was all his own.

"Good genes on both sides," she said, "despite all my drinking, despite your occasional smoke. Aren't we just…so…lucky?"

She punctuated each word with a kiss to his neck and a rough stroke over his cock. He bucked into her grip then abruptly gave in, wrapping his arms around her, one hand on her smooth head and the other stroking down her spine between her secondary legs. He tightened his fingers over her head to guide her to his lips for a kiss. She clung to him, opening her mouth and taking him in until she melted from the inside.

"Imagine," she murmured against his mouth when he let her breathe on her own. She dipped a fingertip into his slit, tantalizing the sensitive opening while smearing pre-cum over him. "Imagine all the things you get away with because you're so damn pretty."

"Goes both ways. I'd never have let you get away with half the things you did if you weren't a fucking demon in the bedroom and a succubus for the camera. Fuck, babe."

That chuckle she heard wasn't from Dez.

She held his cheeks in her prime hands as she showed appreciation for how good he looked to her, how well he kissed, how fine his cheekbones were. "And no one ever believes that you do anything wrong because of that beautiful face, that angelic artist's face."

Her secondary hands went harder over his cock and balls, just the kind of rough and needful that he craved. He drove them against the glass coffin, his hands all over her body, his claim on her mouth, his cock fucking her hands. Elizabeth kept at that pace until he started to groan, getting so close. All she had to do was stroke him up and over…

"Imagine," she whispered, "what might happen if you weren't pretty anymore." She licked the corner of his mouth then reared back and struck, extending her teeth with that audible click in her skull. She sank her fangs into his cheek, the mirror to hers that had swelled up to block the lower part of her eye.

At the same time, she kept him too weak to stop her by wringing him into completion. Semen struck her stomach in thick strings over and over and over, lasting longer than she expected, even as she pumped her poison into him—like a small orgasm from her mouth. It was a release of her own, each sweet taste of her venom shivering through her body.

As soon as Dez overcame the weakness of his orgasm, he tried to push her away, but she still had a grip on his cock, albeit a more slippery one, and her teeth were still in his flesh. Pushing her away meant hurting himself more.

But finally she couldn't stop the manic giggles from bubbling from her mouth, and she let him go, using her extra legs to keep her from falling back when he shoved her away, shouting for a whole new reason.

She wiped blood and venom from her lips while Dez tried to do damage control to the bleeding from his cheek and the light bleeding at the base of his cock where she'd accidentally scratched him with her claws.

"What the fuck did you just do?"

"It's not only arms, legs and armor that make me a Spider, Dez. But I have to give you some of the credit. You're the one who made me want to be the black widow."

She doubted Dez could appreciate the nuance, not as his face started to swell, and much faster than her own. His cheek puffed up to the size of a pear as the toxins infiltrated his flesh.

"What the fuck?" It was the phrase of the hour, the subtitle to Arcanium, and Elizabeth could stand to hear it more.

She bared her teeth in a smile wider than she could remember smiling before. Then she lowered herself to her knees and grabbed his balls between her claws, threatening him with castration if he tried to pull away. Slowly, with relish, she ran her tongue over his softened, messy cock, his blood flavoring the cum.

He kept hitting her the way a girl might try to hit a mouse with a broom, but he knew better than to do anything too hard in case the hand holding his balls spasmed closed. He shouted at her, whimpered like a terrified teenage boy, like the prisoners in the haunted funhouse. And for a moment, Elizabeth understood how the Ringmaster could hear that all day and never grow tired of it.

Yet Dez's cock started to grow in her mouth. Even at his age, even with part of his face now swollen to the size of a small pumpkin, he couldn't resist her mouth any more than she could resist his. She was flushed with power instead of shame, wet against the leather over her pussy, her clit twitching with instinctive appreciation every time he jerked his hips to fill her.

He stopped trying to push her off in fear, pushed her down over his cock instead.

Men. There wasn't enough room in her head for that kind of contempt.

She looked up at him, rolling his sac in the cage of her hand, and sank down to the base. He shoved his cock deeper, which made her gag, but he was the one who'd taught her how to repress her urge to retch—and wasn't he just enjoying that lesson at this very moment? He savaged her mouth and throat, not allowing her more than a bare second here and there to get some air—still trying to regain control, still trying to assert his dominance, even when his balls were in her claws and his cock between her teeth.

"You're going to pay, you stupid bitch," he said as silkily as he could with part of his mouth too swollen to work. His face had to be on fire, but God knew he was getting off on asphyxiating her with his own erection, getting off on the bear trap set around his genitalia because he was confident it wouldn't spring, that she wouldn't fucking dare.

He grabbed her head with both hands to force himself as deep down her throat as he could, groaning in pain and in pleasure.

She started to panic, gasping for breath and getting nothing, tightening her claws into the wrinkly hanging flesh above the sac, but Dez was too far gone into the power trip. Maybe he wasn't even feeling the pain anymore, not when he could murder her for what she'd done, murder her for daring to leave him, for attacking him — for making him question his strength, his power, his control over her and anyone else he called his. She struggled, lost her grip on his balls in her brain's more immediate need to get his cock out of her throat. She scratched at his thighs, tore ribbons from his skin, and still he wouldn't let her go.

"I'm here."

He wasn't inside her like he'd been in the semi-trailer, but Bell whispered in her head, two words to tell her that he wouldn't let this go too far, that he was waiting for her to do what she needed to do, what he so wanted her to do. She sensed his desire for her violence even through the alarms blaring through her head, the graying of her vision, the desperation with which she choked on her own saliva and his pre-cum.

And the sad part was that this wasn't the first time Dez had done this.

With the last of her strength, she looked up at him, peered into those blue eyes that dared her, fucking *dared* her, to do the same damage to his cock that she'd done to his face. Did he really think his penis was so important to the world that she'd spare it? Oh, it was a lovely cock as cocks went, as sculpted and perfect as the rest of him. But she thought about how many women he'd tortured with it, what he could still do with it in the time he had left.

No, this wasn't the first time he'd done this to her. But in the name of God and all his devils, it would be the last.

She sank one venom-filled canine into him. She couldn't do both at the same time, but one was all she needed. The venom from the other hissed against his skin like acid, filled her mouth around him. He jerked back, which tore her tooth through the shaft, but she kept pumping him with her venom until she blacked out.

She came to after only a few seconds or so, opening her eyes to the sight of the base of his cock and his balls swelling into thick, bruised, rubbery skin. His cock had grown to twice its size, but it was no longer nearly as pretty. Dez howled, both hands covering himself in a belated sense of self-preservation.

Elizabeth coughed, clutching at her raw throat.

Bell's hand was there when she looked up, and without hesitation, she took it, struggling to her feet against the lightness in her head.

"Goddamn rotten cunt!" Dez screamed. All traces of the beautiful man—beautiful even in anger—had transformed, distorted, under the effects of her venom.

"What are you shouting about?" Bell said with only a little exasperation, as though Dez was a slightly annoying toddler rather than a grown man. "If it had been me, I would have ensured a long, slow, painful death. As it is, you'll recover. You'll be scarred, and your dick won't work as well as before—in fact, I think you'll think twice or thrice before sticking it into another woman's mouth, knowing that even teeth without poison might do damage. But you'll live…unless Lizzie decides you should die. Would you like for him to go to the clowns? I don't think I could inflict him upon Lady Sasha, and I have more prisoners than I can handle. However, I could always curse him to the carousel."

"It doesn't make a difference to me anymore." Elizabeth reached for the corset off the table, waved to the huntsmen in their long tank. She used the tablecloth to wipe the thickening semen from her abdomen, then put the corset back on.

"No. No, please. Don't kill me. *Please.* Fix me. Fix me, you fucking bastard! I know you can."

Bell curled his lip in disgust as Dez reached for him, poised to grab Bell's neck.

Elizabeth whipped around and raked the blades on her right arms over Dez's chest without any care for how deep the wounds were.

Blood spilled like the red velvet curtains themselves down Dez's chest. Dez stumbled back, stunned.

Bell blinked. "Of course, I can give you the honor of slitting his throat, if you prefer."

"No. He shouldn't die. He doesn't deserve to die." Elizabeth ran her tongue carefully over the blades so that she didn't slice herself while she cleaned them. She was vehemently opposed to cruelty to animals, but the cruelty she tasted now was a small price to pay for all the cruelty he'd dealt.

Bell ran his thumb over her chin with surprising tenderness to catch where blood had spattered against her. He sucked on the pad as he made the entire mess fade until it was as though she'd never been stained at all, by blood or by seed. For a moment, he looked like he wanted to taste what he had left in her mouth for her. But he didn't.

"What's your poison, then?" he asked.

"I don't suppose you can hang him from a cross and open up his ribs for the vultures to peck at. Would that be too many mythological references for one man?"

"Alas, little Spider, the Rotting Man is about as graphic as we allow to walk the circus, and I'm afraid that's too much even for the funhouse. We can lop off limbs and suggest amateur surgery, but we can't just leave a man so opened up for anyone to look at too closely."

"Pity. But I do like the idea of him in one of the smaller funhouse rooms. Shall we inject him with spider venom regularly to ensure he stays so wonderfully deformed? I don't think I have it in me to bite him every week, though. I want nothing more to do with that...thing over there."

"Oh, you won't have to lift a finger. He'll be sequestered from the rest of the circus until he learns not to fight back against me, but even when he is free one day to walk the circus, you'll never have to look over your shoulder. I won't let him near you. As far as you are concerned, he will cease to exist."

Elizabeth didn't remember Bell's eyes quite that color amber before, like dark honey. "Thank you." She owed him nothing, but she thanked him just the same.

"Don't concern yourself with this one any further. Please take your father to the fortune teller tent. I will meet you there." He lifted his hand again as though to stroke her cheek, but he passed it over her forehead instead, like a benediction. "He saw a goldmine and a diamond choker to put on it, but you're worth so much more than that, Elizabeth. Do you see that yet?"

Elizabeth took his hand from where it rested on her forehead. The air charged around them. She felt it like electricity over her skin, like the sudden dampness of a thick fog.

For a moment, she would have let him if he'd asked. A different kind of fear crept underneath her skin from the way he wanted her. She wondered if this was what Maya felt. If so, Elizabeth understood how a mortal woman could bind herself to him, no matter how awesome and terrible the power contained in such an unassuming man.

But he released her, determinedly turning back to Dez.

Elizabeth had to pause for a second near the hissing cockroaches in the glass coffin. Then she gathered herself again and stepped out of the tent, leaving what was inside it for Bell to handle.

Chapter Fourteen

Elizabeth and her father sat on one side of the palmistry table. She wore her father's jacket again, although she'd left the tent in more clothing than she'd come in with.

The Creature had elected to wait outside, sensing that the business at hand was not for him to be a part of.

Bell slid into his usual seat on the other side. This time he didn't eliminate the table between them. It felt more like a business meeting, less personal. However, he did reach under his chair again to pull another bottle of whiskey out of nowhere.

"Excuse my delay. Desmond decided to remain in the land of the living, so he had to be dragged, kicking and screaming, to his cell. After pleading for his life, you'd think he'd be more compliant after I spared it. Care for a drink, Father?" Bell asked, pouring himself and Elizabeth each a glass.

Petros raised his hand in polite rejection. He didn't comment on Elizabeth taking hers, although it was strange drinking in front of him after hiding it for so long. Still, she quickly downed what Bell had given her then poured herself another, all before Bell even started his own. There was a reason she'd drunk Dez's friends to the floor back in the day.

"I believe we're at a bit of an impasse," Bell said. "Mr. Petros came here because you called him for help, and I was prepared to smooth things over with my divine wit and charm, or have Elizabeth do it for me. I didn't expect to be confronted with someone who could see through what Arcanium is. And that leaves me with a dilemma."

"I want you to let my daughter go," Petros said.

Bell raised his glass. "And there's the dilemma. Because you see, sir, she wished herself in, and the rules of Arcanium are quite clear and in the house's favor. I'm technically *capable* of letting her out of Arcanium, but the sheer fact of the matter is, I don't *want* to. I hope to have Lizzie with me for a good long while, and it's nigh impossible to convince me to do something I do not want to do."

"Then if I were to wish myself into the circus in her stead?"

"I'd just keep both of you," Bell replied. "I would find a way. I've been at this game so much longer than you could ever play it. But as much as I want Lizzie to stay, I've already told her I have no interest in keeping you. You wouldn't take to this life as well as she has, and I'm afraid it would end quite badly for you. You're meant to stay with your congregation, Mr. Petros, and Elizabeth is meant to stay here. Surely a man such as you understands that design."

Petros leaned in, elbows on his knees. "I understand that you are a collector of curiosities, a mad scientist playing God."

"Only of my own little domain. I respect you as a prophet, but I've lived all the Scriptures, from the ones you know by heart to those considered apocryphal as well as those not yet discovered or those that have since been destroyed or hidden. I do not advise that you argue theology with me. There are laws within and without Arcanium that I did not set and that I must follow, just as there are laws you cannot break. It's not playing God to do what I was created to do, nor is it playing God just because it's something you're incapable of doing."

He placed his hand palm up on the table, staring at it idly as he spoke. Curls of smoke emerged from the lines he would read on a client. A tongue of flame appeared, hovering over his palm. Then he clenched his fist, snuffing it out.

"Are you actually telling me you're doing God's will by imprisoning Elizabeth here?" Petros asked incredulously.

"It's my will," Bell said with a smile, "and in Arcanium, my will is what matters. So please, sir, let's set aside the possibility of Elizabeth going free. I intend for her to find freedom within these confines. And she has already shed so many of the chains that bound her before she came to Arcanium. Haven't you, my dear?"

Elizabeth occupied herself with her drink. That was a chain she still hadn't shrugged off, and Bell knew it. "Leave me out of this."

"Do you want to stay here?" Petros asked.

"No. I just know better than to expect him to let me go, not after everything he's done. Not after everything *I've* done." She briefly met Bell's eyes over her glass.

She'd grown up in a church that didn't believe in the necessity of confession but of the catharsis of it. Atonement was for oneself, an antidote to the shame of sin that a saint no longer needed to feel once he'd been saved. She'd tried to atone in her father's congregation, but all she'd managed to do was hide, as though she could eliminate her sins by ensuring no one else knew they existed.

Bell had told her that he understood the need for atonement, sometimes achieved through unconventional means. She could almost believe that now.

Petros took her hand. "I'm just a prophet, but I can get you out. There are spiritual warriors for both sides. I can find another way."

"That's what we were hoping to avoid," Bell said. "Because I also have rules for that, and I'd rather not have to kill you. The world could use more mysteries such as yourself. I'm quite fond of them, even when they are no use to me."

Elizabeth tightened her grip on Petros' hand. "I don't want you to die trying to save me. I didn't mean to drag you into this. I just didn't know who else to turn to."

"How can I ignore what has happened to you? How can I turn a blind eye to where you are, surrounded by this darkness, and in that darkness alone? How can I not save you?"

"I won't keep her here forever," Bell said quietly. "It will seem a long time to her, but she will be released, given a chance to start anew. If the uncertain future remains as I see it, you will still be living when I release her. And, as with any family of my people, you may visit her during circus hours or with the right invitation. She won't be kept from you, only from the rest of the world."

"How dare you present her imprisonment in the light of generosity," Petros said.

"If you knew what I know of dungeons such as this one, you would consider me generous, too. When a rabbit steps into a snare, is it better to release it from the trap and let it wander the forest crippled for a less sophisticated predator to snatch it up as easy prey? Or is it more compassionate to bring it home and keep it in a cage, tending the wound, until its leg is strong again?"

Elizabeth lowered her glass. She didn't think Bell had blinked through the entire explanation, and though he addressed her father, she felt him assessing her, like fingers tracing the inside of her skull.

Was that what he had really created Arcanium for? Or was that just the lie he told, another illusion to sweeten Arcanium for those he kept, to keep them warm and compliant in his web?

"I won't let her go. That is a fact you must accept." Bell spread his hands in a gesture that seemed both offer and shrug. "The only question here is whether I let you go or whether I give you the same choice I gave the shriveled scum that damaged her. It would be an insult, Father, to put you on the same level as him. I don't ask you to be happy, to give your blessing to an old jinni, nor do I demand that you forget her. I only need you to preserve Arcanium's secret. I would very much hate to retaliate if you didn't. I've had more than my share of violence in my time, and I am now, at heart, a peaceful man."

"I'm just to leave her here?" Petros said. "How can you expect me — ?"

"What is best for her, Father? Your congregation or my circus? Look at me, in my eyes. Seek the answer there, if you must."

Elizabeth finished her second glass, but she didn't have much taste for it as her father met Bell's unflinching gaze.

Petros finally stood, a pale hand on the edge of the table. "You are still despicable, but your lawlessness might yet serve my daughter better than the law. At least she'll have somewhere to go when you relinquish her. I'll make sure of it."

He turned to her, sorrow etched into the lines around his eyes. He reached out to her, ran his palm over her head, memorizing her face, noting the tattoos exposed over her chest, her legs, perhaps remembering the others he had glimpsed. Black ink, sharpened teeth, silver piercings over her lip, leather and blades — hardly the image of the daughter of a prophet. Yet he considered her with a quiet pride in his expression that her own dad had never shown her — not a trace of the disappointment he had the right to feel, when the sins of her soul were exposed for any and all to witness.

"I will see you again," he said, with the certainty of prophecy.

Elizabeth wrapped her fingers around his wrist.

"And I love you. Remember that. No matter what." He lifted her hand to his lips and kissed her knuckles. "Call me if you need to speak to me or if you need me to come back."

Elizabeth nodded, unable to say anything more, unable to convince herself to get up from the chair and follow him. She was afraid she'd follow him right out the Arcanium gates.

Before he exited the tent, Petros hesitated. "It's not me you have to worry about interfering with Arcanium. Not everyone wants it led by a beneficent master. Others have other designs, and they may be more powerful than you. If my daughter gets taken by one of them, I'll rain heaven and hell down upon you."

"I am often underestimated. They won't be the first or the last to try to take Arcanium." But Bell frowned, troubled.

Petros lowered the tent flap behind him.

"So things just go back to the way they were?" Elizabeth said. "Just the way you like them."

"Do you want things to go back to the way they were?"

"Don't you try that shrink trick on me."

"I was only being partially facetious. *Do* you want things to go back just the way they were?" he asked. "Because they can. I can continue to force you into the spiderweb, and I can continue to close you in the glass coffin, if making me force you to do the job I've given makes you feel more righteous in your God's eyes. I won't stop you."

"What if I don't?" She slowly undid the buttons of her father's jacket and folded it over the back of the chair then leaned back to cross her prime legs. "What if I don't want things to go back to the way they were?"

"Short of letting you go, which you and I both know I'm not going to do, what did you have in mind?" Bell poured himself another drink and offered her a third.

She chewed on the tip of her tongue, but eventually nodded.

He waited for her to say it, waited for her to finish the drink and declare it to be her last. The set of his smirk, the slightest quirk of his eyebrow… He wanted her to say it, craved her wish the way the Creature craved fear.

She could wish that of him, and maybe he would be inclined to give it to her the way she wanted it. No more bottles in her RV. No more going to sleep drunk. No more mornings in the funhouse with whiskey breath and a fuzzy head. It wasn't working anyway, and if she couldn't numb what was happening to her, then what was the goddamn point?

All she had to do was wish the cravings away. If only Elizabeth believed God intended anything to be easy. But making it easy wouldn't take it away, not really. She saw herself coming back to the bottle, even without an addiction to drive it. The compulsion to medicate with what was on hand would be too much to resist.

She could wish it away, but she wasn't going to. She stumbled a bit, her primary feet slipping on the ground as she leaned in to take the glass. But she took the glass, threw her head back then swallowed it all down at once.

"I wish you'd give me my hair back, and that you'd remove the tattoos. All of them."

Bell traced a line around the rim of his glass. "Interesting. Care to explain, my dear?"

"Don't you know why?"

"I like to be surprised now and then."

"You took care of Dez, but that doesn't deal with the problem. The word's spread that Arcanium has Lucy Lewd playing the part of the Human Spider, and these tattoos just confirm it for them. If they start realizing that the limbs are real, that's going to confuse people, and when people are confused, they start investigating. I don't think you want Lucy in your circus any more than I do. If I were you, I'd want my acts to be famous for what Arcanium made of them, not stunt casting."

Bell stood, leaving his drink on the table.

"It's a shame," he said. "I quite like the tattoos you have. You could stand to embrace the fears you've faced, and as art separate from artist, they are quite remarkable. Even the spider and the chains Troy made for you?" He trailed his fingers over her secondary arms along the newer tattoos.

"He can do new ones. I can be spider enough without belaboring the point. The more different my ink is from Lucy's, the more the previous photos shared on the Internet will be questioned." She fingered the silver rings over her lip. "I think you'll eventually have your tattooed Spider again. I'd just prefer to choose what covers me. I want to start with my own canvas, not his."

Bell slid his hands down to hers and led her away from the table. "You'll be starting with mine. But the spirit of your wish has merit. And how considerate of you to remember Arcanium in your choice," he added — with bite, but without breaking through skin.

He placed a hand on her head. Elizabeth's knees buckled under sudden pressure that crushed her under impossible weight. It wasn't painful, but it was undeniably uncomfortable.

"I hope you don't mind if I take the illustrations into myself, should I decide to interrupt this particular skin in the future." He combed through the fine hair sprouting from her scalp. It slithered down to her lower back, as it had been before he'd stripped her of it. "For the sake of ease, this is the only hair I returned to you.

Do ask Kitty if you'd like to change it, but I favor that wig you wear in the coffin. The blue suits you well."

"Thank you." Elizabeth raked her own fingers through it, passing through the silky black and into the blue flames at the bottom.

"You're quite welcome, my lovely girl."

He was so close to her now. She sensed once again the deceptive power that hid behind his mild-mannered façade, the age and cunning in his eyes, the lust far more complicated and fervid than that of man or monster. It was lust that wasn't merely sexual, and that's what scared her—his overwhelming need to possess, to collect, to design and twist and create, the sheer, unrelenting certainty of his desire. Bell was a thing that didn't know shame, which made him alien to her. And all that in the guise of a man, a common fortune teller and magician of a first-rate circus hidden amid second-rate trappings.

She thought he would caress her, like he had in the red tent, but instead he pressed his fingers to her swollen check.

"Visit Troy or Kitty before you return to your RV. They're the ones who keep healing unguent handy. We can't have you going back to work with a black eye. I could heal it myself, but I'm tired."

She nodded.

Bell released her, turned his back. Not a dismissal so much as permission, to leave or to stay.

She left.

Chapter Fifteen

Men still came specifically to see her in the funhouse and were still urged to continue down the corridors by the Gentleman, who was as gentlemanly as ever. None of that had changed.

The only difference was that they quickly discovered she wasn't the Lucy Lewd other people had sworn she was. Because she wore her armor now instead of the latex bodysuit to show off her distinct lack of tattooing, Troy said people online were debunking the rumors with their own pictures. A few people thought Lucy Lewd had only been there temporarily as a promotional gimmick, especially since Bell hadn't sent the red tent into the outside world in a while. Maybe they thought Elizabeth was some kind of cheaper body double, as though any skinny, half-Asian chick would do in the Spider role.

She felt much freer in the armor, though. Nanny Elizabeth would have been mortified at the amount of skin it showed and the fetish style of the costume, but compared to what she'd worn in the coffin, it was positively modest. Her job was still to hang there and look pretty and scary at the same time, but in the less intimate venue of the haunted funhouse, she could live with that for now.

* * * *

She knew something was wrong when the regular chorus of screams and moans ceased, one by one. The strobe lights and soundtrack also quieted, the way they did at the end of the work day when the performances were about to begin. She usually had a pretty good idea how long she'd been in the funhouse, mostly by the cycles of food that guests brought through the corridors. It was just around dinnertime, not closing.

Once the funhouse had gone completely silent, she could hear the dense drumming of a rainstorm on the roof, and thunder shook the spiderweb. Turned out Bell couldn't control the weather, although that had been a pet theory of hers after they'd gone through January and February with not a bit of snow on the ground everywhere they traveled. If the rain was bad enough, Bell had probably herded everyone to the big top to wait it out, which meant they wouldn't have any guests coming through the funhouse any time soon.

She didn't know the procedure for a rainstorm. Usually, when the soundtrack and lights stopped, they'd all be released, but the ropes strapped over her arms and legs hadn't loosened.

She shrugged internally and slumped in the bindings, resting in the cradle of the web with her eyes closed. Strobe lighting had a tendency to pierce through her eyelids and keep her from settling down, a constant stream of visual stimulation. It was much easier in the steady twilight darkness to drift away, drift off.

"Wake up, sweetheart."

The voice was so soft, the stroke of fingers pushing her hair behind her ear so tender, she thought she was dreaming at first, that moths fluttered over her and the words were the beating of wings.

"It's time to wake up." The hand drifted from her ear to the edge of the corset over her breast, stroking flesh all the way down.

That woke her up, eyes flying open in a rush of both arousal and panic.

"Good evening, Spider." The man in a trench coat and fedora smiled and stepped back, maintaining contact with her as long as possible. "Today's your lucky day."

She opened her mouth to call for the Gentleman, even though she still didn't have a voice before closing, but he clicked his tongue as though she were a naughty girl. Then he snapped his fingers.

The ropes holding her released, and she fell to the floor. He grinned rakishly down at her as she untangled her legs.

"They're giving an early performance. Bell won't even realize you're gone until it's too late." He swept an arm toward the entrance with a bow. "The gates of Arcanium are open, and the magic keeping you has been lifted. No consequences."

A tumble of questions piled on her tongue, caged behind her sharp teeth.

"It's a limited time offer, Elizabeth. I'd get going if I were you." He lifted his hat in farewell then backed down the corridor and turned the corner toward the other exhibits.

Is this some kind of trick? Some kind of test?

But it wasn't just quiet. It was like the hum of a generator had turned off, a sound she'd been so used to that she hadn't noticed it until it wasn't there anymore.

She slowly made her way toward the entrance.

The Gentleman hovered a few inches above the ground in his corner, his head slack on a lolling neck. She'd never touched him before, but she tentatively took his wrist between her fingers to try to find a pulse. She didn't even know whether he had a heart.

His skin was rubbery underneath the powdered surface, what she imagined an alien would feel like. There was a pulse, though—faster than the resting rate of a person, but a pulse nonetheless. She didn't feel as bad moving on.

The funhouse entrance was open, and the carnival part of Arcanium was deserted. At least it seemed like that until she noticed furtive movement within Oddity Row, and around the corner of the haunted funhouse, prisoners started to make a run for it.

Still unsure how much she could trust the man in the trench coat, Elizabeth climbed down the stairs and followed them.

As she passed the oddity tents, someone hissed her name from the other side.

Kevin, with his sad cat face and soft, bald body, beckoned her onto the Row. He crossed his arms over his chest, his cat ears flicking fussily as the rain pounded on them.

"Did you see him, too?" He rubbed his whiskers with the back of his hand to brush off the water. "The man in the hat? Do you think it's true, that we can just leave?"

"I don't know," Elizabeth said.

Kevin took a step toward her. She retreated, wary not just of him but of everything. In spite of the storm, it was too damn quiet. And she'd washed her hands of all these people running past her like the hounds of hell were at their heels. It was the prisoners' Walk of Shame from the funhouse in fast forward, with the mostly mobile victims carrying the ones who had been maimed and mauled, Blondie clutching at her vines, the werewolf loping by.

"Kevin, you fucker, come on!"

Elizabeth jerked behind the oddity tent she was next to at Hank's surreptitious shout. She didn't think he'd seen her, but she didn't want him getting ideas, even if he didn't have a dick to do them with. That's when maladaptives like him started using knives and other violent substitutes.

"Did he go through all of Oddity Row?" Elizabeth whispered.

Kevin shook his head. "Just after the performers left to go backstage — the contortionist, the bearded lady, the demons... You know, Bell's people." He backed away, glancing over his shoulder to where Hank was probably gesturing to him. "After what happened...I'm glad he let you go, too. Now come on. We need to hurry. We don't know when Bell's going to realize what's happening. Or worse, the clowns."

He seemed reluctant to let her go alone, but when she avoided him getting even within arm's length, he decided it was best to let her move at her own pace.

She crept around Oddity Row, walking to put distance between her and Hank and Kevin running. She walked briskly but walked just the same.

The Arcanium gates were wide open. No ticket-taker golem, no sword swallower at his platform, no clowns prowling the fence. Just open gates and woods next to the field that had become a makeshift parking lot. There was no sign of the man in the trench coat.

She watched through sheets of rain as the prisoners hobbled, lumbered and helped others across the Arcanium border into the outside. No one stumbled, no one screamed, no one writhed in unbearable pain. They hurried into the dark woods, obscured by rain and shadow. She heard shouts from among the trees, but she couldn't make out what they were saying.

As he and Kevin crossed the threshold, Hank whooped, pumping the air with his fist, his petticoat flouncing. Then they, too, disappeared into the forest.

A few other prisoners passed by her, Blondie choking on her ivy, whipping boys sprinting for the finish line, flesh-eaten invalids shivering with fever but just as eager to get out of Arcanium.

Elizabeth stopped behind the sword swallower's platform, about twenty feet from the entrance.

The prisoners were able to leave without consequences, but they weren't changing back. Blondie still had ivy emerging from her orifices, and the lesions of the flesh-eaten prisoners' bodies were still bloody, necrotic and seeping pus. Hank had still been the Man Doll, and Kevin had still been the Sphynx.

Maybe they'd decided it was worth it. Maybe they thought they'd rather die than stay, rather be a freak than Bell's plaything, rather take their chances with normals than remain in the circus. Maybe they thought the magic would wear off. Maybe they were just so distracted by the prospect of freedom that they hadn't even realized they'd left one hell and stumbled into another.

Elizabeth's throat tightened as she thought about whoever had been maimed by the butcher, operated upon by the surgeon. The whipping boys would heal, but the diseased prisoners would still have bacteria killing their flesh. The werewolf would still be long-armed and hairy.

And she'd still be the Spider.

But she could be free. In theory, she could go under the knife and have the limbs removed, but even if she had to be the Spider forever, she'd still be free. She could run straight into her father's arms and hide in the congregation like the Hunchback of Notre Dame. Or she could join a regular freak show, where the freaks were just freaks and not magical hybrid toys.

Elizabeth stepped toward the open gates, hesitant, alternating between her prime legs and her secondary, rocking back and forth. The rain had soaked her hair into thick ropes, permeated the leather. Now the cold was starting to seep beneath the surface of her skin.

She'd be free. Wouldn't she?

She only needed a few long strides to step across, out of Bell's clutches. She'd already had Bell strip Lucy from her skin. She really could start over again.

"Elizabeth."

There he was again, just like the last time she'd tried to run, back when the gates had been locked and chained against her. The Creature landed on the platform, majestic in the gray haze. He stepped down onto the ground and stood behind her.

"Don't go."

"I might not get another chance, not for years." She wiped the rain from her eyes in a futile gesture. "Decades. Centuries, even. This might be it."

"Do you really think Bell will leave this trespass unanswered? Any good will you've curried, any freedoms you've gained within the circus… It might take those decades or centuries to regain them again. Even if you evade him, what kind of world will it be for you?" He held out his hand. "There is escape and freedom, Elizabeth, but it's not out in that world. Not yet. Please, little Spider. Stay."

Elizabeth looked back at the open gate. The last stragglers from the funhouse stumbled over the borders and staggered into the world beyond to take their chances.

God, how she wanted to leave Arcanium.

He smoothed his hand over her cheek, his breath hot against her hair. "It's not just your fear I desire. It's not just the strangeness of you that I love. There is a future for you here. Bell wouldn't have brought you in if he didn't have greater plans. But even if he doesn't… Stay with me."

His fur was wet, but she let his warmth draw her in, closed her eyes against the false promise of the open gates and enshrouded herself in the Creature's wings. She covered her face and hid herself against his chest. With her secondary hands, she gripped the Creature's sides, holding on to him to tether herself, lest she find herself pulled to the other side of the gates from temptation too great to resist.

Because he was right. There was no way Bell was just going to let her go if she crossed the threshold. Did she honestly think she could run and never be found again? She couldn't even cry anymore. What was inside her was too big, too dark and powerful—to have the outside world so close and now not even the hope of

403

escape in her grasp, denied to her more times than she could count.

"What in the barren expanse of *hell* happened here?"

Bell yanked open the folded cocoon of the Creature's wings.

She didn't think she'd ever heard Bell like this. He'd never shouted, never been angry like...like a regular person.

A regular person who'd lost control.

He paused in his rampage when she raised her head from her hands, as though he hadn't expected her.

"Elizabeth."

"There was a man, a man who never showed me his eyes. He said he'd opened the gates for us, that we could leave and you wouldn't know. Almost all the prisoners and the oddities who aren't performers left. They're out there." Elizabeth waved her hand at the woods.

Bell struggled to contain his rage. He whirled around and pointed to the incubus and succubus, who'd come up from the big top with the clowns behind them. "You! Into the forest. Bring back whomever you can find. I've closed the circus borders again. They'll be easy enough to pluck from where they're screaming and writhing in pain. Take any of the prisoners you want as payment, but the oddities are off-limits and for the Ringmaster to handle. He'll be out to join you as soon as his performance has concluded. Go!"

The clowns darted through the gates, and the incubus and succubus launched themselves into the air as though they had wings, seemingly unaffected by the downpour, though Lord Mikhail teetered as he gained altitude over the woods.

Bell closed his hand over Elizabeth's wrist. "The man. I need to know what he looked like and exactly what happened. Look at me. I need to see through your eyes."

Elizabeth backed into the Creature, who held her shoulders the way he had that first night, giving her another disorienting case of déjà vu. "You never had to before."

"I can't see him. I can't even see him through your mind alone." He grasped her face and peered deep into her. She couldn't feel anything physically, but mentally, it was like he inserted knitting needles through her eyes straight into the frontal lobe.

Bell abruptly let her go and spat to the side in disgust. "Goddammit. I still can't see him." He spun around to start for the woods.

Elizabeth yanked him back to her. "Why can't you see him? Talk to me. What is he?"

"I don't know. I don't know because you don't know," he said with visible frustration. "But I know what he did and how to defend against it. In the meantime, he's tipped his hand. Now I know someone's following Arcanium. Whatever his intentions are, he won't be able to anticipate me any more than I can anticipate him."

"Why can't you?"

"There are only two possibilities, which are really the same at their core. He's either an exceptionally powerful demon or he's an exceptionally powerful jinni. Either way, whether he merely seeks to interfere with my circus or steal it, I intend to remind him why I have two demons just like him serving Arcanium."

This time, what kept him there was his own hesitation. His frenzy softened into a squall, until it was less furious than the rain pouring down over them.

"I apologize for snapping at you. You are not the one I'm angry with. Far from it, Lizzie. I'm exceedingly pleased that you were not one of the fools who attempted to flee."

"It's not because of Arcanium. I didn't do it for you," Elizabeth said.

"I know. But you made a choice, and it was the right one. It will not go unacknowledged." He quickly leaned in and kissed her cheek. "For remaining, and for opening your mind to me."

"But you didn't see him in any of our minds when he let us go. What if he comes back?"

"You didn't even know anything was wrong until I alerted Kitty," the Creature added.

"I do have some blind spots. Very few beings have the means to conceal themselves from me, but they do exist. Of course, there's another, more worrying possibility," Bell replied darkly.

Elizabeth's stomach went as cold as her rain-drenched skin. "Is Arcanium safe?"

"The magic around it was manipulated, but the magical protections are supplemented with flesh-and-blood guards like the Creature and the clowns. Reconstituted magic and retrieval are exactly how Arcanium should work after a breach. And in the failure of all else, I am its last defense, and I have not yet lost a battle." His forehead furrowed, his expression hard. "However, if I cannot see him not because he is too powerful but because he is too intertwined with my own fate, then all I can do now is prepare for another attack and increase Arcanium's protections—which means getting all my prisoners back within the borders and reminding them of the real meaning of wrath. They forget so quickly, though, that it hardly seems worth keeping them now. If you would like to take closer shelter than the caravan, Elizabeth, the red tent should be set up for you to dry off and rest quietly out of the storm."

Bell strode right out of the still-open gate and into the woods, but Elizabeth sensed the barrier's return, the hum of magic vibrating subtly through her skin once more.

Blondie was the first of the prisoners to be returned. Lord Mikhail dropped her unceremoniously onto the ground well inside the fence. Blood dripped down her legs and from her mouth and nose. Running with a parasitic vine in the real world probably hadn't been as safe outside Arcanium as it had been within. Between her muffled screams and gasps for breath, she scratched at her skin and clothes, tearing lines into her flesh without any heed of the damage.

"I should probably join them, retrieve whatever didn't survive the transition, bring back who I can." The Creature pressed his cheek to her sodden hair. "Would you rather I stay?"

Elizabeth wanted him to, but she shook her head. More lives would be saved if the Creature could help Bell bring everyone back.

"I'll come back to you," he whispered.

Weight in her limbs she hadn't felt in weeks made her solo journey back to Oddity Row ponderous, but she slipped behind the curtain of the red tent with some relief. The heat bulbs that kept the tropical specimens warm provided enough light. She opted not to turn on the lamps.

Instead of the glass coffin, a large cot waited for her, with towels to dry herself off and quilts for afterward. Elizabeth stripped off the ruined leather, which she suspected wouldn't be ruined in the morning. Then she wrapped herself in two quilts and lay on the cot, hungry but warming up under the dry blankets.

A golem entered to bring her dinner, unperturbed by the change in venue or her nakedness. Eating helped, but she couldn't sleep until the Creature came to her.

He shook himself free of rain and blood spatter, used the rest of the towels to clean and dry himself off. She watched him, and he watched her. When he was done, she opened the quilts to let him in against her, wrapping her arms and the quilts around him like wings of her own.

Chapter Sixteen

"Do you trust me, little Spider?"

She ran her teeth over the edge of his ear. "More than anyone else in the entire fucking circus. I thought I'd made that clear."

The Creature hooked his hands around both sets of her thighs, digging his fingers in as she rocked against his erection.

The sex demons were in fine form, because the night had barely begun and she wanted the Creature everywhere at once. The whole circus had been like this for weeks. By all accounts, the guests were feeling it, too, getting together behind tents and booths, fingering each other during performances, hiding under the bleachers, making cars rock in the parking lot—and a few inside the caravan as well, with the cast members who took lovers from the outside. Elizabeth was not among them. The Creature satisfied her just fine. She'd discovered that a being who could decide his own arousal could be just as tireless as she through the nights, through the mornings.

"You quickly recover now from your fear of heights, your fear of everything in your red tent, no matter what I do to challenge you." He scratched his claws through her hair with a smile. "It is not a terrible thing to be conquering your fears, Elizabeth. But I purged so much into your ex that I find myself hungry all the time, and no one is as delicious as you."

"What did you have in mind?" They were both still clothed — as much as either of them ever were. She couldn't tear her hands away from him to start pulling off her costume, couldn't bring herself close enough to him just with the movement of her hips. Her heated skin prickled as though in pain. He wasn't touching her nearly enough.

"Do you trust me?" he asked again.

Elizabeth paused in her attempt to wriggle out of her own skin. He was too serious in his query for her to make light of it.

"Yes."

He wrapped his arms around her in the now familiar embrace that signaled she better hold on. Elizabeth tucked her mouth against his neck, closing her eyes at the initial, disorienting sight of the funhouse roof falling away. But she opened them again as he flapped his wings. All she could see from here were the stars. The lights from the midway and picnic tables obscured some of the night sky, but the circus often parked itself in out-of-the-way places, and more stars pierced through than she used to see in the city.

The Creature brought them lower, the canvas of the big top tent rising into her vision. He landed at the backstage entrance.

Taking her by the hand, he led her into the big top. Valorie and the fire-eater passed them on their way out, Valorie doing a similar sort of leading, although by the fire-eater's collar instead of by the hand. Ciarán followed behind them, Moss on his shoulder. Other than the people in the lion and tiger cages, the only one left backstage now was Bell, who was using an anachronistic pink chaise longue to help him unlace his black boots.

He glanced up, halfway through his last boot. The arch to his eyebrow suggested he hadn't been expecting them, but he didn't exactly look surprised.

Elizabeth stopped where she stood, her hand slipping from the Creature's hold. "What is this?"

"*He* scares you," the Creature said. "He is the only one here that you fear who I trust not to harm you. And I know you desire him. Do you trust me?"

"You want him to fuck me while you watch?"

The arch of Bell's eyebrow lifted even higher, and he straightened with his boot still on the chaise, gaze shifting from the Creature to Elizabeth. He waited, wisely not chiming in.

"I want him to frighten you while I feed. While he takes you."

"Why would you ask me to do this? How *could* you ask it? Why would you want me to have sex with another man when you—"

"As you've already observed for yourself, Lizzie, there's a tendency among the people of the circus to take more than one lover. There's more than enough libido to go around," Bell said.

He bent over again to finish untying his boot. He tossed it with the other, then turned to face them. "You already know that Maya is mine. No one touches her without my permission, and no one touches me without hers. But we give our permission freely and often."

He lowered himself to recline like a jaguar on the chaise. "This is Arcanium, not the world, Lizzie. I'm in favor of a few iniquities to smooth through the nights, as you've taken liberal advantage of since arriving. So don't stand there so shocked the Creature would ask this of you. It's merely a request. He doesn't want to pass you around like a glass of wine or a cigarette."

"I notice you're not protesting," she said, crossing her arms.

Bell's gaze didn't lower to her cleavage, but his Cheshire Cat grin deepened. "Why should I?"

The Creature stepped in front of her, blocking her view of the smug son of a bitch. "It's okay to be frightened, little Spider. We needn't stay."

Elizabeth angled her head into the cradle of his palm, closing her eyes for a moment. "What exactly am I afraid of?" she murmured, uncertain she wanted to know the answer.

The Creature brought his teeth to her neck, breathed her in. "I think you're afraid of how much you desire him, afraid of how much he desires you, afraid of how much he'll take if you yield to him. You're afraid you'll want whatever he gives, that you'll have gone from one evil man to another you can't run from. Afraid you need him anyway. More than you need me right now."

"Awfully specific for just a taste," Elizabeth said dryly.

"That isn't what I tasted. I know your fears better than you think I do. I don't have to consume them to observe what is true."

"Well, if you're so smart, are any of these fears real?"

"All fears are real. I can't tell you how to feel or how to protect yourself. But what creates your ambivalence time and again, little Spider, is not letting yourself have what you want because of fear, whether rational or not."

"You want to see me with him." She swallowed. Took a breath. "Have you thought about it before? Fantasized about it when he looks at me like he wants to shove me onto a table and rip my clothes off, the way you did in the tent the first time he confined me? Do you imagine me writhing under him, over him, on my knees, *begging* him—"

He caught the cord of her neck with his teeth like a dog, sucked at the skin, pulled at it. Her head fell back from the ache between her legs. "What do you think I do all day while you're bound to a spiderweb where I can no longer join you?"

"Imagine I was doing those things to you," Elizabeth said, but she found herself breathless.

"Oh, I do that as well. But I'm the fly to your spider, Elizabeth, and I do not believe I could ever truly frighten you. You know that with me there is no risk, no consequence. I can be neither your judge nor your executioner, but perhaps I might learn more what you are willing to accept from me if you yield it to him first."

He fed upon a layer of jitters, but she gently eased his head up from her neck. "You sure you'll still respect me in the morning?"

"Why wouldn't I? I'm the one who made the request," the Creature said.

"You'd be surprised how many men condemn you for doing them in the same breath they're doing you."

The Creature slowly stepped around her, exposing her to Bell's view once again. Despite Bell's casual demeanor, she twitched reflexively when he stood. But she started walking toward him, like a woman walking the plank into shark-infested waters.

"Hello, Lizzie." He smiled, his body as loose as hers was tense. He carried no insecurity, no doubt, none of the fear she held in every fiber of herself. His smile was wicked, but gentler, even kinder, than it had been. He couldn't hide his amusement entirely, but a trace of caution in the set of his eyes and mouth tempered it.

"Are you certain?" he asked.

She stopped, a great deal of space still between them in the large backstage area. With crates piled high behind him, the backstage suddenly seemed immense, and she and Bell very small parts of it. But it didn't swallow him up, and why should it? Mere size wouldn't dare to diminish him.

"No," she replied.

Each step he took was deliberate and measured, without impatience.

"You know, I never used to enjoy the sort of thing you're looking for. But I confess I've developed a taste for it since. I think I can give you what you've been craving, my dear, but you will have to agree to this little unconventional arrangement before I can fulfill it." He didn't hesitate, didn't break his slow stride. Not until she stepped back. "I don't fuck an unwilling woman unless we've agreed to it beforehand."

"Then she isn't unwilling, is she?" Elizabeth shot back.

"You and I both know that isn't entirely true. There are layers of consent, especially in these murky waters, where a woman of mine has a unique craving for domination, but not some bedroom game — damnation in the name of redemption, purgatory in search of a heaven. Just because Desmond is the reason your mind and body respond to pleasure against your will doesn't mean you can't take pleasure in enjoying pleasure against your will."

"That doesn't make any sense."

"Then why do you understand every word I say?" He stopped not ten feet away, opened his arms, offering himself to her. "You can still hate me, Elizabeth, and need me at the same time. I will not abuse your trust, even if I abuse you. Do you understand? If your tongue cannot be honest, then hold it, and answer me."

Elizabeth caught the tip of her tongue between her sharp teeth — not drawing blood but knowing she could. Reluctantly, she nodded.

"Do you understand that I am dangerous?"

She nodded again.

"But do you understand that you are completely safe?"

Elizabeth didn't look back at the Creature, but she clung to the knowledge that he was there, that the fist squeezing the base of her spine would satisfy him. And God help her, she was turned on again, unable to look away from the fortune teller. She remembered all the times Bell had wanted to kiss her, the times his fingertips had lingered, the way he'd embraced her when he created her, remembered his fingers in her mouth as he gave her venom. Remembered all the things she'd submitted to — and with Dez no longer a threat to her, things she couldn't help but want again.

She'd never truly be done with him, but perhaps there was a newer idol to whom she could bow, a new tyrant bound by an odd honor that Dez never had.

She nodded.

"Tonight, I won't stop just because you tell me to. But I will not disappoint you. Do you entrust yourself to me?"

That wasn't exactly asking her to trust him. She curled her tongue deeper into her teeth, but she freed it before she could do any damage. "Yes."

He closed the distance between them with a swiftness that belied his patience before. He took her by one of the straps on her corset and pulled her against him.

She parted her lips without thinking to take him in. He just smiled with hooded eyes, letting her instant submission speak for itself. For a moment, she wanted to push him away for being an arrogant asshole, but she'd have to touch him to do that, and he was such a warm, firm, bare body on hers right now. She was afraid that if she touched him, she wouldn't be able to tear her hands away.

This wasn't like when she'd been with Kevin. She hadn't wanted to touch him, but she'd been compelled to, and she'd liked it though she hated it. This was closer to how she'd first been with the Creature — wanting to touch him so badly she hated herself for it. It was a subtle distinction, but it wasn't lost on her.

He didn't bother with foreplay. Without taking his eyes from hers, he slipped his hand underneath her leather bottoms, running his fingers over the line of her folds up to the front, where he took her clit hard between two rough fingers. She'd had clamps on her labia before, and once on her clitoral hood, and that's what this was like. He pinched her clit at its base, keeping it swollen with blood and sensation, but God, it was painful. She had to grab onto his shoulders and arms with both sets of hands just to stay standing. Her mouth dropped open, but no sound came out.

"You're going to come just like this." Bell relinquished her corset to stroke her face, tease the corner of her open mouth without taking advantage of it. He didn't loosen his hold on her clit, instead pinched it harder in a rhythm that had her clit twitching with arousal in the same beat as the pain.

"You knew this was going to happen, you goddamn bastard," she said through clenched teeth. "You knew I'd eventually give in, that all you had to do was wait."

Bell brushed his nose against hers. "I kept it from myself. I told you I like to be surprised."

"How many of the women you trap here have you done this to?" She tried to writhe away from his fingers under the leather, her nails digging into his skin, but for such a small bit of flesh, he had a good hold on it, and it hurt even more when he used it to pull her back against him.

"You'd be surprised."

"At how many?"

"At how few. But I wanted you the moment I saw you."

He laughed when she drew blood from his shoulders, but it didn't stop him, and her breathing quickened. It hurt like a motherfucker, but the fingers between her legs that weren't pinching her were getting slippery from her arousal. Underneath the cups at the top of the corset, her nipples rubbed against the material as though it were wool instead of buttery leather.

"Why wouldn't you?" Her teeth were still clenched, but for an entirely different reason, and she dug her nails in a little deeper. He still didn't flinch. "You saw a sexually confused, cult-repressed woman with a memory like an extended hardcore pornographic video that you could enjoy to your heart's content, because you knew eventually you'd have it for yourself."

"I knew what you'd been, Lizzie, but I wanted *this* woman. And I liked your tattoos. That's all. I admit I have a weakness for shame almost as great as my weakness for trying to eliminate it, but the conditioning Dez gave you has actually been more inconvenient for me than you believe."

Inconvenient? She ripped one hand from his shoulder and struck his face, drawing blood. In less than a second, he retaliated. The clap against her cheek was deafening. Her head swung to the side, more from surprise than from force, although he hadn't been gentle.

With a laugh, though, he closed his fist over her hair and yanked her face back to him, and when he kissed her, she still opened her mouth for him, kissing him back as though she were the Creature and he the fear she consumed.

He quickened the pulse over her clit. In spite of the pain, she was as horny as her body could hold. Her cunt tightened over nothing, squeezing out her juices, clenching toward an orgasm that promised to be rough, raw, strong as a punch to the stomach.

The climax wasn't pleasant at all, but his kiss made her mouth ache as though with its own. It should have been messy, completely unsexy, the way he took her, but he was somehow always in the right place at the right time, claiming her mouth with his tongue in just the right moment, turning his head to complement the angle of hers. Kissing a psychic apparently had its benefits. He anticipated everything, wasted nothing.

Bell abruptly withdrew his fingers from her clit and folds and shoved her down onto her knees. Elizabeth cried out. Not only did the blood rushing in and out of her clit mean a whole new swell of pain, but it meant her orgasm hadn't released anything. She was still taut with arousal, unsatisfied, throbbing, the aftershocks that followed the climax merely physical rather than pleasurable.

The way he stood over her was so similar to how Dez used to, but he didn't have the stature to loom, nor the posture. However, despite the casual stance, there was tension in his arms and legs that suggested he could show her his power at any time. He stared at her, his attention a caress surprisingly intimate.

She started to get up, thinking he was done, that withdrawal had been his punishment for her, his absolution — this dissatisfaction and profound sense of betrayal.

He placed his foot on her shoulder and eased her back onto her knees before withdrawing that touch as well.

"Don't." He spoke with tenderness that nearly brought tears to her eyes in her post-climax state, made worse by being suddenly denied contact that the Creature had always given her.

"What Dez did to you ensured that the prisoners were given far more leniency in their transgressions against you for so long, because you permitted them. What he did to you meant that I couldn't smite him the minute he came into your tent seeking to remove you. What he did meant that you and the Creature had to subsist on a state of ambiguity for so long. That was inconvenient for me, but I fully understand it was more than simple inconvenience for you. It is inconvenient to have to rebreak broken bones that set improperly, but it is fully necessary."

"Yeah, you're the hero." Elizabeth scratched at her own arms where her skin was exposed, her legs, rending shallow bits of flesh and bringing blood to the surface. The combination of sex-demon lust and his denial made her want to peel out of her skin, and the intensity of his regard wasn't helping.

"Perhaps more of a gray hat than white, darker gray sometimes more than others. Remove your gloves and your shoes. As much as I liked the tattoos, your skin alone is a lovely thing."

She could leave. She could get up and leave, and though she'd agreed to have Bell ignore what she said, she thought he'd let her if that was what she decided. There was a thin line between not wanting something to happen and not liking it when it did. It was a line she'd always had trouble with, and a line Bell was more than willing to exploit — with her blessing.

She could leave, but she wasn't going to.

Her breasts felt too big for the little bit of leather covering them, full when she bent forward to remove her boots. Then she pulled the gloves off and tossed them behind her with the boots.

The Creature had climbed onto one of the crates, partially hidden in the shadows, his red eyes glowing for her to see him. He'd removed his loincloth, and with his legs bent to the sides, he made no attempt to conceal his cock, hard and thrusting outward. That helped, too, remembering why she'd agreed to this. She'd accepted any number of things she wouldn't have chosen for herself because of him. She certainly wasn't doing it for Bell.

The fortune teller crooked his finger for her to crawl to him, his amusement unfaltering, as though he knew what was going through her mind was less than complimentary toward him. There was no glory or honor for her in being just over the line, creeping on the tightrope like his girlfriend. But there was also no victory for him in giving a spider venom, then making himself immune. Her canines extended the closer she came to his leather-bound legs, to the cock that stretched the skins taut.

Bell backed away as she came close to him, forcing her to keep crawling until she anticipated what he wanted from her. Not just submission, no—the full horror display he'd envisioned from the beginning.

She rolled her shoulders and hips the way she had for Dez, but when she'd done it for him, she hadn't had a separate set of shoulders or a secondary set of hip wings. She crawled for Bell like a spider, the way she'd seen Goliath move over her—all joints and jerky grace, each limb moving independently from the rest. She focused so much on the intricacy of the movement that she couldn't think about how being on her hands and knees debased her.

When he let her catch him, he lifted her chin with his fingertips. "There's my darling Spider. Well, my dear, now that you're there, I'm sure you know what to do."

Elizabeth started at his ankles, smoothing her palms up his legs. The leather there was as soft as the kind she wore, his firmness beneath a bit surprising, because it made him flesh to her, made him real. He felt more human than the Creature, a good feeling to hands that had fondled their share of flesh.

"Are you sure you want me to? You saw what happened to the last dick in my mouth." She ran her tongue over her extended fangs.

"I've had sharper teeth around my cock, love. I was even briefly castrated by a particularly voracious female. Flesh is easy to grow back when you're a shapeshifter." He tucked her hair behind her ears, a pretense for sliding his fingers behind her head in a possessive hold.

She stroked his thighs, her thumbs brushing between them, touching everything but where his cock bulged out in dimensions far more alarming up close.

"And this is the shape you chose?" Elizabeth asked.

He led one of her hands from his hip to his cock, closing her fingers around the width, guiding her to stroke him through his trousers. "Why? Do you find it inadequate?"

She swallowed. She could lie, but he would see right through it. And not just regarding his cock, which was as large as the Creature's — an attribute apparently common to demons and monsters. Men had odd ideas about what a girl wanted from them when it came to what dangled between their legs, but Elizabeth had been groomed to take small cocks as though they were large and large cocks as though they were small. All that set aside, the truth was he was an intimidatingly pretty man, and she'd thought so long before she'd known he was the devil.

"Not many have seen my true face, just as most never see what the Ringmaster becomes. In spite of running and working a circus, I much prefer being overlooked." His good humor faltered for a moment, but he rallied quickly, drawing himself back to the moment. "But if you're a good girl, I might one day grant you the fortune of a glimpse. And that's very good, pet."

She worked open the laces to his leather trousers of her own accord. He helped her peel them away, leaving him more naked than her and somehow even more intimidating for his nudity rather than more vulnerable.

He gave her no warning. To warn her would be to let her prepare.

He purloined her body, snatched complete control from her as easily as when he'd still had to pull her from bed to work. Then he took control of her mind.

She brought herself against him, raised up on her knees and all four hands occupied with his body as though in worship, but none as reverently as where he applied her mouth.

She licked up his thigh, breathing in his scent, not as dark and wild as the Creature's, yet not simply that of man. There was spice like ancient incense, as though centuries of burnings in his name had suffused the skin. But a man like him shouldn't have smelled quite so much like a man she wanted to taste. Dez had been the same, chemistry that complemented hers, and while that hadn't made her helpless to him, it had made her much easier to ensnare. He'd brought her many other men with many different smells, some decent, some revolting. But there was no mistaking the right scent, the kind that made even new sweat appealing.

She curled her fingers around Bell's cock, larger now that it had room to grow, as impeccably sculpted as the Creature's. Under his influence, she took one side of his sac in her mouth then the other, teasing with her teeth, stroking his cock as though it were a holy relic seeking satisfaction. She already would have been aroused by the act, even if she'd done it reluctantly, but he made her pleasure to serve him nearly excruciating in her mind, yet the arousal of her body much slower and hotter—as though she would have a mental orgasm long before another physical one.

He physically guided her up to the base of his cock, and she lavished a line up the prominent vein to the head. Her mouth was as wet as her cunt. She let saliva drip down him before moaning her way over the head and down—wanting, needing, desperate to take as much of him into her as she could. And unlike Dez, no matter how far she took him, he didn't block her throat. She seemed to expand to accommodate him, though her mouth and neck felt the same size.

The demons and the human women they distracted themselves with made so much more sense to her now.

Bell's breath hitched as she pulled back up, running the very tips of her teeth over the flesh, her fangs tight on either side of him. She hadn't lost her breath, but she coughed and gasped in reflex as she came off from his cock, stroking over the gleaming shaft as a new, unexpected wave of arousal made her throw her head back with a whimper. The worst part was that she thought that one hadn't come from Bell.

Taking him back into her mouth, moving over him first slow and tight, then quickening her pace with her tongue softer over him, though… That was all Bell. To her commandeered mind, every slide and stroke over her tongue was like a caress through her folds and into her cunt. She craved him more than food, more than air, and she succumbed to his puppeteering with pleasure—except for that one part of her mind that was so fucking turned on and horrified by her actions and feelings in equal measure.

With his control over her, she withdrew her secondary hands from his thighs and forced them underneath the leather bottoms where he'd tormented her. As sensitive as she was, every gentler stroke of her fingers through her folds and over her clit was heightened, more intense and more wanted than anything she'd ever done for herself.

He could do so much more damage than Dez. If he wanted to, he could make her crave him more than pleasure. He could make her his slave, and she would happily serve him. The more she feared his control over her, feared what monster she might have created by allowing him the freedom to use her, the hotter her cunt felt as she slid a finger, then two, inside.

But he knew better than to let her believe that anything she did to herself would be better than his fingers over her or his cock inside her. He gave her that knowledge even as she masturbated to the nearly spiritual oral experience he manipulated her through. The more she feared him, the more he rewarded that fear with pleasure, in the same playbook that had shaped her so long ago.

He withdrew, his cock sliding out of her mouth to snap back against his hip. She nearly cried. She pleaded with him wordlessly, chasing it with her mouth as he held her back by her hair, a makeshift leash. When he allowed her tongue to reach the head, she shivered in brief delight.

This was so much worse than the crawling, and he fucking knew it.

"Normally, I find this quite distasteful, but your fear is exquisite to him. How he keeps from latching onto you every minute of every day speaks to greater discipline than I might have in his place."

She tried to calm herself down in the panic-ridden part of her mind he'd left free. Tried to remind herself that she was safe, because he'd tried to remind her of that, too. But it was difficult to feel safe when she only had a dangerous man's word for it. All it would take was a change in whim for him to decide that what he wanted most was his very own harem to use and abuse to his heart's content. He could do more than rewrite her anatomy. He could rewrite her right out of her own brain, leaving behind nothing but a pliant, lustful shell.

He threaded his other hand through her hair and used the mass of it to guide her up from his cock to her feet. She kept trying to get nearer to him, to have her mouth and hands and her hips against him, but he held her back, occasionally yielding long enough to lick the tip of her tongue playfully, to kiss her neck, to let her knuckles brush his cock as he led her back with him toward the chaise.

She tried to reach for him with her secondary hands as well.

"Don't you dare stop," he said with uncharacteristic harshness. "You're not allowed to come if I'm not inside you, but don't you fucking stop trying to make yourself come. Am I clear?"

"Yes, Master." God, that ingratiating, desperate tone was physically painful to hear.

Bell grimaced, so it must have been unpleasant for him as well, but he followed the reaction with a laugh as he whirled her around and shoved her toward the chaise.

He knocked her primary hands away from him when he reached her again. She obediently held them behind her back as she continued to furiously work her fingers over her clit and inside her cunt. With her secondary arms, the angle for the latter wasn't easy, but it was amazing what a woman could do when she needed it badly enough.

And she was close again. Following his warning, she didn't let herself orgasm, though she wanted so much to increase the pressure over her clit, wanted so much to rub just a little bit deeper in her pussy to reach the right spot, but she denied herself. For him. Everything for him.

He grabbed her corset, arms flexing with inhuman strength. A man wouldn't have been able to rip the thick leather to pieces, but he did. She nearly collapsed back onto the chaise, but he pulled her up again and ripped away the bottoms as well. His gaze crawled over her as though he'd never seen her before, and in a way, he hadn't. This was the first time he'd seen her completely naked without her tattoos.

His amber eyes went dark, his desire for her as fresh, raw and exposed as her. Like the Creature, she didn't think his erection was the best way to measure how much he wanted her. He had complete control over that, as much control as he had over her lack of control. But his desire… She didn't think he could control that, only how much of it she could see. And he let her see all of it.

"Make me mark you." He stopped trying to keep her away from him, giving her primary hands free rein once more. "You don't get to have me inside you until you make yourself filthy with me."

His cock needed no additional lubrication after being in her mouth. She worked both hands over his erection as he took her hair in his fists again, the flex of his forearms in her periphery.

Even with her long fingers, she couldn't cover all of him at once. She still had plenty of his length to twist her hands over, smearing her saliva and his pre-cum. He was hotter than a man under her palms, as hot as the monster, and even with the heat he sent through her, she thought she'd feel his when she had him inside. She dug her fingers deeper in her cunt in spite of the warning not to come. Three fingers weren't enough, but four wouldn't work at this angle, and she wanted him—his girth, his length, his heat, his firmness. God, how she wanted *him*.

Bell traced her lips. "I love your mouth, Lizzie." He canted his hips into her experienced hands that stole some of the strength from his voice. "I love your teeth, the danger I created as well as the danger that is yours alone. I'd kiss you again, because I could kiss you for days, but you haven't earned that yet. I'll give you something else to occupy it."

He curled his fingers into her mouth, hooked over her canines the way he had when he'd given her the spider's fangs and venom. He drew her head back and forth, pressing hard into the soft palate, then turned them around to probe over her tongue, where he'd slid his cock minutes before.

Just the two fingers at first, but as she savored them, the taste of her arousal still strong, he inserted a third, then a fourth, stretching her lips. She didn't magically accommodate his fingers the way she did his cock. It was a strain, yet she took him down to the bottom knuckles, not once letting up on the manual worship of his cock. Her nipples, lips, tongue ached with the same intensity as the nerves being constantly stimulated between her legs.

He brought her head closer to him with his grip on her hair and his fingers in her mouth. "Do you have any idea what you look like right now?"

Bell abruptly jerked his fingers from her mouth and wiped them over her breasts, pushing and tweaking her nipples as though he couldn't care less what he was touching. When her breasts gleamed with her own saliva, he slapped her face, this blow not as strong but with a sharper sound.

"Harder," he grunted, his hips moving with less purpose and more need.

She wrung his cock, twisting up with one hand and caressing the head with the other, panting as she worked herself at the same furious pace. Taking care of both of them at the same time kept her from being able to slow herself down. She was going to come.

Elizabeth bit her lip, forgetting she still had her fangs extended. They pierced through the delicate flesh just to the sides of her silver rings, wresting an unexpected moan from her. Blood coated her tongue, dripped down her chin onto her breasts.

That did it for him. He brought his forehead to hers and groaned through his climax, as irresistible to her as when the Creature did, because it was a choice to allow himself that moment of vulnerability—and even for them, these greater and more powerful beings, it *was* a moment of vulnerability.

His cum spilled over her worshipping hands first, molten, then came a stronger pulse over her breast, over her abdomen. It could have been like what Dez had done, but the way he looked at her lacked any of the contempt. He may have spoken with the haughty demand of a dominant jackass, but his regard didn't lie. His cum diminished to a trickle, which she smoothed over his cock for the last few pumps that brought him to completion.

Bell broke his self-imposed ban, licking a line from her bloodstained chin to her lower lip, where he sucked the blood, traced her silver hardware with his tongue, then kissed her thoroughly and soundly. She thought he'd push her down onto the chaise again, but instead, he whirled them around and pulled her over him as he reclined, held up by the pillows at the closed end.

Fuck, he kissed well, and this time he let her into his mouth, sucking her tongue, catching her aching lip with his own teeth to gently heal it and take away the pain. He nudged her secondary hands from between her legs with his knee, drawing her against his thigh instead.

Her skin heated as his magic swept over her, cleansing the mark he'd sought to make, the saliva over her chest, the wetness on her fingers. But he didn't take the sweat she'd worked for and the heat their bodies conjured, despite the fact that it was nearly as cold backstage as it was outside it.

Their legs tangled, half on the chaise and half off. From this position, she could almost claim dominance, with more room to maneuver and two legs on the ground to give her more leverage. But he moved her, far more capable of multitasking than she. He had her riding his thigh, though not nearly the focused, forceful stimulation she needed to come. He wanted to keep the fire burning, but he still didn't want her coming until he was inside her.

And now he wouldn't be in any hurry, not the way he was kissing her as though that was really all he would do to her for the rest of the night — and she didn't think she'd mind. He mesmerized her, every touch meant to enhance the kiss rather than anything else. She couldn't help how she moaned, this time with desire rather than discomfort, lust as keen as anything anyone had ever given her.

He cupped her breast, rolled the nipple between his fingers without pinching. He stroked over her thighs, as enamored of the secondary as the primary, and both as sensitive as the other. He traced the valley of her spine to her nape and took hold of her hair again. She had no dignity when he kissed away from her mouth, her cries loud and unmistakably sexual.

"You're right, my dear," he whispered into her neck. "Hair is better for you." He pulled her head back, lifting her up to look her over. "It's time, or don't you want me inside you?"

He laughed as she scrambled up, grabbing the top edge of the chaise with her primary hands and positioning him with one secondary hand on his chest and the other on his cock. He hadn't softened at all.

But he stopped laughing as she came down around him. He groaned, arching up to meet her, and for a moment, their moans mingled. It wasn't just the semen and saliva on his cock and her own arousal that made it so easy to take him all the way to the base. The Creature didn't enter her nearly so well. Bell was a measure bigger, yet there was nothing to stop him as he rolled his hips up to fill her.

She started slow, her strong shadow over him, her eight limbs giving her more strength and more control. This time it was she who hovered over his mouth, tormenting herself with the brief distance it would take to let him kiss her again, even though her mouth cried out to be taken, plundered as completely and deeply as her cunt.

"Do you remember the last time our wills were as one, Lizzie? I haven't been forcing you to do or feel anything for some time." Bell tasted the corner of his mouth as she paused halfway down his cock. "We really must do it more often. Did you ever imagine we'd be so similar?"

The sudden sensation of her heart and stomach dropping had Bell raising his hips to finish what she'd started. She couldn't help a whimper and couldn't convince her hips back up. She kept him deep inside her, her clit throbbing with pleasure. It didn't give a fuck about the destruction of worlds, or maybe just a small handful of beliefs. It wanted exactly what it had and took the swirl of fear in the same stride as ever.

Bell looked up and curled his fingers to beckon the Creature. "I believe this is your time, Creature. Terrified enough for you?"

The Creature spread his wings and glided down to the chaise, his cock as rock hard and taut as Bell's. His chest heaved, his nostrils flaring for that which she couldn't detect except for the whirlwind in her mind. Not even his presence could comfort her until he pressed his lips to the nape of her neck to draw a small measure of her fear in, leaving an equally small measure of relief in its wake.

"Yes," the Creature breathed into her, his answer like the groaning of the wind.

"Oh, we aren't nearly finished." Bell slipped his hand down her spine, dipping between both sets of thighs to trace the lips stretched thin around his cock. She twitched helplessly. "I've no inclination to relinquish her just yet. We're both going to have you, Elizabeth. We're both going to lose ourselves in your body, use you for our own pleasure, though with him feeding on you as he fucks you, you might not have the good sense to fear it the way you should."

"You slimy bastard," she said through gritted teeth, but she followed it with another whimper as some kind of lubrication entered her ass, the magic effortlessly stretching her at the same time. He wouldn't want to make any of the three of them wait, not when the Creature was pressed close, a growl through his quick pants like an animal.

"Kiss me, Spider," Bell said. "Let me drink your screams. Don't hold back on my account."

She couldn't have even if she'd wanted to.

The Creature pressed in above Bell's cock, and though magic had prepared her for him, it hadn't prepared her for both of them together, both unbearably thick, the Creature not nearly as smooth to take in as Bell. The way he fucked her was more artless, more real, and to her red-faced shame, she did scream, muffled by Bell's possessive kiss.

Elizabeth had been double-penetrated before, sometimes two cocks in her pussy at once, but she still felt ragged at the edges, stretched to her breaking point. Why the hell didn't she just break? If she broke, she'd never have to be stretched this far again. Why did she have to be so goddamn resilient?

As soon as the Creature had seated himself as far as he could go, he pulled her hair away from her neck and brought his mouth close.

It took only a single manipulative nudge from Bell to get her moving over him again, fucking herself on both of them until she was riding them, the warmth of the Creature's feed and the heat of lust combining until she thought she might burst into flames.

Or at least she thought it was Bell who got her moving, who made her so high and hot that she felt like she was going mad.

"Oh no, this is your desire that burns, your own will that takes me and that monster of yours in. This is you who needs to kiss me, who needs to be given freedom to fuck anything that comes in her path. Do you really think Dez is the reason you are what you are?"

The Creature could barely keep up with her, his groans against her neck almost like those of distress, though his hips quickened to try to meet her furious ride. He caught her flesh between his teeth, sucking at her skin as though it could draw the fear from her faster if he just took more of her in.

"He created the associations, but he wouldn't have been able to do that if you hadn't already had this raw sensitivity, this capacity for desire – 'resilience', as you call it. This is all you, Lizzie. And I won't say what that makes you, as much as you want me to, because you say it enough of yourself. I wouldn't be so cruel as to agree."

Elizabeth tore her mouth away from Bell's, gasping for breath as though she couldn't survive without his air, but she grabbed his throat between her secondary hands, still bracing her primary hands on the chaise for greater leverage as she tightened her grip around his neck.

"That's right, my dear. Kill me harder. Murder me well. It won't change how much you need me, because I let you be the woman you should have been from the beginning – the one your family and your ex tried to bury, because they knew how powerful it would be if they set it free. And it's not that different at all from a demon."

She dug her thumbs in, clutched at him hard enough to snap chicken bones. He just laughed again, as unabashedly cruel as he professed he didn't want to be, his dark golden eyes glowing. The goddamn fucker didn't need to breathe, and he kept meeting her as she rode him, at the same pace as the Creature.

The tighter she throttled him, the tighter she clenched around their cocks.

"Spider," the Creature growled into her.

"You need me," Bell whispered, his words penetrating her mind. "You need Arcanium. You're mine, my venomous little Spider, as much as Maya is mine. But guess what, Lizzie?" He knocked her arms away and lunged up to lick a hot line up the other side of her neck to her ear. He spoke as much in her mind as for her to hear. "*I don't love you.*"

The spike of fear and lust that followed proved too much for the Creature. His teeth pierced her flesh. A burst of warmth followed, a rush of absolute, heady fearlessness that had all three of them bucking fiercely in an orgasm that felt like it was going to explode out through her skin.

Both cocks inside her twitched, pulsed, filled her with cum hotter than her, stroked through flesh that couldn't stop feeling the pleasure of them as long as they were still moving inside her. She screamed with her teeth bared, punching the back of the chaise as it kept going—the pleasure and the power, the tightrope of safety and danger that she walked not just with Bell but with herself, the warning and the warmth all one in a confusion she had no choice but to withstand.

Bell worked his way back to her mouth, kissing her through the violent aftershocks, easing himself from her. Then it was just the Creature inside, both his cock and his teeth, as he fed from her—not only on fear, but on the blood that sent fear streaming through her. Bell stroked the Creature's head as he kissed Elizabeth, his possession still total but the domination discarded in favor of feverish languor.

The Creature wrapped his arms around her in his own gesture of possession, his hips still jerking despite his completion, pulling her back against him to feed more and more deeply until Bell had to relinquish her.

But eventually the Creature realized what he was doing. He froze, stopped feeding from her, stopped drinking.

"Carefully," Bell said, his tenderness back. With his hand on the Creature's forehead, he helped ease the teeth from her flesh, covered the mark to keep blood from spurting out. "I suspected he might be a breed of vampire. I couldn't be sure until now. You can try to use the blue potion, but I don't think it'll do much to eliminate scarring from this bite. When a parasite like the Creature latches onto a human being… Well, it'll be fascinating to learn what deeper mark he's made. There are many different kinds of venom, my dear."

"What did you do?" Elizabeth said weakly. The wound stitched together under Bell's magic, but he was right. His healing didn't reach deep enough—the wound was more than physical.

"I don't know. I've never done it before." The Creature bucked again inside her then eased himself just as carefully out of her body. Both men's semen dripped down her thighs, and she felt that unbearable hollowness and loneliness that followed significant penetration. "I think the danger is greater for me, though."

"What makes you think that?" she asked.

"I think I'm bound to you more than you're bound to me. I'm not sure whether I can now feed from anyone else."

Bell pulled his hand back. She touched the scar left behind, smooth and knotted under her fingertips.

"It's fortunate she has plenty of fear yet to feed upon." Bell stroked away the hair that had plastered against her cheek with sweat. "But eventually she will leave Arcanium, and eventually she will die. Can you survive such a parting?"

"I don't know." In spite of the mystery — and the fear Elizabeth rarely heard from him — the Creature hadn't released her from his arms. He clung to her, still drawing her subtly away from Bell. She doubted he even noticed he was doing it, but Bell did.

"We really must do this again, Elizabeth." He raised himself up for one last lingering kiss. "Perhaps we might be more recreational in the future. I think we would do quite well together without the need for absolution."

Because we want the same things. She shivered. The Creature drew her away again, this time with more purpose.

"Yes, my dear. You needn't fear it as you do. I'm not the devil you believe me to be. Just because I don't love you the way Maya enjoys doesn't mean you are easily discarded. I am willing to kill for you, willing to keep your tormentors alive for you. What more would you ask of me?"

He bowed to her with far more elegance than a naked man should have.

She didn't protest when the Creature carried her back into the shadows that led beyond the backstage and into the quiet night.

"Let me take it all," he whispered. "Let me take it all away."

She nodded, closing her eyes against the darkness. His great wings carried them back to his makeshift bed, where he made her forget what fear was...for a while.

**Want to see more from this author?
Here's a taster for you to enjoy!**

Intervention
Aurelia T. Evans

Excerpt

"Land, what time is it?"

"It's seven."

"What do you mean it's seven? Why didn't my alarm go off?"

"You needed the sleep, Em," Land replied.

"So you decided to go off on your own at night just so I could get a little shut-eye? Land, we've watched enough horror movies to know that splitting up is *not* a good idea."

"I know. But we've also watched enough reality TV to know that not getting enough sleep also isn't a good idea."

"Touché. Did we get a call?"

"No, Em. I found him."

Emily sat straight up in bed. "You found Matt?"

"The lures worked. He's in the trap."

Emily rocked out of bed and yanked on a pair of leggings. Then she did some fancy moves to get a sports bra on without taking off her long tank sleep shirt. "That's great. That's really great. Is he okay?"

"More or less," Land replied.

Emily stopped rushing through their dark bedroom. "Is something wrong? You sound weird."

"The important thing is that we found him. You should come down. We need to do the intervention together. He won't listen to me. He'll listen to you."

"Um, okay. I'll get my coffee and drive right over."

"Love you, Em."

"I love you, too, Land. Are you sure—"

The call abruptly ended.

Land had never hung up on her like this, not unless they were in a knock-down, drag-out kind of fight, and they'd only had that twice in their relationship. And both times, Emily had known they were in one.

Her stomach tightened, but she forced herself not to overanalyze.

That didn't mean she couldn't hurry. By the time she made it to the warehouse, it would be full-on dark.

She grabbed a large bottle of iced coffee from the second shelf of the fridge. Then she hopped into her subcompact. Land had the company car, but hers had an extermination kit or two for emergencies, so she wasn't going out to the warehouse district half-cocked.

As she drove away from the glittery, bustling part of the city, the blue velvet of the sky went black.

"Ladies and gentlemen, lock your doors," she whispered.

* * * *

Three years ago, if someone had told Emily that she was going to be in pest control, she would have laughed in that person's face while spraying a line of Raid around her apartment.

These days, she could pick up a cockroach without flinching. They were nothing in comparison to the kinds of infestations she, Land and Matt had to deal with in addition to the usual suspects. It just so happened that the usual suspects tended to hang around the unusual ones so often that they'd get paid on the books for the usual, then off the books – cash, goods or services – for the unusual. Because how were they supposed to put 'rat-sized cockroach demon spawn' on the invoice without raising some red flags during an audit?

Their unconventional night job had started as an accident, evolved into a hobby then turned into a full-on occupation.

The accident had happened during a bit of urban exploring that had followed Land's side job at the time as an exterminator's apprentice. When rats started having red eyes and a person didn't have holy water on hand, they'd better hope they had a cross necklace or a rosary. Emily had. Land hadn't.

Back then, it had been a good thing the vampire family hadn't really been interested in bothering or being bothered, otherwise Land might have died then and there.

After that encounter, though, they'd felt like they had a responsibility. 'Once seen, never unseen' and all that. Balancing the work with school had meant creative hours, cat naps, copious amounts of caffeine and a few prayers, but it was totally worth it.

They hadn't even thought about making a profit out of the hobby until after Land had gone solo with extermination.

Around that time, they'd stumbled upon Matt at one of those bars that discreetly catered to hunters – demon hunters, vampire hunters, regular hunters looking to score on exotic creatures…the scene took all sorts. Emily and Land had largely been viewed by that community as newlywed newbies, cannon fodder that wouldn't last a year. They hadn't taken it personally.

Matt had been new himself, drawn to the supernatural underbelly of the city by the promise of an unconventional thrill. He'd been the first one intrigued by the idea of not hunting the big game. And he'd been just charming and enthusiastic enough about the idea that Land had eventually welcomed him to the extermination team.

Para-exterminators, Matt called them, for when a job came along that was too small or too damn infested. After all, what did the other demon hunters know about corpse beetles, ectoplasm residue and specter slugs, except that they seriously stained leather boots?

Emily's parents were still trying to figure out why she hadn't gone running the second Land had become a full-fledged exterminator instead of something more ambitious and less icky, and why she'd actually gone and married the bastard. Or why she and Land had opened up their house to another man. Emily knew the whispers, the bets on who was going to cheat first.

But it made financial sense for Matt to contribute to the mortgage and for them to work out of their house instead of renting an office somewhere. Let the hens and roosters cluck in their narrow little barnyards. The three of them were fiscally sound, would be out of debt in less than five years if business kept up, and they didn't drive each other crazy.

If Matt had a crush on Emily and Emily admired Matt too, what did that matter as long as they kept their hands to themselves and out of each other's bedrooms?

That's how it had been, anyway.

It wasn't like Matt to just run off. He was a thrill-seeker, yes, but if he'd decided to go to Louisiana for an alligator-wrestling lesson or to Florida to swim with bull sharks, he would have left them a note. The only clue they'd had was a bunch of bloody footprints at a warehouse where a hunter had said he'd seen Matt. Some of the footprints had been human, some of them not. No bodies to be found.

Emily and Land specialized in the small, but that didn't mean they were clueless to the larger problems. A creature that size wasn't a Texas chupacabra or a werecat. Those paw prints could be nothing other than a werewolf.

Their local urban sprawl didn't have much in the way of werewolves. The small forest area that ran through the center of the city with the river could only ever hold the territory of a single small pack. There were a few in-city packs as well, but they weren't like vampires or other demons. They didn't thrive in a concrete jungle, and those that did take up residence there were usually pretty passive and self-policing, for their own protection.

However, that only meant that werewolf attacks were *less* common. Not that they didn't happen.

In general, most hunters left the city werewolves alone, as long as they didn't start killing things they weren't supposed to. New wolves, however, weren't always good at toeing that line.

And that was the best-case scenario for Matt—that he'd been turned. So they'd set the traps outside the forest, hoping to lead him in with game and blood to one of the many abandoned buildings in the warehouse district, hoping against hope that he was still alive and that he was the one they'd catch.

Well, Matt *was* still alive, and he *was* the one they'd caught, thank God.

Now that Matt had been captured, what she and Land needed to do next was convince Matt that he was still a part of their family, fur and all. That they'd help take care of him.

No matter what.

About the Author

Aurelia T. Evans is an up-and-coming erotica author with a penchant for horror and the supernatural.

She's the twisted mind behind the werewolf/shifter Sanctuary trilogy, demonic circus series Arcanium, and vampire serial Bloodbound. She's also had short stories featured in various erotic anthologies.

Aurelia presently lives in Dallas, Texas (although she doesn't ride horses or wear hats). She loves cats and enjoys baking as much as she dislikes cooking. She's a walker, not a runner, and she writes outside as often as possible.

Aurelia loves to hear from readers. You can find her contact information, website details and author profile page at http://www.totallybound.com.

TOTALLY BOUND

Home of Erotic Romance

www.ingramcontent.com/pod-product-compliance
Lightning Source LLC
Chambersburg PA
CBHW030749030726
47497CB00001B/211